RHYN TRILOGY

Limited Edition

Katie's Hellion
Katie's Hope
Rhyn's Redemption

Rhyn Trilogy: Origins

Lizzy Ford

Edited by Christine LePorte

Copyright © 2012 Lizzy Ford
http://www.guerrillawordfare.com/

Cover design copyright © 2012 by Dafeenah Jameel
http://www.IndieDesignz.com/

All rights reserved.

No part of this book may be reproduced in any form or by any electronic or mechanical means including information storage and retrieval systems, without permission in writing from the author. The only exception is by a reviewer, who may quote short excerpts in a review.

This is a work of fiction. Names, characters, places and incidents either are products of the author's imagination or are used fictitiously. Any resemblance to actual events or locales or persons, living or dead, is entirely coincidental.

ISBN: 1475110081
ISBN-13: 978-1475110081

Author's note:

Because of the popularity of this series with my readers, I've expanded the trilogy into a saga that'll launch in Autumn 2012. This is a testament to both the power of readers in determining what they truly love and the power of a compelling story. I'm humbled by this, and for all the feedback and support from my fans,

        I want to say THANK YOU!

As always, I'd also like to thank my husband for his unwavering support in the face of my often neurotic behavior

꧁꧂

This book would not be possible without my editor, Christine LePorte, who is often left picking up the pieces of this spastic writer when my husband isn't around

And

My graphics artist, Dafeenah, who has become as incredible of a friend as she is a talented artist.

Katie's Hellion

Book I

Chapter One

Gabriel turned the pages of the Oracle's book, watching as words scribbled themselves across the parchment, updating a chain of events that changed with every decision made by the Council That Was Seven. Only the long-dead Oracle possessing the book and the deities could see the Past, Present, and Future.

He saw only the Present, like fractured scenes of a movie where the actors continually changed their lines and settings. Words leapt from the pages to form hologram-like images dancing over the book. Friends and strangers alike acted out their stilted scenes before dropping onto the page as words again.

Show me Rhyn, he told the book.

He always peeked at his friend, whom he'd dropped off in Hell to serve an undeserved sentence. Rhyn's powers were beyond even Gabriel to control, and the unfortunate immortal was a loose cannon that'd accidently almost destroyed the world more times than Gabriel could count.

Gabriel's lover and master, the deity Death, materialized beside him at the Oracle's altar in the center of an ancient fortress in the Sanctuary. Each of the four Sanctuaries sat on an island straddling the human and immortal worlds and housed an immortal treasure, such as the Oracle.

He sensed Death's disapproval.

"I know," he said, and turned the page in the book to continue watching Rhyn.

Death took her human form out of respect for the women of the convent-like Sanctuary that housed the Oracle. She was beautiful, a woman of sunshine, smiles, and eyes that changed from white to black and every color in between. At close to seven feet with eyes and hair blacker than night and a permanent scowl, *he* was what most expected Death to look like. Yet the lithe woman with the transparent skin and glow was exactly what people saw when they went: a bright, beautiful, peaceful light.

"I want to know if--" he started.

"Rhyn?"

"Yeah."

"Immortals aren't so far off from humans, are they?" Death mused. "They share their weaknesses."

"I know what really happened, and I hoped others would figure it out. He doesn't deserve to be in Hell," he replied.

"You can't interfere more than you have. How many times have I warned you about breaking Immortal Code?"

"Does nothing bother you?" he asked without heat, knowing the answer. "And technically, I interfered by making him disappear before anyone figured out he'd saved humanity."

Death smiled serenely and placed her small hand on the book. He met her gaze.

"All things come to me eventually," she said, quoting the familiar words. "You, too, you know."

"Someday."

"And someday Rhyn. He's on my list, Gabriel."

He was quiet, the words and holograms before him blurring as he thought. The only immortals on Death's list were those who were about to become dead-dead. He'd always hoped Rhyn would have another chance, that Hell was a place to stash the dangerous immortal until the world was ready for him.

"He didn't deserve what he got," he voiced, troubled. "In all my time, I've never felt guilt at what I do."

"You're my best assassin, and you're the only one who can trespass in Hell and return. You had to do what you did. If nothing else, you know he's safe, and so are the little humans."

"Are you serious about making him dead-dead soon?"

"Let me show you something," she said, and stepped up beside him. "Keep in mind, you're not supposed to be anywhere near the Oracle. Only--"

"Deities and whatever," he finished with a roll of his eyes.

She gave him a stern glare that made him smile. Her human form was tiny enough that the Oracle's book reached her shoulder level.

Death's hand hovered over the pages, and she turned them quickly without touching them. She stopped and touched a page with her fingertip. An image sprung from the paper before them.

The earth in flames, with earthquakes swallowing whole towns and buildings burning.

Gabriel shifted, well aware Rhyn was capable of this.

Death gave him a pointed look, waiting for him to jump to his friend's defense as he always did. It was hard with the scenes she showed him flickering in front of him.

"The Future isn't set," he managed at last.

"It's not," she agreed. "But if I don't make him dead-dead, there's a good chance this is the fate of the human world."

"I can't believe there's nothing that can be done!" he replied with more emotion than he intended.

"You're going soft, Gabe."

"It's *wrong*."

"Odd, coming from my best assassin," she said.

He said nothing, watching the scene. Death closed the book and looked up at him.

"Do you believe in him so much, or do you feel so much guilt?" she challenged.

"I believe in him."

She considered him for a long moment before turning away. He suppressed a sigh, sensing she was beyond mercy for anyone on her list. Normally, so was he. Death held out her hand, and an hourglass with black sand appeared in her palm.

"He could be such an asset to the Council That Was Seven. Right now, he's useless to them and anyone else, just an immortal whose freakish power should've landed him on my list long, long ago," she said.

She tipped the hourglass, and black sand began to spill.

"I'll give him a second chance," she continued. "For you, my sweet, not for him. But I can't let him stay alive long, or you've seen what'll happen. When the sand is gone, I'll make him dead-dead, unless he can learn to control his power and to work with his brothers."

Gabriel stared, surprised, then dismayed, at her conditions. He watched the sand that was Rhyn's life and met her gaze.

"And, you can't break the Immortal Code to help him."

The restriction smacked him hard, as he'd been ready to drag Rhyn out of Hell as soon as Death was gone.

"How do I get him out of Hell?" he demanded.

"You won't. Someone else will."

"Who?"

"The leader of the Council That Was Seven is about to make a decision that will alter all their paths. It involves a woman destined to be the first Ancient's mate and who's immune to immortals," she said.

"Rhyn has a *mate*?"

"He might, if she doesn't die before the sand runs out."

Gabriel dwelled on this new information. He wasn't really sure Rhyn would consider being sentenced to eternity with a mate much of an improvement over Hell.

She slid the Oracle's book carefully into a satchel and replaced it inside the altar before placing the hourglass in front of him.

"Immortal Code," she reminded him.

"You won't kill me," he remarked, hope and frustration filtering through him. "I'm violating Immortal Code by serving you, by locking Rhyn in Hell to keep Kris from killing him."

"Take him this, and don't you dare break the Code again," she said.

A familiar vial appeared in her hand containing what looked like sand. Rhyn's name was etched in the immortals' tongue across the top. It was his immortal powers, which Death had yanked from him when she ordered Gabriel to take him to Hell.

Gabriel took it and smiled, cheered by the thought of the most powerful immortal ever born cursed with the self-control of a five-year-old in a room with fresh-baked cookies and no adult supervision. Rhyn couldn't do what others wanted, not when he couldn't control his own powers. Gabriel wondered if even a mate and a second chance could help him.

"He tends to destroy the natural balance of everything when he's free," Death said with some annoyance. "Maybe when he's stabilized, he can leave Hell."

He looked at her, and she smiled the same gentle smile she used to greet humans to the underworld.

"But who in Hell is going to become his mate?"

"His brother Kris will take care of it," she said.

"He'll make things right with Rhyn after their nasty break?"

"Not on purpose, but yes."

Intrigued, Gabriel relented from his stubborn position before the altar.

A knock at the door interrupted their conversation. The leader of the convent that cared for the Sanctuary opened the door and curtseyed. Death curtseyed back, gave Gabriel a final look of warning, and followed the woman in grey to afternoon tea.

He watched her go, wondering how he could help his friend without breaking the Immortal Code yet again. Pocketing the vial, he willed himself to the shadow world, the place between worlds. It was hazy and cool, like a beach after the evening fog rolled in. Portals to the mortal and immortal worlds glowed warm yellow through the fog like beacons. He went to the only portal that glowed black--the portal to Hell-- and stepped from the shadow world into the tiny, dark cell holding his friend.

He watched Rhyn's body contort beneath the spells of Rhyn's brother, Sasha. Without the contents of the vial, Rhyn was defenseless against any immortal. Gabriel couldn't help the feeling of deep satisfaction as he gripped the vial in one hand.

Rhyn was being given a second chance, and Gabriel hoped he killed Sasha before the sands in the hourglass were gone.

In Hell, Rhyn didn't even know what shape he was. His cramped prison cell was always dark as, his skin hot and clammy. He'd been fevered for a zillion years, trapped in the tiny cell in ever-changing forms.

At least he wasn't burning or drowning or freezing or watching his skin being pulled from his body and screaming. Sometimes his brother let him out for a furlough, claimed he was free, and then yanked him back. If nothing else, his traitorous half-brother Sasha kept things switched up. Rhyn would stay in this holding cell on the outskirts of Hell until Sasha figured out some new grueling punishment.

A touch of coolness grazed his heated frame, which always grew hotter than Hell when he changed forms. His body contorted, and agony floated through him as the sixty seconds of being whatever he'd been was up and he changed again.

"Still dark in here," said the voice of his only friend.

"You here for me, Gabriel?"

"No, but thanks for asking."

Rhyn growled a painful laugh, appreciative of the death dealer's dark humor. Especially now, when he had no one else.

"What am I?" he asked, panting as he dropped to all fours.

"Not sure. You look like a cross between a were-beast and a bird."

Gabriel's touch was like ice, and Rhyn shuddered. He changed again and this time recognized his human form. One wall of his cell lit up suddenly. He shielded his eyes and gazed into an empty prison cell opposite his. Surprised, he crossed to the bars of his cell but found the whole wall disappeared when he touched it. In darkness again, he dropped his hands.

"Hell sucks."

"Yeah." Gabriel's voice was quieter.

"You and Death fighting?"

"Never. She'd win."

Rhyn snorted and faced the corner, making out Gabriel's eyes, which gleamed darker than a night in Hell itself. The death dealer was his only friend who'd stuck with him since he'd been banned to Hell by his brothers and dragged there by the immortal death dealer before him. Gabriel's visits weren't often, but Rhyn had grown to like him even more during their brief exchanges.

"Brought you something."

Gabriel held out a vial he'd last seen in the hand of a furious Death. A thrill went through Rhyn as he claimed it. He popped the top off and dumped the sandy magic into the air. The sand transformed into a mist and swirled around him before settling into his skin. He felt the magic penetrate him to the core, and the ancient tattoos marking him as both an immortal and an Ancient blazed red in the darkness before subsiding.

For the first time in years, he felt whole again. He tested his ability to control the familiar magic. Hell buffered his natural inability to rein in the magic and absorbed much of his energies.

"Who'd you kill for this?"

"I have other means of obtaining stuff," Gabriel said with some offense.

Rhyn felt Hell's and Sasha's power roll over him like he was a boulder in a river. They couldn't control him once he left Hell; no one could.

Even Kris, the brother who headed the Council That Was Seven. Rhyn's anger made his cell wall shake before the energies of Hell itself began suctioning his power from him.

"Easy," Gabriel warned. "I'm breaking Immortal Code one last time to bring that to you."

"Fuck the code."

"Rhyn."

"Don't bother, Gabriel."

The death dealer chuckled

Rhyn stretched physically and metaphysically, testing the bounds of Hell. They were much older, much stronger than he. He sagged against the wall, exhausted.

"Are there any girls down here?"

Very little surprised Rhyn, but the death dealer's question did. He squinted into Gabriel's dark corner.

"Or…women, I guess," Gabriel clarified.

"You need a woman that bad?"

"No, no. Just thought I'd check."

Rhyn shook his head. He didn't know why the death dealer was distant this visit, and he didn't care. The only thing that concerned him now was killing Kris. And escaping.

Escape first then kill Kris.

"You wouldn't happen to have a key to my cell, would you?" he asked.

"I'm not allowed to break any more Immortal Codes," Gabriel said with some distaste. "Or I'll end up in the cell beside you."

"Better company than I have now."

"Not my thing."

"So you give me my power back but don't free me. This does shit for me here," Rhyn grumbled.

"I'm restricted by--"

"I know, Gabe."

The death dealer shifted but didn't leave, and Rhyn looked again at the corner.

"I need a favor," Gabriel said at last.

Rhyn never expected to hear these words from the death dealer, who needed nothing from anyone.

"Whatever it is, I'll do it," he said without hesitation. "You've done more for me than anyone else."

"There's going to be someone you'll meet soon. I can't break Immortal Code to protect her."

"But I can," Rhyn finished. "Immortal? Demon? If you tell me it's one of my brothers, I--"

"Human."

"*Human?*"

"One of the immortals wrote a book about caring for humans," Gabriel said with some reticence. "It might help you."

"You could've asked me for anything in the universe, and you ask me to babysit a human." Rhyn said, hearing the scrape of book and stone as the death dealer placed the book on the ground beside him.

He reached for the book, convinced Gabriel had finally gone crazy after all his years serving Death. The book was an immortal's, clasped in a flexible, leather-like cover with thin, transparent pages. Rhyn was fascinated by the feel of both after so long with nothing but stone walls beneath his fingertips.

"Where is this human?" he asked. "How do I find it when I'm stuck here?"

"I haven't figured that out yet," Gabriel admitted. "I'll let you know."

Rhyn lifted the book. He had no intention of reading it, but he liked how soft the cover was.

"Why is this human important?"

"Death won't say."

Rhyn snorted and let his head drop back against the stone wall. Death and her pet worked in their own ways. He didn't mistake his returned powers for a free favor. No, Death wanted something from him, and gave him the ability to do her will.

Yet another traitorous woman. He felt some peace knowing that--whatever Death wanted from him--she'd have to free him from Hell to get it.

Katie Young looked at the speedometer, which read thirty-seven when the blue lights flared up behind her, jarring her out of the pre-coffee morning stupor. She guided the car to the lit parking lot near the metro station, her destination. It was four-thirty, and she'd never seen a cop along this stretch leading up to the nearest metro station.

His glaring spotlight of a flashlight blinded her as he walked to the driver's door, and she held her hand up.

"Do you know why I stopped you?" the officer asked as she rolled down her window.

"No," she said.

"You were going thirty-seven."

"Yeah."

"That's speeding."

The light flashed away, leaving her in blackness studded with dim bulbs.

"The speed limit's thirty-five," she objected.

"So you knew that?"

"Yeah. I drive this way every day."

The light returned to her eyes, and she bit her tongue to keep from griping. She couldn't be late again for her job as an assistant general manager of a fast food joint, or she'd be fired.

"You were speeding intentionally," he said with a level of disgust she'd reserved for the revelation of her sister's ex-boyfriend cheating.

"It's just two miles an hour."

He said nothing, but the light disappeared and she heard him scrawling.

"Your taillight is out," he added in a clipped tone.

"I have four. There's only *one* out--the rest all work."

"So you knew your taillight was out."

More scrawling.

"Look, it's early, I didn't get much sleep, and these seem like minor issues," she said in what she hoped was a friendly voice.

"Your pupils are dilated. Have you been drinking?"

"No."

"On medication?" he prodded.

"I took a sleeping aid last night, yes. I have a lot of trouble sleeping lately, probably because--"

"How many hours ago?"

"Four," she said.

"Taking a sleeping aid and driving before eight hours has passed means you're driving while under the influence of a medication."

She rested her head against the steering wheel, frustration making her veins swell. Her headache worsened.

"I have you for reckless endangerment, driving while under the influence, driving an impaired motorized vehicle while dark, and speeding," he summarized, handing her one ticket for each crime. He waited, as if she'd reveal enough dirt to make his monthly quota then added, "They'll probably suspend your license. You'll have to report to court tomorrow morning."

"Sounds wonderful," she managed.

"God bless."

She rolled up her window, watched him return to his car, and cursed.

She beat the rush onto the metro and took up a comfortable position on the aisle side of the commuter train, book in one hand and purse in the other. The train lurched forward, the gentle hum of electricity soon pushing her into a near-doze, until the train lurched to a halt. As usual, the next stop filled the train, and she looked with some irritation at a five-year-old who shoved by her legs to stand next to the window beside her.

He was dressed in worn clothing and shoes and flattened his palms against the window, as if he'd never been on a train before. He turned to her twice and pointed out the window as the scenery whizzed, but she ignored him, reading instead.

Four stops later, she rose and tucked the book away, wading through the throngs of people to the door as the train slowed.

"Mama!"

The cry startled those around her, and she glanced back at the kid, who stared in her direction.

"Lady, that your kid?" someone asked as she stepped toward the door.

"Oh, hell no," she said with a smile.

The kid began crying and she waited, ticking off her mental to-do list to see where she'd start. First off, request the morning off to go to court tomorrow. Second, find out when the general manager of the fast food joint where she worked was returning from maternity leave. Third, call her snotty sister and find a way to back out of brunch Saturday. Fourth--

"Ma'am, your kid," a woman said, taking her arm and pointing with a look of such judgment that Katie reddened despite herself.

"Not mine," she said.

The kid was crying and began tugging on her coat. He spoke in tear-filled gibberish she didn't understand, and she moved away to the door. She was one of the first off the train while the kid wailed and several people around her muttered.

"Lady, you can't just leave him!" the first objector said, grabbing her arm. "You're like that sick lady who put her kid on a plane to Russia 'cause she don't want him no more!"

"How could you leave him on the train? What's wrong with you?"

There were three then five voices with a sixth calling the police and the seventh hugging the sobbing kid.

"He's not mine!" Katie insisted, unable to break away from the mob. She protested until the cops came and took them both to a police station.

Too surprised to understand what exactly was happening, she obeyed the police officer's instructions to sit down and shut up and sat in the quiet police station reception area. The kid sitting beside her made smacking sounds as he chewed on a huge wad of gum. She rubbed her face, certain the mistake would be clarified soon and she'd be released with an apology the size of a bottle of painkiller she desperately needed.

"Fill this out," a dour woman with cocoa skin said, handing her a clipboard. "C'mere, honey." She took the hand of the little boy.

Katie ignored the glare leveled on her while the woman cooed to the little boy. The woman and boy left while she filled out the paperwork and then set it on a counter of what looked like an abandoned reception area. There was no computer, no office supplies on the other side. A single bell sat on the counter. She rang it. When nothing happened, she rang it again.

She looked around her, flustered. The waiting room consisted of two chairs, an empty magazine rack, and a potted plant in the corner. It resembled a doctor's waiting room rather than any police station she'd seen.

She rang the bell again.

"Please have a seat, Ms. Young," an irritated voice announced over the intercom.

She obeyed. Another hour of silence passed, and she started to pace. Her cell phone had no signal, her head throbbed, and the coffee pot was empty. When she felt ready to snap, the same woman returned with the little boy in tow. His dark eyes were glowing, and syrup was on his face.

"Officer David will see you now," the woman told her.

Katie grabbed her purse and walked quickly down a pristine hall to a placard outside an office that read Officer David. The little boy followed her. She knocked and entered with a smile that faded.

Officer David gave her the same glare.

"Have a seat, Ms. Young," he said. "You too, Toby."

"Officer, this has been just a horrible morning," she started.

"For your son, maybe."

"He's not my son."

The officer stared at her then held up an ID card with the boy's picture.

Toby Young.

"It must be some other Young," she insisted. "I don't have a son."

"I oughta call child services on a wack job like you," he muttered.

"Go ahead--call them!" she snapped.

"Parenthood is a responsibility that no one should take likely, even if you're a teen parent! I don't care how..."

She listened to his rant, peppered with language no kid Toby's age should hear. Officer David waved a piece of paper in her face depicting Toby's ID. Toby was quiet, and she snatched the paper, intent on showing him their addresses were different.

Only they weren't different. Toby's address was listed as hers. She set the paper on her lap and stared at it. She'd lived there for two years, since a fight with her sister drove her away from the home her sister shared with her fiancé.

"I don't understand..." she muttered.

"Your record is full of bullshit," Officer David said acidly. "Reckless endangerment? And now child endangerment? You're going to court. You damn well better have a good lawyer, because..."

She sucked in a breath and turned to the kid.

"Toby, kid, whatever. Tell this nice man the truth," she said, meeting the twinkling brown eyes.

The kid was adorable, with dark eyes and hair, sun-kissed skin, and a round face. He was well-fed, though clothed like he'd been going to make mud pies and not to school like he should have been. He smiled.

"Toby, is this your mommy?" Officer David said in tones as sweet as they were bitter toward her.

Toby nodded. Katie's mouth dropped open, and she began to realize something was very, very wrong. This was a dream; she'd fallen asleep on the train and not yet woken up. With any luck, the worst part of her day would be missing her stop.

Toby took her hand. His soft hand was cold. The sensations assured her the surreal situation was really happening.

"Officer David--" she began in earnest.

"Enough!" he roared loudly enough to make them both jump. "I've had enough with deadbeat..."

He ranted, signed her papers with a vicious flourish, then shoved them at her and manhandled her out his door. She stood in the hallway, staring at the door slammed in her face, holding a fistful of papers she didn't know what to do with.

"The car will pick you up." The tone of the woman with cocoa skin left no imagination to what she thought of the latest deadbeat mom in her office.

Frustrated, Katie looked both directions down the pristine, eerily quiet hallway before following the kid toward the far end, where a bright red exit sign hung over the door. Her unease grew as she went. The placards on each of the other doors were blank, the doors closed with no sign of light around the edges. The hallway smelled medicinal and clean, like the antiseptic-laced air of a hospital mixed with pine cleaner.

She'd never been in a police station, but she didn't think they'd be this different from the police shows on television! She paused near the end and turned back to see both Officer David and the woman watching her with disapproving looks and crossed arms. She'd not thought twice about their lack of police uniforms but was now struck by it.

This wasn't a police station. It couldn't be.

"Mama!" Toby called cheerfully.

She turned and stared at him. He shoved the door open with all his might, revealing the steely skies of winter and the grey cement curb outside. Whatever this place was, she--and probably Toby--were better off somewhere else. She joined Toby outside.

The boy was agitated and shivering, skipping up and down the sidewalk while shaking with cold. She'd been too flustered to pay attention to the trip to the police station and looked around, not recognizing the area. It looked suspiciously like the warehouse district near the Annapolis port, and she smelled the sea on the air. She twisted around. There was no handle on the outside of the door she'd just walked through, no number on the building.

She shivered in her wool coat, folded the paperwork, and called her sister. As usual, the phone rang until her voicemail picked up.

"Hey, Hannah, it's Katie. I need some help. Can you give me a call?"

Toby's pattering stopped, and she looked up, startled to see a massive man a few feet away. The sight of him struck her like a frozen water balloon. He was tall and clothed in all black, ominous and large against the slate sky. His trench was long and unfastened, the chilled winter wind whipping back one side to reveal a sword tucked against his leg. He looked like death with his dark hair and cold eyes, his panther-like physique, and gloved hands.

"Toby," she called instinctively.

The little boy ran to her side. The man in black approached. She took a step back, heart fluttering.

"We made a mistake. Toby, you can come with me." The stranger failed to make the cryptic words in any way friendly, and the cold glare seared through her.

"I don't think that's a good idea," she managed.

"You're early," Toby said, unafraid. "I want to go with her."

Katie turned to stare at the little boy, who beamed a smile.

The shadow-man's hand twitched and inched toward the sword at his hip. She stepped back even more and clenched the purse to her body, distracted as a sleek black car pulled up to the curb. A door opened, and Toby vaulted in without waiting for her. She took one more look at the ominous man in black and the sword at his hip and followed, shaking from more than cold. The man shut the door behind them.

"Goodbye, Gabriel!" Toby called from the interior of the warm car. He waved at the massive shadow lingering on the sidewalk.

"You'll be fine. I'll take you home." The soft, firm words of the female in the driver's seat were the first kind ones of the day.

Katie instinctively believed her and twisted, staring with Toby at the man in black who watched them drive away.

"My God," she murmured.

"No," said Toby. "Death dealer."

She looked at him, and he nodded as sagely as a five-year-old could.

"Death dealer, ha! Probably just some bum," the brunette driver said with a forced laugh. "We get lots of them around here."

"At a police station?" Katie asked skeptically.

"Yeah, sure," came the less certain answer. "You know, like, you can't have a cop station in a nice side of town. They kinda have to be in a crappy part of town, where the criminals are. It makes total sense, right? I mean, why would a death dealer be *here?*"

The grey eyes were beseeching, but Katie couldn't manage anything verbal let alone a lie to placate the driver. Instead she looked again to Toby, who'd begun to mess with the buttons on his side of the car.

"Shouldn't you have your seatbelt on?" she asked.

"Okay, Mama," he said cheerfully, and complied.

I'm going insane.

The driver said nothing the rest of the way and dropped them off in front of her apartment complex without asking for directions. Toby darted out of the car and shoved the door to the lobby open with all his might.

She trailed, even more perplexed when the janitor waxing the floor called out a cheerful, "Hey, Toby!"

She rubbed her head, wondering if the kid lived somewhere else in the building while unable to shake the sense that something was really, really wrong. Toby held the elevator for her and pressed the buttons for all twenty floors. She looked at him hard, unable to recall anything at all about the kid.

They reached the sixth floor, where her apartment was. He darted off the elevator and down the hall, stopping in front of her apartment. She opened the door, and he strode in as if he owned the place. Toby bolted to the first room on the right, the guest bedroom.

Katie looked around her apartment, eyes lingering on a drawing done by a child on the fridge. There were pictures on her mantle of the two of them together when he was younger, toys piled into a box near her couch, a school lunch menu and more pictures--these apparently from past Halloweens--on the bulletin board on one wall of the kitchen. She took it all in, feeling as if she'd stepped into the Twilight Zone, and followed Toby down the hall.

The guest room was redone in race cars and Disney characters. His energy sapped, the kid was sprawled half asleep across the race car bed. She stared at the walls, wondering who'd had the time to repaint her guest room. It certainly didn't smell like someone had painted it recently, and there were scuff marks, crayon, and dirt on the walls.

As if it'd been a kid's room for a long time. She hesitated, then covered him with a blanket and walked to the guest bathroom. It, too, was done up in a race car theme with toys lining the side of the tub.

Head pulsing, she retreated to the kitchen and painkillers, staring at a picture drawn by a kid, probably Toby, on the table before her.

She didn't have any kids. She'd never had kids. She'd never met Toby before this day!

Her cell rang, and she stared at it briefly through bleary eyes.

"Hey sis," she said after pressing the answer button. "I've had a horrible day!"

"Oh, hon, I'm sorry to hear that," her sis said in a distracted tone that said she really didn't care. "Toby still sick?"

"What?" Katie asked.

"Is Toby still sick?"

She drew the phone away from her head and stared at it, willing herself to wake up.

"Hello, Katherine?"

"Yeah."

"Ooooh, are you having one of your…issues?" Hannah whispered the last word.

"What issues?"

"You know…your amnesia issues."

"I have amnesia?" Katie asked.

"Hon, call Dr. Williams immediately."

"Who? Hannah, when I left home this morning, I had no kids! None. *None!*"

"God, it's getting worse, isn't it?" Hannah said with genuine concern. "Gio's paying for the best neurologist in the world. You may as well go in."

"So you're still engaged to Giovanni. And I work at…"

"McGillen's, like you have for the past few months. I think it's your third job this fall, which is why yes, we're still paying your rent," Hannah said with some irritation.

"I remember those things. You can't tell me I'd forget my own child!" Katie all but shouted. "Hannah, I'm eighteen! Teens my age don't have five year old kids!"

"Let me guess, you have a headache. You probably did something stupid like leave Toby on the train."

Katie's mouth worked without producing sound.

"We go through this at least twice a year." Now Hannah sounded bored rather than concerned. "Call the doc. You keep his number on the fridge."

Katie looked to the fridge, where a small business card was stuck beneath a cartoon magnet. She plucked it free.

"Yeah," she managed. "Yeah, I'll call him."

"We'll have brunch Saturday. Don't be late this time. I have to get ready for the Kingsly gala," Hanna said. "Oh, and wear something decent this time. You looked like you were in pj's last time."

"Yeah."

Katie set the phone on the table and stared at the kid's drawings on the fridge.

How could she remember everything but *her child?* She felt sick to her stomach.

Chapter Two

Dr. Williams gave Katie a warm smile. "Almost everything looks normal. There's an anomaly in your blood test, but you're physically healthy," he said.

"Just a mental mess?" she prodded.

"Don't be hard on yourself," he chided, pulling a rolling chair up to the exam table. "Your amnesia is trauma induced from the rape you survived a little over five years ago."

"I was *raped?*"

"And beaten near death," he said with a shake of his head. "I don't know how you survived, but you did, probably because you were young enough to heal what an adult probably wouldn't. To protect you, your mind backtracks whenever you feel overwhelmed, overly stressed, mentally threatened."

Katie gazed at him skeptically. Her file--two inches thick--was yet more proof that the world that seemed foreign to her really wasn't.

"So my mind blanks stuff out?"

"Precisely. It's a survival technique. The human mind is so wonderful and so versatile." By his glowing eyes, the doctor loved his job. His enthusiasm and genuine warmth melted more of her resistance.

"But how is it I remember being alone getting on the train, and Toby got on at the next stop?" she challenged.

"It's how your mind wakes up from whatever sleep it went into. You fantasized him appearing at the next stop; it's how your psychosis snaps and brings you back to reality."

"That makes no sense."

"We've gone over this several times," he said. "You'll have to take my word on this."

"Do I usually do that?" she asked.

"No, but I'd like to get home to my wife before midnight. And I called the judge on your behalf and volunteered you to go to counseling. The judge liked that option rather than jailing a young single mom."

Jailing a single mom, like her. She managed a nod. He gave another warm smile.

"Get dressed and take your file to the nurse. Please call me if you experience any other problems. I'll tell my receptionist to make you an appointment for next week. Your blood test results were unusual."

He handed her a business card and left. The antiseptic pine-laced air from the hallway made her nose wrinkle. She looked at the door, the familiar scent disturbing her, then down at her file.

Everything was documented, every visit, every doctor-scrawled record, every prescription she'd ever taken.

It was too real not to be real, yet it didn't feel real at all! She followed his instructions and traded the file for two prescriptions to drugs she'd never heard of. She considered debating with the nurse at the front desk, whose friendly grey eyes were familiar. Toby hopped up from his chair and waved to the nurse. Tired and confused, Katie left without asking what the drugs were for and stepped into the chilly fall evening. Toby trailed silently.

The cold wind felt good against her face and roused her dark thoughts. She breathed out fog, watching it rise to the dark grey skies. Dr. Williams' clinic had a blessedly late schedule; it was nearing eight, and the lights of his building still glowed. Having the world's best neurologist on call was one of the perks of the rich and famous, a world unfamiliar to her except that her sister had been gunning for it since her sixteenth birthday.

Hannah had succeeded in landing a big fish blueblood, a descendant of Italian royalty, whose old money placated the chilly welcome she received into a lifestyle far, far different from her own. The fight that led up to Katie running away had been because of Hannah's insistence Katie attend some refinement school, so she wouldn't embarrass Hannah's new family.

Katie shivered and looked around for a cab. Her eyes settled on a form across the street, so still and dark he would've been a shadow if not for his presence beneath a street lamp. She felt the cold, black glare and fought the urge to run back inside the clinic. He didn't move. For a long moment, she convinced herself he was a statue, not a man too still to be human. He was in black, unaffected by the cold or the light settling over him, outlining him like glitter on black construction paper.

Like one of Toby's drawings on the fridge.

Toby.

She didn't know why she suddenly felt near hysterics. She felt no motherly bond to the kid huddled beside her in a thick coat despite how adorable he was. With the living shadow staring at her, the winter wind sucking the air from her lungs, and the prescriptions clenched in her hand, she'd never felt less a part of her world.

A car approached, and a window lowered.

"You need a lift? Taxis quit coming this way after rush hour."

The voice of the friendly nurse from the nurse's station brought her back from her thoughts. Blinking back tears, Katie looked toward the shadow. He was gone.

"Yeah," she forced herself to say. "Thanks."

The nurse dropped her and Toby off, and they trudged to her apartment.

The shadow man was on her fridge. Toby had drawn him on black construction paper with silver glitter outlining the shape of a man. There was no mistaking the image.

Death dealer, Toby had called him.

Katie stared at the picture for a long moment then emptied her pockets on the table. She attached the prescriptions to the fridge with another cartoon magnet and smoothed out the paperwork she'd been given from the police station. Toby dropped his coat in the middle of the floor and trudged to his room with a yawn. She slumped in a chair at the kitchen table, eyes blurring as she struggled to make out the forms. There were biographical forms and consent forms she hadn't really read, all signed in a loopy, angry signature, and a copy of Toby's birth certificate.

Wiping her eyes, she pored through the rest of the paperwork, growing cold despite her wool coat in the middle of her warm apartment. Biographical information on her and her immediate family, her own medical and employment histories, all forms she'd completed without question. Toby's birth certificate listed her as the mother, no father, and the naval hospital in Annapolis as his birthplace.

The paperwork otherwise had nothing to do with Toby or their accusation that she abandoned her kid on the Metro.

Aside from the birth certificate, there was no way the rest were official police papers!

Dropping the papers on her computer desk, she then stripped off her coat and passed by the guest…Toby's room. He was asleep.

She returned to the desk and scoured the paperwork for some sort of identifying information on the place she'd been or the company that developed the forms.

Nothing.

Frustrated, she searched the Internet for Dr. Williams until she found the eminent neurologist, whose picture she recognized. Somewhat relieved, she read his biography, impressed by his clientele, who ranged from heads of countries around the world to the richest families on the planet. He'd graduated from a Switzerland medical school and practiced extensively in Europe before coming to the United States thirty years before…

…and dying twenty years ago at the age of sixty-four.

She reread the entry, brow furrowed. Yes, it was his picture and yes, his clinic had been located in the same place it was now.

She'd spent several hours in his office talking to a dead man?

"Mama."

She jerked. She had forgotten Toby…again. He stood sleepy and frowning, dark hair tousled.

"I want cocoa."

Did she even have…of course she would. Right next to her tea. She went to the kitchen and made him a cup in silence, glancing at him a few times as he propped his head up with both his hands.

"Do you go to school?" she asked awkwardly.

"Yes," he said, and rolled his eyes. "I have a map. I know you forget."

I can't be this crazy, she thought. She sat across from him, cocoa with marshmallows before both of them.

"Do I forget often?" she asked.

"No."

"Do you like…school?"

"I guess," he said with a shrug. "The teachers are mean to me."

"That sucks, I guess."

"Yeah. I like marshmallows."

She stretched for the counter and tugged the bag off, handing it to him.

"I think the death dealer needs cocoa," he said cheerfully.

"Why do you call him that?"

"Because that's what he is, silly!"

"Oh," she said.

"He's outside my window. Can I take him some cocoa?"

"He's *what?*"

"C'mere." Toby took her hand in one of his, with his other fist wrapped around a large marshmallow. He led her to the window overlooking the street.

The death dealer stood at the edge of the shadows as he had across from the doctor's office, waiting.

"What is he?" she whispered.

"He's a death dealer," Toby said with impatience. "He's not here for us."

The confidence with which he spoke floored her. She wiped her face again, the world around her spinning. Near hyperventilating, she sat heavily on the couch and clutched her head with her hands. Toby chattered, his tone lifting in a question that didn't penetrate the in-between world in which she'd fallen.

There were sounds that should've alarmed her, the feel of hot tears on her face. Something warm touched her back, and a jolt of hot electricity made her sit upright. Her mind cleared, and she wiped her eyes at the massive form in black before her. Panicked, she backpedaled until trapped into the corner of the couch.

The death dealer stared at her, much larger in her small living room than he was in the middle of the street. He was close to seven feet tall, with chiseled features and eyes as black as eternity. His clothing was thick and heavy this night, as if he expected to be standing outside her window until dawn. His sweater, jeans, and trench coat were all of high quality with his heavy boots dwarfing her feet as hers did Toby's. She didn't see any weapons this night. He was muscular and buff beneath the trench.

Of all things, his gloved hands scared her the most.

"Gabriel!" Toby cried happily as he started into the living room, spilled the cocoa, and then retreated to the kitchen. The death dealer moved to follow, silent even over the hollow wooden floors.

She heard Toby's chipper voice as he invited the death dealer to share some cocoa with him.

What the hell was a death dealer? The grim reaper, here in her home?

In the course of a day, her whole life had gone to shit.

She tiptoed to the kitchen and peeked in. The death dealer took up much of the small space, his trench still on despite sitting at the kitchen table. Toby was showing him the glitter drawing he'd done. The death dealer glanced at it, his face so emotionless she thought him a statue again. He sipped his cocoa from a sticky cup filled half with marshmallows.

What kind of mother let her five-year-old son carry on with *death* like he was a favorite uncle?

"...and this is your portal into the shadow world," Toby said proudly, indicating a blob of silver on one side of the drawing. "Do you see where it goes?"

"Elisia."

"Yes!" Toby squealed. "Where the fairies are!"

She was shaking, cold with fear on the inside and fevered skin clammy on the outside.

The death dealer touched a gloved finger to a blank spot on the construction paper, and an orchid sprung up, ethereal and hovering over the paper. Its colors rippled and changed before the flower bent and delicate wings spread apart, revealing a creature that was surely a fairy.

Toby squealed again and bounced to his feet, beginning a whirling dance. She thought she heard ethereal laughter as the fairy danced with him. The death dealer touched the paper again, and another orchid appeared, stretched, and morphed into a second fairy. Toby laughed and whirled.

Katie's vision blurred and grew dark. She heard herself scrape against the wall as she fell and was out before she hit the floor.

So far, he hadn't been forced to change shapes since Gabriel's visit. Rhyn tested the bonds of his cell again until a mage in a brown robe hurried down the hall to repair the damage. Sometimes he could see out into the hallway and the empty cell across from his; sometimes he couldn't.

Today, the cell across from his wasn't empty. A human-like creature sat in the corner making snorting sounds he assumed was weeping. He looked closely at the creature. It was from the healer's guild, one of the oldest guild's in the universe. By the tattooed bands wrapped around his arms--each one depicting a millennium--the creature was nearly as old as Andre, the eldest of Rhyn's brothers.

"Shapeshifter!" someone called from down the hall.

He watched the mage in brown scuttle away. "Yeah," Rhyn grunted.

"I'm bored. Entertain me," the male voice down the corridor said. "Can you shut that healer up by eating him?"

"Yeah," he replied.

The sobbing, slender creature tensed and covered his head, as if expecting an attack from above. Amused, Rhyn stopped pacing and sat, staring the small creature down. The healer quieted.

"Good enough," the creature down the hall, Jared, said with a loud sigh. "What shape are you now, beast?"

"The usual."

"Not much for talking, are you?"

The rest of the freaks collected by Sasha, Rhyn's half-brother who aligned himself with the Dark One, were quiet on the cell block. They normally were, and if they weren't, their screaming was muted by the magic of their cells. Rhyn stretched out on the ground of his cell to stare at the ceiling.

"I heard Sasha's getting promoted by You Know Who," Jared continued. "Wonder if he'll be too important for his personal zoo."

"He'll make time for you, Jared," Rhyn assured him.

"I suppose. Not sure why he has a half-breed like you hanging around when he's got a full-blooded demon like me here."

Rhyn knew why well enough. In Sasha's zoo, he was at the bottom of the food chain of the otherworldly collection of creatures. He intended to keep his relationship to their zookeeper a secret. Sasha had an affinity for collecting the worst of the worst--creatures whose intentions toward humans and immortals alike were as far from the Immortal Code as could be.

Despite Rhyn's fury and occasional diversion from the Immortal Codes, he still believed in them, a *weakness* Sasha was trying to beat out of him since their eldest brother--the peacemaker and enforcer of the Council That Was Seven--sentenced them both to Hell.

"Fuck you, Sasha," he whispered into the darkness, not caring if Sasha heard him or not.

Fuck you, Kris, for making me do what I did, and fuck you, Andre, for pulling the trigger and sending me here with Sasha.

When he was out of Hell, he'd already planned on kicking the ass of their eldest brother, Andre, and killing Kris. The Council That Was Seven would survive without the three of them: Sasha, who'd sold out long ago; Kris, who needed to die; and him, whom Andre'd kill as soon as he killed Kris.

As much as they hate me for aligning with the Dark One, they hate you more for our father's death, Sasha had told him smugly more than once.

It was true, and only Andre supported his petition to be recognized as one of the seven sons charged by their father with protecting humanity against the Dark One. By the time he came of age, his other six brothers had not only come of age but also had each adopted a continent of responsibility. His late birth in the immortal world landed him Antarctica, where he could do little harm with his wild powers.

As much as he hated Hell, he hated Antarctica more.

Restless, he rose and paced again, wondering why Sasha needed an ancient healer in his zoo, a place where creatures came to suffer.

He sensed what Gabriel wouldn't say: things were about to change for him, and he suspected that meant he'd soon be free. Whoever it was he was to protect, even his promise to Gabriel wouldn't stand in his way of revenge.

I'm coming for you, Kris.

Katie awoke and readied herself for the world, convinced everything had been a nightmare caused by exhaustion. Her conviction wilted as she stepped from her room into the living room to find the black-clad death dealer seated in an armchair, facing the door as if on guard, with a lethal black sword across his lap. He'd laid his trench over the couch, though he still wore boots and gloves.

"I was hoping you'd be gone."

His gaze settled on her, and she'd wished she'd never spoken. She hid in the kitchen, cold inside once again. Her hands shook as she made tea. The glitter and construction paper picture was back on the fridge with no sign that any fairies had emerged from its depths. She breathed deeply, struggling to remain in control when all she wanted to do was run for the nearest psych ward and check herself in.

She turned and jumped.

"God, I can't take this! You, out!" she belted at the death dealer, who leaned his hip against the counter and managed to fill up the entrance to the kitchen.

He obeyed, and she gave a growl of frustration. She followed, intent on having her tea by the window as she did every morning.

"Your shit is everywhere!" she snapped. "And what in the name of everything holy are you doing with a *sword*? Is that even legal?"

"As legal as underage drinking," he replied, though he moved the sword off her favorite chair and placed it on the trench stretched across her couch. He sat with his hands on his thighs and his eyes straight ahead, like a statue chiseled in Hell itself. He was perfectly still, and she tried to concentrate on her tea.

"This is impossible."

She marched to her bathroom and yanked out the three prescription pill bottles she'd found in her cabinet, reading the labels. She'd done research on the drugs; they were antipsychotics and anti-anxiety pills. She grabbed a second bottle and went to the kitchen for water, dumping out two of each into one hand. She took a deep breath and opened her mouth, freezing when a black-gloved hand clamped around her wrist. She looked up at the silent shadow, whose chiseled features were unreadable. He swept up the pills and crushed them in his hand, then released the powder into the sink. He dumped the rest in the garbage disposal and turned it on, returning a few minutes later with the other bottles.

Too afraid to challenge him, she watched him destroy everything. He gave no explanation and headed toward her bedroom. She bit back an order to leave her stuff alone but stopped herself, watching him go through her medicine cabinet for any additional drugs. Satisfied there was nothing left, he tore her prescriptions to bits before returning to the chair and stilling again into a statue.

The living room started to spin and she sat, forcing herself to breathe deeply.

"We can talk." His stoic offer made laughter bubble within her.

"I don't *want* to talk! I want my life back!"

"This is your life."

"Absolutely not!" she snapped. "I'm not psychotic, I didn't have amnesia yesterday, I've never had a son! I don't care what anyone says, not Dr. Williams, not my sister, not *you!*"

"You weren't supposed to remember anything before Toby appeared in your life," he said.

"What're you talking about?"

He looked at her, a penetrating stare that made her again regret drawing his attention. She couldn't read his face. He rose and, with methodical patience, swirled the trench around him, placed the sword on the inside with an array of other weaponry and stalked to the door.

All it took was a hissy fit to get rid of him. The door closed behind him. She sagged into the depths of her chair.

"Mama, do I have to go to school today?" Toby called.

She ground her teeth, on the verge of throwing her cup at the wall before her.

"It's not working."

The man in the white lab coat, Ully, jerked from his hunched position over a keyboard, and fear flashed in his eyes. The unease passed quickly as he saw which death dealer stood before him.

"Of course it is," he said, twisting in the chair to face him.

Gabriel leaned his hip against the counter and crossed his arms in physical disagreement. He rarely spoke, and when he did, people rarely failed to take his words seriously. As the oldest and most revered of the death dealers, only the damned millennial generation failed to flinch when he spoke.

"Okay, so maybe it isn't," Ully said quickly. "You're sure?"

Gabriel said nothing but pinned him with a glare that had killed a few men outright.

"Okay, fine."

The brunet scientist leaned forward to hit the intercom button.

"Kris, death dude's here. We need to talk!" he called cheerfully, then spun and started toward the conference room at the end of a lab that stretched the size of a football field.

Gabriel followed, ignoring the rows of delicate glassware, Bunsen burners, machines, and other science toys that employed the two dozen immortal scientists. The lighting was harsh in the lab; he didn't remove his sunglasses until they'd entered the romantically lit conference room. The brunet flipped the overhead lights on, and Gabriel flipped them off.

The conference room was silent, the air purified, the lighting perfect. Gabriel sat opposite the door while Ully flung himself into a cushy chair.

"I wondered where that went," the scientist murmured as he withdrew a vial of violet gel from his lab coat. He whistled as he shook it, and the color went from purple to orange.

"This is bad shit," he said to no one in particular. "It's contaminated."

Gabriel didn't need to understand modern science. Death dealers were immune to disease, poison, and any other thing humans could throw at them. They had to be, because mankind had been trying to outsmart Death since the beginning of time.

"Gabriel."

The immortal Council's leader, a silver-haired man with violet eyes and a face untouched by time, stood at the entrance. He was one of the oldest warriors among the immortals, a man with the body of a thirty-year-old and the soul of the Ancients.

The scientist, whose name was Ully, replaced the vial and leaned back in his chair.

"Death dude said it's not working."

Kris raised an eyebrow and turned to Ully.

"Where did we find her?"

"She was referred by another immortal, Giovanni," Ully replied.

"Then what's the problem?"

"It's not working," Gabriel said.

"Ully, check the info we got from her," Kris ordered.

The scientist hopped up with a cheerful salute. Kris waited until the door closed.

"You should've killed her, Gabe," he said with a frown.

"Sasha wants her as much as Toby."

"Sasha wants a *human?*"

"Yeah. She's an immortal mate, a special one."

Gabriel knew the impact of his simple words just as he knew the impact of his appearance. Kris's normally iced features clouded, his violet eyes going green as he thought.

"How special?" Kris asked, the worry lines on his forehead deepening.

"Special enough she's immune to immortal magic."

"That doesn't make sense," Kris said, and leaned forward. "Unless you're saying…"

Kris looked at him hard.

"Are you saying she's an *Ancient's* mate?"

Gabriel shrugged. Neither Kris nor Sasha was capable of mercy or empathy. For that sake, neither was *he*. But an immortal's mate was off hands. An Ancient's mate had never before been found. As the leader of the Council That Was Seven, Kris would be obligated to take the first Ancient mate.

Kris's features clouded, and Gabriel suspected it was because Kris had been with his current lover, Jade, for hundreds of years.

"This isn't good," Kris voiced. "Keep an eye on her and stay my execution order for now. Ully might figure something else out."

"The Council meets in two days," Gabriel reminded him.

"Trust me, I can think of nothing else. Sasha's planning something big."

"End of the world."

"Your sense of humor couldn't be worse timed, Gabe."

"You'll get to see my place finally."

Kris shook his head, his look of disapproval mixed with amusement. Gabriel liked Kris as much as he'd ever liked anyone despite the bad blood between Kris and his half-brother, Rhyn. They were different men with different purposes, yet both honorable to the core.

"You still think you can leave Death when you want?" Kris challenged.

"I'm a guest."

"No such thing."

"I'm an exception. She took me in as a favor to my father and will release me, if I ever wanted it."

Death had her pick of badasses from every generation of man and creature, and she wooed every one with the promise of endless riches and the ability to leave when they chose. His circumstances were different, and they both knew it.

Kris slid two rare green life crystals across the table, the common form of payment for an assassination not ordered by Death herself.

"Two for the girl watching Toby, in case you're right, and someone else grabs her," he said. "Your choice of death for her."

Gabriel took the crystals with a nod. Kris left, and Gabriel closed his eyes, crossing into the shadow world before emerging on the street outside the woman's apartment building. He watched the people pass as he had every generation of man. He sank into the shadows, at home in the darkness, watching. Always watching. Never a part of the world around him.

Some things never changed, like the blue sky, the sun orb, the grass and oceans. They were constants in a world where humans and their inventions passed through the world, less significant than an exhaled breath. He spent most of his time anymore in the shadow world, except when forced out by Death or called out by someone who wanted to buy an assassination. In the darkness, he was comfortable. In the darkness, he was alone.

In the darkness, he wasn't reminded of an ache he'd killed long ago, that which reminded him he once knew what it was to feel the warmth of the sun on his human skin.

He took up his position outside of Katie's apartment building to protect Rhyn's mate despite his promise to Death not to break any more Immortal Codes.

Katie poured more whiskey into her cocoa. She hadn't been able to shake the cold she felt and was dressed in layers despite the thermostat being set to eighty. Restless, she took her cocoa into the darkened living room and looked out the window, expecting to see Gabriel lurking across the street. He was there.

"I'm a four-hundred-thousand-year-old angel. I'm a baby in my world. More marshmallows!"

Just when she thought things were weird enough, Toby had started to talk to her. She refused to send him to school or to go to work, determined to figure out what insanity was going on under her roof. Toby's eyes glowed as small marshmallows tumbled into his cup. He held out his hands. She ignored them and placed the cup on the table before him, then set down her own.

"You're a four-hundred-thousand-year-old baby," she repeated. "Then you're not my kid."

"I am!" he replied. "I have to have a human mother."

"You get a new one every eighty years or something?"

"I'm kinda reborn every once in awhile to a new mom."

"And the death dealer is…what?" She asked and pinched her arm. She was still awake.

"He's Death's hit man."

"Of course, why not." She poured more whiskey into her cocoa. Alcohol had replaced Hannah in her life when she left.

Toby chewed on the crackers she'd placed before him, crumbs and chunks going all over his pj's. He didn't look like a four-hundred-thousand-year-old angel trapped in a five-year-old's body.

"His name is Gabriel. He's way older than me. I see him every few dozen years, usually when he's coming to kill my mama. He's cool."

She gripped her head.

"Gabriel, fairies!" Toby exclaimed.

She turned and gasped, heart leaping to see the death dealer lingering like the shadow he was in the middle of her living room. His eyes glowed darker than night, two black holes in his otherwise indistinguishable face. She groped for the nearest light and flipped it on, unsettled by the man even in the warm lamplight.

"Toby says you're going to kill me," she said, heart hammering.

"Not yet."

"Not yet?" she echoed. "You have a date in mind you'd like to share?"

"No."

"Soon, not soon?"

"No," he said.

"Look, I get that no one survives life, but I'd like to know when you plan on taking me out so I can plan a few things, say farewell to my sister, maybe prepay for my burial!" she demanded, hearing the hysterics enter her voice.

"There won't be a body to bury."

Her mouth dropped open.

"Gabriel takes people to the underworld, body and all," Toby explained as he grasped the large man's gloved hand. "Fairies!"

The death dealer went obediently to the kitchen. Katie's hands shook. She followed them and set her cocoa down on the counter, grabbing the whiskey and retreating with the intent of drinking herself to sleep. Gabriel's hand snaked out as she passed, and he yanked the bottle neatly from her hand. She snatched at it, and he pushed her away.

"Immortal Code," he stated.

Keeping her away with one hand, he dumped its contents into the sink. She watched, and then stalked out, furious and frustrated. After he destroyed all her drugs, she'd suspected he'd react this way and had hidden another bottle in her bedroom.

She slammed her door and rested her head against it, wondering how long this would continue before her head exploded. Or when Gabriel the death dealer killed her. She withdrew the final bottle of whiskey from beneath the bed. It was wrenched away from her, and she grated her teeth.

"No," Gabriel said. He held up the bottle and retreated to the bathroom.

She jerked her door open and grabbed her coat. She didn't care if she left a five-year-old kid home alone, not when he was a four-hundred-thousand-year-old angel! He had someone better than an army watching him. He had death's personal assistant.

She walked out onto the sidewalk, shivering in the cold.

I usually only see him when he comes to kill my mama.

The words echoed in her head, and she walked blindly for several moments, until the cold burning her lungs made her stop. She'd been seen by a doctor who'd been dead twenty years, was babysitting a four-hundred-thousand-year-old angel, and the grim reaper spent the night on her couch.

Things really couldn't get much stranger.

"Ms. Young, I need a blood sample."

The man who spoke stood behind her. He was tall with glasses, a brunet ponytail, and a goofy grin. His lab coat was all the overcoat he wore, and he hopped in place beside a beat-up VW Bug whose engine coughed as if it were on its last leg.

"Let me guess, you work for a dead doctor," she said, crossing her arms.

"Oh, no!" he said with a laugh. "Technically, I *am* a dead doctor."

"Unbelievable."

"No, no, it's a really good story. I got to meet Death and everything."

She turned on her heel and walked.

"*Please*, Katie!" he begged. "No girls ever visit my lab, and Kris rarely lets me leave. Just one pinprick."

"You know Ted Bundy drove a VW Bug, right?" she challenged.

He opened the passenger door with a hopeful smile. She climbed in wordlessly, not surprised to find it cold. The vents rattled without producing heat.

"It's not far," he said with a cheerful smile despite his shaking body. "I'm Ully."

True to his word, they drove less than two blocks before he entered a public parking garage and drove to the bottommost floor and parked in a dark corner with yellow no-parking lines. He turned off the car and touched the garage door opener on the sunshade above him, whistling as he waited. She jerked as the ground lurched below them, lowering them slowly through the thick cement layers into a tunnel wide enough for a dump truck.

He started the car again and drove through a series of tunnels and intersections, a virtual underground street grid, before arriving at a large garage filled with gleaming cars.

She trailed him to an elevator that took them even further underground. Her headache was returning, her heart beating so fast she knew she'd pass out if she didn't calm down. Her deep breaths drew Ully's dark eyes.

He smiled in encouragement and led her off the elevator and through a series of cheerfully lit hallways with pictures on the walls and wood floors. He swiped a badge to enter what she imagined was the Mecca of all science labs, with rows of stainless steel, machines, computers, and glass. He parked himself at a computer, and she perched on a stool beside him.

"What is all this?" she breathed.

The air was cool and clear, as crisp as a fall day.

"Only the best lab *ever!*"

His enthusiasm for the underground world only made her feel more nauseous. He took her hand and pricked her finger. The pain and the sight of her blood made her vision dim. She fell into the in-between place, only vaguely aware of his panicked response as she sagged against him or of the muscular form that lifted her from the floor and carried her away.

The pungent smelling salts snapped her out of the in-between place. She swiped the hand away, blinking to clear her gaze as she stared into a fire. The hearth blazed opposite her position on a plush sofa with buttery leather in a small study with Persian carpets. She thought the man before her old because of his silver until her vision cleared and she saw his face.

His white-silver hair was long and clasped at his neck, his bronzed face and forest-green eyes displaying no emotion. His features were chiseled, the firelight casting harsh shadows across the planes of his face. He was muscular and tall, clothed in dark jeans, a snug grey T-shirt that hugged his biceps and stretched across his chest and back and then sagged at his slender torso and hips, and a round black medallion that fell from his T-shirt as he leaned over her.

"Ully," he growled, turning to face the scientist.

Ully was pale.

Katie pushed herself up, startled by the stickiness on her hand. She looked down and saw the sleeve of her sweater soaked in blood.

"I am so sorry!" Ully gushed, stricken. "You fell, and I tried to catch you, but then you kind of veered to one side and I grabbed your arm but then you--"

"Out."

Ully frowned but obeyed the white-haired man's command. Katie sat up, wondering why her hand didn't hurt. It shook, and she was even colder.

"I don't know what you are, but I couldn't heal you. You owe Gabriel one," the silver-haired man said. He squatted beside her, wrapping her arm in a clean white towel before he rose and strode to the desk along the far wall. He picked up what looked like a medical file and became as still as the death dealer, as if forgetting her presence completely.

Her eyes skimmed his perfect, buff body before the pain in her hand finally registered. She tugged off her wool coat with some effort. Blood soaked her towel, and she stood.

"Do you have a restroom?"

He jabbed his thumb toward the wall behind him, where she made out the slender nickel doorknob in the space between two shelves of ancient books. He didn't acknowledge her as she entered the surprisingly large bathroom. She winced and pulled the towel free then turned on the water as hot as she could stand. She stared at herself in the mirror, wondering when she'd started looking like a pound dog. She glanced down to watch the blood stream down the drain then held up her arm.

It was healed, just as he said.

She flipped both hands front and back and looked at the blood-soaked towel and the sleeve of her sweater. Her hands both worked. With a sigh, she cleaned up the area as well as she could and pulled off the sweater, as it was warm enough in the study with her T-shirt.

She looked like shit. There were dark circles beneath her light eyes, her hair was in a half-assed lumpy ponytail, and her face was so pale and drawn, she looked ill.

Was this what crazy looked like? She breathed out another sigh and righted her ponytail, then splashed water on her face. Emerging from the bathroom, she was confronted by a pacing Ully.

"I, uh, dropped your blood sample," he said with a glance at the figure with his back toward them both. "Could I get another?"

She handed him the towel. He hesitated then took it and left. The silver-haired man made no move at all.

"I need--" she said finally.

"Have a seat."

His order was calm, the slight accent in his voice foreign. She stared at the back of his head, a chill running through her. Her move toward the fire was reflected in a small mirror behind the desk in front of which he stood.

He had no reflection.

She squeezed her eyes closed and breathed deeply, swaying. His touch made her jerk away and her eyes snap open. She stared at him, backing out of his reach until the back of her knees hit a chair and she dropped into it.

His eyes had changed color to a deep violet-blue, a beautiful shade of tanzanite. She felt cold again on the inside and shivered. He looked away finally and returned to his desk.

"Are you all right?" he asked in a measured tone.

She cleared her throat and said simply, "Yes."

As if sensing the weight of the word, he turned, brow furrowed. He perched on the edge of the desk, the fire casting shadows across his perfect, chiseled features. Any other day, she'd have stared at his hard body and the way his jeans hugged his muscular thighs and the round globes of his backside, or the T-shirt that fit so well.

"What's your name?" he asked.

"Katie."

"How did you get in my lab?"

"Ully brought me."

"From the Outside?" He crossed his arms, displaying his displeasure without his face changing.

She nodded. "You must be Kris."

"I am."

"Ully said you don't let him out much."

"I don't," Kris agreed.

"And that he was once a dead doctor."

"Yeah."

She shuddered. They gazed at each other for a long moment, her shock and exhaustion too deep to fear the man who radiated power and control, even in a simple T-shirt.

Tattoos of interlinked geometric shapes glowed on his arms before fading.

"Why do you need my blood?" she asked.

"Ully's testing it. It's what he does."

"Dr. Williams said my blood tests were unusual."

His eyes turned from tanzanite to deep emerald. She shivered again.

"I need a shot of whiskey," she said.

For a long moment, she didn't think he'd agree, if not because of how young she looked, then because of how shitty she looked. At last he moved around the desk to a dark corner and withdrew a crystal carafe from a locked cabinet.

"Don't give me your good stuff. I don't intend to savor it," she warned.

He gave her an amused look, then poured her three shots worth of whiskey and handed it to her. She downed a mouthful, grimacing at the burn that went down her throat and all the way to her gut.

"I can't get warm any other way," she admitted, and took another gulp.

"You're in shock," he surmised.

"No argument there. I have a feeling you know already what the past two days have been like."

"Tell me."

"No, thanks."

He raised an eyebrow, crossing his arms again. She really didn't give a damn if he wasn't used to being challenged. She finished her whiskey and sat back in the chair, its warmth chasing away her internal chill. For now.

"Do Gabriel and Toby work for you?" she asked.

"In a sense."

"What does that mean?"

"Death dealers don't work for anyone really, just Death, though I do buy assassinations from him on occasion," he said.

Buy assassinations, like he was ordering a new couch for his study.

"Oh," she managed. "And Toby, the baby…angel?"

"I'm his guardian, yes." His gaze had sharpened.

"And you randomly assign him new moms every few dozen years and then send Gabriel to pick them off at the end," she summariezed.

"More or less."

"Do you ever bother to see if the moms want to have a baby angel in their lives?"

"I don't think I've ever had a *human* question me," he stated, eyes flashing golden topaz.

"It's really not cool to use women like this," she replied. "Even if we are puny humans."

"You're the first to object."

"No offense, but I'm under the impression the others didn't have a chance to object."

A light tap sounded at the door.

"What, Ully?" he belted.

She jumped, unaware she'd ruffled him despite the calm exterior. Ully opened the door without entering, his gaze fluttering from her to the angry non-human.

"I, uh, kinda need to talk to you, bossman, if you're cool with that," Ully said.

The man with the jewel-toned eyes strode across the study without a look at her. She waited until the door closed before crossing to the carafe and refilling her glass. His anger surprised her with its intensity, and she judged from Ully's reaction that seeing the lord and master pissed was not something the good-natured mad scientist wanted anything to do with. She didn't know what he was, but if he routinely played with the lives of puny humans and bought assassinations…

She drank the caramel liquid too fast and was soon too dizzy to stand.

"I thought something was weird based on what death dude said," Ully said, stepping back from the rotating DNA molecule on the screen with a triumphant smile.

"Antigens? You're saying she's allergic to us?" a skeptical blonde woman with striking blue-green eyes asked.

Kris glanced at her and then back at the screen. His trusted deputies--the slender blonde Iliana and the raven-haired gigantor Jade with cocoa skin--sat across from him. Death dude sat at the back of the conference room, out of the glare of the screen.

"Sort of," Ully said. "Basically these antigens are acting as a screening agent."

"Meaning…?" Jade waved his hand impatiently.

"Meaning she's immune to many of our talents," Kris supplied with a frown. "How, Ully?"

"It's genetic."

"So one of her parents was like us?" Iliana asked, tapping a hot pink fingernail.

"Not exactly. It's kind of like…" Ully looked around and stretched for the pen on the table. "If immortals are pens, and normal humans are number two pencils, then she's a mechanical pencil."

"*What?*" Jade demanded.

"She's a hybrid," Iliana said, realization dawning on her face. "Kris…"

"Yeah, I know."

"She's also an immortal's mate," Ully added.

Kris studied the DNA molecule, now certain the woman's appearance spelled certain danger for him. His gaze settled on Jade's familiar features, and he studied his companion of so many years. Jade was everything he admired: brave, compassionate, dedicated. Loyal. He didn't doubt his second and his lover would move on, if Kris chose to take the woman as his mate. Yet he wondered if *he* could ever care for another the way he did Jade.

His duty as the leader of the fractured Council always came first. Jade's duty would, too. He'd found peace with Jade after Rhyn killed his first love, Lilith. But Jade was like most immortals: he'd only ever loved other men, whereas Kris valued mettle over sex.

As he weighed if he'd be forced to choose between someone he loved and an immortal's mate with a desirable gift, he couldn't help thinking Jade wouldn't take breaking up well. His love had a temper. It would take him a while to recover.

"We have two issues," Ully continued, sitting. "There's never been a mutation like this in the history of our people. If it's hereditary, then the mutation has been hidden from us for, like, maybe even hundreds of thousands of years. Second, I can duplicate the DNA with some time in my lab and isolate the antigen, meaning I can make someone immune to our enemies' powers."

"Or they can make someone immune to us," Jade said.

Kris felt the intent gazes of both of his deputies, who left the obvious unvoiced. They were in more trouble than he'd thought once the Council convened.

"We know a few things," he started. "One, Sasha probably knows about her by now. Two, someone in our organization knew what she was when they set her up to be Toby's human guardian."

"Good job, death dude!" Ully cheered, earning him the scathing look of Jade.

"She's immune to all but the most ancient of us. The mutation started sometime after our births, Kris," Gabriel voiced.

Surprised, Kris eyed him. "You know more than you're telling me?" he challenged. "This isn't a secret you're sworn to protect."

Amusement flashed across the death dealer's face, and Gabriel shook his head.

"Ully, do a full workup on her parents, grandparents, as far back as she remembers. Find any siblings and get their blood. We need to know how many people have this mutation and where they are," Kris ordered.

Ully bounced up.

"And Ully, be discreet," Kris added. "No more stalking and kidnapping."

The lab rat flushed but saluted and ducked out of the room.

"The Council meets in a few," Jade commented. "Do we return her and pretend we don't know or keep her where they can't get her?"

It's not cool to use women like that.

Kris had never heard anything so ridiculous. No human--nor most of those in his organization--would dream of speaking to him like that. And yet, she had without fear. Shock did much to humans, he knew, but she was either crazy or incredibly stupid to challenge someone like him.

Worse, they'd never run across this type of issue in all their years. That it emerged now, when the Council was on the verge of disintegrating, couldn't be a coincidence.

"Jade, send some men to her apartment and dig around. Check on Toby while you're there. Iliana, we have a Council meeting to attend in a couple of hours."

"You want them to take her back?" Jade asked.

"Yeah. Take her back and post guards everywhere you can. I want to see what Sasha's planning."

"You shouldn't go alone to the Council meeting," Jade warned.

"It's the way it is."

"Someday, one of you is gonna snap and take out the others."

"Let's hope it's me," Kris said with a small smile.

"If you wouldn't take out half the continent doing so, I wouldn't care. C'mon, death dude. Let's get her to her apartment. Travel safely, Kris."

Gabriel followed them out obediently, content to hang around them while bored.

Kris traveled via shortcuts through the shadow world as Gabriel did and willed himself to the in-between world. It was foggy and chilly, like a walk on the beach after the fog rolled in. Several portals glowed, and he strode across the silent domain toward the portal he needed. He emerged from the shadow world in a luxurious penthouse suite in Paris overlooking the Arc de Triomphe.

"You Americans. Jeans and T-shirt, Kris, really?" Andre asked.

Kris dismissed his uneasy thoughts at his eldest brother's accented voice. He shook the hand of his brother and friend, whose night-colored skin clashed with his. Andre was dressed in cashmere and wool, his hair kept short and neat, his loafers more expensive than Kris's conference room had cost to build.

"Got nothing to prove, big brother," Kris said.

Andre snorted and motioned to the pristine white sofa. Kris sat.

"I wasn't expecting you," Andre said. He crossed to the wet bar for two glasses, one with red wine and the other with whiskey. "I keep this cheap shit around just in case."

"I like the cheap shit," Kris replied, accepting his whiskey.

"You obviously clothes shop at yard sales."

Kris smiled, and Andre did as well, the skin around his eyes crinkling in warmth.

"I hate these meetings with our brothers," Andre admitted. "I'd rather stay home. Brother, go change. You're not going to embarrass me again."

Kris chuckled, at ease with his brother despite the unprotected penthouse on the top floor of a building that could be easily leveled by a single explosive charge. Being underground meant he was a much harder target to hit, yet despite his attempts to convince his brother to act likewise, he'd not yet succeeded.

He went through one of Andre's two walk-in closets, choosing a maroon sweater and chocolate suede pants. He knew his brother would disapprove but also knew Andre would view it better than jeans.

Andre pursed his lips in displeasure as Kris reappeared.

"Good enough," his brother grunted. "One of my most expensive shirts with the pants that went out of season five years ago."

"How's your spy network?" Kris asked as he poured himself a second glass of whiskey.

"Eh, not so hot lately," Andre replied. "I've been losing some good ones. Still have an idea of what Kiki and Tamer are doing but no idea what Erik is doing."

"You keeping track of me as well?"

"Part of an older brother's duty."

Kris sat opposite his brother. Their alliance off the Council was as important as their balance of power on the Council. Despite being brothers, neither approved of what the other did. Andre's gift lent him great power and control over the mind, enough so that he had no problem recruiting spies as the others did. He was a pacifist, though, and viewed his position on the Council as balancing out the outwardly aggressive predators.

Andre was no threat to the others yet had a full vote on everything the Council did. It was how he walked easily among all the others, never threatened and routinely confided in. Even Sasha, who'd betrayed them all to serve the Dark One, still sought out his brother's counsel. Kris knew his brother too well to know he'd not betray the trust of anyone, even a man who wanted to kill him.

Next to Kris's whiskey Andre kept at the wet bar was Tamer's favorite vodka, Kiki's rice wine, and Erik's diet soda, as if he were expecting one of them at any time.

"What about Sasha?" Kris asked quietly.

"He's killed my last few spies. Got a good one in there now. Getting a lot of good info out of this one."

"Good to hear. You ready?"

Andre held out his hand. Kris took it and they walked through the shadow world through the portal leading to the Sanctuary where the Council meetings took place. His three other half brothers were already present and waiting, Erik pacing, Kiki at the table, and Tamer busy with his PDA. The conference room was plain, the white walls bare, the harsh lighting and round conference table centered.

"Let's go, brothers," Andre said. He sat, leaning back. "Shall we start with Asia this time? Kiki?"

"We started with Asia last time," Kiki snapped, oriental features, turquoise eyes and towering height marking his mixed breeding.

"Very well. Europe," Andre said, unaffected. "Erik."

"Everything's fine."

"Erik."

"The last time I said anything, all my men in North America disappeared. Kris, care to explain?" Erik challenged, ice blue eyes falling to him.

"Nope," Kris said.

"Erik's right, brother," Kiki said. "We can't talk freely like we used to."

"We have a common enemy," Andre reminded them. "One who would like us divided so he can take over our world."

"I'll start," Kris said. "Today, we found someone who's immune to our powers."

All eyes turned to him.

"What do you mean, immune?" Tamer pounced. "There's no such thing."

"She has a hereditary blood anomaly that makes her immune to all but the oldest of our kind. We just found out and are researching it."

"Bullshit," Kiki snapped. "If you know that much, you know more."

"Think what you will, Kiki."

"Have you tested her?" Andre asked.

"We discovered her when she proved unaffected by one of our typical talents," Kris said.

"She's a spy for Sasha," Erik said. "Probably revealed your entire operations by now."

"Not likely," Kris replied.

"I don't believe any of this nonsense," Tamer insisted. "She's a plant. Like Erik said, she's some mutant Sasha made to infiltrate your operations."

"Maybe you're the mole, brother," Kiki added.

The four stared at him. Kris didn't flinch. He'd long since suspected one of them was working with Sasha, but it wasn't him. If anyone, it was Tamer, whose isolation in Siberia and ability to outsmart Andre's spies gave him the ability to hide his actions.

"Bring her here," Tamer said.

"No," Kris said.

"Then I'm not going to believe a damned thing you're saying."

"And I won't share how to counter her mutation so you don't end up at Sasha's feet."

"Fuck you, Kris!"

"Enough," Andre said with a sharp look at both of them. "Kris, the Council will need some sort of proof that this isn't another ploy by one of you to wipe out the others. It's been calm for the past few hundred years, but I don't think any of us have forgotten that five hundred year period where we were at each other's throats."

And they'd lost two of their brothers to the war. Andre himself had ordered the exiles of Rhyn and Sasha to Hell when it was revealed what they were. He didn't say this, but Kris knew it was on everyone's mind.

"Would you object to my visiting her?" Andre finished.

"Nope," Kris said.

"Good enough, Tamer?"

"For now," Tamer allowed. "No compartmentalizing this info, Andre. It's a common threat to all of us. According to the rules, we get to know everything."

"Everything," Kiki emphasized.

"You are entitled to know of anything that threatens you," Andre clarified. "As you know, I'm the only one here who actually adheres to our rules."

The others smiled. There was one rule they all knew better than to break, or Andre would order them killed. So long as they didn't put out a hit on one another, they could decimate each other at their own battles, lie, cheat, spy, steal, anything and everything.

"Other news," Andre said. "Kiki."

"Everything's fine."

"Kris?"

"Ditto."

"Tamer?"

"Same."

"Erik?"

"Nope."

Andre pursed his lips again. Kris sat back, satisfied. He'd done as required and alerted them about a potential threat. As far as he was concerned, he'd do nothing else, even if he learned how to counter it.

"Same time and place next month," Andre said, standing. "These meetings need to improve, brothers. We are not one another's enemies, and we'll never defeat our common enemy so long as we're squabbling."

No one spoke. Kris remained where he was, aware they'd destroy each other if allowed. Their turf wars and battle against the Dark One--and now Sasha--had stirred up some of the bloodiest wars in mankind's history.

One by one, the others left, until he was alone with Andre.

"No one knows her identity, and no one else sees her," Kris said firmly. "We don't know what she is yet, but I won't hesitate to attack my brothers if they try to take her."

"You know me well enough, brother," Andre replied.

"I'll send for you."

"What are you not telling me, Kris?" Andre pressed with brotherly concern in his voice. "There's something else to this human, isn't there?"

Kris looked away. "She's an immortal mate."

"Not uncommon," Andre replied. "What else?"

Kris chuckled, aware his older brother could wait him out. "She's an Ancient's mate."

"Ah," Andre said softly. "Then you're in a bind, if you intend to claim her."

"Can't leave this one to fate," Kris said in the same quiet tone. "But there's Jade. Do you…"

"You and I have always put the Council and our mission first," Andre reminded him. "Now is not the time to doubt yourself. Of all our brothers, you are the only one who can lead us to victory. If this woman gives you the power to do so…"

Kris said nothing, feeling at once foolish and like he was the child Andre used to chastise for failing to focus on his duties. Andre clasped his shoulder, bowed his head, and disappeared.

Kris willed himself to the shadow world and walked back to his underground refuge, heart heavy. Jade awaited him, as he expected. Kris accepted the glass of whiskey but avoided Jade's extended hand.

His lover of many years sensed his unease and waited for him to speak.

"The woman we found is an immortal's mate," he started.

"I know," Jade said, seating himself. "You have someone in mind for her?"

"I do."

Jade waited, and Kris held his gaze in silence. He watched the expectant look turn to one of disbelief. Jade's jaw grew lax before he managed to speak.

"You're serious?"

"I'm bound by my duty," Kris replied.

"But *this*? You'd leave me for her?"

"Not by choice, Jade. Her talent can--"

"You can mate her to one of our friends! There's no--" Jade pointed out.

"She's an Ancient's mate, not just any immortal's mate," Kris explained.

"Give her to Andre."

"Jade."

His gut twisted as raw emotion crossed Jade's face. His friend and lover searched his face hard, then rose and stalked out.

Kris let him go despite his desire to follow him. There was nothing he could say that would take away the pain he'd just caused.

He poured himself more whiskey and sat on the sofa, feeling utterly alone for the second time in his life.

His gaze strayed to the desk, where Katie's file sat. He'd go to her apartment tomorrow and explain to her what her fate was about to become. He suspected the conversation would go as well as his talk with Jade.

His chest felt tight, but he refused to admit his pain.

Jade stormed out of the study and shoved past two warriors in the hallway. Blinded by emotion, he made his way out of the underground compound without knowing where he went. He broke into a run when he reached the country road leading away from the compound.

He ran until his pounding heart drowned out his pounding feet. Cold air made his lungs ache, and he slowed then stopped, buckling over to catch his breath.

The pain in his chest couldn't equate with the pain and distress shooting through him like cold fire. He dropped to his knees and wiped messily at the snot streaming from his nose and the tears frozen to his cheeks.

Images of Kris, his only love in two thousand years, swam through his thoughts. He remembered everything from where they met, their first kiss, their first night together. The memories collided and tortured him, replaying with painful detail.

He'd never felt pain this intense in any of his battles!

He roared and slammed his fists against the ground.

"Kris's pet."

He whirled at the all too familiar voice and sprung to his feet.

"Sasha!"

"Hello, Jade," Sasha purred.

Jade straightened, eyeing the dark figure with bright eyes.

"Looks like the shape you left me in," Sasha said, "when you ditched me for dear Kris."

"Get away from me!"

"Who'd he leave you for?"

Jade said nothing, pain spiraling through him.

"He left you for someone," Sasha insisted, drawing near.

"What do you want, Sasha?"

"My lover is in pain, and you ask me why I'm here?"

"We've been through for hundreds of years," Jade replied.

"True. I still feel when you're upset. We've always had that bond."

Jade knew he should've walked away the moment Sasha appeared. He found himself lingering, wanting to feel a little less alone. Sasha was their enemy.

Kris's enemy.

He faced Sasha, recalling the years they'd spent together. He broke off their relationship when Kris took interest in him and soon after, Kris convinced Andre to banish Sasha to Hell.

Trying to convince himself he was too angry to think straight, Jade shook his head and turned away.

"Whether or not you still care for me, you care for him. Let me help you, Jade." Sasha's voice stopped him again. "A favor from an old friend who doesn't want to see you in pain."

"I don't trust you, Sasha."

"You did once, long ago. Come and sit with me, like old times. I'll take your pain away."

Jade squeezed his eyes closed and said hoarsely, "No one can help me."

"I can. Come with me. An hour is all I ask. If you tell me to leave at the end of it, I'll never bother you again."

He hesitated, at war with himself. There was nothing Sasha could ever say, nothing he could ever do in an hour. But right now, Jade needed someone who understood him, as only Sasha always had.

"One hour," Jade said. "Then you leave me alone forever."

"Deal," Sasha said. "Come with me, my love."

"Katie, your kid's on line two!" one of the cooks shouted back to her.

She looked from the computer screen to the phone with the flashing red light. She sat in the general manager's office of the fast food joint where she'd worked for a couple of months six months. The office was small but clean and smelled of fried food. The general manager was on maternity leave, and Katie rifled through several drawers before locating a bottle of painkillers. She was hungover and tired, with a roiling stomach and headache, yet she managed to make it to work before the breakfast rush. Only after she tossed back a couple of painkillers did she pick up the phone.

"What's up, Toby?"

"Hi! I didn't want to go to school today and stayed home but we're out of marshmallows and Gabriel doesn't have any money so I told him that we could ask you to pick up more marshmallows because we both really like them."

"You need anything else from the store?" she asked, her head hurting more.

"Nope. Oh, but you might want to get some…Gabriel, what does he like?"

She heard a mumbled response.

"Oh, never mind. Kris will send a car for you."

"Kris? Why?" she asked suspiciously.

"He wants to talk to you."

"Tell him I kinda have a life and don't really care what he wants."

There was a moment of silence, then a child's gleeful laugh. "Can I really tell him that?" Toby asked.

"Please do."

"Awesome!"

"Listen, I've got work to do," she said. "I'll bring you marshmallows. Text me if you need anything else."

"Okay! G'bye, Mama!"

"Don't call me that. We both know better," she grumbled.

He laughed again, and she hung up, pressing the heels of her palms to her eyes. She'd fallen asleep in Kris's library after half a bottle of whiskey and awoken in her own bed with a throbbing headache and dry mouth.

She'd dared to hope again that everything was a hallucination brought on by too much alcohol, until Toby burst in chasing a cat she didn't remember owning. The boy had clambered across her bed, shrieked happily, and chased the cat under the bed.

"Katie! Visitor!" one of the cashier girls said with a jarring knock.

Katie sighed and sat up straight a second before the door was pushed open to reveal someone she didn't know. The stranger was well dressed, tall, and handsome with eyes too dark and still for her comfort.

"Ms. Young, I'm David Kingsly, from Kingsly Enterprises."

Surprised, she rose and shook his hand. His multimillionaire father's picture was on the wall, and he owned two dozen restaurants in the Annapolis area, including this one.

"It's a pleasure, sir. I apologize for the mess. I wasn't expecting you. Are you here for the GM?" she asked, flustered the GM hadn't warned her about his visit. "I can call her."

"No, no. I drop by on occasion to check on my father's restaurants," he said with a quick glance around. "The GM said your team came up with the latest marketing campaign. I wanted to thank you in person. It's increased profits about seven percent over last quarter."

"Thanks," she said, smiling. "We have a good group here."

"A good leader makes a good team the best, as my father says."

Despite the honor of his visit, she couldn't help but feel a trickle of familiar coldness at his still gaze. He smiled but his eyes did not. He resembled his father in height and narrow face, though there was warmth in his father's face she didn't see in his. For a moment, she thought she saw tattoos blaze across his neck and then disappear.

"We intended to invite the GM to our fundraiser tomorrow night, before I was told she's on maternity leave. My father feels it's important to recognize all those who support our family's success. We'd be happy if you attended our gala in her place." He reached into his jacket and produced an embossed invitation in peach and brown.

"I'd be honored," she said, accepting it. "Thank you, Mr. Kingsly."

"David," he said with another smile that didn't reach his eyes. "I look forward to seeing you there."

He rose and left, and she stared after him, excited for the first good day in months. She dialed her sister immediately.

"Sis, I need some help," she said as soon as Hannah answered.

"Oh. Another issue?"

"No. I was invited to some Kingsly gala. I need something to wear."

"*Some* Kingsly gala or the biggest event of the fall?" her sister asked with a laugh.

The sound of Hannah's voice made Katie long for something more familiar than her world had become.

"Hey--you mind if I come over after work?" she asked. "Toby's...going to a friend's house for the night, and I'm sick of my apartment."

"Yeah, sure. You were supposed to come for brunch tomorrow anyway. I'd planned a spa day tomorrow before the gala. We can add shopping to that; I know you don't have anything nice to wear."

Katie rolled her eyes. A day and a half with her sister was as much as she could tolerate; faced with the alternative of returning to her creepy apartment with its creepy occupants, she'd tough it out.

She survived the day of bitching customers and employees alike and arrived late in the evening to Hannah's, a mansion in the outskirts of Annapolis where her sister lived with her fiancé, Giovanni.

Hannah opened the front door before Katie reached it, took one look at her and frowned fiercely.

"You couldn't change before showing up?" she asked, looking past her out at the street.

"It's not like you have neighbors, sis," Katie replied impatiently. "Afraid I'll make you look bad in front of the 'hood?"

"With the money Gio paid for you to go to Georgetown, you'd think you could last a full semester or at least get a better job than this!" Hannah started.

Katie sighed. Hannah stood aside as she entered the large foyer, lecturing her as they ascended to the second floor. Katie knew the mansion well enough after living with Hannah and Giovanni for a year before the fight that made Hannah force Gio to rush out to get Katie an apartment, for fear she'd run away to Europe like she swore.

"...how expensive Georgetown is, Katherine!" Hannah continued.

"I know, Hannah."

"You're eighteen, a single mom, and you've got a shitty job and frankly, a shitty attitude about your future. Why do you smell like alcohol?"

Katie pushed the door to her designated guest room and stripped out of the grease-stained, French fry scented clothing. Hannah continued on the same speech Katie heard every time they were together.

"You know I'm just concerned," Hannah finished. "Toby--"

"He'll be fine," Katie bit off. "I came here for a break, Hannah."

"Gio and I are worried. Everywhere you work, you're recognized for being the brilliant person I know you are. Why can't you pick an office job or at least try to go to school?"

"I don't know, Hannah. I'm not sure what I want to do with my life," Katie said. "And with Toby in the picture ..."

"Well, do something! You owe your child to keep him off welfare."

Katie flung herself on the bed. Despite Hannah's criticisms, she would still rather be here than at her apartment, even knowing Hannah would never believe her story about Toby and the death dealer.

"I'm assuming you already ate," Hannah said, nose crinkling. "Take a shower and come down to say hello to Gio. He's letting me buy your gown for tomorrow, so you might as well be nice to him."

With a sigh, Katie pushed herself off the bed and obeyed

Chapter Three

Katie maneuvered her sequined ball mask into place only to see her sister on the verge of disappearing in the masses of women in custom gowns and masks. The women's coatroom was off one side of the entrance of a mansion even larger than that of Giovanni.

"Who throws a Halloween gala where no one dresses up?" she grumbled, uncomfortable in her formal dress. She'd last dressed up for Hannah's engagement party two years ago.

"Masquerade, not Halloween," Hannah replied.

Katie didn't reply, gaping at a woman in her sixties with enough diamonds to reverse world hunger.

"Stop it!" Hannah hissed. "Pretend to fit in. Don't embarrass me."

Hannah struck off, and Katie lost sight of her one again. She emerged from the coat room in time to see her sister stop beside her fiancé. Katie moved toward them steadily, self-conscious in the snug teal gown that displayed the curves the slender women around her didn't have. The neckline was plunging, revealing the curves of her full breasts.

Her sister had chosen the gown and--thankfully--paid for it. It was three months' salary for Katie, though Hannah had added it to the black AmEx her fiancé paid in full every month without a second thought.

Just like their four-hour trip to the spa, the wardrobe Hannah bought Toby, the jewelry they both wore. Within a four-hour period, Hannah had dropped $50K. For once, Katie was beyond grateful. She felt almost human again after the drama of her week. She fully intended to return the gown and tanzanite jewelry dripping off her ears and neck, but for the night, she enjoyed feeling like Cinderella.

She trailed Hannah into the massive foyer with a dangling chandelier, regally arcing stairway, and an army of wait staff in tuxes circulating alcohol and hors d'oeuvres. Massive ballrooms flanked either side of the foyer, one whose orchestra filled the mansion with calming music, and the other devoted to a buffet unlike any Katie had ever seen. The swirl of gowns of dancing couples drew her attention to the ballroom with the orchestra. She walked through the masses, comfortably hidden behind her mask. No one would know she didn't belong among the blue bloods in this crowd. Beyond the main room were two hallways, also packed, and opened doors along both where men and women circulated.

Katie paused to look around. She'd lost Hannah in the crowd. Her sister wore maroon, as did many of the other women in masks around her. She fingered the small teal evening purse hanging around her wrist, where her cell phone was. Worst case scenario, she'd call her sister.

Completely free, she relaxed and accepted a glass of champagne from one of the wait staff and waded toward the buffet. She paused in the doorway, realizing she was squeezed too tightly into her dress to eat anything. Instead she crossed to the full bar and traded the champagne for a triple shot of whiskey on the rocks. She sipped, surprised at the smooth flavor. It wasn't cheap like the stuff she bought.

"Triple shot of whiskey, no ice."

She shifted as the male form attached to the voice squeezed into the area behind her. Saluting the bartender with her glass, she started to move away when a warm hand on her forearm stopped her. She turned, surprised, and looked up into eyes the color of her jewelry. Most of his face was hidden behind the mask, but his silver-white hair was too familiar to be anyone else's.

"We have similar taste in alcohol," he said, and lifted his glass to her.

"Did you follow me here?" she demanded, refusing his salud.

"I got you invited."

She suddenly felt foolish for believing David Kingsly. No blue blood like the Kingslys gave a damn about some deadbeat assistant GM at a fast food joint! She tossed the whiskey back and gulped it down, then slapped the glass on the bar before turning away.

She searched for half an hour before spotting her sister sitting in one of the airy rooms off the hallway near the buffet. There were several women sitting and talking while choosing delicacies from large silver trays. They'd all removed their masks.

Hannah glanced up with a smile at her approach and patted the seat beside her. Katie sat, irritated to see who followed with a confident stride and two glasses of whiskey, one with ice and the other without. He drew the eye of every woman in the room and silenced those around her with his presence.

"Excuse me, ladies. Katie, you forgot your drink at the bar," Kris said, holding out the iced whiskey to her.

She didn't miss Hannah's stunned look, as if it were a miracle her homely sister could catch the eye of anyone!

His move was too deliberate to be other than planned. He stood far enough away that she had to stand and walk a step to reach him. When she accepted the glass, he followed with a quick and confident, "Let's take a walk around."

If not for Hannah's surprised silence, she would've refused him. He held out an arm she ignored, instead marching past him. He caught up to her in the hallway.

"Whatever it is you want, the answer is no," she told him. "I just want you to leave me alone."

She felt his gaze and suspected she'd pissed him off again with her directness. He placed a hand on the small of her back and led her through the crowd to the ballroom with the orchestra and the dancers. He snatched the whiskey from her hand and placed their glasses on a table.

"I don't dance," she told him.

"Hush."

He spun her to face him and pulled her against him with one arm while his other took hers to the side for a waltz pose.

"Where you been hiding?" he asked casually.

"None of your damn business!" she snapped, craning her neck back to look up at him. Even in her heels he towered a head above her. His eyes flared amber then faded to tanzanite as he gazed down at her.

"You drop off some sort of demon in my house, try to convince me I'm either completely crazy or suffering from amnesia, stalk me to this gala, and expect me to tell you where I spend every minute of every day?" she demanded at his silence. She tugged at her captured hand and was squeezed against him even harder.

"You weren't supposed to remember anything," he replied calmly. "You have a genetic--"

"Don't want to hear it," she cut him off. "Take Toby and the damn death guy and leave me the hell alone."

"I can't."

"The hell you can't."

"You're in danger," Kris said.

She studied him.

"Some very bad people know who you are now," he added.

"So what? You feel guilty for dragging me into this and are obligated to help me?"

"Guilty, no. Obligated, yes. You're destined to work alongside us immortals." His honest answer silenced her. She stepped out of his embrace, the two of them freezing in the middle of the dance floor like rocks in a flowing creek. "Katie, I need to talk to you about something very serious."

He made no move toward her. At his severe tone, she took another step back, ready to exit as fast as she could in the snug dress and high heels.

Suddenly, the lights flickered and went out. A murmur went through the dancers, several of whom sounded as if they ran into each other before pausing. The orchestra fell silent, and somewhere someone--possibly the host--called for the generators to be turned on. A woman gave a cry, and the sound of jostling grew closer.

A man walked calmly through the crowd, strange red tattoos glowing all over his body, similar to the tattoos she'd seen on David Kingsly's neck when he invited her to the gala. She didn't know what he was, but she felt cold inside.

He was evil.

Kris rested one hand on her shoulder. She started to pull away.

"He can't sense you while I'm here," Kris whispered.

She watched as the creature neared in the shadowy darkness. Katie's breathing grew shallow. Her eyes stayed on the creature, which joined several more tattooed beings in the hall before they all struck out in different directions. As if on cue, the auxiliary lighting came on, casting a romantic glow around her.

"No one should know you're here. We gotta get out of here," Kris said.

His hand gripped her neck loosely. A pulse of warmth dispelled the tunnel vision that had begun to form.

"We'll take a shortcut."

He took her hand and led her through the crowd at a steady pace. She looked over her shoulder, uncertain where the men with tattoos were. She didn't know what they--or *he*--

wanted, but if the man before her was worried, she should be terrified. Kris reached an alcove out of sight of the crowds and faced her.

"Close your eyes," he ordered.

She stared at him. He gripped her arm. Before she could shove him away, the sounds of their world fell silent. She looked around, stunned. Their surroundings looked as if someone had left a fog machine on too long in a gym. Several doorways glowed around her, and Kris yanked her toward one. She opened her mouth to speak and then clamped it shut, her stomach turning. He all but dragged her through one of the glowing doorways before she vomited.

Kris muttered curses and touched her shoulder.

Warmth and cold shot through her, righting her stomach but bringing intense pain to her head. She pushed his hand away, unable to stabilize the hot and cold racing through her blood. Her teeth chattered and her body felt so hot she wanted to scream.

"Stop it!" she all but shouted. "God, my head!" She gripped it, vision blurred and balance precarious atop the four-inch heels.

Kris reached for her and she stumbled back, holding up her hand to ward him off. He snatched both hands in one of his, balancing her with his body as he placed his other hand against her forehead. The sensations stabilized and then dissipated.

"Enough, enough, enough!" she belted with a shove.

Her vision cleared to reveal she now stood in a luxurious living room with several people in front of her displaying varying levels of alarm on their faces. She wiped the tears from her face, feeling more torn up than she had the day before. Tattoos flared on the arms and necks of the people in front of her before fading and growing invisible again.

"Whiskey?" Ully was the first to speak.

"Two," Kris replied.

Katie caught her balance against the arm of a sofa.

"Your rescue mission went well," one of them commented with a half smile. He was built like Kris with dark hair. The similarities stopped at their tanzanite eyes and chiseled features; the speaker's skin was as dark as night.

"Well enough," Kris replied.

"Are you all right?" the night-skinned man asked her. He rose and motioned for Katie to take his seat in a plush armchair.

She didn't answer, concentrating on figuring out where the hell she was.

"I'm Andre. This is Jade and Ileana. You know my brother Kris. You also know Gabriel and Ully, I believe."

She lowered herself onto the sofa. "Feels like I've been on a drinking binge," she murmured.

"Kris, real people aren't supposed to go through the shadow world," Ully said, wide eyes on the man with glowing amber eyes.

"No shit, Ully," the man named Jade responded.

"I went through the shadow world?" she asked, brow furrowing.

"Technically, you may have died," Ileana said with a sip of wine. "Death gets pissed when mortals go through the shadow world."

Built more like the beauties Hannah surrounded herself with, Ileana was a natural bombshell with pillowed lips and large eyes.

"Hey, we're alike now!" Ully said, handing her two glasses of whiskey.

Katie took the glasses from him and downed them one at a time, then handed them back.

"Glad to see you're taking this so well," Kris said.

Fury lit her insides at his calm words, as if he wasn't responsible for destroying her life! She rose, wobbled, and pulled off her heels. She looked around until her eyes met those of the death dealer.

"Gabriel, you're taking me home," she ordered.

The death dealer rose.

"Sit, Gabriel," Kris responded.

Gabriel obeyed, and Katie flung a shoe at the domineering man with the jewel-toned eyes. He caught it with reflexes too fast for her to follow.

"You *will* send me home, and you'll remove Toby, Gabriel, and every other interference you placed in my life, down to the scuff marks in the hallway, which I know weren't there on Tuesday! No more dead doctors, no more kidnappings, no more blood draws, nothing!"

The angrier she got, the calmer Kris looked. His eyes went from emerald to tanzanite again.

"When you calm down, we'll--" he started.

"No. Now. I'm going home *now*. Back to my boring life, my horrible job, my tiny apartment. *Now*, Kris!" She saw the white of his knuckles as he gripped her shoe hard and sensed she was pushing a wild animal. His jaw was clenched and ticking as the muscles jumped.

He wasn't going to budge. Neither was she.

"Let's take a step back, shall we?" Andre said, stepping in front of her. "We shouldn't take you through the shadow world to return you. If Kris didn't kill you on the way here, he might on the way back. I'm going to send Kris away and bring you a bottle of whiskey. Then we'll talk. Is that okay?"

His presence and words were as soothing as Kris's were not. She felt herself relaxing at his even tone and the words that seemed logical enough. She didn't want to be dead, and she definitely needed more whiskey. At her hesitation, he motioned for her to sit again and turned, continuing to block Kris from sight.

"Brother," he said with gentle command. "Jade, you, too. Gabriel, do whatever you do."

The death dealer disappeared. She heard Kris stir, and the cocoa-skinned Jade followed. Andre relaxed and sat on the couch near her while Ileana drew close as well. Ully reappeared with a carafe of whiskey and set it down, taking Andre's head nod as a cue to leave. Andre poured her whiskey and sat back. She sipped it, rubbing the back of her neck.

"You are handling this well," he said.

She eyed him. His words appeared genuine, unlike Kris's.

"You'd have to be pretty mentally tough to go through all this without cracking."

"Oh, I'm cracking," she shot back.

He chuckled. Despite her fury and fear, she found his presence oddly calming, like sitting in a spa surrounded by incense with her feet in a salt bath. The air around her felt heavy and still.

He was doing something to her. Even with her precious whiskey, she shouldn't feel like she did. She shook her head, trying to clear it of the fog he'd placed there.

"I don't need you to placate me!"

He leaned forward, curiosity flaring in his tanzanite eyes. Whatever fog gripped her dissipated suddenly, and she breathed a sigh at the palpable release. She tossed back the whiskey, meeting his gaze only when he placed his hand across the top of the carafe.

"You've had enough," he said with genuine concern. "I apologize. I won't do it again."

Katie pulled the carafe from his hand and poured herself another two shots. He pursed his lips then poured himself a shot and sat back to sip it. They gazed at each other for a long moment.

"Did I really die?" she asked at last.

"No. But mortals shouldn't travel through the shadow world. It's hit and miss on what'll happen."

"What exactly is going on?"

He leaned forward and placed the glass on the table. "It's a long story, one you don't necessarily need to know to understand your circumstances. My brother's people found you and identified your unique gift for...blocking their natural talents. It makes you valuable and dangerous. If our enemies find you, they can take your blood and modify the creatures who work for them to make them immune to us."

"Back up a sec. Natural talents?" she echoed.

"Our ancestors were immortalized--albeit incorrectly--in myths. Mages, vampires, elves, immortal creatures with extraordinary powers who battle evil for supremacy and the ultimate fate of mankind."

"And my unique gift could make the bad guys immune to the good guys."

"Correct," he said.

"Why is your brother so pissy when he interfered with *my* life?"

"My brother is never pissy," Andre said with polite offense. "He's unaccustomed to having his authority challenged. We nicknamed him the Phoenix, which is notorious for not only rising from ashes but also for taking down everyone and everything around them in flames. He's forever in that stage that precedes a perfect storm."

"Highly combustible, I get it," Katie said and rolled her eyes. "Send me home, get rid of everything that shouldn't be there, and move on. Everyone will be happy."

"I wish it were that easy."

"Why isn't it?" she prodded.

"Because our enemies have your blood and know everything about you. This started out as a mission about us but has turned into a mission about *you*."

"How did you trick my sister Hannah into thinking I had a kid, when you and I know I don't?"

"Angels must be raised by humans in the mortal realm," he said patiently. "It's something immortals learned long ago. Angels are mortals' allies, but they can't appreciate the intricacies of mortals without the years of exposure. When we placed Toby with you, we altered the minds of those in your immediate family circle. We learned that those outside of this circle are less likely to be concerned about the appearance of the child. The human mind is quick to find excuses to accept such things."

She gripped her head, feeling sick.

"Go and rest. We'll talk in the morning," Andre said with genuine warmth.

"I could use some food, though. Too much alcohol on an empty stomach."

"I'll send dinner. Your room is the third on the left." He indicated a narrow hallway off the large formal living room.

She stood, wobbled, and then went the direction he indicated. The room was dark, the floor-to-ceiling windows displaying the incredible views of the Eiffel Tower , whose frame was outlined by lights against the dark Parisian sky. She was about to step onto the balcony when a knock at the door drew her attention.

Andre entered, followed by a second man carrying a large tray of food.

"I included the whiskey, though I advise you to stop drinking soon," he said with brotherly firmness. "We'll be going to a soiree across the street in about an hour. You'll have some peace, at least until tomorrow morning."

Katie offered a watery smile, eyes going to the roast lamb, bread, and custard. They left, and she sat and ate leisurely. When she finished, she crossed to the balcony.

She'd never left the country and couldn't help but stare in wonder at the romantically lit Arc de Triomphe. The street below was narrower than it appeared on TV and packed with cars and elegantly dressed men and women walking to a gathering across the street--probably the soiree Andre had mentioned.

In the distance was a dark swath of park leading up to the lit-up Eiffel Tower, which was larger than she'd imagined. The air was chilly, but she left the window open to the street sounds and the cold, wanting to feel normal.

Wiggling her toes in the plushest carpet she'd ever felt, she leaned against the window sill, exhausted yet wired. Andre was the only gentleman in this outfit and the only to take pity on her.

Her headache was gone, her stomach full, and another glass of whiskey in her hand. By the end of this ordeal, she'd be an alcoholic.

If it ever ended. Andre and Kris seemed to think she was there for the long haul. Her chest tightened again, and she sipped more of the warming liquid. She wondered if this was what immortality felt like, watching humanity progress down a road unable to join them in soirees or understand how precious every second of life was. Did humans understand both their universal significance and their individual insignificance?

She shook the thoughts away, suspecting they weren't hers. Whenever Andre tried his shit, her head felt foggy, and right now, she was foggy.

"Stop it!" she hissed at him, suspecting he'd hear her, even if he was one of those in attendance at the soiree.

The sense eased. She slumped against the sill, hot from the inside out while the late fall breeze chilled her skin. Her eyes fell to the entryway in front of the elegant building in which she stayed, then to the street further down, where several forms moved from beneath a canopy, trailed by a shadow darker than night. She saw Kris and squeezed her glass to keep from hurling it at him. Andre was with him, the beautiful woman, the dark man Jade. All trailed by Gabriel, who paused to look up and wave at her.

She waved back, wondering how the most damning of them all was also the only who seemed anywhere able to feel sympathy. Gabriel disappeared. She imagined he went to her apartment to check on Toby and was struck by her longing to return to the tiny, cluttered mess of a life that was hers. She closed her eyes, desperately wishing the whiskey would take effect and knock her out.

The boom of thunder and a bright glare made her eyes open. It hadn't come from the sky but from one of the buildings across the street, diagonal to her. She suspected fireworks and saw something streak into the sky. It didn't explode into lights but fell to her side of the street. She watched in fascination, not understanding what it was until a floor several below hers exploded into flying stone and fire. The impact of the rocket knocked her on her backside. She heard another boom, then a third.

The building shuddered, one explosion hitting close enough to her room that her windows shattered. Fear lit her insides, and she scrambled to her feet, darting to the door. It was still locked.

"Let me out!" she shouted, beating on it.

It wasn't a cheap plywood door with a simple push lock but a thick, wooden door as ancient as the hotel with deadbolts, as if Andre regularly locked prisoners in his guest room.

The door didn't even flinch as she beat her fists against it as hard as she could. She stepped away, sweating from whiskey and fear. Another boom, and the edges of the door lit up and spit fire as the rocket exploded in Andre's apartment. The impact knocked her back. The door groaned but didn't give, though the wall on one side crumbled enough to leave a large opening.

Andre's apartment was black and fiery. The rocket had exploded as it landed on the floor, leaving a gaping hole. She squeezed through the hole in the wall to find there wasn't enough of the floor left to walk on let alone make it to the door across the apartment.

She wriggled back into her room, mind working quickly. Another boom, another flash of light outside the window, another shudder as the building struggled to stand upright. Screams and blaring horns came from the streets. She tiptoed through the glass and leaned out the window, eyeing the wide ledge. There were balconies along the far side of the building that hadn't been destroyed. Any thought she had at Andre's apartment not being the target fled as she saw the damage done to her side of the building.

The booms stopped. She saw dark figures jump from the top of the building across from her to the ground, unaffected by what seemed like a thirty-story drop. They wove their way through the panicked crowds toward Andre's building.

Coming for *her*.

"Shit, shit, shit!"

Half drunk, shoeless, scared shitless, she had no option for escape except to crawl from her balcony onto the ledge. She wiped the glass shards from the ledge and carefully stepped out, standing against the outside wall. The ledge was just wide enough for her foot to fit fully. The wind was harsher, colder than it was just a few minutes ago. She pressed the front of her body against the building, dug her fingertips into indents in the stone, and slid her foot along the roughened ledge to the right, stepping slowly and forcing her head up.

"I don't even speak French," she muttered. "No passport, no identification, no shoes."

She moved along, foot-by-foot, focusing on the next stone and on her anger to keep from sobbing and falling to her doom. The sounds of chaos below grew as emergency vehicles responded.

Boom. She tensed and held her breath. The rocket slammed into an ambulance parked in front of Andre's, the brilliant explosion throwing heat and light that reached her on what she estimated was the twentieth floor. She started moving again, panic rising as she realized not all the attackers in the building across the street had jumped to the street. She was vulnerable, exposed. If they wanted her dead, she'd given them the best target imaginable.

A shuffling drew her attention, the sound at odds with the chaos below. She looked back toward Andre's apartment, surprised to see two dark forms on the ledge following her.

She reached a balcony and lowered herself carefully onto it. The French doors were locked, and she beat on them, looking around wildly for deck furniture to break the glass. The patio was empty.

Boom. She dropped instinctively to the ground. The rocket smashed into the floor below, shattering glass and pulverizing part of the balcony. The impact was close enough to deafen her to everything but her own breathing. She stared at the broken glass before her and then at the men nearing on the ledge. Across the street, she imagined the man with the rockets taking careful aim at her. Her only chance at safety was across a swath of broken glass.

For the second time that night, she began to think she hadn't drunk enough whiskey. She rose unsteadily and brushed some of the glass away with her bare foot, near tears.

Boom.

She ran, crying out as glass shredded her feet. She forced herself to continue to the apartment's entrance and flung open the door, revealing a hall with auxiliary lighting reflecting off a white marble floor. She stepped inside, sagged against the wall, and lifted one bloodied foot. She pried glass free with shaking hands between sobs, then set her foot down and did the same for the other. Familiar dizziness assailed her. She shoved herself away from the wall and staggered down the hall. A hole in the floor was between her and the elevators.

Boom. The lights went out. She clung to the wall, at a loss as to what to do. Right about now, she'd be happy to see Kris and would even risk going to the shadow world!

She felt two tiny bites on her arm, and suddenly electricity flew through her. Her mouth opened in a frozen scream as the burning pain paralyzed her. The current stopped, and she convulsed on the cold marble floor.

Red flashlights blurred before her eyes. Gloved hands snatched her. A hood went over her head, and she was flung across someone's shoulder hard enough to make her ribs flare with pain.

Dazed and pained, she couldn't help but wish she'd just jumped off the ledge instead.

Chapter Four

Sasha himself, followed by two members of his guard of immortal badass creatures, delivered the new, bloodied tenant to the cell across the hall. They were trailed by a man Rhyn recognized well.

Jade. One of Kris's warriors. With some satisfaction, Rhyn wondered if another of Kris's men had gotten as fed up with Kris as he had.

Sasha left without even a smartass remark, and Rhyn rose, gazing with interest across the hall. The scent of blood made his blood sizzle. The bloody mess in the next cell was a human. There was something very different about the human's blood, like comparing warm, homemade bread with stale crumbs out of the garbage.

He *drooled* at the smell, his gums and body aching for a taste. In all his years as an immortal, he's never *drooled* over anything!

Immortal mate. There was no mistaking the sense, just as there was no mistaking this human was so much more than a mate for the average immortal.

Ancient mate.

Surprised, he cursed Death for dumping the vulnerable human he was meant to protect into Hell before freeing him!

The cell block fell silent, and he sensed the others also smelled the human blood. The cowering healer left his corner of the cell for the first time in a while and approached the human on the bed. Its tongue flickered out as it rolled the human. Gently, the healer began its trade.

Rhyn watched, even more fascinated when the healer hesitated suddenly and withdrew.

"What is it, Rhyn? And why does it smell like the best hamburger earth can make?" Jared broke the predatory silence.

"Looks human," Rhyn replied. "Smells human."

"My left arm for a bite…" Jared groaned. "What's that freak doing?"

The healer's nervous gaze flickered to Rhyn. It drew the human off the bed and dragged the body into the corner, as if to protect them both from the immortal prisoner.

"Nothing right now," Rhyn replied. "Worst healer I've ever seen. Should be done by now."

"N…no!" the healer replied, agitation crossing its features. "Not a normal h…human."

"Looks and smells normal."

"N…no!"

It said nothing more but ducked its head and began to clean the human with its long tongue, shuddering at each lick. Rhyn felt suddenly jealous, wishing he could taste what smelled so wonderful.

He paced again, wondering why Sasha would put a *human* in his zoo, unless this was the worst human in the world.

The more he watched, the less likely this seemed. The human was a female, and a young one. Her dark, curly hair was matted with blood, her features pale. The healer stopped to rest and pushed immortal sustenance--small square water and food cubes--into her mouth.

Her draw was insane. Her blood smelled sweet, and the oddly charged aura around her made his brow furrow. In all his years, he'd never seen anything like her.

Ancient's mate. His *mate*.

He froze. He'd heard how other immortals stumbled upon the humans meant to mate with them. There were few humans who could stick it out with an immortal; something in their blood made them different from all the others. He'd felt a familiar sense around…

Lilith. The woman whose death by his hand had landed him here in Hell.

Only the draw around this woman meant for him was much stronger. Much more dangerous.

He growled deep and low, glaring at the woman across the hall. The healer pulled her into its arms, his gaze flickering around again.

Rhyn had thought himself in love with Lilith once, and so had Kris and half their brothers. Fools, all of them! She'd been a siren, a human whose black heart lured any immortal she encountered into the hands of the Dark One! The woman across the hall held the same beguiling aura.

Rhyn retreated to the wall and sat with his back against it, staring at the healer that held the woman protectively in his arms.

Every human had its own special power, similar to immortals. He wondered what hers was, and if it was the same gift of treachery that had doomed Lilith.

Katie awoke on the lower bunk bed in a prison cell with no windows and a tiny metal toilet and sink. Her blurred vision fell to the corner, where a creature with glowing emerald eyes crouched. She jerked back, pain shooting through her.

"You brought much blood," the creature said, its voice trembling a little with excitement.

She closed her eyes and pushed herself up, her breath catching at the sharp pain in her ribs. Her feet felt swollen and fiery.

"What are *you?*" the creature asked. Its voice was hoarse, and it spoke with a small lisp.

She braced herself and opened her eyes. The lighting was harsh. Aside from its large, glowing green eyes, the creature appeared near-human with a lean body covered in some sort of leather jumper. She couldn't distinguish whether it was male or female. The voice sounded like the sultry growl of a woman, but it had short hair and no breasts. And four fingers on each hand. Its skin was porcelain pale, as if it never saw sunlight.

"I'm a human," she said.

"A *mortal* human?" it replied skeptically.

"Is there any other kind?"

The creature looked confused but shifted from its guarded crouch to a kneeling position.

"Does the mortal human have a name?" it asked.

"Katie."

"Katie," it repeated pensively. "Kaaaaaaaaaaaaaaaaatie."

Her feet were swollen and shredded, as she expected. The creature repeated her name several more times while she examined her body. She was bruised all over and wondered if her ribs were broken as well. She'd be lucky to walk again soon, and without medical supplies…with her luck lately, she wouldn't die from infection, just suffer for the rest of her life.

"Kaaaaaaaaaaaatie."

"Would you stop that?" she snapped, her head aching.

"Katie."

"Do you have a name?"

"Lankha," it said promptly.

"Where are we, Lankha?"

"In Hell. Heeeeeeeeeell."

She looked out of the front of the cell into a small corridor with equally harsh lighting. Across from them was another cell, this one darkened. Its occupant stared back at her with glowing silver eyes.

"He drinks blood. He smells yours," Lankha volunteered.

"What is he?"

"Don't know. From the mortal human realm like you."

"What…realm is this?" she asked.

"Heeeeeeeeell. It's in the underworld, the only place where immortals can't come."

If no immortals could save her, she wondered who could. Who'd have ever thought she'd *want* to be found by the jackass, Kris?

"I need whiskey," she said, and rubbed her head.

"Whiiiiiiiiskeeeeeeey." Lankha's voice was almost sing-song. It stood and retrieved small blue pellets from its bed, offering them to her.

"What is it?" she asked, accepting them.

"Water for mortal human. Warden says one every moon cycle."

She eyed them doubtfully but popped one into her mouth. It tasted like a plain jelly bean, until she swallowed, when it felt like a stream of water spilled from the back of her mouth to her gullet. Within seconds, she felt refreshed.

Lankha retrieved a small satchel from its bed and sat cross-legged on the floor beside her feet, withdrawing small vials and balled gauze.

"What're you doing?" she asked, watching.

"I'm a healer. Heeeeeeeeeeeealer. Warden put you here so I could help you. I cleaned your blood. I started but grew tired. Now, I finish."

Lankha licked its lips in satisfaction. She feared asking more and braced herself when it took one foot in its hand. Lankha's hands were covered in what felt like soft, feathery, cool micro-suede. Its touched eased the heat and pain. She watched, astonished, as it carefully cleaned her feet without hurting them and then slathered on oil from one vial and wrapped them in gauze. When it'd finished, she felt little pain, and the heat was completely gone.

"That's amazing, Lankha," she voiced.

"Amaaaaaaazing," it agreed. "I'm the oldest male healer in my guild. There's one female older. Your body is stubborn, but you will heal."

Male, she noted mentally.

His hands traveled up her legs with the expertise and gentleness of a doctor, all the while spreading the soft coolness through her. His touch lingered on bruises, and he retrieved a small tool when he reached the hem of her dress. He sliced through it, and she pushed his hand away.

"You're hurt," he said, surprised.

"I don't have any other clothes! You can't be cutting up the only set I do have."

He looked concerned and stood again, retrieving something else from his bed. He dropped a leather jumper similar to his on her lap and then returned to his cutting. The creature across the hall growled. She didn't let herself think too much about what it might be, how she ended up in Hell, or why she'd just let some otherworldly creature with fuzzy hands cut off her clothes. No, those were not thoughts she could handle in her current condition.

Lankha's hands remained on her ribs for a long, long time. He appeared satisfied at last and touched her breast. She slapped his hand away, and he looked at her, confused again.

"What *are* these?" he asked.

"Just ignore them and finish up."

He obeyed. He finished at long last and replaced all his things in his satchel. She pulled on the jumper, not expecting it to fit and surprised to find the leather-like material as flexible as spandex. It fit snugly, though it was so thin, she still felt exposed.

"What do you do?" Lankha asked, sitting back.

"I'm in the food industry. I help them with marketing, which would've been my major, if I didn't quit school on the fourth day."

"You make vegetables? There's a marketing guild?"

"Oh, no," she said, realizing his meaning. "I don't do anything…special like you."

He frowned.

"Rather, doing nothing *is* my apparent talent," she clarified.

"You are not a normal mortal human."

"No. I'm, um, apparently unaffected by the…talents of other…guild guys, unless they're, like, really old," she fumbled.

"Ooooohhhhh. Old like me, oldest in my guild."

"Yeah, I guess."

"Very nice talent," he said. "Very rare. Not good for you, though."

"Why not?"

"The Ancients are very rare. I've been in Heeeeeeeeeeell forever, and if I wasn't here, I couldn't heal you."

"Only the Ancients can offer any protection," she murmured with a frown. "Interesting."

"You'll die soon."

"Shouldn't I be dead already if I'm in Hell?"

He shrugged, not nearly as concerned with her life or death as she was. She set the blue water pills on her pillow and stretched back. Her ribs were sore but no longer painful. Amnesia was looking like a good option compared to Hell.

"Now you pay me," Lankha said.

"Excuse me? Pay you *what*?"

He smiled, revealing fangs among the neat row of white teeth. She shivered, cold inside.

"Blood," he confirmed.

She stared at him.

"Not much. I don't have the appetite of the *beast*," he said, lifting his chin to the glowing silver eyes across the corridor.

He took her hand gently in his feathery, cool hands and pressed a finger to the inside of her forearm. It fell numb. She said nothing, the world too surreal for her, and turned her head away as he dipped his head. She didn't feel his fangs sink into her, but she *heard* the sound of punctured flesh. He sipped quietly. As promised, he did not drink long, and she felt him press another finger to the wound to seal the seepage.

Her stomach turned. She didn't know how she could ever eat again.

The beast across the hall roared and threw itself against its prison. The cell wall buckled and bent. She scrambled toward the back of the cell, huddling with Lankha in a corner. She couldn't see what was there but knew it was on its way to get her.

"He likes mortal human blood," Lankha whispered.

"No shit!"

A man in a robe hurried down the hall as the beast battered itself against the weakening cell. The man paused and whispered something in a harsh tongue. The cell repaired itself until it stood straight again. The beast within continued to throw itself at it, ceasing finally when it saw the prison had been reinforced.

The robed man strode away, and Katie and Lankha eased from the corner. She sat on her bunk while Lankha climbed atop his. She stared at the beast across the hall staring at her and soon heard Lankha's snores. He was fed and happy. She shuddered, looking at the tiny scars of his teeth on her forearm.

One day, she'd wake up and find herself on the Metro again.

"Hey, human."

She glanced up. The voice came from a cell down the hall.

"Lunchmeat," the male voice called.

She moved to the bars at the front of her cell, aware of the beast across the hall doing the same with a growl. Pale hands draped through bars two cells down from the beast.

"Did you just call me lunchmeat?" she asked.

"Oh yeah. A little mortal meat, some cheese and crackers. How ya doin', lunchmeat?"

"Pretty shitty. Is there anyone here who doesn't want to eat me or drink my blood?"

The masculine voice gave a surprised laugh, and he pressed his face to the bars. He *looked* human, aside from the fanged smile.

"Sexy lunchmeat," he said. "You'd enjoy what I'd do to you."

"Never really been a fan of being eaten alive," she returned.

"Spunky. Me likey."

"Thanks, psycho."

"You talk big behind those bars, little girl," another voice said.

She stared with surprise at the low growl from the darkened cell across from her.

"The rabid dog speaks," she noted. "I'm already in Hell. I'm thinking death might be a bit more to my liking."

The pale, fanged man laughed again.

"Which one of you will promise me a painless death?" she baited, at her last wit's end.

"I'll make it less painful than usual," the pale man said.

"I like pain," another voice down the block growled.

"Less pain than Jared."

"More pain than Jared but less than Khakhala."

"No deal."

"No death, just pain."

"Mortal blood rocks."

"Can I get some action and then give you a painless death?"

The immortals in the cell block threw out their best offers, and she couldn't help the sense of terror settling into her gut.

"No," she replied. "No action. Just the pleasure of killing me. You can do whatever you want to my body afterwards."

"No good to me dead."

"Only good to me dead. Not allowed to kill."

The voices down the hall were all male, though she doubted any of them were human.

"No pain," the beast across from her said.

"Don't you want to drink my blood?" she asked skeptically.

"It won't hurt, little girl." His menacing growl chilled her more than any of the others'.

"I'll think about it," she replied, and stepped away from the bars.

"Hey Lunchmeat," the pale man, Jared, called.

"Yeah?"

"Don't stick your hands outside the cage."

"I have no intention of doing so."

"Rhyn might grab one and pull you out. You'd be cut into pieces by the bars, and then no one would get their snack," he continued.

"Yeah, real shame, shithead," she retorted, feeling more ill by the second.

He laughed. "What're you doing here, Lunchmeat? Humans don't come here unless they're dead, and even then, only a couple make it onto our supermax zoo."

"No idea."

"Why aren't you crying, little girl?" the beast, Rhyn, asked in his gravelly, low voice.

"Maybe she's a spy," a voice farther down the hall called. "Here to listen to our secrets."

"I'm not a spy."

"Wouldn't matter if you were," Jared said, unconcerned. "The beast is right. You're holding up well. Maybe when they start the torture, she'll cry. Then she'll negotiate on that no-pain thing."

"How I ache to be there," another voice moaned.

"You taste as sweet as you look, little girl?" Rhyn mocked.

"Like soggy gym socks," she snapped.

"I like you, Lunchmeat," Jared continued. "Will be a shame when they break you. Or when one of us gets loose and kills you. Not sure what'll come first, though Rhyn there has almost broken through his cage twice now."

Supermax, inhuman predator wing of the zoo. Torture.

It figured. Her heart was beating fast, her palms sweaty. She returned to her bunk and lay down on her stomach facing the hallway, cold fear filling her. She stared at the silver eyes staring at her, slowly falling into an exhausted, restless slumber.

The sounds of Rhyn slamming his body into his cell and snarling awoke her sometime later. Lankha was huddled in a corner, but she rolled to watch. She popped one of the water cubes into her mouth, head pulsing from a nasty hangover.

Rhyn had bent his cage again. Though she tried hard not to fear death, she wondered what kind of creature was capable of breaking through bars made of materials she'd never before seen and held in place with some sort of magic. She wanted to see what the beast looked like, what kind of monster he'd be, yet knew if she saw him in full light, he was on his way to kill her.

The robed man came again and repaired the damage. Rhyn fell quiet, and the robed man turned to her. His eyes were black and empty, his frame small and wiry. He wore a glowing talisman on a leather chain around his neck.

"Hey Lunchmeat," Jared called.

"Yeah."

"If you take the amulet, no pain, guaranteed."

Her eyes dropped to the talisman around the robed man's neck. The robed man sent what looked like a lightning bolt down the hall. Jared cursed.

"Come with me," the robed man ordered her.

The bars of her cell dissipated at his command, and she stepped into the hall. A narrow, lit walkway extended all the way down the corridor, the only part of the hall out of reach of the arms of the prisoners on either side.

He led her toward Jared's direction. The pale man was tall and lean, and he hung his hands again through the bars of his cell. He winked as she passed and licked his lips.

"Nice ass. Wouldn't mind a bite of that."

She ignored him and crossed her arms. Some of the cells were black like Rhyn's, some with bars, and others with glass.

Some appeared empty while others…she stopped looking when she saw the fanged moth man. The predators were silent, watching their lunch parade by them.

She trailed the robed man through two doors and into a hot, dry night. He led her through a fortress too ancient for her to date, its blackened walls and well-worn stones massive and thick. There were two moons in this realm, one full and the other a sliver.

The robed man led her into the fortress and wound his way through bright intersections, down stairs, and into a more opulent part of the building. The halls grew wider, and the stone turned to carpet beneath her sore feet. She was surprised she could walk at all and knew a few ounces of blood had been a small price to pay for Lankha's work, which she'd never have gotten for all the money in the world at home.

She nearly leapt past her escort when he entered the banquet hall, the scents of roasted meat and a million other things making her stomach roar.

Until she saw the spit with the human-like body roasting above it. She stared, knowing no amount of counseling would fix her when this was over.

"My lord, Sasha, I have brought the human," her robed escort said in a monotone voice.

"Perfect. Absolutely perfect."

The robed man bowed and retreated to the door. She turned as the man called Sasha lifted one of her curls from her shoulder. He was a lean man with gleaming silver-blue eyes, teeth filed into points, and an aura so cold she stepped away.

"Like a doll," Sasha said, admiring her. "So full of life. Perfect."

"I told you, Sasha," a familiar voice said.

Katie looked past him, gasping. Jade stood near the spit, dark eyes blazing.

"And you were right," Sasha replied. "Now go, my love, before they notice you're gone."

Jade's glare stayed on her as he hesitated. Sasha turned to him with a smile, and Jade's gaze softened. He bowed his head and left her alone with the madman. Sasha faced her. Katie took another step back, the stillness of his gaze unsettling.

"I've been waiting for a long time to claim you. We knew you'd appear eventually."

He motioned to a seat at the table loaded with food she feared eating. The seat was at his left, and he waited until she accepted before sitting. There was already food on her plate-- meat from an unnamed source, vegetables, bread.

"I know you're hungry," he said.

She was starving. She took the roll and bit into it, surprised to find it tasted perfect. She ate the whole basketful while he watched. When he motioned to the meat, she looked toward the spit and then lied.

"I'm vegetarian."

He ate nothing. When her stomach was full, she allowed herself to look at him. His eyes gleamed. He took her wrist and raised his pinkie, where she saw the nail had been filed to a point and reinforced with metal. Before she could draw her wrist away, he pierced it. The pain surprised her after Lankha's gentle ministrations. The creature twisted her wrist and squeezed, capturing her blood in a small vial. The robed man who had led her to the hall strode forward and took the vial, then backed away silently.

"Verifying your identity," Sasha said with a polite smile.

"What do you want with me?"

"You know what. Your blood is rare. It can lead us to victory."

"You're the bad guys," she said with a frown.

"We serve a different master."

He said nothing more, as if unwilling to say more until the identity verification was done. Still hungry, she ventured to try the vegetables. The broccoli tasted normal, and she ate all of them. She looked up at Sasha, her heart hammering under his hungry look.

The robed man returned and spoke in the harsh tongue. A look of satisfaction spread over the face of the creature before her. He gripped her wrist hard, lowering his head. She wrenched away. His reflexes were like Kris's, too fast to follow. He snatched her neck and rose, jerking her off the chair. Her air supply cut off, she tore at the hand holding her until the skin on his arm fell away to reveal smooth, black skin more akin to a reptile's than a human's. When the world narrowed, he released her. She fell, gasping for air.

"I want you alive, but I don't care how much you suffer. You will find I'm a reasonable…man. I offered you the easy way, you refused. Now that choice is forever gone. You are stuck with a way less comfortable for you. You're in complete control of how much I hurt you."

His calm words terrified her. She rubbed her neck, sensing the evil and determination in his tone. He paused a moment for the words to sink in. She caught her breath and waited. When he reached for her, she flinched but didn't fight him. He pulled her up and gripped her neck, pushing her head aside to expose the vulnerable skin.

She closed her eyes, telling herself she'd survive this and figure out how to get the hell out of there, even if it meant bartering with the monsters on her cell block. Her resolve to grit her teeth and bear it lasted until the pain.

He tore into her neck, and agony seared straight through her.

Rhyn's impotent frustration subsided some when they returned the human. He didn't know if Sasha would recognize her for what she was, or if only the immortal meant to mate with her would see.

She came back in the same shape as when she arrived: bloodied beyond recognition. He was surprised she came back at all--Sasha had no mercy and rarely left his victims alive.

Unless he wanted her for something else. What would Sasha want with her? What was her gift?

He slapped the wall of his cell, cursing Death again for not freeing him. He couldn't protect anyone from Sasha in Hell, and he itched to taste the woman meant to be his mate.

The robed man dropped her body on the bed, sealed the cage, and turned to Rhyn.

"Your master will see you now," he said.

Rhyn growled at the robed man, who hurried away. Sasha's servants wouldn't get within a foot of Rhyn; instead, they shaped the magic of Sasha's realm around him and gave him only one direction to go, that which Sasha wanted.

"Ooh, come out as something different!" Jared exclaimed.

He'd amused them and himself by emerging each time in some other shape. Today, however, he was more interested in seeing Sasha and hearing about the human than amusing the zoo creatures. He waited for the barrier before him to lift and then strode out.

"A half-breed! Worst one yet!" Jared exclaimed, hanging his hands through the bars in his cell.

"Fuck off, demon," Rhyn growled.

He made his way through the castle with the black stones as he had many times during his long stay. The twin moons of the outer banks of Hell were bright. It was always dark here, and the moons rose and set each day instead of a sun. The fresh air was welcome after the musty scents of prison. He found some of his wired energy dissipating at the long walk and change of scenery despite knowing nothing good had ever come from a meeting with Sasha.

Sasha was waiting for him in his study, sitting beside a fireplace that burned with black flames. Blood had dripped down his face to speckle his shirt. His silver-blue eyes glowed with no warmth as he smiled.

"Time for our periodic chat, little brother," he said, and motioned to the other chair before the hearth.

Rhyn refused it and threw himself onto the comfy couch farther away from Hell's flames.

"How are all my pets?" Sasha asked.

"You know how they are, fuckhead."

"Another month and you're still defiant."

Normally, it was as far as they got before Sasha flew off the handle, had him tortured, and threw him back into his cell. Rhyn waited for it, determined to put up the same fight he always did.

It didn't come. Sasha was calm. In fact, Sasha was *happy*!

Rhyn sat up, eyeing his brother warily. Sasha sipped blood from a goblet, content.

"I've decided to take a mate," Sasha said.

Rhyn laughed, thoughts flying to the spunky human in the zoo. Sasha glared at him.

"You, brother, will take a mate?" Rhyn goaded. "It's the human you threw in the cell across from me, isn't it?"

"She's beautiful and she's an immortal's mate."

"Beautiful? No. Not ugly, yeah. Our family has no luck with immortal mates. Traitorous bitches, all of them."

"Sounds like *brotherly* concern," Sasha mocked. "You know, if you hadn't joined our family, I wouldn't be here, and Father would still be alive. You think I want to be in Hell at the side of the Dark One?" Sasha flung his arm around.

Rhyn rolled his eyes and got up, grabbing an orange off the fruit basket on Sasha's desk. Sasha's moods were varied and fickle, never lasting too long. Of all the brothers, he'd always been the one to begrudge Andre's role as their leader.

"As long as I keep her out of your reach, so you don't kill this one, too," Sasha added.

"If she's yours, I'll kill her faster." Even as Rhyn spoke, he was disturbed by the thought of the frazzled but sweet woman across the hall from him falling to his brother. She was a smartass worthy of any of his brothers, and yet, no human deserved *this*.

Especially not the immortal mate meant for him.

His gaze took in Sasha before sliding to the black flames. He'd forgotten what color real fire was, but he found himself thinking it was orange, like the fruit in the basket on Sasha's desk. Sasha was staring into the fire, pensive.

"She's different," Sasha muttered. "Easy to break. Still human."

"What's her gift?"

"Fuck off, Rhyn. Who would you rather see her with, Kris or me? Kris must be livid I've stolen her from him."

"She's better off dead," Rhyn replied.

He wanted to keep Sasha talking, to find out what it was about this woman that was so special that both Sasha and Kris wanted her. And to spend more time outside his cell. He'd long since stopped trying to escape, knowing the magic of Hell and the Dark One was too old for him to break. He'd still rather be humoring Sasha and eating his oranges than sitting in the damned cell!

"You don't seem too thrilled yourself," he added.

"The timing is bad," Sasha said with a glance. "I may need something of you soon."

"You know I'll refuse."

"We'll see," was the growled response. "I do have news for you."

"I don't give two--" Rhyn started.

"Andre is dead-dead."

Rhyn fell silent. The only brother who'd accepted him and treated him half decently was gone?

"Thought that might mean something to you," Sasha said, searching his face. "I guess not. Maybe I've succeeded in breaking you after all."

"Never, fuckhead."

"Without your protector, you'll never be welcomed at the Council."

"I never was," Rhyn growled. "One of you was always trying to kill me."

"And now you've got no one to protect you. You've got nothing, Rhyn, but a place by my side. Think about it."

"Done. No," Rhyn said without hesitation.

"Get the fuck back to your cell."

Sasha left, pissed this time. Rhyn watched him, even more curious after the odd interaction. Sasha had told him many things before to try to break him, but this time, he sensed the truth behind the words.

Andre was gone. He felt heaviness sink to the pit of his stomach, and regret trickled through him.

Of all the brothers, Andre had been the only who believed in him. The eldest and wisest had found him when he was a child, wandering the immortal world, alone. Andre had raised him as much as anyone, sponsored his petition to be recognized by the immortals, cleaned up all the messes he'd never meant to make.

Regret turned to sorrow, and Rhyn gazed around him. Whatever killed Andre would never have succeeded if he weren't trapped here!

He snatched two more oranges before the magic constrained his movement. He took his time going back to the cell block.

Sasha was not a hard creature to understand. This time, Rhyn couldn't figure out why the creature wanted a human so badly he'd bring her here yet didn't seem eager about her becoming his mate.

He retreated to his cell and sat against the wall again, troubled by a familiar feeling of helplessness.

He could've saved Andre. He had the magic, the strength.

He simply didn't have the control. His brothers didn't hate him just because of his lineage. They hated him because he couldn't focus his magic. It came out when it wanted in what form it wanted.

They'd always said he was a danger to the human world because of this. In the darkness of his cell, he admitted this was true, but he also knew no one could've saved his brother but him.

He hated Kris even more. Fury and sadness made him loosen control of his magic. He didn't care that Hell would suck him dry.

He slammed himself against the cell walls, roaring.

"Still alive, Lunchmeat?"

She never thought she'd want to hear the monster's voice. Her world was one of agony and blurred colors. Someone had dumped her into a heap in her cell, and she felt Lankha's cool, fuzzy hands.

"He took too much," the healer chided.

She smelled her own blood. It covered her by the time Sasha had finished his sick games with her. Her heartbeat was shallow and fast; her head felt like it was in a clamp. He'd forced her to stay awake through it all despite her fainting spells, tearing open her veins and feeding until she was too weak to fight him.

He *wanted* her to fight him, to ratchet up the levels of agony. He got off on it as he dry humped her and sucked her life from her.

Rhyn made a racket in his cell. She wished, prayed he got free and ended her.

Lankha's cool magic worked quickly. He took away her pain first then shoved a water cube between her lips. It melted in her mouth and ran down her throat, soothing it after her screams had rendered it raw. The healer's soft hands took away her headache, then the throbbing in her neck, and worked on the other parts of her body until she felt whole again.

She was too weak to move. He gently removed the blood-soaked jumper and cleaned her. His touch was so soothing and cool, she vowed to give him whatever blood he wanted for taking away such pain. He tugged on another jumper and then lifted her onto the bed with strength that seemed at odds with his small form.

Still, she couldn't sleep. She relived the bloody scene in the banquet hall, heard the creature panting her name as he came against her thigh and then tore through the other side of her neck. He'd spent hours on her, disabling her and then hurting her.

Lankha shoved another cube in her mouth, then a third. They melted and trickled down her throat. They weren't water cubes; they tasted of nothing she could identify. They were metallic and sugary. He smoothed out her hair and finally rested a feathery hand on her eyes, easing her into a restless sleep that didn't last long enough.

It felt like mere seconds later when she opened her eyes but guessed it'd been much longer. Her body was weak but working, and there were more of the odd sugar cubes beside her pillow. Lankha was asleep above, and the clamoring of the cell block was gone. She rubbed her head, shaking despite the rest. She ate two more of the sugar cubes and a water cube, eyes lingering on the bloody mess that was her jumper in the corner.

She had to get out of there. She understood Jared's warning about torture and being willing to bargain. But she didn't think any of them could escape, or they would have.

"Not so brave anymore, are you, little girl," Rhyn said.

Her eyes fell to the dark cell holding Rhyn.

"If you were half as tough as you sound, you wouldn't be stuck in here," she retorted.

"Lunchmeat's still kicking," Jared said. His hands appeared through the cell bars.

Rhyn smashed himself against the cell, as if to prove his strength. She ignored him and rubbed her forehead.

"What does the amulet do?" she asked Jared.

"Now you want to talk."

"Keeps us here," Rhyn growled.

"Yes, that neat little trinket is a source of constant magic that traps us. I hear you're immune to magic. You could get one of us out," Jared said.

"If that's the case, why on earth would I bother to free any of you parasites?" she asked, too tired to stand. She sat next to the bars on her cell.

"I guess you wouldn't if you didn't plan on leaving Hell. Sasha's men would kill you twice before you reached the front door."

He had a point, but she knew she'd be in as much danger from the monsters as from Sasha's men. If she had the amulet and could bargain for protection--and one of them not eating her in exchange for her freedom--she wondered if she couldn't escape.

"No pain," Rhyn said with a husky chuckle.

"Not too much pain, and I'll raise you a promise not to fuck you till you're dead," Jared offered.

"Jesus," she muttered.

"He ain't coming here," a voice down the hallway snickered.

"But I am!" another chortled.

She touched her neck delicately, tracing the scars. They were jagged and ugly, similar to those on her arms. Lankha was a lifesaver, but she didn't intend to spend the rest of her years being torn apart by some sadistic vampire with a hard on.

"We'll see," she said at last.

She hoped no one ever came for her, and she'd never have to choose which predator to end her life. The monster across the hall was no option, and Jared was little better. The others...she wondered if Lankha could defend her. Based on his cowering every time Rhyn roared, she doubted it.

Even Kris was better than any of these creatures, and she'd barely tolerated him! Her thoughts turned to him with some bitterness. What kind of human protector allowed one of his own men to turn her over to something like Sasha? Did Kris even know about Jade's betrayal?

"Hey, Lunchmeat, what do you call a human running down the street?" Jared called.

"What?"

"Fast food."

Several of the monsters snickered. She rolled her eyes and retreated to her bunk, hoping Sasha planned to give her time to rest before attacking her.

"Damn you, Kris," she whispered.

"Kris?" one voice echoed.

"The Council's Kris?" another snarled.

"Yeah," she answered.

"He sent you here?" Jared asked.

"Don't know. My luck's gone to shit since meeting him."

"Rhyn, you hear that?"

She glanced toward the dark cell and saw the silver eyes flash dangerously.

"You know Kris and Sasha are brothers, right?" Jared continued.

"No, I didn't."

"There were seven of them. Sasha betrayed the others and aligned with the Dark One. He goes through Hell and collects us freaks down here."

"Hate Kris."

"He must die!"

"Kris." Rhyn's low voice was the most sinister of all the monsters' complaints. He drew out the name, and she sensed a personal connection to the white-haired man.

"Kris's not stupid enough to send you here. My guess is Sasha snatched you. This is the only place immortal pets can't get you, or anyone else," Jared theorized. "Hey Rhyn, bet Kris wants this one back."

Rhyn smashed his cell hard enough for the walls to shudder.

Her luck grew worse. She heard the hisses that preceded the robed man's approach. She tensed and waited, willing him to continue. When he stopped at her cell, she sighed.

"Come with me."

The inmates began cheering. She hesitated, reviewing what the inmates had told her about grabbing the robed man's necklace. As she emerged, both of them jumped back as Rhyn smashed into his cell.

"Less pain," Jared reminded her as she passed.

"A million dollars."

"No pain but some fucking."

"I'll just eat you."

One by one the inmates made their offers as she passed. The robed man was small. Surely she could punch him hard enough to knock him out. She balled up a fist and looked at it, wondering how to hit him.

She wasn't going back to Sasha. Ever.

Hands darted from the cells to swipe at them, and she saw why the robed man kept to the center of the corridor. He reached the end, and she readied her fist. Once she had the amulet, she could bargain harder with the inmates.

Punch him, grab the amulet, bargain for her freedom. The plan was quick and easy.

The robed man opened the door for her as he had before. She waited for him to face her then punched him as hard as she could in the nose. It *hurt*! She shook her hand out.

The inmates erupted into cheers. The robed man didn't fall to her feet unconsciously as she planned but stared at her in surprise. She saw lightning forming in his hand.

"Hit him again!" Jared yelled.

"In the neck," another seconded.

She raised her fist to lay a right hook to his throat, beginning to panic when the lightning arced between his hands. He raised a hand to block, but she kicked him in the groin, and then in the neck. He bent over, coughing. She jerked the amulet off his neck, and the lighting flickered. The robed man stretched for her. She danced away from him and the hand of a monster that brushed her calf back to the center of the hall.

She raised the amulet to stare at it, the cacophony around her rising as the excited inmates glimpsed their freedom. They began beating against their cell walls, and the lights flickered again.

The robed man was coming for her.

"Make me an offer!" she shouted, backing away.

"No pain!" four voices chimed at once.

"No pain and escape to your world!"

"A million dollars."

"NO pain!" Jared shouted at last.

"If you're Kris's, pain like you've never known."

"That's not how this works, Rhyn!" she snapped.

The robed man tackled her, and the amulet went flying. Arms, tentacles, and antennae stretched for it. It landed dead center in the hall, out of everyone's reach. She wrenched away, only for the robed man to snatch her ankle and drag her down. He shot lightning at her that bounced off and hit an inmate. The screams added to the chaos. She kicked the robed man, and both launched themselves at the amulet.

She snatched it. He grabbed her waist. When she dropped it, he bent. They tumbled to the ground, one foot--she wasn't sure whose--knocking the amulet away.

Silence fell. She and the robed man both stopped moving, watching in disbelief as the amulet skittered, rolled, and disappeared into Rhyn's cell.

Rhyn gave a chilling chuckle.

"You better run," Jared advised. "Both of you."

The robed man scrambled to his feet and darted for the door. A dark arm darted from Rhyn's cell and snatched him mid-stride. There was a small scream, then the crack of bone and ripping of flesh. Silence.

Katie rose, heart hammering. Weakened already, she struggled for her balance.

"C'mere, little girl." His throaty chuckle scared her more than the thought of returning to Sasha. She eyed the door at the end of the hall, then her cell, and turned 360. There was one way out.

"Give me a head start, Rhyn. It's only fair since you're free because of me," she ventured.

"Go for it." His noncommittal response and stillness worried her more. She started forward.

"Farewell, Lunchmeat," Jared called in resignation.

This couldn't be how she died! She'd lived through too much the past few days to be eaten by some boogeyman in a dark cell! She straightened her shoulders, determined to approach her fate without fear. She'd been terrified since being told she had amnesia, but she'd stayed strong.

"Do your worst, you rabid dog," she challenged as she approached the point where the robed man had disappeared.

Another smoky chuckle. She sensed his movement and closed her eyes, willing her death to be as fast as the robed man's. Rhyn snatched her into the darkness, and a familiar fog appeared around her.

Suddenly, the shadow world released her. She gasped and dropped to her knees, unable to see in the inky blackness around her. She didn't feel sick this time, only weakness. The scent of sea was in the air, a rough circle of lighter darkness before her, as if she had landed in the back of a cave and looked towards its mouth. The ground was rocky beneath her hands and knees, the air chilled.

She shoved at Rhyn when he grabbed her again and hauled her up. He certainly felt human with a massive male body expending heat and warmth.

"I haven't eaten in thousands of years," he rasped, holding her easily despite her struggles.

He gripped her neck and tilted her head. She fought him harder, tears in her eyes.

"Not so tough now, are you, little girl?" His voice was husky.

She slammed her elbow into his ribs, and he chuckled, locking his other arm around her. His body was warm compared to the chill of the sea. Immobilized, she waited with panicked dread for an attack like Sasha's. He nuzzled her neck, his breath hot against her skin. She squeezed her eyes closed, heart slamming in her tight chest.

There was a pinch and numbness as his fangs sank into her neck. He drank for a long minute then threw his head back, roaring with pleasure.

"You do taste as sweet as you look," he said, voice thick with need. "In the name of the Seven, I claim you as mine."

His words confused her. He released her neck, touching it with a thumb that burned hot enough to singe her skin. Her legs were too weak to hold her, and he lowered her to the ground. She saw his large frame against the night sky outside the small cave, human one moment, then decidedly not the next. He growled a warning and peered back at her through the silver eyes of a cat-like beast the size of a large horse.

And then he was gone.

Chapter Five

Dawn came slowly, followed by the brilliant blue sky of morning. She shifted from her seat in the cave to stand at the edge of the cave, furious at him for leaving her in a small cave on a sheer cliff overlooking the sea. She hadn't slept all night, afraid of what other secrets the night held.

She looked down. The churning sea below was littered with jagged rocks that looked small from her perch a hundred feet above them. Not only could she not escape, but she could just as well starve to death if he decided never to return.

She braided her hair to keep the stiff sea breeze from tossing curls in her face and squinted upward again. She was closer to the top than to the waves, but the cliff had too few hand and footholds for her to try to climb. She perched on a boulder near the entrance, wondering how many nights of Sasha-type treatment she'd take before tossing herself off the cliff.

Bored, restless, fearful, she retreated to the back of the cave, searching it again for any sort of door or anything that might aid her escape. There was nothing. *Nothing* she could use to escape.

Which was why he chose this spot, and she couldn't help shivering at the thought that this place was too perfect for this to be the first time he'd imprisoned someone here.

"What're you doing?"

She jumped but replied without turning, "Looking for a way to escape."

"One way out."

She steeled herself and turned, expecting to find a monster.

He looked human. He was taller than average, over six and a half feet, built like a rock with wide shoulders and tapered abdomen and hips beneath a jumpsuit similar to those worn by the prisoners. Its snugness drew her eyes to his crotch and lean thighs. His hair was dark, his eyes liquid silver, his complexion olive and unshaven.

He tossed fish tied together on a rope into the center of the cave, ignoring her inspection.

"I can't eat them raw," she objected.

"Then you don't eat."

He walked to the edge of the cave and dived out.

She followed, startled, only to see a massive black bird the size of a pterodactyl coasting along the tops of the waves. She shook her head, convinced she was going crazy. Her eyes fell to the fish, and her nose wrinkled.

Rope. She knelt beside the fish and unwrapped them with a grimace, cheered to find the section of rope nearly five feet long. She tossed the fish back to the ocean and coiled the rope, hiding it beneath several small rocks in the back of the cave. She napped, paced, and stared up at the ceiling. The sun crossed the sky, and an hour before it would set, he returned.

With more fish. She sat up and crossed her legs, eyeing the rope. He walked out again, and she tossed the fish and hid the rope, straightening just as he reappeared.

His eyes flashed silver as he glanced at her. He sat on a boulder near the entrance, as if he were the bouncer trying to prevent someone like her from exiting.

"C'mere, little girl," he growled.

"I *hate* that!"

"It's how this works."

"How what works?" she asked.

"I feed you, you feed me."

"Can't you eat a cow or a rabbit or something?"

"You taste better."

She didn't know what to think. She needed more rope to reach the top of the cliff, yet being dinner for any creature wasn't the way she'd like to go. And what if he attacked her as Sasha did, and she had no Lankha to heal her? She'd bleed out in this cave.

"I've claimed you as my blood slave," he said, as if reading her mind. "You're worth more to me alive."

"In that case, then, if you ever hurt me, I'll throw myself to the ocean!"

"Whatever."

She wasn't ready yet to prove it to him, not before she at least tried to escape. He gave her a look that warned her he'd get her if she didn't come to him. She rose, angry, and knelt beside him.

He gripped her neck in one large, roughened hand, tilting her head. She squeezed her eyes closed, heart quickening and her breathing fast and shallow. She gripped his wrist hard, wondering why he insisted on tormenting her by taking his time. At long last, she felt the warmth of his breath on her neck. He bit, and she stifled a cry. The pinch was less today, and the pain gone instantly, replaced by heat and warmth. He didn't drink long, and when he was finished he touched his thumb to the wound, cauterizing it again.

Only when he released her did she sit back on her heels and open her eyes. He was gone again. The blood loss and lack of food made her dizzy. She reached into her pocket and pulled out one of the three water cubes and the remaining sugary cube. She popped one water cube but replaced the sugary cube with some hesitation. If he brought her more fish tomorrow morning, she'd have rope enough to reach the cliff edge ten feet above. She'd need her strength for what she planned.

She lay down on her back to watch the sun set and didn't move until he returned early the next morning to toss stinky fish beside her. She rolled to face him, squinting in the grainy dawn. His silver eyes flashed from the darkness at the back of the cave, alarming her.

"You slaughter a party of Girl Scouts last night?" she asked, unnerved.

"Brave little mortal," came the growl. "Don't know the size of the storm about to hit you, do you."

She hated how he spoke to her, like he knew exactly what to say to terrify her. She was normally good at covering emotions she didn't want to display, but he read them all and threw them back in her face.

"What's it to you?" she groused.

"Need a mortal blood monkey. You owe me. Easy blood."

She rolled her eyes and crossed her arms. She'd like to think she was saving poor souls every day she spent with him donating her blood, but she couldn't help thinking she really wouldn't care what he did to get blood if she was gone.

"I owe *you*?" she echoed. "Who wrestled the crazy guy in a robe for the key? You wouldn't be free if not for me."

"You'd be in a thousand pieces if not for me."

"Like being a mortal blood monkey is soooooooo far above lunchmeat!"

"You're alive, you're fed, and you're free," he pointed out.

"I am deep in your debt, my most gracious lord and master."

"Fuck you."

She skulked and imagined him doing the same in the back of the cave. He rustled around, and she wondered what he was doing so close to her precious rope. She feared asking him, not wanting to tip him off that she was plotting.

"And I'm not free," she added under her breath.

He stalked past her, his anger palpable. He dived off the ledge, and she scampered forward. The pterodactyl dropped and caught itself, coasting in the sea breeze.

She watched him until he disappeared, then freed the fish. She tied the lengths of rope together and hunted for and found the perfect boulder in the cave: a loose, rounded rock the size of both her fists that was light enough for her to throw. Tying her chosen anchor to one end of the rope, she sat to eat her sugary cube, checked again for the monster, and leaned out of the cave.

The cliff edge was around ten feet from the cave. She looked down, stomach unsettled by the distance. This was worse than ledge walking in the hotel; there was no balcony to catch her!

She swung the boulder up, ducking as it slapped the side of the cliff just short of the ledge and fell back to her. She tried again, releasing more rope this time. It clattered along the top of the cliff and fell. She continued to throw it until it stuck. She pulled hard on the rope, feeling some give, then tautness as the anchor lodged itself between unmovable objects.

Sweating already from the effort, she braided her hair to keep it out of her face and then leaned her full weight on the rope. It held. With another look down, she found her first foothold along the side of the cave and began to climb.

The ten feet to the top felt like it took hours, though the sun had barely risen when she finished. By the time she clawed her way over the edge, she was soaked with sweat and panting, her muscles burning from effort. She rested on her back for a short time before forcing herself up to sit up and look around.

Wherever she was, it was beautiful. Cliffs stretched as far as she could see in either direction with uneven stone and shale between her and the rest of the island. Some sort of goats watched her from the distance. Far, far, away, beyond the stone and shale, she thought she saw a swatch of green.

She might not be on her street or even in her neighborhood or city, but it certainly looked like she was back in her world. She trotted away from the cliff, slowing when she felt far enough from the edge. She walked through shallow stone valleys and hopped across boulders and shale toward the sun, casting frequent looks over her shoulder to make sure she wasn't being stalked by a shape-changing demon with an attitude.

She found a narrow, rocky road and hopped from rock to road, surprised to see an older man leading a donkey pulling a cart ahead of her. There were small white houses here, one with a dog that barked as she passed. Fences that looked like nothing more than stacks of rock shingles edged each property. She followed the man at a distance, slowly confirming she was somewhere on her planet. She didn't know where exactly, but by the man's pale skin, she guessed Europe, maybe one of the Slavic countries.

The road rose, and she stopped at its peak to stare at the small village edging a wide bay below. The word "HOSTEL" was emblazoned across the side of what looked like a large red barn in the center of the village. There were several small vehicles, several more men with donkeys, and a slew of boats departing the harbor for the morning catch.

The old man was waiting for her on the other side of the peak. He spoke a smattering of words she didn't understand.

"English?" she asked hopefully.

"Aye," he said with a chuckle. "Bit early fo' the tours to be comin' up this way."

"I wasn't on a tour. Could you tell me where I am?"

He looked her over, eyes lingering on her neck. She covered the bite marks self-consciously.

"Ye drinkin'?"

"Um, yeah," she said slowly. "I had all my…things stolen."

He gasped and crossed himself.

"Mother Mary," he murmured. "This is the second time in a year some thug's attacked a tourist. The world is going to shite."

"It is," she agreed. "Listen, I need a phone. I have to call my sister and tell her to send money so I can get home."

"Come, come with me," he said, resolution on his face. "Not all us here are thugs."

He led her back the way she'd come and to a small house with a couple dozen fluffy sheep in a pen in back. She paused on the sagging porch until he beckoned her in. The house was cozy and simple, with creaky wooden floors covered in rugs, a pot-bellied stove still warm, and worn furniture.

"Toilets are there," he said, pointing.

She grimaced, expecting an outhouse, and was pleasantly surprised at the cozy but modern bathroom. She looked first in the mirror and froze. Aside from the scarring, a maroon tattoo seemed to wind all the way around her neck. She turned slowly and craned her head to confirm the design covered every inch of her exposed neck.

"Son of a bitch!"

Rhyn.

He'd not just claimed her in deed but had the nerve to brand her like chattel as well! She'd never in her life wanted a tattoo, but to have some blood-sucking, shape changing, ill-tempered, *inhuman* beast's name on her neck was infuriating! She tried to scrub it off with no success.

When she emerged, she saw tea and cookies on the small table tucked into a corner of the living room. She joined him, hesitating before gulping down most of the cookies.

"Here ye go," the old man said, handing her a cell phone. "Yer American?"

"Yeah."

"Dial oh-one-one then the number." He eased into the chair across from her and poured them both tea as she dialed.

"Hello?"

"Hey sis!" Katie exclaimed, never as happy as that moment to hear Hannah's voice.

"Oh, god, Katherine! Where are you? What happened? Gio had the police looking everywhere for you! They said you'd been kidnapped from the--"

"I'm fine, I'm fine. I was…taken. Not sure where I am now, but I'm free and okay," Katie said.

"Are you in the city? We'll come get you!"

"No, I think I'm in some other country."

There was a pause as Hannah waited for her response, and Katie covered the mouthpiece.

"Where am I?" she asked the old man.

"Innisheer."

"I'm in Innisheer, sis," she relayed. "You know where that is?"

"God, no. How did you get there? Did someone take you or….maybe you forgot?" Hannah asked in a hushed tone.

"Sis, I have no money, no passport, no identification, and I haven't eaten in a few days. I didn't forget anything. I even remember Toby, the Masquerade, and some guy snatching me when the lights went down."

"Thank god!" her sister sighed. "Toby's been staying with us. You really let him eat that many marshmallows?"

"Don't tell him where I am," Katie said quickly. "I don't want to worry him. Just say I'll be back soon."

"I don't even know where you are. I'm Googling it now."

"Sis, can you send me some money to get back?"

"Yeah, sure," came the distracted response. "Ireland? You're in Ireland?"

"I don't know where I am."

"It says it's an island off the coast of Ireland. I bet it's nice," Hannah said.

"I really don't care, Hannah."

"I'll send you money. It doesn't look like the place you're on has an airport. Can you get to Dublin? I'll book you a flight."

"I'll figure it out," Katie replied. "Thanks, Hannah."

With the old man's help, she caught the last ferry across the channel just before sunset. She stepped off the ferry and stood in a mostly empty parking lot, wondering how the hell to get to civilization from there. There weren't any cabs or buses like in the city; she didn't even see a town nearby. Just a road leading to the small parking area and a closed ticket booth for the ferry. The lone two people on her ferry got into a car and left. She stood for a long moment before striking out after them on foot.

The old man, Liam, had fed her and given her a handful of euro coins before putting her on the ferry. Grateful to him, she was likewise anxious to leave the island before the beast returned and flew off the handle.

She scratched at the tattoo winding around her neck, furious with him. She didn't walk far before someone in a tiny car speaking only Gaelic pulled alongside her and motioned to her. After several failed attempts to communicate, they proceeded in silence to the nearest town, a coastal resort-like town. As if sensing she was some poor tourist, he dropped her off at a youth hostel located above a bar already teeming with people. For an extra few Euros, the hostel manager gave her a clean though worn sleeping bag that matched the clean but worn bunk beds in the women's section.

The two German women sharing her room ceased talking when she entered and looked her over before one said in halting English, "You're American."

"That obvious?" Katie returned, tossing the sleeping bag and a small shaving bag filled with basics on one bunk.

"I like your clothes," the other said, gazing at her jumpsuit. "Very fashionable."

At least Hell kept up with the latest styles, she thought darkly.

"Your..." the other woman said, motioning to her neck. "Very nice."

Katie snatched the shaving bag and a towel, stalking to the bathroom. She bathed in the unisex shower room, grateful for the lukewarm water and the chance to scrub herself down and assess the damage. Her arms and legs were only faintly scarred despite the glass shards from the rocket attacks and the damage done by Sasha. She marveled again at Lankha's healing skill.

Her first shower in days made her want to stay in the hot water forever, until one of the men staying at the hostel entered the bathroom. Self-conscious, she turned off the water and wrapped herself in a towel before crossing to the sinks lining one wall with bright mirrors hanging above them.

Her eyes were drawn to the *Rhyn* tattoo snaking around her neck like a collar. The name was black against a band the color of red wine, both intricate and bold, with odd characters etched into the edges of the band. The geometric shapes changed as they circled her neck rather than stuck to a pattern; she assumed it was some kind of writing.

She wore a collar like a dog with her master's name on it. There was no other explanation. She'd never wear anything but turtlenecks ever again!

"Son of a bitch!" she muttered.

"Awesome tat," a male voice with a distinctly American accent said.

She dropped the hair she'd been holding up and wrapped the towel around her tightly. She met his gaze briefly in the mirror. He looked like any normal nerdy American with big glasses and a scrawny frame. She thought she saw tattoos flash across his exposed chest. She blinked, and they were gone.

After her time in Hell--where most of the monsters looked human--she didn't trust this one. He shrugged as she ignored his hello smile.

She returned to the room, where the two Germen women still sat and talked while cleaning their camping gear. She dressed quickly to avoid comments on either her collar or her scars and flung herself into her bunk, reminded of her cell with Lankha.

She'd never had an opinion of bunk beds until this moment. She *hated* them!

"American, you like beer?" one of the Germans asked.

"Yeah."

"We're going down to the bar. Come with us?"

She hesitated. The Irish rock blaring from the bar below was loud enough, and cigarette smoke already curled in through the window. A shot of whiskey sounded heavenly!

"Yeah, I'll go."

She joined them at the door with enough loose euro change for a couple of beers and dinner. The women with her spoke in German as they made their way down the narrow wooden stairwell to the packed bar. The music blared louder, the smoke became thicker, and the scent of food intermingled with body odor. They stopped to join a small group at one side of the bar and squeezed their way into a booth meant for four and already holding four. They made room for her and pushed fries at her, which she accepted.

Katie's gaze took in the crowd. She looked for Rhyn. She looked for Kris. She looked for any face she knew.

She was done with them. All of them. When she got home, she was kicking Toby out, buying a gun, and taking back her life. Her paranoia faded with the first round of beers and disappeared completely by the third. She joined the Germans and other backpackers in an Irish dance as the cigarette smoke thickened and the rock band grew louder.

"Fire!" The shout went unnoticed until the panicked bartender grabbed the mike of the lead rocker.

"Everyone get out!"

Katie stared at him dumbly until the crowd forced her toward the exit. She let the bodies pressed against her shove her into the chilled night and blinked back her blurred gaze until she saw her German friends. Smoke billowed blacker than night above orange-yellow flames that mesmerized her.

The whole top of the building--where the hostel was housed--was on fire. The flames were beautiful and entrancing. She and the Germans stood in silent awe, too drunk to feel the cold.

"Rhyn, is it?"

She blinked and turned at the voice, not recognizing the American nerd until her vision cleared.

"Funny name for a girl."

"Whatever," she said curtly.

"I told my friends about your tat. Mind showing it to them? My friend Ziggy's a tattoo artist in San Francisco. Thought he'd like yours. It's kinda unique."

She sighed, her instincts too dulled by beer to warn her. She had nothing better to do, not with her source of alcohol gone and her bed in flames.

"You guys got any whiskey?" she asked, trailing him through the crowd.

He held up a bottle. "I grabbed this when everyone started panicking."

"Vodka? No way."

He lowered the bottle. She didn't notice how far they'd gone until the blazing bar disappeared around a corner. Only then did her senses register the three men before her, the alley, and the familiar bloodlust in their glowing eyes. This time, there was no mistaking the tattoos on their bodies.

She spun, the action rocking her precarious balance, only to come face-to-face with the American nerd.

"You don't want to do this," she blurted out. "I taste like shit."

One laughed.

"You should be used to it, or you wouldn't wear your dead master's mark," the nerdy guy said.

"Dead? He's not dead," she replied. "In fact, I'm expecting him any minute."

"No one leaves his mate in a place like this. Penniless? Alone? Obviously too long under his keep to know what to do with herself in the real world?"

Mate?

"He's bigger than you," she warned.

"Bigger than this, bitch?" the American nerd demanded, shoving her against a building and riding his erection against her backside.

"I've seen popsicles bigger than you, jackass!" she snapped.

He pulled her away from the wall and backhanded her hard enough for her to feel nauseous. She was too drunk to feel the landing. He licked his hand, where blood from her lip remained.

"Sweet," he whispered, closing his eyes to savor her. "The Ancients always choose the sweetest blood monkeys."

"You can lie there still like you did for your master while we do our thing, or we can tie you and beat you into submission and then do our thing. Either way, we do our thing," another reasoned, kneeling near her.

"Let me think," she said, and rolled her eyes. "Why don't you walk away now before a certain Ancient tears you into pieces."

"Nice try, sweetheart. We've seen your type before. You won't last the night anywhere you go. He made his mark; it draws us to you."

She frowned, wondering when someone would explain the rules of this game to her. Wobbling, she rose, familiar coldness replacing the alcoholic warmth inside her.

"Sweet, little, defenseless, bet you're wet and taste just as sweet," the man who'd tasted her said. His eyes glowed more unnaturally than the others, the taste of her addling his senses. He looked like the rabid dog she'd expected Rhyn to be.

"Chill, Dean. First we all drink, then you can fuck her up," another warned.

"Appreciate the chivalry," Katie retorted.

If ever you were going to appear, Rhyn, now's the time!

Dean backhanded her again, following her to the ground. He pounced, tearing at the jumper. Her head spun. She batted at him with clumsy arms, at last landing a punch in the neck, as the creatures in Hell had taught her. He gagged. She tried to shove him off, but he snagged her hips and dragged her down, pinning her hands over her head.

She squirmed. His knife cut through her jumper, slicing into her skin.

"Dean, fuck, chill man! She's gotta last the night! We're all famished!"

She cried out, and the other three pried him off. She scrambled up, watching them wrestle Dean until he shook them off. She looked down at her newest cut. It wasn't deep but it stung. At their silence, her gaze returned to them.

She saw their expressions change as they got a whiff of her blood. Whatever control they hoped to maintain slipped.

"I'm warning you," she said again, backing away. "If you…"

She heard the beastly snarl and caught the blurred mass of darkness, punctuated only by two flashes of silver, as Rhyn flew by her. A new terror filled her. As if the four fledgling vampires weren't enough…She turned and ran. One of them snagged her, but his attention shifted at the strangled cry and sound of snapping bones. Dean's head sailed over them. She stared in horror and launched forward. The vampire holding on to her didn't fight her but joined her, running with her from the possessed shapeshifter. She followed him, praying he knew the town better than her, until they ran into a dead end.

Rhyn shoved her into the side of the building with a massive paw, holding her there for a split second as a warning before he launched himself at the vampire. She heard the kid scream and hunched her shoulders, nearly vomiting at the sounds of his body being torn apart. When there was silence, she felt the beast approach her, its bloodied fangs at the same level as her head.

"Is it too late to say sorry?" she managed.

He growled low, and she jumped, squeezing her eyes closed. Swallowing hard, she tilted her head to one side in a display she hoped he took to be an apology. There was a long pause before she sensed him change forms behind her. He gripped her throat roughly and pulled her against his body. Her body shook, but she didn't dare fight him, not when he was so pissed.

There was no pain this time when he bit her, only numbness. She almost cried in relief. He didn't hurt her, even when she had obviously infuriated him. He drank longer than he had before and withdrew at last with a satisfied growl.

"Can't take you anywhere without you beheading folks," she whispered.

"That I let them die fast is not something I'll do for you if you betray me again."

"I'd rather die than be stuck in a cave."

"You think I can't replace you with a *willing* nymph who knows her place?" he demanded.

By the stillness of the body at her back, he was deciding her fate. She waited, her breathing growing shallower and faster.

"Now you have nothing to say," he snarled. "You taste like cheap whiskey."

His words were accompanied by a push. He walked away. She gasped in air, heart soaring. She'd escaped death again, but how many lives did she have? Near hyperventilating, she bent over and drew in deep breaths until moonlight revealed the dismembered hand near her feet.

She darted after him, cold on the inside yet still buzzing from whiskey. He walked through the town to a large bed and breakfast near its edge. She didn't look up as they walked through a comfortable living room with several guests talking loudly about the fire. They grew silent as Rhyn entered and stared her down as well.

She followed him up a set of regal stairs to the second floor, where multiple rooms lined a hallway. He disappeared into one without turning on the light. She trailed, groping around the wall nearest the door until she found a light switch.

There were two beds in the room and a single bathroom off to one side along with a small living area. He said nothing, and she sensed his simmering anger. She sat on a trunk at the end of one bed. He flung off clothing soaked with blood, stripping with his back to her without one concern about her watching.

He was muscled like the panther-beast he turned into. She felt both awed and terrified watching his rippling, shapely muscles move beneath the olive skin. His shoulders and upper arms bulged while his long torso was lean and chiseled. He changed mechanically, as if accustomed to removing bloody clothing several times a day. He tugged on loose judo pants and flung himself on his back on the bed nearest the door.

"You're acting like you're normal," she objected, tears rising. "What the fuck is wrong with you? You run around turning into animals and tearing off people's heads and then just...a bed and breakfast? Come *on!* Now you'll just lay there and go to sleep? Is this where you hung out while I was in that cave?"

He pulled a pillow across his face, ignoring her. She stood and glared at him, wanting to cry, scream, and sleep all at once. Instead, she marched to the bathroom and took the hottest shower she could tolerate to try and take off the alcoholic edge. Her shot nerves calmed until she rubbed a towel against the misty mirror and saw the tattoo again.

Rhyn.

Fury at her situation rose hard and fast. She suppressed it with deep breaths. She'd been to Hell and back; Ireland with a moody predator was far better than that. She put on the jumpsuit she hated and emerged, expecting her first night of good sleep in a week.

Her nose wrinkled at a familiar scent, and she looked first at the plate full of raw fish on the table and then at the silver-eyed predator with his roped forearms displayed across his wide, bare chest. His look was calculating and judging.

"That's it!"

She crossed to the table and lifted one from the plate, flinging it at him.

"You miserable son of a bitch! You all deserve to be in Hell! Damn you, Toby for ruining my life, and Gabriel and Ully and Andre..."

With each name, she flung a fish at him. He was unaffected, batting the dead creatures away like flies.

"...and you, Rhyn, who should owe me something for freeing you from the depths of Hell! Fuck you all! I swear to God, I've had it with all this shit. One week ago, I had a shitty life alone but I was normal. *Normal!* I know you don't know what the fuck that is, but it means no immortal monsters sucking my blood and tearing up my body, no tattoos, no four-hundred-thousand-year-old angels in the bodies of five-year-olds, no buildings exploding when I get near them, no trip to Hell. And no raw fish!"

He stared at her, and she flung the plate at him, furious at his lack of reaction. He didn't care. He *couldn't* care. Monsters couldn't care!

Tears stung her eyes. "Kris was right. I need to help him save the world from jackasses like *you*."

His eyes flared then narrowed. He moved toward her slowly, body tense.

"Oh, now you give a damn!" she snapped, backing away. "It's personal, isn't it? Like it's been for me for the past fucking week! Kris, Kris, Kris!"

With each mention of his name, Rhyn's eyes flared hotter. A low growl started deep in his chest, a warning that penetrated her rampage. She stepped back and whirled, darting toward the door. He snatched her around the waist and lifted her.

"Damn you, Rhyn!"

He flung her on the bed, and she launched up, meeting a wall of pure male. His solid, warm body atop hers immobilized her and he pinned her wrists to the bed, silver eyes blazing and elongated fangs resting on his full lower lip. She strained, unable to move but no longer caring if he did kill her.

"Fuck you, Rhyn," she said again, his silver eyes blurry through her tears. "I want my life back!"

"This. Is. Your. Life." His words were controlled with effort, his body so tense, she thought he'd snap any second. "You. Are. Mine."

"No!"

"You. Are. Mine."

She began to cry, no longer able to deny what she knew deep down: she'd never get her life back. Even without some sadistic creature's name around her neck, things would never be the same.

"There's nowhere you go where I cannot follow," he added. "Kris's *pets* can go anywhere but Hell. I can find you even there, and I will. I claimed you. You. Are. Mine. Forever."

She sobbed, her emotions from the week's events breaking free. He released her without another word, and she curled onto her side, weeping not only for the bizarre world she'd entered but from the realization she'd never, ever, *ever* return to hers.

Rhyn stormed out of the bed and breakfast. The streets of Dublin were too busy for him. He felt claustrophobic in the city, needed air and space. Without a thought as to who might be watching, he ducked into an alley and flung himself into the air. Pain blazed through him as he took the shape of the ancient creature. He beat the air mercilessly with his wings, rising high above the city and coasting on cold wind currents until he reached the ocean. He floated on the updraft of air off the water and then drifted to the beach below, changing into his human form as he landed with a gentle thud on rocky sand.

You. Are. Mine

He hadn't believed the words himself until he said them. He hadn't wanted them to be true. He wanted to fulfill his promise to Gabriel, piss off his brothers, and then walk away. It wasn't quite as easy as he thought, especially since she was so helpless.

The doll with the large blue eyes crying on the bed bothered him on more levels than he wanted to admit. He'd meant to piss her off earlier, keep her from developing any sort of affection for someone who had no intention of keeping her.

That, too, was more for him than her. The minute he found her missing from the cave, he'd felt an uneasy, unfamiliar sense of concern. He didn't just notice she was gone--he found himself wishing she wasn't.

He sensed the death dealer's presence.

"What, Gabriel?" he said without turning.

"Brought you another book," Gabriel said, handing it to him.

"Hope it's better than the last."

"This one was written by someone in the human realm. The other one was from a bitter immortal."

Rhyn accepted the book, glanced at it, and flung it into the ocean.

"You're right," Gabriel said, unaffected. "That one was probably bad, too."

"I burned the other one. *How to Train a Pet Human.* Really, Gabe?"

"It was worth a try. I don't know anything about them."

"They don't eat fish," Rhyn grunted. "You never did answer my question about Andre."

"You know I won't."

They stood in silence, watching the waves fling the book around before sinking it.

"I fucking hate Kris," Rhyn snarled. "I've been waiting for someone to tell me what to do with this human."

"She's your mate."

"So why did you insist I protect her? Death doesn't have something up her sleeve?"

"Death always has all the cards," Gabriel grunted. "But the woman is yours."

Rhyn frowned, not sure whether he wanted the woman or not. Gabriel cocked his head to the side and then shifted.

"Death's calling. Talk later."

He disappeared. Rhyn sat and draped his arms over his knees, staring at the horizon. He'd been furious when Katie mentioned Kris. He didn't understand why the self-proclaimed guardian of humans would drag such a helpless creature into this web of evil.

He remembered little about how to deal with humans and nothing of how to deal with their women. The women he remembered were docile and *silent*. The men of his time had been harsh with them, and he thought he was doing well by tolerating her.

Even so, his own conviction to keep what was his made him uneasy. A human was weak. A human mate was a liability he couldn't afford.

Yet he'd done what Andre always warned him about: he'd acted without thinking and affected someone he hadn't intended to. He'd claimed her as his, and the tattoo around her neck proved it.

You can't protect someone so fragile from what's coming.

Maybe there was a way out of it yet. Maybe he could undo what he'd done.

He dwelled on her scent, the taste of her, the kiss. He'd never felt such a connection with anyone. The sight of her being attacked by the lesser immortals infuriated him like nothing else ever had. He'd wanted to go back and tear apart the pieces he left.

Maybe there was a part of him that didn't want to undo whatever he'd done. She was destined for him. His mate.

He couldn't shake the sense he'd reached the first challenge in his life he didn't know how to handle. He'd never been entrusted with anything to care for, not when he was unable to control his powers.

And now he had a mate who infuriated him as much as she turned him on.

For the first time in years, he doubted himself. Could he really protect her, since he was now bound by Immortal Code to keep her? Or was this another Immortal Code he dared break, for the sake of another, and take whatever consequences came his way?

He'd been to Hell. The only thing worse would be to make him dead-dead.

Rhyn dropped back to stare at the sky. He wasn't ready to be dead-dead yet, not after all the time he'd spent in Hell and all the unfinished business he had.

Chapter Six

Katie ate gingerly, her head aching from both her hangover and her mental breakdown. She'd cried herself senseless before falling into a sleep too heavy to bring her any real rest. Five cups of coffee later and a full Irish breakfast settling in her stomach, she still couldn't shake the throb. The breakfast room had cleared out an hour before, but the patient matriarch kept her coffee cup full.

"Blood puddin'?"

Katie almost lost her stomach at the innocent question from the middle-aged matriarch of the bed and breakfast.

"No, thanks," she managed. "More coffee, please."

"Aye, I see that."

Because she looked like shit. She knew it. She wore a jumper that reeked of her own body odor. Her eyes were puffy and bloodshot, her hair in a half-assed braid.

"I need to get some clothes," she said, turning to where the woman had moved to sit and read her paper. "You know a cheap place around here?"

"Consignment store down the road."

"Thanks. I'll bring this back."

She carried the mug with her down the street to a store that smelled like an attic. The sun was too bright, the people around her too friendly. She sorted through the clothing, finding a pair of jeans, another pair of cargo pants, a scarf, and a few shirts. She paid the cashier with the remainder of her Euros and returned for a hot shower.

New clothes had never felt so nice, even if they were used! She wrapped the scarf around her neck and almost felt normal. The room was straightened and the fish removed, though the scent of them lingered.

The owner had left a bottle of painkiller and a snack on the nightstand, and Katie smiled at the first piece of thoughtfulness she'd received in what felt like a year. The whiskey she'd asked for. She downed her painkillers with a swig of alcohol. Before she could take another drink, Rhyn appeared out of nowhere and snatched the bottle from her.

"What is it with immortals and alcohol?"

He ignored her question and tossed it out the opened window.

"My sister is expecting me to call and then to actually show up in DC in the next week."

"I don't give a fuck." He looked her over and then strode to her again. She took a step back, but he only snatched the scarf and flung it, too, out the window.

"I don't need the reminder every time I look in the mirror!"

"Not for you. They'll leave you alone when they see it," he replied.

"Just like the goons last night?"

He gave her a warning look. "You look like shit."

"I feel like shit, no thanks to you," she said, sitting on the bed. "My head hurts, my body hurts, and I was nearly sliced open before you decided to show up last night."

"You learned what you needed to."

"I already knew you could tear people's heads off."

She refused to admit he was right. She had learned her lesson. He'd find her no matter what, and he wasn't going to be swayed by her neck next time. And, he'd slaughter anyone near his property.

"I'm not chattel," she muttered.

"You are what I say you are."

"No, I'm not," she countered. "If you want an obedient nymph, then go get one. You're stuck with me otherwise."

She thought she heard him grind his teeth and frowned.

"If you really don't want me around, why did you go through that effort to *claim* me?" she asked, crossing her arms and taking a step toward him. "Why not go get a stupid nymph, whatever those are?"

In daylight, he was almost approachable. Almost. He fidgeted with a couple of pens and doodled geometric shapes similar to those around her neck onto stationery bearing the seal of the bed and breakfast.

"You freed me. I repaid you by not killing you," he replied.

"That doesn't explain why you keep me around."

"I don't have to," he said, voice lowering into a growl.

"Those idiots last night said Ancients always pick the best blood monkeys."

"You were the only one around."

"So, this was an opportunity too good to pass up and isn't about getting back at Kris?" she asked.

One of the pens in his hands snapped, and she took a step back. The tension eased from his frame, and he said with effort, "No."

"The idiots also said that anyone--I assume monster--can sense me 'cause you did claim me."

"Wouldn't go out walking alone after dark if I was you, little girl."

"Then they said I was your mate, because I bear your mark. I don't know what--"

Snap. The other pen and pad of paper went flying out the window. This time the tension didn't leave his frame. He rose from his kneeling position and faced her. Wordlessly, he pointed to a spot on the floor before him.

"You just ate a little while ago!" she argued.

His eyes flashed, and she hurried to stand before him with her neck craned back to meet his gaze, toe-to-toe with the beast. He took her throat in one large hand, his thumb stroking the sensitive skin of her neck. They locked gazes, his intense silver eyes boring through her. Last night, after he'd beheaded the four, she'd innately known he wouldn't hurt her. Even when he spoke of replacing her with a nymph. Whatever claim he had on her, she was more than just a blood monkey, especially when he had his choice of blood monkeys outside of Hell.

What did he want from her, if more than her blood?

She closed her eyes and offered her neck, surprised to find her pulse quickening in excitement.

"You spit fire one moment and submit the next," he said, his voice thick with need.

"We are both complex creatures." She gasped as his fangs pierced her throat. The pain subsided, replaced by familiar warmth. He didn't drink long and sealed the wound after.

"No more whiskey," he snarled, turning away.

When she opened her eyes, he was gone, and she was just as confused as ever. She caught her reflection in the mirror, and the sight of the tattoo around her neck infuriated her. She strode from the room through the house to the alley to retrieve what belongings she had.

She was on her way back to her room with the scarf securely wrapped around her neck and the whiskey that had fallen mercifully into an outside trash bin without busting when she felt the change in temperature. Not as severe as traveling through the shadow world, but close. She pushed the door to her room open slowly, surprised to see who awaited her.

"Gabriel?"

He lifted his chin in greeting from his spot at the table.

"You here to kill me?" she asked.

"Nope."

She closed the door. His dark eyes dropped to the whiskey.

"What is it with whiskey?" she demanded. "You're immortal--can't kill you."

"Mortals need the power of reason to deal with us. It's Immortal Code. You have free will." He took the bottle and tossed it out the window. This time, she heard it smash.

"A choice?" she echoed. "I haven't had a choice yet with you people."

"But if you did, you'd need to be sober."

Was he amused? She couldn't tell.

"Well, what do you want?"

He offered a hand. She took a step back.

"That's not a good idea," she said.

"Kris's orders."

"Why doesn't he come get me then?"

"I'm not allowed to tell him where you are," he said.

"Why not?"

He took her hand. "We aren't to interfere in mortal happenings."

"Bullshit."

Her curse was lost as she was sucked into the shadow world. She wobbled. Gabriel steadied her. She turned around, but saw no doorway behind her. Forced to follow, she couldn't help wondering where the other portals went as he disappeared through one. She stepped from the shadow world back into her world and waited for nausea or pain. This time, there was none.

She looked around. They were in a burnt-out room…with the Arc de Triomphe a short distance away.

She had no good memories of Paris and crossed her arms. Kris rose from his squat nearby, flanked by Ileana and Jade. He looked her over intently while she stared speechlessly at Jade.

Jade withdrew his knife with a warning look.

"You look awful," she said to Kris. She wondered what it took for an immortal to look as if he'd been through Hell and back.

"So do you."

"I went to Hell."

He snorted, then looked back at her when she didn't break a smile. His gaze went to Gabriel.

"Hell?" he asked.

Gabriel shrugged.

"And you escaped?"

"Long story. Not about to relive it," Katie said, crossing her arms. "You dragged me into this shitty world."

Kris rubbed his face and glanced at Jade, whose frown was more pronounced than Ileana's.

"We'll talk about it later," Kris said. "I asked Gabriel to find you days ago. Didn't realize why it took him so long. Andre's dead."

"Oh." She softened. "I'm sorry, Kris."

His gaze lingered on her, as if he smelled her perfume and was trying hard to identify it.

"You summoned me here. Do you want something or were you curious if I'd survived the bombing after you all ditched me?" she asked at the uneasy silence.

"There isn't a creature in this realm that talks to me like you do," Kris muttered. "How the fuck did you survive Hell?"

"Made some friends. Met the devil himself and decided I'd had enough of this shit. Used my newfound power to steal a key from some robed freak."

"You met Sasha?" Ileana asked, interested for the first time.

"Intimately acquainted," she replied, cold gaze on Kris. "Not a fan of yours, either."

"No one has to like me. My job is to protect the fate of humanity, and I do it well," he snapped. "You can't possibly have somewhere else to be. My brother, Andre, was the mediator on the Council That Was Seven on which my brothers sat. World War Three is about to break out and the Council will dissolve if I don't introduce the human who's immune to us."

"You want me to meet the Council?"

"You will meet the Council this evening."

Rhyn'll be so pissed. Yet the thought of the alleged good guys losing the ultimate war because she didn't attend a stupid meeting didn't sit well with her. Her gaze again went to Jade, who looked ready to pounce. Whatever happened, she couldn't be alone with him.

"I need some coffee," she said.

Kris relaxed, as if expecting a refusal. He motioned toward a hole in the wall, and he and Jade and Ileana trailed her out of the destroyed building.

"I really am sorry about Andre," Katie said. "I liked him."

"He kept the Council focused on defending humanity and not killing each other," Kris replied. "I'll miss my dear brother."

"There are...were seven of you, right?" she asked.

"Who told you this?"

At his sharp tone, she quickly changed the subject, saying, "After the meeting, I have to go."

"No. You're staying where my brothers can't get to you, which is with me."

"No can do," she replied. "Gabriel knows where I'm staying. You can send him when you want."

"It's too dangerous for you alone," he said firmly.

"I'm not alone, and I'm leaving."

They squared off, glaring at one another. His gaze dropped to the thin, stubborn line that was her mouth and then to her scarf. Understanding crossed his features, and he unwound it, ignoring her attempts to slap him away. His stunned look was accompanied by Jade's alarmed exclamation.

"That son of a bitch claimed you? I thought he was dead-dead!"

"Betrayer of humanity," Ileana whispered. "Almost succeeded in destroying the world."

Ileana's reaction scared her. Jade's look turned to one of horror. Katie knew Rhyn was a monster, but of this magnitude...

"Thank god Gabriel got you away from him. There's no telling what he'd do to you," Kris said. "He's been in Hell for hundreds of thousands of years. He and Sasha betrayed the Council and humanity long ago."

She gazed at him, confused. Rhyn had been a prisoner like her.

"There goes that plan," Ileana said with a sigh. "Kris had planned to claim you. Ully found out Kris can use your power to make him immune from the other Ancients."

Jade glanced sharply at Ileana, then at Kris. Kris met his gaze, and the intensity of the exchange left Katie no doubt as to their relationship. A red flush rose in the normally unflappable Council leader's face.

A chill went through her. Was this why Jade sold her out? And did Rhyn know of her gift? Was that the plan of the betrayer of humanity, to use her to destroy the world?

But he'd treated her so differently than Sasha. Sasha she could see raping and bleeding her nightly to mask him from the Ancients. Rhyn had been…nice. Almost.

"Kris, what time is the damned…"

The voice was unfamiliar. She turned to see a tall, lean man with olive features that more closely resembled Rhyn's.

"Tamer, this is our Katie. Katie, my brother Tamer, who's in charge of Africa," Kris grated. "The meeting's at seven."

"So you weren't lying, brother," Tamer purred. His gaze fell to her neck. He frowned. "Kris, you have enough immortals to destroy Rhyn again? He can't be allowed to betray us again."

…destroy Rhyn again…betray us.

"I'll keep an eye on her," Jade offered.

How did she tell Kris his closest advisor had betrayed him? She was panicking, recalling the horrors of the hours at Sasha's hands. She met Jade's gaze, unable to look away. Her throat felt raw again, and the scent of her blood returned. If she looked, she'd be covered in it…

She had to get out of there before Jade found a way to alert Sasha.

"You look sick, Katie. I'll get you some whiskey," Ileana said. "And a bottle for me as well."

Katie nodded stiffly, unable to speak. She sensed Rhyn's presence before any of the others and braced herself, almost hyperventilating.

"Fuck," Kris whispered, rigid.

He stared past her. She feared looking at Rhyn, feared knowing what shape he'd taken. Instead, she tried to keep her trembling body upright and her vision from growing tunneled.

"You have something that's mine, brother," came the familiar, low growl.

"You should be in Hell with your fuck-buddy Sasha," Kris snapped.

"You couldn't defeat me and Hell couldn't hold me."

By the look on Ileana's face, Katie knew Rhyn spoke the truth. Katie faced him and saw that he was dressed like Gabriel, all in black. His chiseled features were sinister in the fractured light, his eyes glowing with quiet fury. He was as tense as she'd seen him, ready to morph and attack.

Without looking at her, Rhyn pointed to the spot beside him.

"No, Katie," Kris said quickly, starting forward. He stopped at the growl that came from deep within Rhyn's chest. "Stay with us. He'll destroy you and then the rest of humanity."

"Stay with us, Katie," Ileana seconded.

She hesitated, her gaze turning to Tamer.

"Stay with us," Jade echoed.

"*Now.*" Rhyn's tone made her jump.

She went to him, shaking with the thought of being vulnerable to a creature like Sasha again. Kris didn't know what Jade had done. He couldn't protect her. Rhyn could protect her from anything. Her head was spinning, her vision narrowing, and she paused close enough to Rhyn to lean against him.

"Take us away, take us away," she whispered.

He steadied her with one hand, and a second later the cool dampness of the shadow world swallowed her. He guided her through the fog, and they emerged in a dark room with the light of streetlamps filtering through two windows across what looked another hotel room. She rested fully against him, shaking too hard to stay on her feet. He pushed her head to the side. She didn't object when his fangs bit into her, instead sighing as the comforting warmth consumed her.

When he'd drunk his fill, his arms remained around her. She rested her head on his chest, listening to his strong heartbeat. Her shaking subsided. While she feared him, she feared the rest of the monsters more. At least this monster had indicated he was interested in keeping her around.

"Not so tough anymore, are you, little girl," he murmured.

"You're not exactly the greatest protector!"

"You're still alive."

"Is that your standard? Me surviving?" she asked incredulously.

"If they turn that beautiful face ugly, I still get blood."

She opened her mouth to retort but stopped. In his own twisted way, he'd just called her beautiful. He smelled of rain and night, a masculine musk she found as soothing as his bite. He seemed at once disgusted by the fact she was a difficult mortal blood monkey and yet primitively protective, holding her as she quaked after her run-in with a man who wanted to kill her.

"Why on earth did you choose me over a nymph?" she demanded.

He released her, the peaceful moment over. It was dark wherever he'd brought her, and she looked around in wary curiosity. He didn't answer but crossed to a window and flipped on a light.

"No more warnings," he growled. "You go nowhere without my permission."

She raised an eyebrow.

"Nowhere," he emphasized. "I don't care if Death herself comes for you."

"It's not like I have a chance to call you when you disappear," she pointed out. "You want me to tell Death to wait till you get back?"

His silver gaze swept over her. "No more scarves. Or alcohol."

She rolled her eyes. There was one bed--a California king--in what she now realized was a plain hotel room. She flung herself onto her back and stared at the ceiling. He sat at the window overlooking the street two dozen stories below.

"You need only say my name, and I'll come to you," he grated at last, as if the words cost him a hefty bet. "Like you did when those immortal sons of bitches attacked you in Ireland."

"Some sort of monster psychic connection between us?"

He gave her a scathing look.

"Thanks for rescuing me again," she said and sighed, exhausted. "You can teach me how to defend myself against monsters if you get tired of bailing me out."

"It's my duty," he said, eyes returning to the street.

"Thank you anyway."

He bristled. She assumed he was angry with her again for some reason. When she felt the cool touch of the shadow world, she sat up straight.

"Gabriel!" she exclaimed, her gaze going to Rhyn.

To her surprise, the monster didn't leap up and attack him. If anything, he ignored the death dealer.

"Sorry, Rhyn. I should've asked first," Gabriel said with a glance toward the window.

Rhyn shrugged.

"Gabriel, you have to tell Kris that Jade is working with Sasha!" she exclaimed. "He can't know."

"He doesn't," Gabriel confirmed, and sat in an armchair near Rhyn.

"Do *you* know?"

"Of course."

"Why the hell...is this that damn I-don't-interfere-in-other-people's-business thing?" she demanded.

"Something like that," Gabriel said with mild amusement.

"Can you tell him I told you to tell him?"

"No."

"Can you take him a note?" she pushed.

"Why do you give a fuck, girl?" Rhyn snapped.

"He's your brother, Shapeshifter," Gabriel chided.

"Brother?" she repeated. She stared at Rhyn. "You're one of the seven Ancients."

"Who spent the last million years in Hell, thanks to Kris."

At the warning note in Rhyn's icy tone, she fell quiet. He wasn't a patient creature, whatever he was. She crossed to the small desk and rustled around for the complimentary paper and pen.

"Marriott, St. Louis?" she said with a frown. "Never wanted to go to St. Louis."

Neither spoke. She glanced up. Gabriel's head was tilted to the side, as if listening, and Rhyn's form had relaxed.

They were communicating silently. She wrote Kris a short message and folded the paper, presenting it to Gabriel. Rhyn snatched it and read it before tearing off the strip at the bottom with the hotel's address.

He gave her a dirty look. She rolled her eyes at him.

"I'll let Kris know not to worry about Katie," Gabriel said.

"He only need concern himself with his head," Rhyn responded. "The girl is mine. Nothing anyone can do about it."

"Unless someone kills you permanently," she said. "Right?"

Both looked at her, fleeting amusement on Gabriel's face but Rhyn's gaze flaring.

"Try it, and you'll spend eternity with Sasha," Rhyn snapped.

"How much do you charge for assassinations, Gabriel?" she asked, ignoring Rhyn.

"A life for a life."

"Defeats the purpose, doesn't it?"

"Not if you're already dead or immortal."

"Out, Gabriel," Rhyn growled.

The death dealer disappeared. Rhyn gave Katie a long, withering look that she bore with crossed arms. Looking ready to explode, he rose, snatching his trench coat.

"What does it mean that I'm your mate?" she asked.

"It means I can't kill you, as much as I'd like to!"

He breezed by her and wrenched the door open, slamming it closed. Frustrated when he was around, she couldn't help but feel unusually alone when he was gone.

Gabriel returned to the Sanctuary in the Caribbean and paced in front of the hourglass perched on the altar. He wasn't able to shake his unease. Rhyn wasn't as far along as he'd hoped.

The sand in the hourglass had begun to fall faster the past two days. Rhyn didn't have a week.

He needed more time.

Gabriel crossed to the window and stared at where the dark ocean and night sky met in the distance. He willed his friend to learn the lessons he needed to, and fast.

Of all the mortals and immortals alike Gabriel had ever known, he'd never considered one a friend, not since his father's death. He'd often wondered if he had more family somewhere. If he did, he hoped he had a brother like Rhyn, who had been no older than Toby when Gabriel stumbled across him long, long ago. Gabriel delivered Rhyn to Andre and left him, though he always checked up on the half-demon whenever Andre hired him for an assassination.

Feeling helpless, Gabriel glanced again at the hourglass. For the first time since he was a child, he was worried.

Katie awoke in a sweat, the blurred scenes of gore and screams of dying from her dreams fading. The room was dark. She was alone. Disoriented, she leaned over to turn on the lamp. It was almost two in the morning.

St. Louis. She was in St. Louis.

Rhyn was still gone.

A tremor of dread slid through her. She'd had an impending sense of doom since meeting Gabriel on the street outside the faux police station, but this feeling was…defined.

"Rhyn? Can you hear me?" she called, feeling foolish when nothing happened.

She rose. As she bent to tie her shoes, a gory vision made her stagger. It was her dream all over, the flashes of light, darkness and blood, the scent of sulfur and death. She landed on her knees, horrified yet knowing something was very wrong. Rhyn was in trouble.

She glanced out the window and spotted the Arch. It flashed, silver glinting off its graceful curve. She closed her eyes, and dampness slid through her, over her. She opened her eyes and froze, recognizing the shadow world. Portals to other places glowed around her.

"Rhyn?" she whispered, close to panicking.

One of the portals flickered as if in response. Terrified of what she'd find on the other side, she stepped through and tripped. Grass tickled her hands, a chilled wind nipped her neck, and the scents from her vision intensified until she was near gagging.

She pulled her shirt over her nose and mouth and sat back on her heels. She sat on the river bank across from a series of wide, large steps leading up a hill to the park where the Arch stood, framed against a black sky.

Death. It was everywhere. She rose, trying hard not to look or touch anything. The grass, the road, the steps…all were littered with bodies and soaked in blood. She didn't know what kind of massacre had occurred here--was it even real or was it a dream? She stepped through masses of flesh and body parts, holding her mouth, until she reached the road. It was less cluttered with bodies. Some of the tattoos of the dead still glowed, the eerie red tribal patterns punctuating the landscape.

She didn't feel cold inside; she felt frozen. She'd grown up never having seen death, and in the past week, she'd seen it in its most gruesome forms. She felt something squish beneath her shoe and almost vomited.

The sounds of heated discussion made her look toward the river. Three forms with glowing tattoos were moving slowly toward the road, stopping to sift through the dead bodies. One grabbed an arm and took a bite.

"Not here."

The words were loud. She looked around, panicked, and darted to the massive stairs. Keeping along the long wall, she inched her way upward, sticking to the shadows. The three creatures continued to hunt through the fallen, sometimes eating, most of the times pushing body parts aside in search of something.

In search of Rhyn. She reached the top of the stairs and stared at a similar scene leading past the Arch and all the way up the park toward the city.

She heard a shout and whirled. The three creatures made a run for the stairs.

"Rhyn!" she called, darting forward. "Rhyn!"

Another vision, one of the Arch through the branches of a tree. She staggered and looked around widely before going to the right. She stepped on something squishy but didn't let herself stop to think about what it was. Instead, she half ran, half leapt through the piles of bodies into the treed area lining two wide walkways.

"Rhyn!"

She was closer. She *felt* him. No vision came to her and she continued. The creatures had reached the top of the stairs and were looking around, trying to figure out which way she'd gone.

"Rhyn!"

Her shout drew their attention, and they started toward her.

"Goddammit, Rhyn!" she said, tears rising to blur her path.

The taste of death was in her mouth and if she looked, she knew her shoes would be covered in blood. She ran, eyes blurry and stomach turning.

Stop. His command was weak, yet the air around her stiffened until she hit an invisible wall.

She dropped, surprised and disgusted when one hand landed in what was a human or creature at one point. She wiped her hand on her shirt and leapt up.

"Rhyn?"

Katie.

She turned, not sure if she heard his voice or if he was in her head. She hopped over another mess and searched the darkness. His was the only form in one piece; he was propped up against the base of a tree. She dropped beside him, crying, shaking, terrified, and found he was unconscious.

"C'mon, Rhyn, they're getting closer!" she said, and shook him.

He sagged against her. She smelled his blood, felt the weakness of his body when their skin met. The sensations surprised her.

The creatures were coming. They'd kill her. They'd kill him. He wasn't waking up.

She choked back a sob and saw the glint of starlight off a knife on the ground. She crawled over him and snatched it, wiping its blade on her clothes before she hesitated.

She'd never cut herself before. She looked at her wrist, where Lankha had bitten her, closed her eyes, and hacked. Pain made her gasp as blood welled and spilled. She placed her wrist to Rhyn's mouth, willing him to awaken, to drink her. She'd never thought she'd find a reason to want some creature to suck her blood; if ever, now was the time.

At first, nothing happened, and she readied herself to run. He groaned softly, licked his lips. His body tensed so fast she didn't have time to blink.

His silver eyes opened, glowing almost crazed in the night. Uneasy, she started to move away, but he grabbed her arm to keep her wrist in place and tore into it. She screamed, the creatures came closer, and sheer will made her close her eyes to envision the hotel room.

The shadow world…she staggered and floated through it, hauling him with her toward a pulsing portal that grew blurry fast. She toppled through it into their hotel room. It was silent aside from her choked gasps. Rhyn was unconscious again, his face marred by her blood.

There was nothing left of her forearm but a mangled mess. Horrified, she stumbled into the bathroom for a towel, wrapped her arm in it, and collapsed, sobbing.

Rhyn stared at Katie's still body, uncertain what to do. Her breathing was shallow, the scent of her blood making him shudder. He was weak but alive, his body covered with his blood and hers.

His little mortal had come after him. No one had ever come after him before.

The thought shocked him. He watched blood ooze from her arm. He wasn't a healer, and the only healer he knew was trapped in Hell. Humans had their own kinds of healers. Gazing at her, he doubted a human healer could help her.

He scooped her up, not knowing what else to do. He opened his senses to locate the immortal he wanted, and then willed himself there. It was the only place he knew where someone *might* help him.

He stood in the gently lit bedroom of his brother, Kiki. Kiki whirled from his position before the hearth, his oriental features set off by electric turquoise eyes.

"What the fu--*Rhyn?*"

The only brother not to declare outright war on him, Kiki was a distant second to Andre in his tepid support of their black sheep of a young brother.

"Gods, what'd you do to her?" Kiki demanded.

Rhyn ignored the accusation and pulled her away when Kiki tried to snatch her.

"Tell me where to take her before she bleeds out," he ordered.

Despite the animosity boiling at the back of his brother's gaze, Kiki's pragmatism snapped to the forefront. He whipped off his T-shirt and wrapped Katie's arm.

"No one told me you were out of prison," Kiki muttered as he worked. "You hear about Andre?"

"Why else do you think I'm *here*?"

Kiki glanced at him and whipped out a mobile phone. His conversation was short and curt before he tossed the mobile.

"I'll take her somewhere safe," he said, holding out his hand.

Rhyn pulled the scarf he hated from her neck. Kiki stared, even more stunned.

"Fool," he said, eyes narrowing. "What--"

"Kiki!" Rhyn growled.

His brother snapped his mouth closed and extended his hand, pulling Rhyn and Katie with him into the shadow world. They crossed through the fog to a destination Rhyn had never been before. They emerged from the shadow world and stood on a narrow, winding road. The fragrant ocean was too dark to see. The sound of waves rushing the shore and the firm sand beneath his feet indicated its location a few yards from them. A sprawling castle with thick walls, an old portcullis, and torches glowing along the walls rose up before them. The road leading to the castle was modern blacktop.

"What is this?" Rhyn asked suspiciously as Kiki started toward the arched door beside the portcullis.

"There are four immortal Sanctuaries on earth. This is one. Hurry."

Rhyn followed, painfully aware of the limp mortal body in his arms. Kiki didn't knock the door down as he could, instead beating loudly enough for the sound to drift down the road.

A small, older woman in severe grey opened the door. Kiki clasped his hands and offered a small bow.

"We seek your assistance, good guardian of the Sanctuary," he said.

The woman curtseyed deeply in response and stepped aside. Rhyn shoved past Kiki into a small courtyard. The woman motioned them to follow, her quick steps echoing across the cobblestones. Another woman in grey emerged from a hallway. She bobbed her head and darted off at the murmured instructions of the first woman.

They stopped at a wooden door, which the woman flung open. The room was tiny, but Rhyn didn't care. He carefully lowered Katie to the small bed. Immediately, the second woman reappeared with a small basket full of medicinal wares.

"You must leave. You cannot be here," the first woman said, pushing Rhyn toward the door.

He ignored her order with a glare.

"Rhyn, come on. Ancients aren't welcome in Sanctuaries," Kiki said.

Rhyn resisted for a moment longer, watching the woman expertly slice Katie's shirt open. Kiki gave him a shove, and the older woman closed the door behind them.

"This is the best you can do," Kiki said. "Don't piss these people off by breaking their rules, not when they're probably the only ones who can help her."

For once, Rhyn agreed. He trailed Kiki out of the castle to the boulders a short distance from the walls.

"What the fuck are you doing, Rhyn?" Kiki turned on him at last. "*You* are the last person in the entire fucking universe that should take a mate!"

"Back off, Kiki," Rhyn replied, knowing the words were true.

"No, Rhyn, I won't. I've never been as strong of an advocate for you as Andre, but I always thought you decent somewhere on the inside."

"Thanks for your faith, brother!"

"But you, Rhyn, have somehow managed to kill every mortal you run across! How the fuck did you--"

"Enough!" Rhyn roared.

Kiki fell silent, but his gaze was accusing.

"I don't know, Kiki!" Rhyn snapped. "Leave me the fuck alone."

"You don't know what?"

"I don't know why I did it. I wanted to piss off Sasha at first. Now..." He stopped, not sure how to explain the fact he now wanted something he shouldn't.

"This isn't...is it Katie?" Kiki asked, gaze sharpening.

"Yeah. And?"

"We lost her the same night Andre died. She was with you?"

"Sasha dragged her down to Hell. He wanted to make her his mate," Rhyn said.

"So you did before he could," Kiki finished. "Real smart, Rhyn."

Rhyn ignored his brother as the lean man paced and pulled at his hair in frustrated silence. Rhyn looked toward the walls, unable to quell the flutter of worry within him.

She'd almost died to save him. He'd almost died many times, and in many cases, for the sake of his brothers. He never thought twice about walking into danger and rarely cared if he survived or not.

But no immortal—let alone human—had ever risked his or her life for him. For the first time in his life, he didn't know what to do.

"What do we do?" Kiki demanded at last. "You can't keep her."

"What do you mean I can't keep her?" he returned, facing his brother.

"I mean, you don't have what it takes to keep a mate alive, let alone safe. You're your own worst enemy, as Andre always tried to warn you."

Rhyn clenched his jaw, hearing the truth in Kiki's words.

"Do you have any idea how fucking pissed Kris will be?" Kiki muttered.

"Like I give a fuck what he thinks."

"He intended to take her as his mate, Rhyn. This is going to reopen that wound…"

Rhyn said nothing, giving his brother a bitter smile. Part of him felt triumphant to know he'd piss off Kris as well as Sasha. Kiki ceased pacing and stared at the walls.

"You can't keep her," Kiki said again.

"Yes, I can. And I will, Kiki," Rhyn said through clenched teeth. "She's mine. I've claimed her under Immortal Code. Why the fuck does everyone want her anyway? She's just a little human."

"Yes, but she's…" Kiki's retort drifted off.

Rhyn met his gaze, as Kiki became suddenly considering.

"You haven't blown anything up yet," Kiki said. "Hell tame you?"

"Nope."

"Something did."

Rhyn shrugged. He hadn't noticed until Kiki's words. Nothing had blown up or gone wrong since he'd returned from Hell. His power felt the same, but maybe his time in Hell had mellowed it out, made it more responsive to his command.

"I'm bound to tell Kris you're here," Kiki reminded him. "And the others."

"I don't give a shit."

"As for your mating…maybe you can find a way to undo what you did."

"Fuck you, Kiki," Rhyn said.

"You're welcome, Rhyn."

And Kiki was gone. Rhyn took a deep breath before perching on a boulder outside the walls. He'd never been to a Sanctuary. He was glad Kiki brought him and just as troubled by his brother's doubt.

Katie had proved herself to him by doing what even his blood-brothers never would. No, Katie was his. He wasn't going to *undo* anything, especially not if it was something his brothers wanted!

Chapter Seven

Katie awoke in a mental institution. At least, that was her first impression of the eight-by-eight room with its steel-framed bed, simple mattress, and no furniture. The wooden door and whitewashed walls--along with the open window above the bed allowing in balmy air--soon brought to mind a more tropical place. She rose and flinched, expecting agony as she moved her arm. It was bandaged and stiff, but there was no pain.

She tugged the heavy door open by its old iron handle and gazed into a large square of grass, a courtyard, around which many similar rooms with heavy doors were arranged. Airy hallways led through the hacienda style structure on either side of her. There were more buildings past the hallway to her right. The hallway led into an open area with one car in the large parking lot and a medieval stone wall and turrets surrounding the entire hacienda. The heavy wooden gates marking the entrance to the compound were closed.

Stairs traced the inside of the thick wall, and she walked up them to figure out where exactly she might be. The effort made her dizzy. She leaned against a wall, overlooking a stretch of rocky terrain punctuated with patches of yellow-green grass. In the distance, she saw the blue of an ocean meet the horizon.

And one dark form seated on the rocks, staring at the walls like an angry puppy thrown out of its master's house. She touched the tattoo at her throat.

Serves you right, she thought darkly then said outloud, "I've saved your life twice now, jackass."

He flipped her off, confirming he heard her.

"Vile creature," a cool, crisp voice said.

She turned, surprised to see the middle-aged woman in grey robes and sharp brown eyes.

"But he did save you," she allowed. "There's something in that."

By the austere clothing and stern features, Katie assessed she was in some kind of religious convent.

"Come. We'll feed you real food. You needn't worry about him," the woman said in her crisp voice, leading her down the stairs. "He can't come in the walls."

"Is this a holy place?"

"It is."

"Will he burst into flames or something?" she asked.

The woman chuckled. "No, we'll just kick him out again."

Katie trailed the fit woman through the hallway, past her room, and down a second corridor. The scents of fresh bread and some sort of meat cooking nearly nailed her to the ground as she rounded the corner. The woman led her straight into a small cafeteria with rustic tables and benches, an open fireplace, and a sagging buffet table along one wall. The windows were open with no glass, and heavy iron chandeliers hung from thick wooden rafters and were burning real candles.

"What is this place?" she asked.

"Have a seat. This is a Sanctuary, one of four remaining in the human world."

As soon as she sat, another woman in similar robes with a flushed face appeared, serving tray in hand. She placed warm rustic bread, whipped honey butter, and water before her. Katie bit into the bread, determined not to eat like a heathen that would shame her sister. At the first taste, she wolfed it and three more pieces down until the edge of her hunger disappeared.

"Wow," she murmured, and gulped her water. "What exactly is a Sanctuary?"

"We're like the Switzerland of the immortal world. All four Sanctuaries are neutral territory, governed by Death," the woman said with a small smile. "Any immortal who comes must check their weapons--and their talents--at the door, or be rendered dead-dead by Death. Only the Ancient Ones and Death may pass with their powers intact. We normally expel the Ancient Ones. They disturb the order here."

Katie sat back with a contented sigh, gaze dropping to her arm. She frowned. Rhyn had never hurt her until then. Granted, he wasn't exactly himself at the time, near dead, starved, weak.

She'd never thought a creature like him weak. Yet she'd felt it when their bodies touched. His guard was down, and she'd felt just how weak he was despite taking her blood. She knew he could've taken so much more, made himself stronger by bleeding her dry. He didn't, instead taking only what he needed to survive.

"He brought you here," the woman said, her eyes on Katie's bandaged arm. "We have a member of the healing guild on staff, but her skill wasn't old enough for you. We did what we could. You'll have full use of your arm, even if it's scarred."

"I've gotten so many...marks...the past couple of weeks. Don't think another really matters at this point," Katie said.

The woman's gaze dropped to her neck, and Katie caught the troubled look in her eyes before she hid it. There was reason to fear the Ancients, especially *this* Ancient, who seemed to have no alliance to anything good or bad and was so unpredictable. At least he'd thought enough of his blood monkey to bring her here, if only to keep her healthy so he had a food source.

She frowned, troubled by her thoughts. Rhyn was weak but drew only what he needed to survive; he was both hunter and hunted. He'd claimed her, whether in a fit of jealous fury after hearing Kris's name or for some other purpose. In her mind, dragging a human around seemed like a pretty serious liability.

She didn't understand him. Or this world. Or why she couldn't just go back to her life and be normal again. Her throat tightened. Willing herself not to cry, she pointed to her neck and said instead, "Do you know what this means?"

The woman hesitated and took a slice of bread, toying with it.

"You're his mate," she said at last, as if this should mean more than it did.

"I know. So?"

"You're *his mate*."

"Assume I never knew this underworld existed before a little over a week ago," Katie said dryly.

The woman studied her for a long moment. The second woman with the flushed face returned with a plate heaped with half a cooked chicken smelling of garlic and spices, rice, and fried plantains. Katie dug in, unconcerned with the woman's silence while there was food in front of her.

"If it helps, I'm allegedly special somehow," she prodded around a mouth full of food.

"Of course. You were born an immortal's mate," the woman replied. "Still, you'd have to be something more to attract an Ancient."

"Why?"

"It's just the way things are." She paused then shook her head. "I'm Daniela."

"Katie."

"Welcome, Katie. Your mate dumped you on me in the middle of the night. I knew he was an Ancient--a powerful one--but he wasn't much for talking."

"Yeah, he's like that. Drags me around the world without telling me where or why we go anywhere," Katie said.

"You said you've known him a week?"

"I've known him a few days. I was introduced to this world a few days before that. I don't know anything about either."

"Very, very unusual. No Ancient would…" Daniela drifted off, thoughtful.

Katie held her breath, awaiting the awful news. Daniela shook her head again and smiled.

"What's so significant about being his mate?" Katie asked.

"It's hard to explain to an Outsider. There are only so many immortal mates born into the human race, far fewer than there are immortals. It was believed that no Ancient would ever take a mate, because none ever have. For all other immortals, they get only one shot at a mate in its life cycle. One mate. That's it. Many immortals go extinct without taking a mate at all. They wait so long, they forget they can have one, or they choose not to have one, or they simply just don't."

"Why would any Ancient creature choose me?"

"I don't know. I'm sure he knows."

"I'm not so sure about that," Katie said with a shake of her head.

"There is the theory that the mates of Ancients are predestined like those of other immortals, that if the Ancients don't find their mates during the mates' life cycle, they never will," Daniela said.

"That's kind of sad."

"Yeah, it is."

"I buy into this preordained theory. Rhyn wouldn't saddle himself with a blood monkey he had to actually take care of voluntarily. Doesn't seem like the type who wants to be slowed down by a liability like that," Katie mused.

Daniela shrugged.

"Or he wants to use me for my talent," Katie added. "I could see that."

"Unlikely, since he only gets one, unless he planned on dying dead soon. If he doesn't die-dead, he'd have to spend eternity with you. Maybe it is predestined. He's the least friendly Ancient I've ever met."

"He's been in Hell for a long time," she replied. "Wait, did you say *eternity?*"

"Of course."

A familiar headache started, and Katie stuffed the last few bites of food down her throat, feeling ill for a different reason. She hadn't been able to keep a job or a boyfriend for more than a few months, let alone an eternity!

"You got whiskey?" she asked.

"We make our own alcohol. It's closer to brandy."

"Bring it out."

As if on cue, the flushed cook returned for her plate, and Daniela ordered the brandy and two glasses.

"I don't get this whole free will thing," Katie complained when the cook returned. She poured herself amber liquid and took a long swallow. "It's not really free if the choice is made for you."

"The immortals must give humans a choice. It's Immortal Code. They've been working for millions of years to get around this one; they're quite crafty at it. You may have wished your life to be different or made some statement in anger. They're better than lawyers when it comes to taking things out of context, and there are no judges keeping track of what really happened," Daniela explained.

"It's a sham."

"It exists to protect mortals, and in many cases it does. In some, it doesn't. It just depends on the immortal and how he or she chooses to interpret the Code."

Katie wasn't sure if the homemade alcohol was stronger than normal or if her weakened state made her more vulnerable to its effects. After two shots, she felt woozy.

"Are there any benefits to being an Ancient's mate?" she asked.

"Prestige. You move to the head of the immortals' hierarchy. Immunity to Death, children with magical powers--"

"*Children?*"

"--protection from enemies, a really comfortable lifestyle, and some mates even are able to tap into their immortals' talents."

Eternity. Children. She couldn't have one day without some sort of surprise or other? As if sensing her distress, Daniela poured her another two shots of brandy.

"Where are we?" Katie asked.

"In the Caribbean on an undeclared island."

"Undeclared?"

"Protected by magic. No one knows we're here, except those seeking refuge," Daniela said.

"Is refuge…free?" Katie asked.

"Always. We sell our liquors and also are the beneficiaries of various immortals. The Ancient Andre, who became dead-dead recently, left us his fortune, as have many others before him."

"I met him. He seemed like a good man. Ancient. Whatever."

"He was the glue that bound the Council That Was Seven. Seven brothers with one common immortal father and seven separate mothers. Their father fought the Dark One and left his children to carry the torch. Only, the siblings couldn't ever get along. It was said two of them turned on the others, aligned with evil, and only Andre had the power to kill any of the others. He was their elder, the peacemaker, and the executioner. He sentenced both brothers to Hell for eternity."

"Sasha and Rhyn," Katie said quietly, touching her throat again. "What did they do?"

"They turned on their brothers and against humans and the order of good. Massacred millions. The human race barely survived. The legends are thick in every culture, from floods to plagues to volcanoes and the ground rising up to swallow people, to the influence of men who slaughtered whole nations for entertainment."

"They did all that?"

"According to the legend. Sasha was the first to align with the Dark One, and Rhyn…"

"Rhyn what?" Katie demanded, holding her breath.

"They say he went mad when the woman he'd chosen as his mate chose Kris instead. She died at Rhyn's hands. The legends don't say what happened, but after Rhyn killed the woman, he tried to kill Kris. Andre stopped him, and Death made him disappear."

"How awful," Katie breathed. "Does that mean your theory about mates is wrong, if they fought over one woman?"

"Maybe, maybe not. It's hard to know. Maybe she was an Ancient's mate, too."

Rhyn was a mass murderer, a creature who had tried to wipe out the human race. The story didn't sit well with Katie. It explained his and Kris's palpable animosity, but it didn't explain why Rhyn was a prisoner. Or how Sasha swayed Jade. Or how Andre died.

Or why Rhyn kept her around, unless it was purely for her ability to make him immune from the magic of other immortals.

Katie drank more brandy, a familiar sense of panic deep in her chest. It and impending doom had been with her since meeting Gabriel. Her headache pulsed and she felt hot from alcohol.

"Think I'll go for a walk," she murmured. "Thanks for the talk. Mind if I take this?"

Daniela filled her glass with two more shots and smiled. Katie raised the glass in a salute and left. It was muggier than she was used to, the air clinging to her already hot skin. It was near dusk, with the sky growing dark in the distance. She made her way to the wall, needing to feel the cool ocean breeze. Rhyn was gone, and she leaned against the wall.

A hand took her brandy and flung it and the glass over the wall. So he wasn't gone after all. She glared up at him.

"You're not allowed in here," she told him.

"You're not allowed alcohol."

"If I didn't keep learning how insane this world is every second of the day, I wouldn't have to drink!"

His eyes glinted rather than flashed, his copper skin tight across perfect, chiseled features. He didn't have Kris's noble look or Andre's delicate features. Rhyn was a wild animal with a wild beauty, harsh angles and planes, a body built for survival. He said nothing, and she offered her good wrist.

"You're weak," he scoffed.

"So are you."

She dropped her arm and gazed up at him, troubled and lightheaded.

"You don't look like someone who could kill millions," she murmured. "Then again, I saw what you did at the Arch." She shivered involuntarily. "Did you really almost annihilate the human race?"

He said nothing and mirrored her position, leaning against the wall in what she knew was irritated mockery.

"I don't believe it," she went on.

"You're a fool," he replied. "I killed over a hundred of Sasha's creatures at the Arch with only a fraction of my power. You think I can't do the same to a bunch of weak humans?"

"You can't hate humans so much if you chose me as a mate. Why did Sasha send his creatures after you?"

"I took you from him and escaped. He's pissed and wants us both back. Probably heard you're my mate." His silver gaze went to her neck and flared. She didn't know how to interpret his look. His eyes slid away to the distance.

"Is it your duty to protect humanity?" she asked, cocking her head to the side.

"More or less, as long as they're not in my way."

"And I know firsthand how you take your duties."

He gave her a sidelong glance.

"You take them pretty seriously," she added. "You could've killed me a million times over, but I'm your mate. You haven't, yet, because protecting me--albeit poorly--is still your duty. No, you didn't try to kill humanity off. One stupid little human is so much easier to kill than a few billion, and you chose duty instead."

"You drink too much and talk too much. You should've died in Hell," he said.

"Tell me about it. Might have made life easier."

At her bitter note, he looked at her again. She felt angry tears welling and forced them back, soon distracted by the warmth in her blood. Other thoughts collided with her emotions, ones that reminded her that she was forever trapped with some otherworldly creature that viewed her as a food supply and nothing more.

"Eternity's a long time," she whispered.

"Longer than you know."

"You're welcome for saving your ass, by the way."

"You interfered," he replied.

"It's not how I remember things! I saved you from Hell, and I saved you from those things at the…at the Arch." Memories of the massacre made bile rise and her chest clench. "I'll be a raving lunatic at the end of another week!"

He didn't disagree. She wanted to scream at him, hit him, send him far away. Instead, she slumped against the wall, defeated by alcohol and impotent rage. It didn't matter what she said or did; he wasn't going anywhere. He'd made his claim clear.

You. Are. Mine.

"You chose me," she said. "I want to know why."

He was silent.

"You owe me this, if nothing else!" Her words were accompanied by a punch to his arm, one that merely earned her an impatient look.

Still he said nothing.

"Tell me why, Rhyn," she ordered, pushing him to face her. She glared up at him, swaying toward him.

His gaze slid over her face and down her body to her breasts. She gritted her teeth and waited. It was hard to reconcile the man before her with the creature that tore apart bodies like meat in a blender.

"I wanted you," he said in his low growl, the one that gave her chills.

"Why? So you could block others? Revenge against Kris? An easy food source following you around for the rest of all time?" She jabbed him in the chest with each question, unwilling to back down.

He snatched her upper arms and pushed her against the wall, his body close enough for their chests to brush when either breathed in. The silver eyes were fiery, and apprehension fluttered through her. His scent tickled her senses, his nearness making her warm body warmer.

"I. wanted. You." His words were forced through clenched teeth.

"There's gotta be more!" she returned. "You're immortal. You could have any woman you wanted in any time you wanted, including one who'd be far more docile than I am."

"You came after me at the Arch."

"Yeah. So?"

"Why?" he demanded.

"I knew you were in danger."

"You could've left me to my fate, and you didn't. You were a loyal blood monkey."

The thought of leaving him to die had never crossed her mind. However, the thought of swan diving off a cliff the next time he called her a damn *blood monkey* was getting more tempting with each day!

"I can't do this much longer," she whispered. "I can't deal with all this shit."

"You're strong. You'll survive."

"I don't want to *survive*! I want to be happy and not worry about creatures trying to kill me or how often I'll be wandering into one of your massacres!"

"This—"

"I know, I know! This is my life, and I belong to you. You're such an insensitive bastard."

She strained against him. He didn't budge. Exhausted, she rested her head, then her body, against him. She was tired of fighting, tired of his attitude, tired of everything.

He'd hugged her before, an anomaly, she was sure, until his arms now moved around her again. Would she *ever* understand him? He didn't give a damn about her, and he sounded as if he'd rather she jump from a cliff than bother him.

And then he brought her here to be healed. He held her. At one point, he'd called her beautiful and tonight, he'd called her strong. He rested his chin on her head. She liked the way he smelled, how strong and solid his body was. It was more than comforting; she wanted to melt against him and stay there.

The intense sensation startled her. That a mass murdering *demon* was the only man she'd ever felt so comfortable with made no sense. She'd risked her life to rescue him because it was what good people did. After all, in his own twisted way, he'd tried to help her.

"I still don't believe you," she murmured. "There has to be another reason you chose me."

He said nothing.

"If you're hungry..." *...you should eat.* She couldn't bring herself to say the words.

"Whiskey tastes like shit," he replied.

"Now who's whining?"

"Careful, little girl," he growled.

"You're not going to kill me. Might try to chew through my other arm. That *hurt*, Rhyn. You owe me for that. And for rescuing you twice."

"More fish?"

"You won't even apologize for my arm, will you?"

"You should've left me," he said.

"So you repay me for rescuing you by eating my arm."

"You can't face those things. You were a fool to follow me."

"I didn't follow you," she snapped. "I traveled through the shadow world, which is also how I got you back! You think I lugged your heavy ass for two miles?"

"You found your way through the shadow world on your own?" His words were measured enough that she looked up.

"Got a problem with that, too?"

"It's as it should be."

She studied him. There was some satisfaction in his response, the first shred of positivity she'd heard from him yet. Their gazes locked, and she felt a different kind of warmth slide through her.

Could she really be sexually attracted to an immortal mass murderer of millions? It was not a stretch, not with his muscular body pressed against her and his rugged features so close. Even the liquid silver eyes that once terrified her were hauntingly beautiful, when not glowing like some hell-beast's. She liked his smell, his warmth, his strength...even his snarkiness.

She was crazy. There was no way a monster like him would ever be interested in his blood monkey!

He touched her neck, and she waited, assuming he'd take blood from her despite his distaste of alcohol. His thumb traced the line of her jaw lightly, and heat skittered through her. He lowered his head, and she bared her neck. Though his hot breath tickled her, he didn't bite her. The pad of his thumb traced across her lower lip. She closed her eyes, breathing growing shallow.

He nipped her neck, and she gasped, embarrassing herself. Her blood was thrumming even faster than the alcohol alone would have caused, her body growing too warm for comfort.

His lips traced the line from her neck to her jaw with small, hot kisses, sending exquisite shivers through her. There was a pause before he kissed her lightly on the lips, his full lips oh-so-warm. God help her, she responded! She tried to tell herself it was the alcohol scattering her thoughts and not the growing feeling of respect or concern she felt toward him.

Sensing her yield, he deepened the kiss. It became less of a request and more of a demand, with his tongue flickering to taste her. He tasted like he smelled, rich and musky, his kiss intense enough to dispel the fogginess of alcohol. She'd never felt anything like his kiss or the warmth that flowed through her. She wanted more of him, *all* of him, and the heat of need settled into her lower abdomen.

A throat cleared behind him. Rhyn twisted his head away with a warning growl, and the world crashed down on her.

What in the name of everything holy was she doing? Getting ready to tear her shirt open and throw herself down for a monster? She felt the heat--his heat--within her, branding her from the inside out.

"Sire, you've been warned," Daniela said in her crisp tone.

Rhyn turned to face the robed woman, and Katie slid away from him. Her thoughts jangled in her head, some desperate for him to continue, others claiming she couldn't go home if she started down this path, and still others saying she was screwed either way, figuratively and literally.

Chapter Eight

Whatever Daniela said to him after she fled worked, and Katie didn't see him for the rest of the day. The next morning, she leaned against the wall and stared at the dark form crouched on a rock a good distance from the Sanctuary. He was staring at her. She didn't know what he thought from the distance, but she imagined him pissy as usual. He deserved it for kissing her and making her feel things she never, ever, ever imagined she'd feel for any man, let alone a monster like him.

"Katie."

She whirled. "Gabriel!" she exclaimed. "Are you here for me?"

"No, but thanks for asking."

"You're not funny, Gabriel."

His amusement was fleeting. He leaned his elbows on the wall with a wave at Rhyn. He wore his customary all black, his dark eyes hidden behind dark shades.

"I gave Kris your message," he said. "He wasn't happy."

"His problem, not mine."

"It *becomes* your problem if he doesn't believe you."

"Does he?" she asked.

"I don't know. Not yet."

"You can't take me to him, you know. Rhyn will kill everyone in his path."

"You can choose to come with me," he stated.

"Would cause an even worse rampage."

"Very well. He said to give you this." He handed out a note. She took it and read the single sentence.

I'll return your life to you. She expected joy at the offer but felt wary instead.

"Andre said Kris planned to do what Rhyn did and make me his mate. Can I ever *not* belong to Rhyn now that I do?" she asked, considering.

"Not unless Rhyn is dead-dead."

"And Kris doesn't believe me about Sasha," she mused. "He's not really offering me anything. He can't wipe my memory—even Andre couldn't and he's older—and he can't fix what Rhyn's done. Does he think me so naïve that I'd leap at some empty promise?"

Gabriel met her question with silence and another look of passing amusement.

"He must've forgotten I went to Hell already," she said. "I'm not the idiot he took me for when he assigned a certain baby angel to my guardianship. Of all the screwed-up men…*beasts* I've met, I'd trust Rhyn before Kris, even not knowing what Rhyn really is or if he really did try to annihilate mankind alongside Sasha."

"Do you believe he did?"

"I don't know," she admitted.

"What do you feel?"

"Doesn't matter if I'm sorta stuck with him, does it?" she replied icily. She knew what she thought and suspected he did, too.

"The answer's not for me. I know what happened."

"Daniela called him wild. I'd say that's true, but I don't think him capable of walking away from a duty so great."

"Then you'd be right," he agreed.

"Was he always so wild?"

"Hell made him worse. What shall I tell Kris?"

"Tell him to leave me alone."

She handed back the note, more determined not to give the white-haired man what he wanted now that she had confirmation--and somehow she believed Gabriel--that Rhyn hadn't destroyed millions. Her hand rested on her bandaged forearm. She'd peeked at the healing wound the night before and found the scar not just ugly but hideous, a jagged seam between two lumps of uneven flesh.

"Gabriel, who was the woman they fought over?" she asked. "Daniela said this was what spurred their fighting."

He was quiet. She thought he'd refuse to answer until he said slowly,

"A truly unworthy woman. She was the first Ancient's mate born and should've been Kris's mate, if she hadn't first promised herself to the Dark One. She played them against each other and betrayed them both to Sasha. Rhyn killed her to protect Kris and his brothers. Kris never knew and never forgave him for killing the woman he meant to take as his mate. Rhyn probably saved humanity by doing so but was sent to Hell and nearly lost his mind."

"Why didn't he *tell* Kris she was evil?"

"Rhyn's not a talker."

She stared at him, astonished. "So he'd spend eternity in Hell because he couldn't sit down with Kris and tell him what happened?"

"It's complicated," he said.

"No, it's not!"

"There's more to the story. The woman, Lilith, was pregnant with Kris's heir. No matter what Rhyn would've said, the damage was done. To be quite honest, he was so abrasive anyway, even if he hadn't killed the woman, they'd have broken paths. Though all seven were constantly fighting, Kris and Rhyn were always at each other's throats."

"That's dandy, but it doesn't sound like he deserved Hell!" she insisted.

"He's not exactly a pure angel, Katie. He did a lot of bad things, and his mother was a demoness, a powerful one who seduced his father. After they mated, she killed him. The brothers on the Council were looking for any excuse to expel or kill him, and Andre was his only advocate. Despite his demon powers, despite his wildness, despite his struggle to remain dutiful to their cause, he was a danger to anyone around him."

She couldn't imagine an upbringing with no parents, a clan of brothers who hated him, and no ability to change his nature.

"Gabriel, he's protected and helped me more than once since the dungeon and done it out of some sort of sense of duty. Even if he's done bad things…I don't know. I don't think he's the lost cause you're making him out to be," she said, disturbed.

"You saw what he did in St. Louis."

Her gaze shifted from him to the dark form seated on a boulder. She assumed…she *hoped*…all of the dead were bad guys. Even so, she'd seen what he could do to a human-esque body in a few seconds.

"Are you saying I *should* go with you?" she asked.

"I believe your choice to be the right one."

"Do you think…why do you think he chose me as his mate?"

"Daniela seems to think it was preordained. You're an Ancient's mate, and maybe you were meant for him and only him," Gabriel said.

"He told me he chose me."

"You didn't ask why?" he challenged, amused again.

"Of course I did. He said he wanted me. He's not a man of many words, Gabriel."

"Maybe that's the truth of it."

"I know there's more," she said.

"Maybe you stabilize his wild power, though he doesn't know it yet."

She considered the new possibility. Rhyn certainly didn't seem to have much control, as far as she could tell. He'd massacred every human she'd run across to date.

"You mean he was *worse* than this before?" she returned, surprised.

"Much. Would've wiped out the island by now and half of Cuba without realizing he'd done so."

"He's using me."

"He needs you and wants you," Gabriel said. "He needed his brothers and still left them. As much as he's done wrong in his life, he's not a liar."

The information filtered through her skepticism until she admitted he spoke too logically to be anything but right. Her disbelief that Rhyn had chosen someone like her over a supermodel was softened by the rationale that he would also innately recognize his intended mate, even if he didn't recognize her ability to help him control his power.

What a horrible life he'd lived, if this was the best it'd ever been for him! Yet he didn't seem too affected by a life of pain, exclusion, and conflict. If anything, he seemed absolutely sure of himself and what he wanted, even if his nature didn't allow him to control his own wild talents.

"Kris may want to come here to talk to you," Gabriel added. "He knows he can't take you anywhere, but if he asks…"

"I don't care if he comes to me. I can't trust him enough to go to him. And he comes alone, Gabriel."

"Understood."

He was gone before she could tell him goodbye. She leaned against the wall, eyeing the distance from her position to the rock on which Rhyn sat. She doubted he'd come if she called.

The conversation with Gabriel turned over in her thoughts as she descended the stairs and left through the opened gate. She felt bad for Rhyn, though she suspected the emotion was wasted on someone who didn't have a drop of self-pity. She crossed her arms as she neared. Rhyn watched her, unmoving, like a predator watches its prey.

"You don't have anywhere else to be aside from sitting here day and night staring at the wall?" she asked.

"I'm immortal. I have time."

She drew a deep breath. Instead of retorting, she said, "That's not how I wanted this conversation to go. I came out to thank you for bringing me here and saving me more than once from those things."

He stared at her.

"So, thank you. If you're hungry, just let me know."

He said nothing, his tense frame never relaxing. At the silence, she turned away and started back to the compound, irritated.

"What did Gabriel want?" he asked before she'd gone more than a few steps.

"Kris sent him to fetch me," she replied without turning.

"And you said *what*?"

"I said no."

She didn't hear his silent step. He gripped her arm hard and stepped in front of her, his size sending a tremor of unease through her.

"Why?" he growled.

"He can't make me, and I don't want to go," she said archly.

"Until he offers you something you want."

"He did. He offered me my life back."

He bristled more.

"You're the lesser of two evils," she said at the unspoken command. She pulled her arm away and returned to the Sanctuary. As she walked, she began to wonder how to train a wild animal. She'd had cats before, but she'd never even owned a dog. She couldn't imagine potty training one let alone training some ancient creature to contradict his nature. She didn't realize he was following her until he spoke.

"You turned down returning to your life to stay with me," he stated with one of his low, evil chuckles. "Foolish human."

"Maybe I know he's promising more than he can deliver. Really, why do you all think we mere mortals are all idiots? I'm so sick of this whole better-than-thou attitude you all have!" she snapped, facing him with her hands on her hips.

"I never said you were stupid."

"Whatever, immortal overlord of the universe! Every time one of you opens your mouth, you patronize me. It gets old and I think I've done damn well in this sick world of yours."

He said nothing, and she raised an eyebrow. He was impossible to read. He wore all black, though he was dressed more simply than she'd seen him, in dark jeans and a black long-sleeved T-shirt and heavy boots. His hair was tied back, his jaw and chin scruffy from a couple days' growth of hair. His liquid eyes were assessing but not flared, his large frame still imposing.

"No smart-ass comment about your blood monkey?" she challenged.

"Nope." He looked amused, if a statue could look amused.

"What *are* you waiting here for?" she asked.

"Nothing a blood monkey could understand."

"Son of a bitch!"

She marched back to the Sanctuary, wearied by the exchange. Daniela stood just inside the entrance, and her normally calm face took on an expression of sudden irritation as Katie passed her.

"Oh no you don't!" Daniela cried, and flew out the gate toward the rocks. "Sacred ground!"

Katie couldn't imagine what Rhyn had done and hesitated to look. Curiosity drew her to the gate again, where tiny Daniela was animated and angry as she stood between Rhyn and Kris. Katie couldn't help but pity the woman; it was her fault they were both there. She felt beat already but forced herself to once again leave the confines of the Sanctuary.

Kris's white hair, fair complexion, and amber eyes were at odds with Rhyn's darkness and glowing pewter gaze. Both were outwardly calm, though tense enough that a hair landing on their arms would make them snap.

Daniela finished her lecture on the Sanctuary's rules and waited. Neither spoke. Katie approached uneasily.

"What do you want, Kris?" she asked, crossing her arms.

"I came to talk to you. Alone."

"You're not allowed in the Sanctuary, and I doubt Rhyn will agree to disappear. He's a stubborn jackass like that."

Both looked at her. Daniela paled.

"It'd do you well in our world to learn some respect, especially for the Ancients," Kris snapped.

"What do you want, Kris?" she repeated.

Kris looked at Rhyn, who refused to take the hint. Kris lifted his chin at Daniela, and the woman offered a curtsey before hurrying back to the Sanctuary.

"I couldn't believe you wouldn't want your life back and wanted to hear it from you," Kris replied, facing her.

"You don't have the power to offer me that."

"Of course I do."

"Obviously one of us is confused," she said. "I haven't lived for millions of years in your world, but I believe Rhyn here would have to die permanently so his claim on me was nullified. And then you'd have to find someone older than Andre to wipe my memory and put everything the way it was. All of this would assume that you've decided you have no further use for me."

"You've learned a lot but not everything. There are ways of releasing you from Rhyn's claim, and there are ways of erasing your memory," Kris replied, agitated.

"But are you done with me, Kris?"

He didn't respond. She frowned.

"You don't seem to understand how important you are," he said at last with barely restrained impatience. "You can right the imbalance of our world so that evil is held in check. Do you want humanity to go down the toilet because you didn't feel like helping?"

"You had no intention of returning my life to me."

"Eventually, yes."

"Kris, you can't use people!" she exclaimed. "Do I want to help you save the world? Yes, I do. But I don't trust you. If you lied to me about everything so far, why the hell would I trust your word about anything, even saving the world?"

He wiped his face, and she sensed again he was unaccustomed to being challenged. Andre had claimed Kris was highly combustible. She didn't want to find out, but she wasn't following him blindly.

"You used Jade, too, didn't you?" she accused. "Look where that gets you!"

"I trust Jade with my life! You think I believe the word of some stupid mortal?"

"I know what I saw, Kris!"

"So, what is your solution?" he ground out between clenched teeth. "You stay here with *him* while the world falls apart around you?"

"He's the only reason I'm alive, Kris," she reminded him. "You dropped me into this world, and he's kept me alive."

"How noble of the beast that nearly destroyed the world once!"

"You didn't come here to talk. You came here to do the typical immortal thing and boss me around."

They stared at each other. His gaze turned from amber to fire, and she wondered if she'd pushed him too far. Rhyn, for once, was quiet. She'd never seen his attention stay any one place for long, but today, he was actually calm. His arms were folded across his chest, his frame growing more relaxed as his brother grew tenser. With effort, Kris drew a deep breath and blew it out.

"I am one of the leaders of the immortal world," he said. "Yes, I am used to giving orders, orders that *everyone* follows. I understand that you don't know our world, and that you have the disadvantage of having been through some truly awful things since being thrown into our world."

Despite her anger, she recognized the physical effort he put into his words.

"For what it's worth, I apologize for treating you like you were subhuman. I need your help for the sake of humanity."

She softened at his obvious struggle. Her gaze went to Rhyn, who looked almost amused again, then back.

"And how can one puny little human save humanity?" she returned.

"Sasha and the Dark One will destroy everything they can. Ully is experimenting with your blood to find a way to create a sort of antidote we can inject into our immortals to render them immune to the powers of Sasha's creatures. He's close but needs more time and more blood."

She took in his words, surprised he'd admit to needing a human.

"Thank you, Kris. I'll help you on two conditions."

"Name it."

"You take the bounty off Rhyn's head and readmit him to whatever weird immortal society you belong to AND I get to leave whenever I want."

"You gave me three conditions, not two. I'll allow you one in the name of *compromise*," he said with distaste.

She sensed a brick wall and hesitated, considering. She really did want to help humanity, and she really did want her freedom from stupid immortals bossing her around. Her gaze settled on Rhyn, who was waiting as tensely for her response as Kris.

"Remove the bounty on Rhyn," she said with some effort. "No more hunting, tracking, targeting, hurting, killing, or anything else. He's your brother, for God's sake."

Kris's gaze flared again, and she assumed he'd expected her to ask for her freedom. She heard him grate his teeth, then say, "Rhyn, bring her to the compound."

He turned and stalked away, disappearing with a puff of cool breeze.

"Foolish human," Rhyn said more quietly.

"Everyone deserves a second chance, even you, you jackass," she responded. "I'm going to get my things."

He was silent as she turned and walked away. He was watching her, a predator who'd either figured out his prey wasn't edible or needed more study to kill. His penetrating gaze gave her a different kind of chill, one that made her blood quicken as well as her step.

She gathered her things and searched for Daniela--or anyone--but no one was around. She left the Sanctuary one final time. Rhyn stood in the same place she'd left him, unchanged in any way. She stood before him and waited. This time when he reached for her, she knew it was for blood. She closed her eyes and tilted her head, anticipating the pinch. He drank long, until she was swaying and leaning against him. When he released her, he touched her arm. Warmth shot through her, energizing her.

She looked up at him. She hadn't noticed his pallor beneath his copper skin, but she saw it now. He returned her gaze, steadying her with a possessive hand on her hip.

"Were the guys you killed in St. Louis all bad?" she asked in a measured tone.

"More or less."

"What does that mean?"

"Trust me."

God help me, I think I do.

As if hearing her thought, he gave a slow smile. Before another insult could leave her lips, he kissed her, a commanding, intense kiss. One arm looped around her and she braced herself against his chest, vaguely realizing that--by not refusing him the day before--he'd taken her response as a blank check. The familiar warmth, his intensity--both lit her blood afire, and she couldn't help but imagine what his hot, talented tongue could do to other parts of her body. The vision in her mind made her bones too weak to hold her on their own.

He drew away with a satisfied growl. She wanted to be angry at him but was too dazed, too surprised at the sensations running through her. He'd pursue her like a predator its prey, and he'd consume her. All of her.

They gazed at each other for a long moment. She sensed he was reading her thoughts, and she wondered what he was thinking.

"You're not wearing any underwear."

Then again, maybe she didn't want to know.

"Aren't you supposed to take us somewhere?" she snapped, face hot.

He bared his teeth in a grimace, then turned her so her back was to him. She didn't know why until she felt the fog of the underworld followed by the warmth of wherever it was they went this time. He tensed as they stepped through the portal, clutching her against him with one arm, and she blinked.

Only to find herself staring at the bubbles of blood forming from within his fist, which was clamped around the blade of a knife a few inches from her face.

"Jade, no!" Kris shouted too late.

Silence surrounded them, not the good kind, but the heavy kind that made her want to hold her breath lest she break it and all hell erupt. There were many still forms around them, with only Kris moving. She saw Ully, Jade, Ileana, Gabriel…and a dozen more she didn't know. The walls were made of uneven, massive stones, the same kind beneath her feet. The air was chilled, still and damp, like she imagined a castle dungeon would feel.

"Rhyn is our…guest," Kris said, as if eating glass shards. "And Katie."

Rhyn tossed the blade back to Jade, who caught it with a look that made Katie want to hide. The tension in the room ratcheted up a notch.

"Katie," Ully hissed, as if they were kids hiding under the porch and not in the obvious line of sight of everyone in the room. "C'mon."

He held out a hand, motioning toward the door. She went. Rhyn refused to release her, and she sighed, leaning her head back against his shoulder in defeat. His arm loosened, and she hurried to Ully, who grabbed her hand and pulled her from the room.

He shoved the massive oak door closed.

"I do *not* want to see what happens next!" he said, breathing out hard. "Kris told us you both were coming. I think they have some things to discuss with your…" His gaze went to her neck as he fell silent.

"As long as he's okay," she said with a frown.

"You don't know much about us yet, do you?" he asked. He gave her an odd look and started down the hall, waving for her to follow.

"Nope."

"Rhyn's mother was a powerful demon, and his father is the same as Kris's. There isn't an immortal out there who'd face off against Rhyn now that Andre's gone. Have you done much to civilize him?"

"There's no civilizing a man like him." Even as she spoke, her thoughts went to what Gabriel told her. Compared to how Rhyn had been, she *had* made him civilized.

"Probably not," he agreed. "I'll show you to the women's wing. I'd stay there if they let me!" His step grew quicker, and his face brightened as they wound their way through the compound.

"Are we underground?" she asked.

"No. This is just a really huge place. It's pretty easy to navigate after a few decades of trying."

"*Only* a few decades?"

He didn't catch the sarcasm in her voice; his gaze was trained on a woman clad only in a towel and trailed by steam, emerging from a door along one wall. Katie heard the sounds of laughter and talk from behind the closed door. They followed the woman, who looked like a fitness warrior if she ever saw one. The black-haired woman had dark Mediterranean skin and tattoos down her back and across her shoulders. She was barefoot.

"Ully, you're not supposed to be down here!" she called over her shoulder in a distinct British accent.

"I have a reason," he said quickly. "I'm showing a new member to her room."

The woman turned, interest then puzzlement on her serene, chiseled features. Her eyes were almond shaped and clear amber.

"Not a warrior," she said, her questioning look lingering on Katie's neck. "Wow, really?"

"Yeah, really," Ully said. "Megan, this is Katie. Katie, Megan. Megan is one of the chic fighters."

"Female warriors," Megan said, raising an eyebrow in warning.

"I'm too wimpy to beat up," he reminded her.

"Right. I'll take her from here."

"But I—"

"Out."

Katie almost smiled at his fallen face as the stern voice of the Amazonian-sized woman before them. Ully was too harmless to be angry at, like a kid brother. He turned and smiled at her, then retreated, lingering at the door to the shower room.

"You're…" Megan trailed off, as if debating what to say while trying to figure out what was standing in front of her.

"Short? Human? Disrespectful? Not accustomed to the rules of this world?" Katie supplied with no heat. "You can say it—Kris won't let me forget I'm a square in a round hole."

"I was going to say you look like a living doll," Megan said with a half smile.

Katie smiled in return, deciding she liked the Amazon with the British accent and wild tribal tattoos.

"Nearly all of us girls here at the castle are warriors," Megan said. "None of the Ancients have mates, though some other immortals do. C'mon. I need to change, then I'll show you around."

Katie trailed her. The women's wing was a beehive of activity. They crossed through a common area with a kitchenette and large, flat-screen TV, past a gym, a library, and a few other common rooms, and into the barracks area, which bustled with activity.

She crossed her arms, self-conscious with the looks the others gave her. Her arrival silenced conversations and made most everyone do a double take. Even if not for Rhyn's name scrawled across her neck, she'd draw attention. None of the other immortal Amazonian warriors were below six feet. They came in all colors and complexions, some slender and graceful like dancers while others were muscular. She heard several different languages spoken before those she passed fell silent.

"This room's empty. Go ahead and make yourself at home. I'll come get you in a minute," Megan said, pushing a door open near the end of the hall.

The room was more welcoming than Katie expected, the stone walls covered and smoothed with Sheetrock painted a light green and edged with pumpkin orange. The room contained two full-sized beds and two large wardrobes along with military-style trunks at the foot of each bed. She had yet to see a window. She sat on the bed, placing her small satchel of belongings on the nightstand. The room smelled of vanilla mixed with some other exotic scent, the beds covered in soft white duvets with pumpkin-colored pillows.

She looked at her belongings and then at the room around her. It was nice, but *eternity*?

She felt a deep sense of loneliness and longing. For the first time in years, she wanted her sister around. Tired and conflicted, she lay back on the bed, taking great satisfaction out of a real bed after the few days on the flimsy bed at the Sanctuary.

"You need to rest, or do you want to see more of this place?" Megan asked, chuckling as she leaned against the doorway. "I'll show you where to go for logistics."

"Logistics?"

"Clothing, bathroom stuff, anything. They have all kinds of good stuff. You can order things out of magazines or from your favorite stores or pick from what they've got."

Megan led her again through hallways that fell silent when she passed. They crossed more intersections, descended to the level below, and stopped outside of double doors.

"Clothes, rations, gear," Megan said with a toss of her hand down the hall toward several other open double doors. "Cafeteria's on this level, too, all the way down at the dead end. This is the women's clothing department."

Katie braced herself to see a storage room full of military uniforms and was surprised to see what looked much like a women's department section.

"Cold weather, transitional, summer weather. In the back they have more exotic clothing, like Indian saris and the like. Pajamas, underwear, socks, bras in that corner. You know what hemisphere you'll be in when you leave?" Megan asked.

"No idea."

"It's always chilly here, more so now that it's autumn. We're in northern Europe, so you can't go wrong with sweaters."

Megan wandered, looking through piles of sweaters and pants. The walls were lined with blouses, formal wear, business wear, jackets, and other kinds of clothing, while displays of knit shirts, sweaters, jeans, and slacks spanned out before her.

"Megan, how much do these cost?" Katie asked, lifting a cashmere sweater.

"Free. One of the perks of our job."

She replaced the sweater and began hunting in earnest. She selected a few items, enough to get her through a few days in the new world. Light sweaters, long-sleeved shirts, a couple pairs of jeans. Megan helped and stacked socks and underwear in her pile and then brought her a light wool jacket, leather gloves, hat, and scarf. The Amazonian picked out a couple of T-shirts, her thick upper arms exposed in the tank top and jeans.

Katie gathered her clothes into a wool satchel and slung it over her shoulder. Megan led her down the hall to a room dedicated to shoes. Most were either boots of various kinds or running shoes, but there were a few more stylish pairs. Katie chose a pair of wool-lined clogs, shower sandals, and waterproof ankle boots.

She almost felt normal. Next Megan took her to what looked like a large drug store, where she plucked a few items from a shelf filled with top of the line skincare products. Katie's eyes widened in surprise as she recognized a brand of moisturizer that cost a few hundred dollars.

She grabbed the moisturizer and its cleansing counterpart and eye moisturizer. When she'd gathered everything she needed for bathing, she trailed Megan through the maze of hallways back to her room. Megan left her alone, and she unpacked. Then she grabbed her shower gear, sandals, and a plush towel and headed to the showers.

Steam and dampness clung to her as she set foot in the bathing room. No less than twenty showers separated by waist high walls lined the area before her. Another door led to a chamber with several bathing tubs. Still another door led her to a locker room with mirrors along two walls and another door to the restrooms. The final door led to a sauna. Several women bathed in stalls, the easy banter between them marking their camaraderie.

The hot water pounded over her body. She sighed deeply as it beat against her sore muscles. They responded and began to relax. She stood for a long time, letting the hot water pour over her, before she lathered herself up from head to toe. When she finished, she felt refreshed for the first time in weeks. She shut off the shower and wrung out her hair, then wrapped herself in the thick towel. She turned and gasped.

"Rhyn, you ass, how long have you been there?"

He looked her up and down in approval from his position leaning against the wall nearby. His glance went to the other women in the showers, who either ignored him or weren't going to say something to someone whose mother was a demon.

Exposed, irritated, she pointed to the door. He didn't budge. She tossed her hair over one shoulder and walked to him, pushing him toward the door.

"This is the women's locker room!" she said. "Give me ten more minutes of peace, and leave these poor women alone!"

Katie didn't notice the amused glances the women gave her, but she did see their appraising looks at Rhyn. He made no attempt to hide his perusal of the tall, athletic women around her.

"Missed a spot," he said, looking pointedly at the tattoo around her neck. "Might come off if you scrub hard enough."

"Jackass," she muttered, pushing him again.

She told herself he'd gotten there after she'd wrapped the towel around her. She didn't want to think of him watching her bathe naked. The idea made her body thrum with something she didn't want to feel.

He left, though she sensed he sought her out for a reason and wasn't about to grow patience. Determined to enjoy her first relaxing experience in a few weeks, she watched to make sure the door closed behind him and went to the locker room. She hadn't thought to bring her clothes. It was, after all, the *women's* wing. Her clothing from the Sanctuary was in a garbage can. She'd taken great pleasure in stuffing it there. Left with her towel and her toiletries, she took her time applying the thick moisturizer and lotion over her entire body, then finished by combing through her hair.

"*That's* the Ancient Rhyn?" Megan asked in disbelief, appearing through the door leading to the hall. "The girls wanted me to ask since they haven't met you yet."

"Unfortunately," Katie grated.

"Wow. Not what I expected."

"What did you expect?"

"A demon or something," Megan admitted. "He's quite a looker. You are one lucky woman to go to bed with that one."

Katie ignored her, irritated. She looked at the tattoo on her neck and slathered lotion on it, wishing it were paint.

"I'll tell Aisha not to hit on him," Megan said.

"She can have him."

"Trust me, if he weren't an Ancient and he looked that good, she'd snatch him up, even if he had a mate," Megan said with a laugh. "That girl knows no bounds and can land any man."

Megan's words pissed Katie off. She didn't want to feel attracted to Rhyn. She wanted him to find someone else, but the thought of that happening made her furious. No one else would share his incredible kiss…or anything else that might happen between them. Her heart fluttered at the thought, and she wondered if it was her teenage hormones talking or if there was something else growing between them.

"Aisha wouldn't want him," she said with more calmness than she felt. "He's…you know, small."

Megan looked ready to laugh but smiled widely instead.

"You can say you haven't slept with him. I won't tell," she said. "I'll tell Aisha to back off anyway."

Katie flushed without answering. She gathered her things and left. Rhyn was standing outside the door, and she passed him without a look. He trailed her through the halls. She wasn't the only one who stopped traffic and conversations. She expected someone to be angry that there was a man in the women's wing. Instead, the women gave him open looks of lust and approval, as if he were the hunted and they the lionesses lining up to take their turns at him.

She was scared to turn around, almost afraid he'd be passing out his phone number to every lithe, beautiful Amazonian they passed. She wouldn't put it past him. He wasn't known for his morality or virtues. They reached her room, and she threw down her shower things on the bed, agitated. The door closed softly behind him. She was surprised he made it and wasn't screwing one of the Amazons in the hall.

"I need to put on some clothes. Please turn around," Katie said.

"Nope. You're my mate."

She faced him, suddenly overly aware of how small the room was and the fact that he leaned against the only way out. He watched her with an intensity that made her blood quicken and her nipples harden. She crossed her arms. He wore the long-sleeve knit shirt, snug enough to show his physique without clinging to it, the snug jeans low on his lean hips.

"What do you want, Rhyn?"

"My room, too," he said.

"What? No. You have to go to the men's wing."

"Nope."

He lowered a backpack from his shoulder to the bed, nearing her. She all but jumped away.

"Scared, little girl?" he growled without looking up.

"Scared, no. Suspecting you're in the women's wing to get something other than sleep, yes."

He looked at her closely, a slow smile spreading across his face. He pulled out a small stack of clothing from the backpack and peeled off his shirt, displaying the lean, muscular body beneath. She stared, awed. He caught her and said nonchalantly, "Only one woman in this wing I'll fuck."

"I see you've met Aisha," she said stubbornly, flushing.

He took a step to close the gap between them, and they were kissing again. Emotion and desire fueled her. She responded as aggressively as he. He wrapped one arm around her and pulled her against him. The feel of his warm skin against hers thawed her resistance, teased her with the image of his naked body against hers. He smelled of sweet rain and dark grasses, his taste just as exotic.

His strength, his heat…in seconds, she couldn't think of anything more than feeling more of him, tasting more of him. His arousal rose solid and thick against her belly, and the soft towel agitated her suddenly sensitive skin. She met his aggression with her own, nibbling his lower lip, tasting him. Her hands roamed his chest and back. He pressed her against the wall, moving against her slowly while intensifying the kiss.

"Say yes," he ordered in the low growl.

"Yes," she said breathlessly.

He chuckled and lowered her onto the bed, his body atop hers. She surrendered to the heat in her blood.

Chapter Nine

They made love twice, then once again. When her mind had cleared and her body no longer thrummed with need, she tried to figure out what the hell had happened. She felt too sated to move. She breathed deeply of his scent and listened to his heart beat from her position sprawled atop him. She'd never felt such a connection to anyone. It was so much more than their physical joining; she'd felt him from the inside. For the first time since she could remember, she felt at peace, whole.

She didn't exactly understand the sensation except that she didn't ever want that feeling to end. She felt alone when he was gone, and while he frustrated the hell out of her, she still felt better when he was near.

"Rhyn…" she whispered. "Was this supposed to happen?"

"Don't start."

"Don't start what?" She lifted her head to look at him. He propped his head with one folded arm, silver eyes glowing at her.

"You're my mate."

"So…that's permanent."

"Yep."

"Guess that means I'll have to stop sleeping around," she retorted.

"Go ahead. Don't ask where I hide the bodies."

She chuckled. His confidence was too strong to shake, and she suspected he knew just how damned good in bed he was and how unlikely any woman who'd had him would choose another man over him.

"Don't expect me to sleep with you at your bidding," she warned. "You're still a jerk."

"Only have to say yes once."

She sighed, content to rest atop him. His confidence was the only rock to stand on in this forsaken world of immortals. She didn't know if she could trust him, or Kris, or anyone yet, but she could at least know the man beneath her was probably the only man she was safe from. It wasn't much, but it was more than she'd had in what felt like a lifetime. He'd protected her and made it clear anything that got near her would die a nasty death.

Albeit everything he did was on his terms. Always on his terms. She couldn't swallow his ability to be a fierce beast shredding human-like creatures with no regard or morals. She didn't understand why he'd chosen her of all people. She feared knowing what he truly was, that she'd married a *demon*. There really couldn't be any kind of good demon, could there?

Troubled, she dozed, waking when she heard the knock at her door. Her demon lover was gone and her body covered with a sheet. She and her bed still smelled of him, and she breathed deeply.

"Hey, Ully wants to see you. Something about science experiments," Megan said, poking her head in.

"I'm coming," Katie replied, stifling a groan as she shrugged out of the sheet to stand. Her legs were wobbly, the muscles of her inner thighs stiff.

Megan disappeared, and Katie changed into one of the outfits she'd chosen. She almost felt normal in the jeans and light sweater. She slid her feet into clogs and left the room, meeting Ully just outside the girls' locker room. He beamed a smile and offered his arm, which she accepted.

"All hell's broken loose," he said cheerfully.

"What do you mean?"

"I mean, Sasha's created some sort of funky monster that even an immortal can't kill."

Her thoughts went to Jade, and she frowned, troubled.

"Awful."

"Yeah," he agreed. "The tests I did with your blood came back promising, but I can't nail down the right genetic code."

He led her down a floor to a large gym where a group of men stood in a loose cluster on a mat. Her eyes found Rhyn first, then Kris. Jade was there, another man with Kris's eyes but whom she didn't recognize, and a fifth man. All but the man with Kris's eyes and oriental beauty were sweating and bloodied in at least one spot.

Ully stopped a short distance from them, as if expecting them to launch into a battle despite their relaxed poses. The oriental man held a PDA and was frowning as he read through notes while the others waited for him to speak. Ully cleared his throat. The five turned, and Rhyn winked at her. She crossed her arms, forcing herself not to cover her neck as four sets of eyes landed there. Her gaze settled on Jade, whose dark eyes still held the fire of danger.

"Kiki, this is Katie, Rhyn's mate," Kris said coolly. "Katie, Kiki, one of our brothers."

The oriental man looked her over, almond-shaped turquoise eyes assessing.

"Pleasure, Katie," Kiki managed before returning his gaze to his PDA. "That's five, brother." His voice held an accusatory note that Kris ignored.

"Your theory looks legit, Ully," Jade voiced at the tense silence. "Rhyn is immune to everything. Kris was for all of five minutes."

"Five minutes?" Ully repeated with a frown. "That would mean…"

"Either we get an emergency five minutes or you figure out how to make it work longer," Kris said.

"It'd take *all* her blood at this point," Ully said absently.

Five sets of predatory eyes fell to her, as if realizing there was a lame lamb in their midst. She moved closer to Ully, even while knowing the skinny nerd was the least likely to defend her.

"Is it because she's his mate or because her blood sustains him?" Kiki asked, agitation on his face.

"Both, I'd say," Ully said. "If my serum worked, then we know her blood will give immunity. Rhyn's bond as her mate amplifies her natural ability. He needs less to do more."

"Sasha's figured it out," Kris said. "His monsters are tearing through our warriors like they're made of cotton candy."

"I know, I know."

"He drank her blood," Rhyn said.

"Sasha?"

"Yeah."

Once again, the predatory look from all. She wanted to shrink away and hide. Instead, she drew herself up to her just above average height, and confirmed, "He nearly killed me. He brought in a healer who pieced me back together when he was done."

"Before or after your mating to Rhyn?" Kris asked.

"Before," Rhyn volunteered.

"Would have to knock you off for that to work now," Kris said with thinly veiled hostility.

Kiki rolled his eyes, and Jade inched away from Rhyn, who bared his teeth in a humorless grin.

"Like children on a playground," Katie murmured.

"Worse," Kiki agreed. "In any case, it looks like Ully needs to go back to the drawing board, and we use Rhyn for now to take out Sasha's henchmen."

"Have you learned some control of that demon power, little brother?" Kris asked.

"Didn't have to," Rhyn said.

"Katie stabilizes him," Ully offered. "I did some tests and then asked Ginny for some research help. The mates of old balanced out the powers of your badass predecessors."

"Let me rephrase. Have you learned any sort of *discipline?*" Kris asked.

"It doesn't matter, Kris. We don't have much of a choice," Kiki said pragmatically. "I'll go with him."

"I don't need a babysitter," Rhyn snapped.

"Yes, you do," Kiki said firmly.

Both Rhyn and Kris sulked. Katie smiled, deciding she liked Kiki's no-nonsense attitude.

"We'll report back nightly," Kiki added. "In person. Jade's coming with us."

"Very well," Kris relented.

Katie frowned at the thought of Rhyn being gone all the time but was glad Jade would be with them and not around to try to drag her back to Sasha.

"I'll introduce you to the mates of the immortals in residence later. Your place is there," Kris said to her. "Ully, take her to the royal wing."

She bristled, feeling as if she'd been sentenced to nothing more than a sewing circle for good little wives. Before she could object, Kiki took charge again.

"Rhyn, go get ready. Kris, can you spare a few warriors?" he said.

"Yeah," Kris replied.

"We'll test this out and see how it goes."

Ully stepped aside as the massive men passed. She scowled. Rhyn slapped her on the butt as he passed. She cursed him quietly. When they'd gone, she turned to Ully and demanded, "What do the mates of immortals do?"

"A lot of things," he said. "They take on the roles the Ancients and immortals can't, like working with human counterparts, touring the Council's facilities all over the world. They're into the arts, and charities to raise money for our war. Most…well, all but you come from the elitist circles of their times. The Ancients and immortals could choose anyone they wanted as mates, and they chose from among the royalty, the wealthiest, and most influential."

"I really won't fit in," she muttered.

"It really doesn't matter what they were when they were mortal," he assured her with an uncomfortable chuckle. "The rank structure in the immortal world is based on your mate."

She'd never in her life wanted to be a princess. She'd always wanted to be in marketing, and the thought of becoming a socialite with no real responsibilities made her gut sink. Eternity?

"Sounds awful," she said.

"You'll be the envy of us lesser immortals," he assured her.

She wanted to go home. In the face of a fate she doubted she wanted any part of, she felt homesick again.

You. Are. Mine.

There really was no chance of it. She felt she'd been a good sport since entering the immortal world, but she knew she'd never fit into a world where her sister surely would.

"When you see your room, you'll totally feel better," Ully said, and held out his arm.

She went grudgingly. He led her to the uppermost floor of the castle, to a hallway with magnificent views of a green valley with towering trees. She felt immediately out of place, even in the hall. The ceilings were gilded, the chandeliers dripping with crystals. Ensconced lights glowed in the midday, and antique furniture, rare paintings, elegant marble sculptures befitting a museum, silk Persian rugs underfoot, and many other priceless displays of prestige lined the wide hall.

He pointed as he walked, indicating the dining room, the library, the reception room, and others, each sounding stuffier than the last and all marked by polished oak double doors. They left the common area for the bedchambers wing. His voice grew hushed, as if the all-important guests behind each door might hear him. He paused at one room toward the middle of the hall and pushed it open.

No one in this place believed in locks. She crossed her arms and followed him in. Her bedchamber was half the size of a small house, with a domed ceiling replete with vibrant paintings of the sun progressing across the sky. The bed was the largest she'd ever seen, with a finely spun silk bedspread of pale yellow. The bedchamber was done up in pastels, soft rose drapes, light blue and green rugs, yellow pillows and highlights, which seemed to take the chill out of the stone walls.

She wondered if she'd freak everyone out with a few Hello Kitty posters to take away the severity of the rooms. They strode through the bedchamber to a small living room to the side with a flat-screen TV and comfortable-looking couch. The windows all faced east, over another valley, and a terrace was decorated with dainty iron-scrolled chairs. Off the living room was a private dining area.

Opposite the living room was a massive bathroom with marble floors, a Jacuzzi, small sauna, and a large shower with multiple shower heads.

"Doesn't this make you feel so much better?" Ully asked, envy in his voice.

"It's the most beautiful place I've ever seen." She saw the glow of his eagerness and tried to be more upbeat than she felt, for his sake.

"I know!"

"And this is mine?"

"Yep! And Rhyn's, unless he wants to stay with the other Ancients in their hall."

She didn't think he would but remained silent. At least, she *hoped* he wouldn't.

"I'll leave you here. Make yourself at home."

She didn't fully register his words until the door closed behind him. The bedchamber was silent. She looked around, feeling very much alone in the cavernous room. She couldn't help but think the barracks and all their activity and life were far more appealing than the solemn, stately apartment that was hers.

Her sister would be in heaven.

Katie felt like crying again. She roamed the apartment again and opened all the closets and drawers, not surprised to find them filled, as if she'd lived there all her life and hadn't just arrived.

It was creepy. She left the apartment and walked down the silent halls, turning down the hall with the common areas in time to see the back of a silk ball gown disappear into opened doors. She slowed until she smelled the scents of dinner. Suddenly ravenous, she quickened her step despite her dread of meeting one of the elitist mates.

Her gaze landed on the dining room, which looked much like that of a fancy restaurant. Small tables seating four were well spaced for privacy, with candles lighting each table and an assortment of flatware she'd never seen before. The room was warm and cozy, its walls done up in dark lacquered wood, the warm glow of chandeliers non-imposing. The soft sounds of talk drifted to her, but it was the dress of the women within that drew her eye.

Few women wore similar fashions from similar eras. There were wide eighteenth-century ball gowns, women in little black dresses, one in a fifties poodle skirt, and several in dark dresses with ornate brocade on the bodice, like that of wealthy Middle Age royalty. One woman wore rustic battle wear from an era she couldn't name, another flowing Grecian robes, yet another robes of a different era. While their dress was different, their faces were similar: stunning beauties from across history.

"Ms. Katie?" The maître d' asked and looked at her skeptically, as if the woman passing in a revealing Middle Eastern belly dancing costume ahead of her was normal and jeans were not.

"Yes," she replied, her gaze going from him to the grand buffet in the center of the dining room.

"Shall I seat you?"

She nodded, hungry enough to set foot in the room with the most beautiful women in history. He led her to a private table in the corner near the buffet, as if sensing her unease. She had barely sat when a servant bearing a tray of coffee and diet root beer--her favorite--set down the drinks in front of her.

How was it possible they knew everything about her?

Rather than go to the buffet herself, the servant joined several others selecting morsels and food for her to try. He returned and set it before her. She looked at him, then at the silverware, and picked a fork she recognized.

The food was heavenly, the duck crisped to perfection in a light, tangy sauce, the vegetables still fresh. Even the honey butter was a perfect balance between sweet and rich, and the rolls still warm when she bit into them. Dessert was a slice of five different kinds of pies, and she dug into everything, eating fast.

"…only fitting he'd choose a classless barbarian. He's a demon."

Katie froze at the cultured voice with its rich accent, knowing the woman at the nearest table spoke about her. She shouldn't care, but part of her did. She was alone in a world she didn't fit into, and she wanted more than anything to escape.

She glanced around, abruptly aware of the number of looks she received. Some were politely curious, others pitying, still others resembling that of the maître d'. More than one went beyond polite disdain and glared to the point of hostility.

Declining seconds, she finished her meal and rose, suddenly wishing she hadn't been seated in the far corner. Those at the tables she passed quieted and watched. Ignoring the looks on their faces, she marched to the door. Once she was out of sight, she ran. She didn't know where exactly she went aside from down from the top floor. She followed what she thought was the path Ully had brought her on and found her way to the women's barracks.

There was life here, and friendly looks as she passed. She made her way through the common areas to the dorms and cautiously opened the door to the room that had been hers. It was blessedly empty.

She flung herself onto the bed, tears in her eyes. It still smelled of *him*, and she couldn't help wishing he was there, even if all he did was piss her off.

"Katie."

She wiped her eyes and twisted, surprised to see Kris in her doorway. He gazed at her for a long moment, an odd gleam in his eye. She sat uneasily. He entered and closed the door.

"What do you want, Kris?" she asked.

"Why aren't you in your bedchamber?"

"I like it here better."

"Did Rhyn make you cry?" His gaze slid to the floor, and he shook his head ever so slightly, as if trying to shake free an unpleasant thought.

"No," she said, crossing her arms at the odd question. "Rhyn's been the only man to take care of me in this godforsaken world."

His eyes flared amber. Before she could blink, he snatched her and shoved her against the wall, pinning her to it with his body.

"By all rights, you should've been *mine*!" he snarled in a low growl.

"Kris--"

"Shut up! He stole *her* from me just like he did you."

She said nothing, afraid to move, afraid to speak. She rested her cheek against the cool stone wall.

"The only human who can help us defeat evil, and you chose *him*."

"Kris, you're not yourself," she whispered.

"You think I give a damn about one stupid, feeble, weak human, especially one mated to Rhyn? You think I'd let you stand between me and my fate?" Kris demanded. He wrenched her head back and gripped her neck, nuzzling it.

"Kris, don't do this," she managed.

"Whatever is in your blood can tame evil."

She tried to pull away, but he pressed her harder against the wall until she could barely breathe. His fangs sank into her neck, and she jerked, feeling her skin and muscle tear. She cried out and arched, blinded by pain as he held her against the wall. He didn't take blood gently as Rhyn did; no, Kris *wanted* her to hurt!

He drank deep and long until she began to grow woozy. His erection pressed hard against her backside, and tears slid down her face. She shook from pain and fear of what he'd do next, if he was more like Sasha than Rhyn.

She closed her eyes and wished herself home. The shadow world appeared hazily around her. She willed herself there, concentrating hard to keep from losing the connection.

Kris released her and stepped away. "Oh, god, Katie…" His voice was hoarse, a mix of pleasure and horror.

She sagged against the wall and gripped her bleeding neck. The shadow world swallowed her in its fog. There were several portals, and she hesitated, focusing on the mental image of her apartment. One of the portals grew brighter. She staggered toward it, stumbled, then fell through it and landed flat on her back on a familiar, faded red rug. It was dark, the spinning world lit by the kitchen and hallway light.

"Mama!" Toby cried.

She closed her eyes, terrified of bleeding to death right there in her own home.

"Wait in the kitchen." It was Gabriel's voice. He was blurry as he knelt beside her. His black gaze was still visible in the dark living room.

She felt him assess her by running his hands lightly over her limbs before he pried her hand free and rested his there, sealing the wound.

"Juice, Toby!" He propped her up, and she sagged against him, unable to keep from crying at the thought of one sworn to protect humanity nearly killing her!

Gabriel lifted her and carried her down the hall. She shied away from her reflection, from the paleness of her skin and the stark red of her blood soaking the cream sweater. The death dealer set her on the bed. Toby clambered up beside her, spilling the juice.

"Rhyn's mate?" he exclaimed. "Wow, Katie, wow!"

"Go make cocoa," Gabriel said, expertly rescuing the juice before more spilled.

Toby obeyed. Gabriel waited until he was gone before pulling a chair to the side of the bed.

"Rhyn didn't do this," he observed, handing her the juice.

She wiped her face again and shook her head, pain thrumming through her body. Rhyn could make it leave. She didn't know how, but she knew he could. Gabriel touched her forehead, and cold lightning buzzed through her, absorbing the pain. She released a tight breath. His hand remained, and she felt the cool lightning in her mind, ruffling through her memories.

"Gabriel," she objected.

"Kris?" he asked, surprised

Katie said nothing.

"Rhyn needs to know."

"It's the last thing he needs to know!" she replied. "He and Kris are barely working together as it is. I think Kris is right-- the fate of humanity is more important than me."

"Doesn't give him a right to break the Immortal Code. You don't touch another's mate."

"The Immortal Code has done me no favors yet, Gabriel," she said, beyond exhausted. "Can we talk about it in the morning? Please?"

Gabriel fell silent, and she closed her eyes, exhausted.

"His time is up, my pet," Death said.

Gabriel replaced the hourglass after several unsuccessful attempts to shake it. The sand at the bottom didn't move.

"He's almost there," he replied, facing the bright figure that was Death.

She offered one of her warm smiles and approached him, looking up at him with a mischievous twinkle in her gaze. The heavy Caribbean air rustled the pages of the Oracle's book. A storm brewed on the horizon, visible through the window behind Death.

"What?" Gabriel asked warily. "The last time you looked at me like that, I lost a bet."

"I guess it's cheating when you can see the future," she mused.

"Damn right it's cheating."

"Then you better answer this question right."

He crossed his arms, aware she was the only creature not intimidated by his displays of strength. She whirled away and crossed to the Oracle's book, closing it after his failed attempt to see Rhyn's fate.

He watched her grab the hourglass and toss it in the air. It disappeared before it could hit the ceiling. He felt dread knot in his stomach at the sign she wasn't going to give Rhyn yet another chance.

"Would you do *anything* for your friend?"

His jaw clenched at the question. She'd been trying for years to have his voluntary service revoked. Long ago, she'd given him the choice to serve her, the only one of her assassins offered a choice.

"I've always done everything you asked," he replied. "I've served you longer than any of the others. You'd put me in the position of choosing my freedom or my friend's life?"

"I sensed a thaw in you. The moment one of my assassins hesitates--or starts to care--I make them dead-dead. I don't own you like I do them, and I like you, Gabriel," she said.

"You're threatening to kill me now?" he asked, bemused.

"We both want something. Just say yes, you'll do anything for your friend, and I'll spare him a little longer."

"How much longer?"

She looked at him knowingly before saying, "You don't trust me?"

"You know I do."

"Then say yes, Gabriel. You've served me long enough to know what I am. Unless you were considering leaving me?"

He said nothing, aware the thought had crossed his mind more than once lately. His gaze went to the incoming storm. His life wouldn't change drastically if he agreed. He just couldn't walk away.

Ever.

He'd taken the boy he'd watched over his whole life to Hell. He'd betrayed Rhyn. This sacrifice was the least Gabriel could do for his friend.

"Yes. Give him more time," he said softly.

Death smiled slowly, satisfied with the prize she'd won.

Katie was thinking of how much whiskey it'd take to dull the edge of her headache when the phone rang. Irritated, she would've ignored it if not for Toby, who snatched it in excitement.

"What're you doing?" Toby yelled into the phone.

She looked at him. In four hundred thousand years, he hadn't learned to answer a phone right? He carried on a conversation for a few minutes, and she rested her head back, staring at the ceiling.

Though she hated to admit it, she'd hoped Rhyn was calling. Her heart leapt then dropped to her feet when she realized a man like that didn't call. He'd just appear whenever he felt like it. If he ever felt like it. If he cared AT ALL that his blood monkey and mate had been totally abused. Again.

"It's for you!" Toby called, holding out the phone. Katie took it. "It's Auntie Hannah!"

"Heya, Katherine."

The sound of her sister's voice made Katie's throat tighten. She'd never been truly happy to talk to her.

"Heya, Hannah."

"Toby said you've been under the weather. You're interested in coming to see me for a few days?"

Katie glared at Toby at the skeptical note in Hannah's voice.

"Gabriel said--" Toby started in a loud whisper.

"I would," Katie replied. "Been having a rough time on my...medications or whatever."

"Oh, I understand. Will Toby come?"

"No, he'll be with a friend," Katie replied.

"I'll send a car to get you!"

"Thanks. You spending the weekend with your...friends?"

"Don't start, Katherine. I know you don't like them," Hannah warned.

"Hate them, actually."

"You'll get used to them. Maybe one day they'll rub off on you, help you get a decent man."

Katie touched her throat. *Decent* wasn't the word she'd ever use for Rhyn. Her sister would have a heart attack once she saw the tattoo and found out she'd basically married the type of man Hannah'd always warned her about.

"Will you be ready in an hour?" Hannah asked.

"Sure."

"See you soon!"

Katie clicked the phone off and looked at the five-year-old doing wind sprints across her apartment. She waited for him to finish before crossing to her room to change. The effort of a shower left her even more exhausted. She dressed comfortably and packed her overnight bag, then searched the room, certain she was forgetting something.

"He's not in the closet," Toby said, then laughed.

She rolled her eyes at him and snatched her stuff before leaving her apartment for the sidewalk in front of her building. She waited in the cold winter day until the familiar Lincoln

Town Car arrived. She dozed in the car during the forty-five-minute drive to coastal Maryland, where her sister's fiancé owned a mansion secreted behind towering shrubbery and a gate that swung open to welcome her.

Her sister waited in the reception parlor, sipping tea and flipping through a magazine. She looked as healthy as Katie didn't feel. Hannah looked up as the butler let her in, her smile turning to a frown.

"You look ghastly," she said. "How long have you been…"

Too late, Katie realized she'd not thought to wear a scarf. Hannah's eyes widened, and she rose, angling her past the butler and a maid dusting a painting to the second floor. She closed the door behind them in the massive bedchamber that was hers and whirled.

"You know how trashy tattoos make women look? Why on earth…Gio will be so angry!"

"I don't care what your man thinks," Katie replied, agitated already. "I had it done in Ireland. It's some sort of Celtic…thing."

"What's a *rhyn?*"

"I'm not having a good turn, sis. Can we please just…do something?"

"The girls and I are going to brunch."

Katie didn't bother hiding her grimace. Hannah rolled her eyes and looked her over. Her gaze lingered on Katie's face, which Katie knew was pale. It was this that saved her from some snide comment about her less-than-fashionable clothes. Hannah gathered her things and led her down to a warm, waiting car. Katie pretended to listen as Hannah discussed the Paris fashion show she'd attended and the month in Monte Carlo she'd spend in January to escape the coldest weather.

Katie watched the world go by as they drove, half-listening to Hannah's chatter. The grey skies of winter and grey cement of the city depressed her. This place had nothing to the castle in the Alps, though she never wanted to go back.

In fact, the normal world--while comforting--seemed a bit boring after her trauma. She relaxed and sank into the soft leather seats of the Town Car, telling herself she was being granted a chance to be normal. She didn't doubt that the only creature Rhyn would listen to was Gabriel, and that Gabriel had told him to leave her be. She was grateful.

Sorta. Part of her ached with loneliness even her sister's presence did nothing to help.

They reached the trendy teahouse in the wealthy section of DC, Hannah still talking about Paris fashions. Katie trailed her into the stately Georgian mansion and glanced down as the polished wood beneath her feet creaked. A butler took her coat. She forced herself not to cover her tattoo with her hands as she followed her sister to the second floor, where the private rooms were.

Hannah warmly greeted her friends, four coiffed women in expensive clothing with diamonds the size of her thumbnail on their ring fingers. Most wore trendy boots and coats, sat in designer jeans and sweaters worth a month of her salary, and wore make-up that coordinated perfectly with their expensive clothing and hair.

Katie felt frumpy the moment she stepped into the room. The women--even if not beautiful--were dressed beautifully.

"I think you all remember my sister, Katherine?" Hannah said, fully knowing they did. "She just returned from a trip to Ireland, where she got her tribal tattoo. She's a bit jet-lagged though."

Katie bit her tongue. Hannah was apologizing for her pale features and dark-rimmed eyes. The four women looked at her, one gasping as her gaze fell to the tattoo and another paling, while the other two looked down their noses at her.

As usual. She'd shocked them all. Hannah sat and began talking about Paris again to an audience eager to hear her.

Except for the one who'd gasped, Molly, the half-Asian, half-Italian with beautiful coffee eyes and olive skin. She was tall and willowy, a former model that'd made it big. Her gaze stayed on Katie's neck until one of the others addressed her.

Katie wondered if she'd shocked her that badly or if there was some other reason Molly was so surprised. She knew very little of Hannah's friends, except they were all richer than sin.

"What took you to Ireland this time of year?" Molly asked.

It took her a moment to realize one of them had addressed *her*. It wasn't normal for them to acknowledge her existence, let alone address her.

"Sightseeing," she managed, unable to think of any other excuse.

Molly appeared skeptical while the others exchanged knowing looks with each other. *Another wild adventure by the black sheep of a sister that was dear Hannah's*. She'd heard them say it.

"It's an interesting tattoo," another said with forced interest. "What does Rhyn mean in Gaelic?"

"Nothing, I don't think," she responded.

"Is it Old French or English?" another asked.

"No," Katie said. She glanced at her sister, who seemed interested as well.

"What is it?" Hannah pushed.

"It's a name," Molly said.

Katie met her gaze. Amusement was deep in Molly's gaze, though she made no effort to come to her rescue.

"Oooooh, you had some sort of fling over there, didn't you?" one asked, interested for the first time.

"Not exactly." Katie sipped her tea, hot from head to toe. Sensing some sort of lurid story, all five of them waited for her to speak. "I actually got married while there."

"No!" Hannah exclaimed.

All four women gasped in unison.

At the end of her patience, Katie rose. "Going to the little girl's room." And she marched off, chest tight.

It was not the relaxing day she'd hoped for. She sat on a couch inside the gold lacquered bathroom, rubbing her face. She ignored the door opening until someone spoke to her.

"You're that new, aren't you?"

She looked up at Molly's voice. The svelte model wore towering boots and a one-piece cat suit that left nothing to the imagination. Molly rolled one legging up to display a tattoo similar to the tattoo around Katie's neck. It read *Fendril*, apparently the name of Molly's mate. She replaced the legging and perched delicately on the loveseat beside Katie. Molly dug through her purse to retrieved a familiar brownish cube, like the ones Katie'd eaten to stay alive in Hell.

Shocked, Katie hesitated and then took it, the sugary taste soothing her headache as she swallowed.

"Your Ancient drew too much too fast," Molly said. "He needs to learn some control. It's worse than a hangover."

"He's always gentle," Katie replied. "For whatever reason, people like to attack me."

"The first Ancient to take a mate," Molly said with both awe and disappointment in her tone. She offered Katie a food and water cube, both of which lessened the pain throbbing through her. "Rhyn? Isn't he in Hell for trying to wipe out mankind?"

Katie sighed.

"I didn't have much of a choice, either," Molly admitted. "I'm among the youngest of the immortals' mates, only a hundred years old. They allow us to lead as normal of a life as possible. You'll find your mate will move around a lot, but you can still make friends wherever you go, and immortals' mates are an amazing group. It's an incredible life! You must be thrilled."

"No."

"Well, it does take some getting used to. It's an honor to be among the first to welcome you officially to the family."

Katie glanced up, surprised to see Molly was genuinely smiling. The beautiful woman pulled a card from her small purse and handed it to her.

"You're always welcome to call me, and I hope you think of me when you're prepping for the Spring Gala."

Molly rose and left. Katie watched her go, feeling better with the otherworldly sustenance in her system. She composed herself and psyched herself up for a day of shopping, awkward questions about Rhyn, and Hannah's flaky friends.

Hours later, Katie dropped onto the plush guest bed, clad in a T-shirt and underwear after a hot shower. She was barely on her feet and debated whether or not she'd get up to turn off the light or fall asleep right there.

A touch of coldness made the hair on the back of her neck rise, and she sat up, fearful Kris or Sasha had come for her. Rhyn emerged from the shadows near the window, dressed in black with his hair tied back. His eyes flashed silver, his rugged features covered in a few days' growth.

Fear flashed through her at the memory of what someone his size could do to her. Kris had been of a smaller, leaner frame, and she'd been helpless against him. And then she relaxed. Rhyn was the only man who'd never hurt her.

"You look worse than usual," he observed.

She flushed and pulled her T-shirt over her bare legs, resting her chin on her knees.

"How's the war?" she asked as he neared.

He growled deep in his chest in response. He sat beside her and reached for her, his gaze on the newest scars given to her by Kris. Despite her determination not to, she flinched as he gripped her neck.

"Who hurt you?" he growled.

"No, Rhyn."

"You will tell me."

"No."

His eyes flashed. She waited for him to explode. Instead, his hand dropped to her shoulder, and he pulled her against him. Her body sang in happiness at the closeness, and she felt herself relax. She breathed his scent and released her knees, wrapping her arms around him.

Embarrassed, she felt tears in her eyes. He pulled her into his lap, his possessive touch and warmth soothing her.

"You will tell me," he said.

"Nope."

"You're not supposed to leave without permission."

"I wasn't going to bleed to death on the floor, and you weren't around!" she snapped.

"You know how to call me."

"It's no big deal."

"I don't know what the fuck you're smoking," he said.

She gripped him harder. He reciprocated.

"You're not one to talk about not breaking sacred rules," she pointed out.

"No one hurts what's mine."

"Everything hurts what's yours!" she retorted with feeling. "I'm not going to survive your world for long, Rhyn!"

He said nothing. He smoothed her hair and rested his chin on her head. She loosened her grip on him, sensing he wasn't going to leave, whatever his mood was. Her eyes were heavy, her anger draining her last bit of energy. She breathed in his scent and closed her eyes.

When she opened them sometime later, he held her tightly against him. They lay in bed beneath the covers in the dark room. She couldn't help but feel grateful he was there. She didn't feel up to the challenge of finding out what other creatures lived in the darkness of the immortals' world.

"Why wouldn't you just tell Kris the woman he loved was evil?" she asked the question that had been plaguine her.

He growled.

"Don't you dare!" she said. "You owe me some explanations. Every time I turn around, I'm getting my ass kicked by some beast, many of which are probably after you!"

"I like you better when you're quiet."

She gritted her teeth, unwilling to leave the sanctuary of his arms and cursing herself for her weakness.

"I broke the Immortal Code." His words surprised her.

"You don't follow rules, though," she said, confused. She twisted, trying to see him in the dark. His eyes glowed pewter.

"I respect the Code. Doesn't mean I always have to follow it."

"That makes no sense. You break the Code when you feel like it?"

"When I must."

She pushed herself up despite his grip, staring at him hard. Despite his monstrous habits of shredding anything in his path, he had a sense of honor more deeply ingrained than she'd ever suspected. He'd broken the Code for a brother who'd never cared one ounce for him and accepted his place in Hell.

"Isn't there anything in the Code about doing a better job of protecting your mate?"

"I've never had anything to take care of," he snarled. "You're weak and foolish and Gods, if I could find a magic pill that'd knock some sense into you—"

"I have a great deal of sense! What you fail to realize is that--whatever I am—I draw good and evil to me. Nothing corrupts someone like the temptation of invincibility."

"It was one of Kris's warriors who hurt you," he said, his voice lowering into another feral growl. "I knew when Gabriel summoned me to you and went to Kris. You tell Gabe but not me?"

"I didn't tell him. He went through my memories," she said with a note of anger. She felt his tension slide away as he became thoughtful. "No, Rhyn. Have some respect for my mental privacy!"

He snorted and pulled her down into his arms again. Resistance was fruitless. She allowed him to wrap his arms and one heavy thigh around her body.

"What's Kris supposed to do to someone who broke the part of the Code about someone else's mate?" she asked quietly.

"Don't care."

"What?"

"Don't care what Kris does. I'll kill whoever it is," he said with conviction that left her no doubt he was serious.

Her heart slowed. She didn't like Kris, but he did what he did for some greater cause than himself. He wasn't a bad man, just a misguided one.

"Is this Code written down anywhere?" she asked.

"Nope."

"Can you tell me what it says?"

"Nope," he said again.

"Rhyn, I--"

"Shut up and sleep. Nothing else bad will happen to you."

She fell silent. Her body was still exhausted from Kris's attack and a day spent with Hannah and her friends. Though she fought sleep, it started to claim her anyway.

"Rhyn?" she said drowsily.

"What."

"I think I'm falling in love with you."

"*What?*"

"I'm smarter than you, too."

Chapter Ten

Gabriel's soft cluck of disapproval filled the air around him as Rhyn sat in the corner, watching the most vexing woman in the world--his mate--sleep. He sensed another immortal in the house but couldn't place where exactly.

"You just don't listen," the death dealer said, materializing, a shadow darker than night.

"Why would I start?" Rhyn replied.

"Thought you'd learned something after all those years in Hell."

"Nah."

Gabriel was his only friend who didn't judge him. Rhyn patted the chair beside him. The death dealer sat, his trench coat rustling.

"You're lucky you don't have to defend Death against anything," Rhyn grunted. "Much more complicated than it looks."

"Free will's a bitch," Gabriel lamented.

"Yeah."

They sat in comfortable silence, the quiet room filled only with the woman's soft snores. She was tired, frustrated, and, worst of all, scared. She'd been scared since Hell, if not before, for which he blamed Kris.

"Kris--"

"Don't start," Gabriel warned. "At some point, you two need to trust each other."

"Not gonna happen."

"Immortals are about as imperfect as humans. I don't know about much of anything any more.'"

Rhyn looked squarely at the death dealer, sensing unease for the first time in their long history.

"It never sat well, what I did to you," Gabriel said.

"I never held a grudge," Rhyn reminded death's top assassin.

"Maybe you should have."

"Nope."

Gabriel chuckled then said darkly, "How can you be so sure?"

"I know," Rhyn replied. "I know what I am, I know what you are, and I know what my brothers are. The rest I don't care about."

Gabriel lifted his chin toward the bed.

"Work in progress," Rhyn replied with a grimace. "She's mine. The rest will follow."

"Wish I had your faith."

"I think you mean narcissism," Rhyn said.

"Big word for you."

"It was Kris, wasn't it?"

Gabriel said nothing, and fury unfurled within Rhyn as his gaze went to the sleeping woman.

"I know my brothers," he repeated more softly.

"You are quick to assume the worst," the death dealer said at last. "She refused to tell you."

"Yeah."

"Then leave it be. Listen to me this time."

Rhyn didn't want to leave it be, not when his own brother had attacked his woman. Maybe Kris thought turnabout was fair play. Or maybe he'd succumbed to the weird draw around the woman. Or maybe to his own desire for power. In the end, it didn't matter.

"She never feared me before tonight," Rhyn said in a growl.

"I'm sorry, Rhyn. I've wanted to protect her, but Immortal Code--"

"Not your fault."

"I didn't know he would hurt her. I would've broken Immortal Code and interfered had I known," Gabriel said.

"You broke Immortal Code what? Twice in your life? Both times for me," Rhyn said with a shake of his head. "No, Gabriel, don't do me any more favors."

"I righted a wrong, which required another wrong of sorts."

"Don't grow a conscience now. One of us has to walk the straight and narrow. It won't be me," Rhyn assured him.

"You can't go after Kris. That's strictly forbidden."

Rhyn said nothing, aware the penalty for an Ancient killing another Ancient was death-death and eternal Hell. He was sick of Hell, yet Kris's crime deserved punishment.

"And you have to realize that he didn't know about Lilith's betrayal," Gabriel added. "You're lucky all he did to your mate was take her blood."

"He made her fear me. He was an idiot to fall for Lilith. She wasn't even his mate--she had no protection from Immortal Code. My mate does!" Rhyn replied.

"She's barely made it this long, Rhyn. Before you run off and kill your brother, you should probably see her safe. Because of her, you can control and channel your power. You aren't surviving day-to-day anymore as you have your whole life, and for the first time, you're fighting for something other than you. You have a second chance, Rhyn. Not many get that."

Gabriel's words struck hard. Rhyn thought hard for a minute, then said with effort, "I don't know how to be a mate, let alone take care of a human, Gabriel."

"I gave you books to read," the death dealer said, bemused. "It's the best I can do. I'm not human."

"You were once."

"Too long ago to remember. You'll just have to figure it out on your own."

Rhyn grimaced. He didn't know a thing about being a mate. His gaze drifted again to the woman whose pale features made him feel both proud and worried. He was the only line of defense she had against the immortal world. Thus far, he'd barely managed to keep her alive.

He didn't know what else to do. She couldn't defend herself, and every immortal she drew to her ended up hurting her. Even Kris, the protector of mankind.

His thoughts darkened as fury blinded him for a moment. Gabriel clapped him on the arm, and Rhyn shook his head to clear the anger.

"Kris sent a message for her," the death dealer said, withdrawing a folded sheet of paper from his pocket.

Rhyn reached for it, but Gabriel pulled it away.

"Only for her. If he's apologizing, let him do so in peace."

Rhyn wanted to destroy the letter. Instead, he watched Gabriel cross the room and leave it on the pillow beside Katie. Rhyn's gaze fell to her again.

What drew him and others to his mate? It was her curse. He had to protect her while keeping her from those who could help. He had to protect her from Sasha and the Dark One; he had to protect her from Kris and his people.

I think I'm falling in love with you.

The woman was crazy, and yet, a part of him liked that about her. She'd proven herself to him in a way no immortal ever had.

He couldn't *not* believe her to be his match!

Gabriel was right--he had to figure things out before he lost his mate.

The assassin left him in peace, and Rhyn stayed awake the rest of the night, watching over Katie. He braced himself for more syrupy love sentiments when she awoke but was relieved when she gave him a warning look and disappeared into the bathroom, the letter clutched in one hand.

He stripped off his clothing and changed into what Gabriel told him was *normal* for this place: jeans and a sweater. And steel-toed boots that would go right through any bad guys who got in his way.

Katie emerged still pale, her gaze troubled. Her skin was scrubbed clean, her dark hair wet. He saw no sign of the letter.

"Hannah won't approve of you being here," she told him.

"Who's Hannah?"

"My sister."

"You have a sister?" he asked.

"You know, we mortals have real lives, too, or do you immortals assume we're all just sitting around waiting to have our lives intruded upon by the likes of you?" she snapped. She whirled and marched to a closet, wrenching it open.

Despite her ordeals, she still had her spark. He wasn't sure if he liked that or not about her. She reached for a scarf, and he growled. Her hand dropped, though she didn't acknowledge him otherwise. He took in her shape. She wasn't beautiful, but she was pretty enough with a body she plainly took care of.

"Don't you have somewhere to be?" she demanded.

"Someone's gotta keep you outta trouble," he replied.

"Like you've bothered to do that yet!"

"It's a new day."

At his quiet response, Katie faced him, searching his gaze. She frowned and he breezed past her, pulling the door open before the woman on the other side could knock. The woman he assumed was Hannah stared at him, her mouth dropping open.

"Hannah, this is Rhyn, my...the guy I met in Ireland," Katie said.

Hannah was beautiful in the model sense, with a slender form and large eyes that grew wider when they swept over him.

"*Really?*" Hannah almost gaped.

Rhyn felt Katie tense. She crossed her arms.

"Yes, *really*," the smaller woman said in a sharp enough tone to draw Hannah's attention.

Hannah wasn't the immortal he sensed, though she exuded a calming power that stabilized his powers, similar to Katie's, though weaker. He began to believe Kris was right about the bloodline of his mate's family. There was something unique about them.

Hannah shook herself visibly and said, "I didn't hear you come in last night. Are you staying for long?"

He felt Katie's gaze settle on him at the question.

"No," she said firmly.

Hannah waited for more. When nothing came, she mustered a smile and motioned down the hallway.

"I'll take you to meet Giovanni, my fiancé. He's interested in meeting our Katherine's husband. Katherine, I have a small breakfast waiting for us with the girls," she offered.

Katie grumbled beneath her breath and pushed past him to join Hannah, whose gaze never left him. Katie cleared her throat loudly, and Hannah started down the hall. Rhyn hesitated then followed. Hannah paused a few doors down along the wide, tall corridor with plush red rugs and gilded cornices. It was the kind of place his brothers would love: opulent and openly displaying signs of wealth. With her carefully crafted outfit and makeup, Hannah fit right in.

She tapped at a door and ducked inside.

"Really, how long are you staying, and what do you want?" Katie hissed as they waited in the hall.

"No rush. We're immortal."

"I told Gabriel I didn't want you around. You couldn't give me some peace?"

"I'm your mate," Rhyn grated. "I'm supposed to…take care of you."

At the effort he put in the difficult words, she looked up at him, her clear blue eyes vexed.

He hated how pale she looked, hated the scars on her body. He admired her strength but knew everyone had a breaking point. Hell had taught him this, if nothing else. He wasn't sure what he felt toward the woman, but he didn't want her to come to harm, and he didn't want her out of his sight.

"Come on in, Mr. Rhyn," Hannah said, pulling the door open.

Rhyn went. The immortal he sensed sat inside a large library. The man's stunned look didn't change at Hannah's quick introduction or when she left. Even the sound of the door shutting did nothing to jar the man before him.

Rhyn studied him, taking in the tattoos only other immortals could see. The immortal was relatively young, maybe a thousand years old, with Mediterranean features tinted olive and thick black eyebrows. At that age, he was relatively low on the immortal totem pole, though his obvious wealth indicated he had powerful connections somewhere.

"Forgive me," the man said, and stood, shaking his amazement away. "I'm Silvestre Giovanni. I never expected to meet one of the Council That Was Seven, let alone have the honor of hosting you."

"It's fine," Rhyn said.

"Is there anything I can procure for you? Please, my home is yours for as long as you like."

Rhyn almost wished he had even a fraction of Andre's manners. He hadn't dealt with lesser immortals since before he went to Hell.

"I'm fine," he said again. "My mate and I won't be here long."

"Hannah told me about Katherine. I didn't realize her Rhyn was…"

An awkward silence fell, and Rhyn knew what the immortal wasn't saying by the look of half-alarm, half-curiosity on his face.

"I get that a lot," Rhyn said. "You're house is…nice."

"Thank you," Giovanni said, pleased. "I purchased it because it reminds me of my beloved Venice. I left many years ago and haven't gone back. Hannah and I plan on taking our honeymoon there."

"Does she know what you are?"

Giovanni gave a half-laugh at the blunt question, and Rhyn sat. The lesser immortal relaxed some and joined him, pouring him a glass of ice water. Rhyn took in the small marble statues and portraits of wealthy Venetians on the walls.

"Not yet, no. I planned on telling her soon. Does Katherine?"

"Yeah."

"You *chose* Katherine?"

Rhyn glanced at him. Giovanni appeared genuinely puzzled.

"She's a good girl," Giovanni said, "but she's a bit of a lost cause. We've been trying to help put her through a good school, so she can start working some place decent and make enough money. She's never known what she wanted to do, unfortunately. Just seems to float from job to job. Hannah gives her all her old clothes, which aren't cheap, and she never even returns Hannah's phone calls. I know Katherine is still young. I'm hoping in a few years, she'll appreciate all we've done for her."

Rhyn bit his tongue out of respect for Katie. Giovanni pitied Katie, and yet, Rhyn suspected he knew more about the woman than either the man before him or Hannah. Part of him was gratified to find she, too, was the black sheep.

Part of him was pissed.

He knew if he did anything stupid, Katie would suffer. She was here because she chose to be here, and he wasn't going to make her life uncomfortable. Again. So he clenched his teeth and nodded.

"Maybe that's all in the past. The immortals can polish her up a little. It'll make Hannah so happy," Giovanni said with genuine warmth.

Giovanni took Rhyn's silence as encouragement and began to discuss his pedigree and which immortals he knew. Rhyn found he didn't need to respond. Giovanni was capable of discussing himself—and his Hannah—without any sign of stopping.

Instead, Rhyn began to wonder where exactly his mate would fit in. It wasn't here, in a place best suited for privileged immortals accustomed to wealth. It wasn't in the barracks of

Kris's fortress. Gabriel had told him just how small and cluttered her apartment was.

She was like him: someone who didn't fit in anywhere she should.

He had nothing, no castles or gold like his brothers. He had nowhere else to go. It'd never been a problem when it was just him. Now, he had a reason to care what tomorrow brought, and he wasn't certain he liked the newfound feeling.

Hannah returned a short time later, the only thing that interrupted Giovanni's ramblings. Rhyn pulled himself from his thoughts as he stood. He didn't like thinking--he preferred to act.

"…my greatest honor to meet you," Giovanni said with a warm smile. "You're welcome here with Katherine anytime."

Katie, Rhyn corrected him mentally.

Hannah appeared puzzled by the invitation but smiled when Rhyn turned to her.

"Hannah, dear, please instruct the servants that Rhyn and Katherine are given whatever they ask for."

"Of course, darling," Hannah replied. "Katherine's waiting for you, Rhyn. She said you were interested in taking a walk around the estate."

Rhyn said nothing and followed her out of the study. They strode through the opulent mansion down a stairwell spilling into sunlight and swaths of green grass at the side of the main house. He was unaware how tense he was until Hannah left him, and he breathed in deeply. His muscles were so bunched, they ached when he shook them free.

"They can be pains in the ass," Katie said from her seat on a stone bench beneath a massive oak tree. "They mean well, I think."

He gazed at her, at once hungry and pensive. He didn't know much about the woman staring at him except that she was the strongest person he'd ever met. She was genuine, straightforward, and sweet. He wanted her in his life, permanently, only he'd need his brothers' help. To keep her, he'd go to them.

"I have to go somewhere," he said abruptly.

She frowned, and he couldn't tell if she were more disappointed or relieved at his news.

"You'll be safe here. Giovanni is an immortal."

"Giovanni?" she echoed, surprised. "Hannah must not know. She can't keep secrets like that."

"She doesn't. I'll be back soon enough."

She looked as if she wanted to say something, then crossed her arms with a glare. He didn't want to try to interpret the look or await her scathing return, not when he needed to find a place for them go to. Instead, he started walking away and summoned his powers, wondering which of his brothers could be coerced into giving him what he wanted.

"Rhyn, wait!" she called.

He faced her. She approached him, gaze troubled once again.

"Kris sent me an apology," she started.

"And?" he asked impatiently.

"He said he knows someone older than him who can put my life back the way it was." Her words surprised him. She didn't meet his gaze. "He said he only needed two months of my time, and even if he didn't do what he needed to at the end of it, he'd let me have my life back."

"You trust him after what he did to you?" he demanded.

"He's not a bad person, Rhyn. If he's making the offer, he'll keep his word. Besides, he owes me, for more reasons than one," she said. "I can't live like this, Rhyn. I won't make it in your world. I've barely survived my first week."

Stunned, he waited. She fell silent.

"You said you loved me last night," he said at last. "I'm leaving now so I can find a safe place for you."

"I was tired and probably half-drunk," she whispered.

"I read your mind."

"And you wonder why I want out of this world?" she snapped, fire lighting up her features. "It doesn't matter what I feel, Rhyn, when I know I don't belong in this world or here with you, and I know without a doubt I won't survive, even if you find some place on another planet to stash me! I don't want that, Rhyn!"

"Gio and Hannah say your life sucks as it is," he pointed out.

"But it's my life, even if it does suck. You try but you can't protect me, Rhyn, which you've proven a dozen times over. Two months is all Kris asks, and I'm free. What do you have to offer?"

He said nothing. He had nothing. They both knew it. She turned away, but he saw the tears gathering in her eyes. He'd never felt inadequate in his long existence until he stood before a mere mortal with the knowledge he had nothing to offer her.

"Don't come back, Rhyn," she said softly. "Please."

"You said you're giving Kris two months. How about me?"

"How about you *what*?"

"If, at the end of those two months, I haven't fixed things, you'll go back to your world. If I make things right, you'll stay. With me," he said in a hushed tone. "As my mate."

She was quiet briefly, considering, before she said, "Fine. Sixty days."

Emotions spiraled through him. He wasn't sure what he felt, but it wasn't gratitude. If anything, he was stunned she agreed so quickly. It meant she didn't believe him.

She walked away. He watched, hurt and then fury filling him.

He'd never had anything worth fighting for until now. Just when he'd accepted he needed to find a way to keep her safe, he was about to lose her. He'd spend the rest of his existence in Hell before he'd let her go without a fight.

Katie's hope
Book II

Chapter One

Three Weeks Later

The dream took shape as it did every night. Even when she knew she was dreaming, she couldn't wake herself up or shake the fear that this time, Rhyn wasn't going to come.

Katie stood between the assassin and the demon. Her choices were plain: Death or Hell. Bad or worse. Screwed or *screwed*. One of them was taking her to his underworld. The other would kill her. As the two stared each other down, she wasn't sure who had the better chance of winning: Gabriel, an Immortal sworn to serve Death, or Darkyn, the leader of all the demons in Hell.

Her hand went to her neck, where the name of her Ancient Immortal mate, Rhyn, had been until he broke their mating bond two days before. Desolation unlike anything she'd ever felt made her want to sink into the ground and stay there.

A shadow blocked the hot Caribbean sun, and she looked up to see Rhyn in his pterodactyl form circling above them. She gasped, hope racing through her as he dove toward the ground, switched to his human form in mid-air, and landed hard on the stony island's ground. He met her gaze, and her body bloomed with warmth in response to the possessive gaze that swept over her from head to foot before his eyes settled on the demon. Evaluating each other, the three creatures stood in tight silence before Rhyn spoke at last.

"What the fuck are you doing here, Darkyn?"

"Half-breed," the demon leader sneered. "Negotiating with Gabriel over who gets your former mate."

"Death ordered her dead-dead," Gabriel said. "And Death always wins."

"Brother, I'll kill you both if either of you tries to take her," Rhyn replied. "You have a contract on her, Gabe?" The assassin nodded. "Let me guess, Darkyn, the Dark One, ordered this."

"We'll just say he doesn't disagree with me."

"All right." Rhyn drew a knife from his boot. Katie watched, her optimism fading. "I'm challenging you, assassin, demon. You can have her when I'm dead."

"Rhyn, no!" she cried.

"I can handle it," he said.

"Rhyn—" She started forward, and Gabriel held out an arm to block her. Furious and terrified, Katie planted both her hands on his arm to push it away with no success. "Back off, Gabriel. It's not like I can run anywhere!"

"Two minutes," he warned. "By Immortal Code, Darkyn and I are obligated to accept his challenge."

She hurried to Rhyn and stood looking up at him. His silver gaze was on his foes then dropped to her.

"This is the stupidest thing you've ever done," she said.

"Letting you go was the stupidest thing. I'm doing something right for once." The resolution in his face was unmistakable. He wasn't backing down. His eyes returned to the demon.

"They'll kill you," she whispered.

"If they do, go with Gabriel. Death's a bitch, but she's better than Hell."

Her eyes watered. She'd barely known what to do when he un-claimed her two days ago, but at least he was alive. If he left forever …

"This isn't right," she said, her throat tightening. He looked down at her again, his gaze taking in her face. He cupped one cheek with his roughened hand and rubbed away a tear with his thumb.

"I'm not dead yet," he said, amused. She wrapped her arms around him, comforted by his scent and tormented it was the last time she'd smell him.

"Can't we just run away, right now? Turn into a bird and carry me with you?" she asked.

"Even if we did, they'd both come after us."

"You can go. I'd rather know you're safe than live without you."

"No, Katie," he said softly. "I know where I belong, and it's right here with you. I have to make things right. I couldn't live if I lost you."

"Katie," Gabriel called.

"Rhyn, I love you," she said.

"I know." He pulled away from her and pushed her hair from her face. With a tender kiss on her forehead, Rhyn stepped away. Gabriel drew a long sword, and Darkyn pulled two free. She felt cold from the inside out. The assassin motioned her over. She went woodenly, her stomach in turmoil.

"Break the bond, and Death will save you both. Rhyn will die-dead otherwise," Gabriel whispered then left her standing by a group of boulders. The words struck her as odd, but she had trouble concentrating when the men launched into a three-way battle.

Break the bond, and Death will free you both. She tried to decipher his meaning as she watched them fight, terrified to take her eyes off Rhyn. Rhyn already broke their bond, unless … she had to break it, too.

Death would free them. *Her* death. She was the only one who had the power to end this before he died. Her attention turned to a different direction, the way she'd walked half an hour ago from the beach. She hesitated only a second more before she started running. She ran hard and left the sounds of the battle behind her, her thoughts on Rhyn and nothing else.

The distance to the beach was short in her dream, her body full of fear and adrenaline. She made it to the sand before being forced to slow to a walk by the ankle-deep, loose sand. Agonizing over how much time Rhyn had, she finally reached the water's edge and sucked in ragged breaths as she knelt for a moment of rest.

"Death will free us both." Heart hammering, she rose, took a deep breath, and waded into the warm water.

Trust my Gabriel, human, a woman's voice whispered into her mind. *This is the only way.*

Katie awoke sweating in her bed in the cavernous room to which she'd been exiled upon arriving to the Immortals' castle in the French Alps. The fire had died down, and someone had turned off the light to her bathroom, rendering the room completely dark. The dream had seemed so real. In it she had even recognized where they were: the Caribbean Sanctuary, where she'd been before coming here.

A movement from the balcony caught her attention.

"Another nightmare?" The voice of Gabriel was as dark as the room. He stood in front of the glass French doors of the balcony, taking up the whole space with his massive frame and heavy trench coat.

"Yeah," she whispered. "Every night." Her hand went to her neck, and she threw off the covers, crossing the cold stone floor to the bathroom. Flipping on the light, she confirmed the tattoos and Rhyn's name still circled her neck. He hadn't left her. She looked tiny and frightened in the large bathroom's mirror, and her gaze was drawn to the lumpy scar marring one arm. She rubbed it as she'd begun to do whenever she was upset.

"You okay?" Gabriel asked.

"Just making sure …" *he's still alive.* She couldn't finish her thought in front of him, partly because it made no sense and partly because she didn't want to admit her soul felt Rhyn's absence like the draft from a cracked window on a winter's night.

"You ever find it odd you feel comfortable waking up to find *me* here?" Gabriel asked.

She rolled her eyes at his twisted sense of humor, which normally teetered on lethal. As Death's best assassin, Gabriel wasn't the type of person anyone ever wanted to run into, let alone when awaking in a dark room after a nightmare.

"I want the light on, Gabriel," she said.

He shook his head. "I don't like it, and you'll have bad dreams either way," he reasoned.

"Makes me feel safer."

"Nothing safer than hanging out with someone who can't be killed."

"Gabriel," she chastised. She left the bathroom light on and returned to her bed, chilled by the drafty chamber that was now hers. It had the combined square footage of every apartment she'd ever rented. It was cold and large, not the kind of place she'd ever choose to live.

"Mama!" Toby's grumpy voice drew her gaze toward the small bedroom whose door was near the bathroom. She'd stopped gritting her teeth whenever he called her that and—God help her!—she'd even started responding.

The five-year-old angel, whose appearance in her life several weeks ago plunged her into the Immortal underworld, squeezed through the cracked door. He trudged across the bedroom, climbing into bed with her without asking.

"Toby, you're too old to be sleeping in my bed," she said. He ignored her and snuggled deep beneath the covers. If not for the nightmares, she'd carry him back to his bed, whether or not he liked it, but she found some comfort in having the angel so close. Despite her efforts to stay awake, she fell into restless sleep again.

Her alarm clock woke her at dawn, reminding her it was time for her morning run. She turned it off and eased out of bed, stopping to gaze out the French doors. Verdant forests stretched to the steely sky, a swath of green, brown, and grey. Uneasy after her dream, she dressed in running clothes and padded out of the room. Gabriel was gone and Toby still sleeping.

She walked through the castle quickly, not liking the quiet, and emerged into a courtyard leading to an expansive cobblestone driveway. The courtyard bordered a small grassy park off which several trails ran from the grassy area into the still dark woods.

Her running partner, Ully, wasn't there. She shook out her arms and stretched, cold in the early morning air. The trails appeared muddy even from the distance and the air smelled of snow.

She heard the soft step of someone approaching and turned, surprised. Her mate, Rhyn, stood in heavy boots, running pants, and a tank top. Relief trickled through her to *see* him alive. His snow cloud-colored eyes were piercing, his muscular frame making her warm from the inside out. The tank top displayed his thick biceps and shapely shoulders. If she stepped just an inch closer, she'd feel his body heat.

"Ully's not coming," he said.

"Why not?" she asked, disappointed. Her morning run was the only moment of peace she would have during the day.

"I saw your dream."

"You're not supposed to be in my head."

He said nothing.

"Are *you* running with me?" she asked.

"Yeah."

Her gaze went to the sky again as she recalled the nightmare. She'd been avoiding him for the same reason her dream revealed: she might just care too much about him to leave when the time came for her to go. The sense of loss from her dream returned, and she was embarrassed to feel her throat tightening.

"I haven't seen you since we arrived," she said. "Are you in the dungeon with the rest of the warriors?"

"Do you wanna run or not?" he asked.

"Are you really running in boots?"

"I can run naked."

She turned away before he saw the flair of interest accompany her irritation. Her face felt hot as she recalled the one night they'd spent together. How could she forget the experience that had effectively doomed her, branded her as his forever?

Rhyn growled low in his chest. Suddenly, a massive black jaguar leapt past her toward the nearest trail. Its back reached her shoulder, and it moved with restrained, lethal power. She'd seen a couple of Rhyn's shapes, but she'd never get used to the fact he could shapeshift.

Rhyn turned to peer at her through silvery eyes, flicking his tail in impatience. She started forward with a sigh and joined him at the beginning of the muddy trail. She picked her way through the first few steps, startled when he launched himself at a tree, clawed his way up, and bypassed the muddy section by leaping to the next tree.

"Stupid cat," she muttered. Rhyn leapt down from the tree a few meters in front of her and sat to await her as she slid and maneuvered the muddy trail. When she reached the other side, he trotted forward. She followed, expecting him to disappear into the trees at any point and reappear with a herd of deer clenched in his jaws.

They ran through the forest toward the cliff, then ducked deeper into the forest before the trees gave way at the cliff. She stopped at the edge, where the trail was nothing but mud. Puffing and energized, she paused for a breath when cold fingers brushed her neck.

Darkyn. He spoke to her, and his cold presence was close. She jerked away, surprised, and slid in the mud toward the cliff edge. Rhyn snatched her and wrapped his arm around her, lifting her out of the mud and farther back onto the trail. Almost immediately she wished he'd let her fall off the cliff. She'd rarely seen him—and never touched him—since arriving a few weeks ago. The warmth of their bodies pressed together made her forget Darkyn, the cold, and the nightmare. The silence was thick and awkward. She sensed him waiting to see what she'd do.

"Thank you," she managed. "For coming with me today." His warm breath on her neck made her shiver, and she instinctively tilted her head. His grip tightened around her, but he didn't bite her.

"Did you mean what you said?" he asked in a husky tone.

"About thanking you? Yes," she said.

"You know that's not what I mean," he growled. "In your dream, you said—"

"I don't know, Rhyn. I've got a lot to figure out."

"Fine. Then tell me you *don't*."

She sighed. She belonged here in his arms, and yet she feared what that meant. She'd lose her sister, her only family, and Rhyn hadn't yet proven he could keep her safe.

"You can't say it," he said, satisfaction in his voice. He turned her to face him, and she gazed up at him, once again awed by his size, heat, and intensity. His silver eyes were molten, his rugged jaw line shaded by two days' growth. His hands were hot on her hips and his body blocked the cold wind whipping up the cliff.

"Can you?" she challenged.

"Don't need to."

"Rhyn—"

"I've done almost everything you asked me to the past few weeks. I need a reward, before the demons in the forest attack us."

"Demons?" she echoed. Any fear she might have felt disappeared when he rested his hand on her neck and brushed her cheek, then her lips, with his thumb. Her blood was already on fire from their bodies being pressed together, and heat pooled in the base of her belly.

"I watch them watch you," he said. "You draw them out on your runs, and I kill them. We're a good team."

"Until the day you're not there." Her words escaped before she thought to filter them. The sense of loss returned. Warmth passed through his gaze, and the skin around his eyes softened as he took in her expression.

"I win," he said. He withdrew, and the cold wind swept over her. She started after him, senses scattered.

"You didn't get your kiss," she objected, her blood humming with need and frustration. She followed him back to the trail. Her eyes swept over his muscular form, from his shapely shoulders and wide back to the thick thighs outlined by the sweats. He whipped out a curved knife from the small of his back and tossed it in the air, catching it easily.

"You better start running. They're coming," he said.

"You weren't joking." She eyed the forest around them. It was quiet and cold.

"I don't do much right, but I can kill things," he said. She turned to see him gazing at her again. His eyes traveled to her neck and lingered. "Hate demon blood."

Fear made the wind seem colder. She wasn't about to stick around for this one. She started past him. He gripped her arm and pulled her against him once more. His kiss was hot, demanding, and quick, his lips warm and soft. Just as her body melded against his, he pushed her away. Stunned, she stared up at him. His gaze was on some point in the forest. She heard them coming, the sound of creatures crashing through the forest.

"Go, now," he ordered. "Don't stop running until you're back at the castle."

Lust turned to adrenaline. He slapped her backside to jar her into gear, and she bolted forward. The sound of fighting erupted behind her, and she stopped before the trail curved out of sight to see Rhyn standing over his first victim, a demon in a jaguar form. He wiped the bloodied knife on its pelt and straightened, meeting her gaze.

She wasn't sure if she should thank him for protecting him or curse him for the kiss. He lifted his chin in dismissal. Intent on fleeing him as well as the demons, she ran as hard as she could back to the castle before doubling over to catch her breath. Her eyes went to the number she wrote on her hand each morning.

She had exactly five weeks left in her bargain with Kris, the Immortal's leader. She squeezed her hand closed to hide the number and faced the forest, waiting for him to reappear.

"What're you doing out here?" Kris's cool voice made the hair on the back of her neck stand up.

"Finishing up my morning run," she answered.

"You were told to take Ully with you."

"I went with Rhyn."

"You don't have much longer here, if all goes according to plan," Kris said and moved beside her, his eyes the color of tanzanite, his white hair the color of snow.

"I know, Kris."

"You're better off without him. That may be the only good thing that comes of returning you to the mortal world."

She looked up at him, anger heating her blood again. She'd never understand how Kris could treat his own half-brother as he did. Rhyn was all she would take away from the twisted Immortal world.

"Go inside. Ully's waiting for you in the lab."

"I'm nothing but a means to an end to you," she muttered. "So tired of all this." *At least I have Rhyn.*

She didn't wait for Kris's response but trotted inside.

Rhyn lopped the head off the last demon and wiped his knife again. He'd fed on the first one and was full but not satisfied. No blood could sate him as his mate's could, and he hadn't tasted her in weeks. Gabriel said she needed space. Kris said she needed anyone but him in her life. She had no idea what he wanted. For once, Rhyn was the only one who made any sense. His blood still raged from their kiss. If not for the demons' interruption, he and Katie would be doing a different kind of mud wrestling.

He growled, irritated as much by demons as he was with the cold weather. Snow fell in lazy, fat flakes, sticking to his clothes and hair. He swiped at the flakes then braced himself to change into his jaguar shape. Hot pain slid through him as his body contorted into the new form. He released a sigh when he'd transformed and shook snowflakes from his thick coat. He loped along the trail through the forest and trotted into the park around the castle, where the person he least wanted to see awaited him with a glower and crossed arms.

"You had somewhere to be half an hour ago," Kris said.

His tone reminded Rhyn that coming here had been Katie's idea and no one else's. He'd come to keep an eye on her and, allegedly, to help his brothers on the Council, though not even he believed he had a decent bone in his body.

"I thought it important for you to see our father's crypt," Kris continued. "He's been interred here since he became dead-dead at the hands of your demon-mother."

Kris waited for him to change forms. Rhyn breezed by him, much warmer in his jaguar shape than he'd been in his human shape.

Hell was a bitch, but at least it was warm, he thought darkly.

Kris strode past him and led him through the castle's ground floor, whose wide, carpeted halls felt nice on his paws. The massive halls were chilly, with ugly stone walls and wooden beams far above. Kris's décor was similar to his ever-changing eyes: jewel-toned drapes, pillows, and tapestries, edged with gold.

Several people stopped to stare or skirt them as Rhyn padded through, and one startled gasp drew his attention briefly to a stairwell. A child-angel—the first he'd seen in hundreds of years—gazed at him with large brown eyes before darting up the stairs. He wondered what poor fool was stuck babysitting the high-maintenance angel as he followed Kris.

"I'd prefer you didn't act like such an ass around here," Kris muttered as one of the servants dropped a tray of dishes at the sight of the massive cat.

Rhyn stayed in his form until they reached a narrow, winding set of stairs. He changed shape before descending behind Kris. They walked down and through an unused part of the dungeons. Their path dead-ended at a large wooden door. Kris produced a key chain from his pocket and unlocked the five locks before pulling the heavy door open.

"You afraid Pop's gonna escape?" Rhyn asked, amused by the security.

"The magic lingering in our father's blood renders the ground here sacred. I've sealed off the crypt with magic to keep Immortals from entering through the shadow world, and installed locks for those who wander where they shouldn't be," Kris said.

"We should just toss him in the deepest hole in Hell."

"I don't expect *you* to understand what it is to care about someone else."

Rhyn said nothing. His brother had no idea the depth of emotion even a half-demon could feel. When he'd looked into Katie's eyes and dared her to admit she didn't love him, he'd seen everything he needed to know. He didn't feel like the half-demon bastard he was when he was with her.

"Pay your respects, brother, while I allow it," Kris said, and pushed the door open. The chamber beyond was dark, lit by the soft glow of a single torch beside a clear sarcophagus. Rhyn's eyes lingered on the body on the altar before he took in the seven statues of descending size surrounding the altar.

Kris lit another torch to shed light on the murals on the floor. There was one beneath each statue representing a continent. The largest statue was Andre, their eldest brother who had recently become dead-dead, standing over Europe. Kris was next in size, standing on a mural of North America.

The smallest statue was Rhyn as a child of five or six, standing on Antarctica. He circled his statue, barely recalling his life growing up. Each of the Council That Was Seven was represented, dutifully overlooking their father's corpse. Rhyn faced the sarcophagus, surprised to see his father looked as he had when he last saw him thousands of years before. Their father had Andre's dark skin, and his hair was grey at the temples. His features were most like Rhyn's: heavy and roughly hewn, while his body was lean like Kris's.

"This might interest you more," Kris said in a cold voice.

Rhyn bristled and turned. Kris lit another torch to display a darkened case on the wall. Rhyn's fists clenched as he took in the beheaded, dismembered body hung for spite on the wall.

"My father's killer," Kris said, taking in the demoness's body.

"You kill my mother," Rhyn snarled. "Yet you've never come after me."

"Andre killed your mother and kept me from destroying you as I should have," Kris replied. "You're a cancer on everyone around you. Andre was too kind to kill you. Even Katie is better off without you."

Rhyn heard without listening, instead taking in the tortured features of his mother's face. He'd gone from being tormented by his own mother to the *affection* of an abusive father who regretted ever having him. What small maternal instincts a demon could have had led her to destroy the man who took her son; then she in turn was killed by Andre.

Andre had taken Rhyn in when he was five and he fled his bullying brothers when he was ten. Andre, however, unanimously approved Rhyn's petition to be recognized as a son of their father when he was old enough, despite his brothers' objections.

"They both deserve what they got," Rhyn said. "Andre alone has ever shown me any kindness."

"And look where that got us all. If he'd killed you, he'd be alive and Katie would be safe."

"Safe?" Rhyn echoed. "You'd force her to become your mate."

"I wouldn't force a human to do anything."

"But you'd hold her down and take her blood." Rhyn's voice lowered dangerously and he faced his brother. Kris fell silent. "Did you think I didn't know?"

"She told you."

"She didn't have to."

"I didn't intend for it to happen," Kris said.

"You're no better than Sasha," Rhyn said.

"And she's better off with you? You have nothing to offer her."

Rhyn faced his mother again. The words were too familiar. Katie had said the same. He hadn't even been able to keep her safe when they were together, and he had nothing—not even a home—to give her.

"Don't destroy anything while you're here," Kris said and left.

Rhyn ignored him, turning from the mother who'd never wanted him to the father who'd wanted him dead-dead. He'd had one friend in his life, Gabriel, and his mate, a woman tough in spirit but vulnerable in flesh. He didn't belong here with Kris's kind, yet she was safe. People around him had a way of dying horribly, and he wasn't entirely sure what to do about it, now that it mattered. He wished Andre had stuck around a little longer, so he could've asked him what to do.

He sensed the entrance of another before his companion spoke.

"She looks like the Council, dismembered beyond recognition."

Rhyn snorted and faced Sasha, the brother charged with governing Australia, and the first to abandon the Council in favor of serving the Dark One. Sasha was lean and pale, his gaze turquoise.

"You're not surprised to see me," Sasha surmised.

"If Kris let me in, he'd let anyone in," Rhyn replied.

"Miss Hell, brother?"

"Warmer than this place."

Sasha chuckled, his gaze taking in the sarcophagus. He neared it with a small frown. Rhyn stayed where he was, wary yet unafraid of Sasha, who'd been the zookeeper among the animals with him in Hell.

"I wonder if he were still alive if things would be the same," Sasha mused, his eyes on their father.

"I'm glad the asshole's gone," Rhyn said.

"I suppose."

"What're you doing here, Sasha?"

"I'm here to see Kris, of all people."

"You can't manipulate him like you do everyone else," Rhyn said, well aware of his brother's ability to twist the minds of others.

"No? Wanna bet?"

"People like us don't pay up."

"True. We are more alike than the others. How's your little human treat?"

Rhyn eyed him. Sasha gave a faint smile.

"I'm not here for her," he said. "Wouldn't you like to have Kris out of the way, so you and your human treat can live in peace somewhere?"

"I wouldn't trust anything you offered."

"Very well, then, how about we make a deal for you to come back with me as my personal bodyguard, and I'll make sure she's safe and happy the rest of her life? I learned in Hell how you can un-mate her. She'd be better off without you, Rhyn."

She'd be better off without you. He'd heard these words more than once over the past few days and couldn't help the small part of him that agreed. The rest of him didn't give a shit what anyone said: Katie was his.

"You know Kris'll kill her when he's done with her. One human is nothing to him in his version of the big picture," Sasha continued. "Not sure which of us is more twisted."

"Fuck off, Sasha. You did me no favors in Hell, and you'll do me no favors here."

"Think about it. I'm off to see Kris."

Rhyn watched him go, wondering just what his brother was planning, and how he'd figure it out before Katie was hung on the wall next to his mother. Agitated and chilled by the chamber, he transformed into his jaguar form to terrorize more Immortals on his way to hunt the demons in the forest.

From the shadows of the crypt, Gabriel waited until the half-brothers were gone to dump the contents of the velvet dice pouch into his palm. Two small green gems—holding the dust of human souls—glittered in the torchlight of the dead-dead Immortal's chamber. Kris had given them to him weeks ago as payment for two assassinations. Wanting to give his friend, Rhyn, a moment of peace with his dead-dead parents, he waited until Rhyn was gone before withdrawing from the shadows.

"He looks so un-dead-dead," Death said, a rare trace of interest in her sweet voice.

Gabriel put the gems away and looked up to see her slight frame standing beside the sarcophagus. Her white hair and snowy skin glowed in the dim chamber.

"I wondered where you'd been going," she said.

"You always know where I'm going," he replied. "You can read my mind."

"You come here a lot."

"I do."

She turned and raised an eyebrow at him, her rainbow eyes flashing with every color between white and black. "I want to hear you say why," she ordered.

"To see my friend and protect his mate."

"You're not independent anymore, Gabriel. I own you now," she reminded him. "The other assassins go nowhere without my permission."

"You know where to find me when you need me," he said.

"You can't influence destiny, Gabe," she said. "You shouldn't be here at all."

"I have one friend in the universe. There's nothing wrong with—"

"You sacrificed your immortal soul for him. You've done enough."

He clamped his jaw shut.

"And he's still not doing what he should be," she continued. "I think you wasted your freedom. Poor choice, but you were a human once. Maybe your human compassion led you astray."

"I thought you appreciated my *human* perspective."

"I *did*. But I think you've become a liability to me, Gabriel."

He'd heard the speech before, though this time, it was different. Three weeks ago, he'd bargained his soul in exchange for her taking Rhyn off her list of those to be made dead-dead. In all the years he'd served her, she'd never owned him until three weeks ago. He still didn't doubt his friend or his decision, but he was the only one.

"I'll stay away," he said. "If it pleases you."

"Stay today, Gabriel, but know that the next time you return, you will take the lives of two of them," she said. "Kris paid for Katie's death and the death of another, whose name he did not mention, but I will."

Heaviness settled into the pit of his stomach. He wondered if Death would've been more lenient if he stayed home with her and played nice instead of spending half his day in the mortal world.

It was too late for him to know.

"Who else would you have me take?" he asked in a monotone. Death smiled, and when she spoke, he looked away. "You would ask this?"

"You're lucky this is all I ask. Normally, when an assassin goes soft, I make him dead-dead. You've been my lover for ages, and I am doing you a favor."

"Next you'll say you've kicked me out of your bed."

She said nothing, and he met her gaze once more, genuinely surprised.

"I guess you no longer interest me, since you're just another of my slaves. You're no longer exciting and different to me," she said with a shrug. "I am sorry for this of all things, Gabriel. You are still my top assassin, assuming you don't fail in your executions."

"I wonder why you agreed to my deal, if it rendered me boring!" he snapped.

"Everything comes at a cost, Gabriel, which you know. I broke Immortal Code to grant your favor of not killing Rhyn. You had to pay the price for it, and so did I."

Her words did nothing to quell the anger boiling within him. It'd been too long since he'd felt such strong emotion, and it caught him off guard. At his silence, Death went on.

"Today's your last day here. Next time, you make them dead-dead."

"I understand, mistress."

"Very well."

At his tone, she softened. "Gabriel, you know there are things I cannot tell you. You must understand there is a reason behind what I ask of you that will not become clear for some time. Trust me. This is the only way."

"As you wish, mistress."

She left him alone in the dark with his thoughts, and he began to understand more how his friend Rhyn felt in a world that was pitted against him. He'd expected things to change once he pledged his soul to Death, but he hadn't expected anything so drastic, so soon. He clenched the pouch with its gems.

Instead of going to see the Immortal leader, Gabriel crossed through the shadow world, squinting as he emerged into the bright mid-morning sunlight. He put on his sunglasses, which did little to alleviate the headache sunlight gave him. The lush Scottish Highlands around him were covered in a blanket of snow that stretched for miles, the white world interrupted only by a few narrow roads snaking in different directions.

It was rarely sunny in this part of the world, and he chalked the irritation up to his sudden plunge in luck. He breathed in deeply of the scent of snow. The chances of him ever returning were slim to none. He was early this year, but he'd rather visit now than risk he'd be grounded during winter solstice in a month.

He'd miss the smell and sight of his homeland and yearned already to stay here rather than return to his dark corner of the Immortal underworld! He began to think Death was right—he was going soft. Before he gave his Immortal soul to death, he'd never noticed how sweet the air was or how the grass sang as the wind whipped through it. He missed the smells and sounds in winter.

He walked a familiar path to a graveyard so old, not even legends remained about its location or the importance of those buried there. A stone cottage up the road was the only sign of inhabitation, and a herd of sheep raised their heads as he neared. He ignored them and went to a place only he knew, stopping when he was atop the graves he sought.

"Mother, Father," he said quietly, "I may not be able to come back again."

He never expected his long dead parents to respond but waited anyway. When only the winter wind greeted him, he continued.

"Father, I did as you told me not to do long ago. I gave Death my Immortal soul. It was for a worthy cause, and I don't regret what I've done," he said.

His gaze lifted, and he recalled vividly the last time he'd seen his parents in this very spot, when they were cut down by bloodthirsty demons during the only period in Immortal history when demons attacked humans. They'd been led by the demon leader Darkyn, whom the Dark One had punished when Death discovered what the demons had done. He didn't know what happened to Darkyn, but Death adopted him, raised him, and trained him to be the most ruthless of all assassins.

Rhyn had become like a brother to him, and the idea of killing his mate reopened wounds that hadn't bled since he stood in this place thousands of years before. He tried not to think of that sad time, instead blinking away dark memories and focusing on the snow at his feet.

"I'll come back whenever I'm allowed," he said with resignation. He gazed around once more and then turned and walked away, back into the shadow world.

Still in her jogging clothes, Katie made her way to the super-lab on one of the castle's upper floors. She knocked and waited.

"You stood me up this morning. Kris yelled at me for it," Katie said, leveling a glare on Ully as he opened the door. His bright features turned pink beneath his wire-rimmed glasses and straw-colored hair. At barely above her height and slender, the mad scientist was very unlike the Immortal warriors that filled the castle.

"You know, I just … well, Rhyn …"

"You can say he scared you shitless," she said.

"Yeah, he did," he said, then brightened. "But I have good news for you!"

"You figured out how to make an immunity injection?"

He whirled away from the door and strode into the lab. She followed, uninterested in the sterile glass and stainless steel landscape. As she did every day, she went to the table near his cluttered desk to await her blood draw and any other experiments he wanted to do. He scampered across the lab to a fridge that held cold tools and bottles of mysterious serums, everything except what a normal person put in a fridge.

"Nowhere close." He retrieved a small bottle of what looked like perfume and brought it back, holding it out to her. She took it skeptically.

"I was hanging upside down this morning with Rhyn snarling at me and I thought, this doesn't just suck, but it's gotta suck even more for a little human like Katie," Ully said. "Kris said the normal Immortals aren't allowed around you, because they tend to attack you. This will help. Try it."

She sprayed the perfume on her wrist and coughed.

"Oh, god, Ully, this smells like a skunk crawled into my clothes!"

"I know!" Ully said, excited. "I created a pheromone repellant. It should cause temporary blindness in Immortals as well as mask your pheromones."

"I can't wear this."

"You don't have to. Just spray any Immortal that gets too close."

She looked at the bottle anew, thoughts going to the long list of Immortals she could've used it on instead of bearing their attacks.

"This is the first useful thing I've seen you do," she said. "You have more of this?"

"I have travel-sized, too. Sit down. Time for some blood."

She sighed and held out her arm, setting the perfume on the table as she sat. She still couldn't watch Ully draw her blood and covered her eyes with one hand. He was quick about it and placed a Hello Kitty Band-Aid over the small puncture before dropping the vials into his coat pocket.

"And you're no closer at all?" she asked, holding her breath for the answer.

"Nope. I had to start over yesterday. I told Kris I don't think it's possible to duplicate the antigen that makes you immune to Immortals. I can probably get close with a few years of research, but not in two months."

She suspected Kris might override his promise to let her go in five weeks, if Ully couldn't figure it out. She released her breath, satisfied on more than one level to postpone her return to the human world.

The wind chime above the door tinkled. Kris entered, followed by someone whose appearance made her gasp. Sasha looked over her, uninterested, and both her hands went to her throat at the memory of what he'd done to her in Hell. Fear fluttered through her, and her gaze flew to Kris, whom she trusted little more than his sadistic brother. Kris's gaze was amber, a visual indicator of his anger despite his calm features.

"Ully," he said in a clipped tone. "Test this." He tossed a vial whose contents were the color of blood. Ully caught it and held it up.

Katie snagged the perfume off the table as the two brothers neared and eased off the chair, placing it between her and them. Sasha seemed to be ignoring her, though a small smile of amusement was on his face.

"What is it?" Ully asked curiously.

"The solution to our problem," Kris answered.

"My lab in Hell didn't have the ethical reservations you do in using Immortal or demon test subjects," Sasha said.

"How could you let him in here?" she demanded of Kris, unnerved by his sudden appearance in a place where she was allegedly safe.

"I came bearing gifts, namely the immunity blood you all need to fight the Dark One's army. I seek an alliance against my former employer and to regain my place at the Council," Sasha answered.

"Cut the shit, Sasha," Kris snapped. "I haven't decided what to do with you yet, and you may end up with an assassination contract on your head."

"As you wish," Sasha said in a voice so calm it drew the gazes of everyone in the room.

"Ully, test that now," Kris ordered. "Sasha, you'll follow me to your room."

Sasha bowed his head in a mocking show of respect. Katie watched him go, her nightmares in her thoughts and her heart pounding. When the door closed, she looked at the vial of blood.

Suddenly, she feared a new fate. At least before, Kris had a reason to keep her around, because he wanted something from her. What happened if he got what he wanted elsewhere, before she knew what she wanted?

"Ully, how long will that take you?" she asked.

"A few days, maybe a week."

She gripped the perfume bottle more tightly. She couldn't help but think Sasha's sudden appearance was related to the demons in the forest and her dreams. Her thoughts went to Rhyn.

"I'll see you later," she heard herself say.

Ully nodded, already seated and scribbling at his desk. She exited the brightly lit room into the hallway, crossing to look out the nearest window at the falling snow. A dark figure in the snow-covered park area caught her attention. Gabriel was sitting alone on top of one of the half dozen picnic tables. She made her way to the back entrance to the castle and stepped into the quiet, chilly day. The snow fell straight from the sky without the wind and was soft and fluffy beneath her feet.

"Gabriel?" she called, crossing her arms at the chill. He didn't face her. "You okay?"

"Better than you."

She paused a short distance from him, sensing something wrong. He didn't speak much. She knew nothing about him, except he'd been a friend to Rhyn.

"You're early today," she said.

"I can't stay tonight."

"Oh. You've got, um, work?"

"Yes."

"You'll be back tomorrow?" she asked at the ominous note in his voice.

"No, Katie. I'm not coming back."

"Ever?"

"For your sake, not if I can help it."

"So when you come back, you'll be back for me for good?" she asked.

"Yes."

She was struck by his words, feeling as if the one person she relied upon was not only running out on her but would chop her into pieces the next time she saw him. Her hand went to her neck. He looked away as his words sank in.

"Take care of Toby and Rhyn," he said, and stood. "And … take care of yourself."

"Gabriel, maybe you should just take me with you now and save us all some grief," she said.

"Humans have free will," he reminded her. "You have some other decisions to make first."

"But if I choose Rhyn and you come back for me tomorrow, it doesn't seem very fair to him."

"You're not making this easier on either of us!" he said, a flare of emotion in his voice for the first time since she'd met him. Taken aback by his anger, she watched him run a hand through his hair in an unusual sign of agitation.

"Guess I don't understand the rules," she said quietly.

"I'll stay away as long as I can. I may not have a choice, though."

"What do I do, Gabriel?"

"I can't tell you that."

"But you can tell me you're coming back to kill me," she said, anger rising.

He looked up at the sky. Dressed all in black with his dark eyes and hair, he looked like a living shadow in the snow-covered world.

"Rhyn is my friend," he said after a long pause. "He cares about you. I've never thought twice about any life I've taken until now."

"I understand but I'm having a hard time sympathizing, considering it's me you're gonna kill."

"It's not just you. The next time I visit the human world, I'll be leaving with two souls."

"Okay, so you're taking me and someone else, but this still doesn't help me figure out what to do!" she said.

"I can't tell you that."

She drew a deep breath. Her hands shook as she stood there discussing her own death with a creature that resembled the Grim Reaper.

"It's not Toby or Rhyn, is it?" she ventured.

"No."

"Good. They're both growing on me."

"I have to go, Katie," Gabriel said.

"First the nightmares, now this. Why do I feel like something really bad is happening?"

"Sometimes things get worse before they get better. Most of the times, things just never get better. Doesn't help that I got demoted. No alcohol," he reminded her.

"Kris tossed it all out after he found me knocked out on the bathroom floor last week," she admitted, rolling her eyes.

"Good. You're going to need your head clear."

She searched his face. The snow began falling harder, and he met her gaze again finally. The regret in his dark eyes made her want to beg him not to kill her and comfort him for the pain he'd surely feel hurting his own friend. Her throat tightened, and in the end, no words came out. She wondered how accurate her dream had been, if her only way to save Rhyn was to sacrifice herself.

"Farewell, Katie," Gabriel said in a hushed voice.

"Farewell, Gabriel."

Death's assassin turned and walked away, disappearing into the shadow world. The coldness of fear within her grew stronger. She rubbed the lumpy scar on her arm, her attention caught by the sight of a jaguar dropping from a tree branch to the edge of the park and the forest a short distance away. It was not all black but had a white patch around one eye. It stared at her through green eyes, and she frowned, uncertain why the sight of the creature bothered her.

A gust of wind flung snow into her face. She retreated to the castle, up the back stairwell off limits to everyone but her, and to the warmth of her chamber. Toby's giggles reached her before she opened the door. She walked in to see Rhyn's jaguar form sprawled across the bed, shredding a down pillow. Her bed looked as if a flock of geese had combusted over it, and she counted at least ten dead pillows.

Toby laughed and tossed Rhyn another pillow, delighted when he snatched it from midair and shredded it in an explosion of white feathers. Reining in her emotions, she tried to distract her dark thoughts by focusing on Toby.

"Toby!" she exclaimed. "Where did you get all these pillows?"

The baby angel and half-demon turned toward the door.

"From our neighbors," Toby said. "I had two and you had three and the fat lady down the hall had four, so then I got hers and that mean man's pillows."

"Just what I need," she grumbled, wondering what other insults the castle's Immortals' mates would fling at her after this incident. She didn't fit in; they made it clear every chance they could, just as their leader did. "Wash up for dinner."

"Okay, Mama!" he sang and sprang away. She bent down to pick up a yet unscathed pillow, startled to stand and see Rhyn had changed to his human form.

"*You* got stuck with the baby-angel?"

"Maybe that should be *we* got stuck with the baby-angel!" she shot back.

"He's all yours. What smells like shit?"

"I think I like you better as a jaguar. Much easier to get along with," she said with a shake of her head, unable to help the warmth that spread through her whenever she saw him. "Gabriel left for good today."

"He always comes back."

"Not this time."

He was quiet, digesting the news. Still shaken from her discussion with Gabriel, she couldn't decide if she wanted to run to the comfort of Rhyn's arms or send him away for good, before Gabriel took her away.

"Mama, I'm ready!" Toby said, reappearing.

"Okay, come on," she said. She held out a hand. He took it and tugged her to the door. Rhyn gazed at her, and her whole body responded despite her fear. The memory of his kiss made her insides warm. "If you want, you can come by later."

His gaze flared with heated interest.

"For tea," she clarified. "And to talk or whatever."

"I like whatever," he said.

"I'll get more pillows," Toby said.

"You're not invited," Rhyn growled.

"But how can we play?"

"You'll be in bed."

"*That*, no, Rhyn," she corrected him. "I mean tea. Daylight tea."

"Breakfast tea."

Toby giggled, and she glanced at him, afraid Rhyn was going to dive headfirst into a discussion Toby shouldn't hear.

"Afternoon tea. C'mon, Toby," Katie said and turned away, allowing Toby to pull her down the hall to the dining chamber, which had yet to fill up. She braced herself for the resentful looks and whispered insults she was glad Toby was too young to understand. They made their way unscathed through the dining room to their own little corner, where Toby's favorite food combination of mac-n-cheese and French toast waited for him on the table.

She couldn't eat, feeling more stressed than she had in the past three weeks. Sasha was somewhere in the castle, and Gabriel was gone. She'd cracked the door to her heart for Rhyn to shove his foot in the door and now needed to close, lock, and deadbolt it closed again.

I do love him, she admitted silently.

Chapter Two

In Hell, the Immortal Jade, formerly the most trusted lieutenant to the leader of the Council That Was Seven, looked around his new bedchamber with a shiver. It was a posh room for Hell, carved of smooth ebony stone that was characteristic of all the buildings in Hell. The room consisted of a massive bed with black bedding and white pillows, a wardrobe and trunks, and yawning windows to the sky that light never touched.

"This was Sasha's bedchamber," a demon said from the doorway. "You will be comfortable here. It has many Immortal comforts we care nothing for."

I care nothing for this either, Jade thought. The demon closed the door—one of the Immortal comforts, for there were no doors in Hell—and left him to wonder how many men and women Sasha had in the bed before him. He'd only spent one night there last month before Sasha flung him to the side in favor of a demoness.

Like Kris had flung him aside to make way for a mortal. His sense of loss was so deep, he thought it'd kill him some nights. He'd done what anyone would do: he'd found a way to get even with one of the men who hurt him. He might even get rid of both of them!

A sound from a trunk in the corner drew Jade's attention. Surprised, he crossed to it and opened it. The woman's face was hidden behind a mass of blonde hair, but he recognized the hot pink fingernails instantly.

"Iliana?" he asked. She stilled. He pulled her gently from the trunk and untied her. She was shaking and bloodied, and the bindings left deep marks around her wrists. She pulled off the gag.

"Did Kris send you for me?" she whispered, her gaze darting around. "Did the demons see you?"

"I didn't know you were gone," he admitted. "What happened?"

"They caught me when I went through the shadow world and brought me here, to Sasha." He didn't have to ask what Sasha did to her when her pretty blue eyes flared with white rage and then filled with tears. "Where is he? I want to kill him!"

"He's not—"

"No matter, we need to escape. Come on, Jade!"

He watched her stride to the door without following, heart heavy at what Kris's lieutenant and his colleague of a few decades would soon discover. She stopped at the door and turned to him.

"Jade, come on!"

"I can't go with you, Iliana," he whispered. "I'm here by choice."

Surprise, then disbelief, crossed her features. "Oh, God, Jade, what did you do?"

"I took care of Sasha," he said somewhat defensively. "I deserve better than how he treated me. How Kris treated me."

"You betrayed us."

"No, I didn't cross that line! I'm just here … there's just two people who I want to avenge myself on!" he said. "I'm not going to hurt anyone else!"

"Anyone else? You can't destroy Kris. It's like beheading the Council!"

"You don't understand. You wouldn't understand."

She crossed to him, furious. "You are a traitor of the worst kind. I will kill you now, before you hurt anyone!"

He blocked her first punch but not her second. Light exploded into his thoughts. He'd tried to reason with her, to tell her what happened. She didn't listen. She was as cold as Kris! Maybe she wanted Kris, too. He'd seen the way Kris looked at her and had long suspected the Council leader had two lovers, not one.

"No!" he roared and picked her up. He threw her against the wall, blinded by pain and rage. She hit the wall hard and landed on the ground, unconscious. "Iliana!" He knelt beside her, horrified at what he'd done. She was alive, though the back of her head bled.

Jade looked around in case someone else saw what he'd done. He picked her up and replaced her in the trunk, and then locked it. No one had to know, not even the demons. At least this way, she'd never have Kris. That left him with one less body to bury.

None of this would've happened at all if not for the Ancient's mate, Katie. Kris never would've sent him away, Sasha wouldn't have stumbled upon the immunity blood, and the demons wouldn't be amassing an army to send to the human world. Darkyn, the most powerful of all demons, wouldn't have returned from the pits of Hell, where the Dark One banished him to lead the army to the Immortals' front door and wipe out the Council.

Without Katie, Jade's world would be perfect.

Katie hid a smile. Rhyn, whose large hands all but swallowed the tea cup, had made an attempt to be civilized. He'd spilled it twice already. Despite his irritation, he'd been as patient with Toby as a half-demon could be. Toby had fallen asleep in front of the fireplace. Rhyn set the cup down and sat back, gazing at her hard. Well aware afternoon had faded into night, she kept her cup in her lap to keep from fidgeting under his intensity.

"You'll tell me to go, won't you," he said.

"I think so," she replied and cleared her throat.

"I'll behave, but I'm staying." He rose and crossed to Toby, looping his arm around the baby angel and resting him on his hip. She cringed as he disappeared into Toby's room, hoping Rhyn didn't waken him.

True to his word, he stripped off his boots and shirt and lay on top of the covers. She hesitated, her blood burning and her confused thoughts terrified of what might happen. Katie crawled under the comforter. Rhyn made no moves on her, simply rolled to tuck her against his warm body.

"Maybe you'll keep the nightmares away," she whispered drowsily.

"If I knew how, I would."

"Is Darkyn stronger than you?"

"Yeah."

"If you and the Council worked together, you could take out anything," she said.

"If I could protect you alone, I'd take you somewhere safe from the demons and the Council."

"I don't think you can. Kris is your brother, and family should stick together."

"You have no idea how my *family* works."

"You'll need your family when I'm gone," she said, thoughts drifting to her impending death. His body and scent felt too nice. She'd enjoy this tonight and then do what she must the next day. She'd spent the day in thought after her talk with Gabriel, and there was only one solution that might drive Rhyn away before she and Gabriel hurt him.

"You're not leaving."

"I know I am, Rhyn."

At the dangerous note in his voice, she said nothing else. She'd seen the acrimonious relationship between him and Kris and understood some of what made them enemies. As she fell asleep, she couldn't help thinking Rhyn was the only Immortal on the Council she'd trust to keep humans safe.

Her nightmares that night involved her sister, Hannah, being eaten by the jaguar with the white patch over his eye. She awoke long before dawn, and her eyes went to the corner where Gabriel no longer sat.

"Rhyn?"

He, too, was gone. Toby's snores drifted into the bedchamber from his room. She tossed the covers off, crossing to the French doors. The half moon's light made the snow-covered forest glow eerily. Checking the time, she counted backwards. It was afternoon in Maryland, where Hannah was.

Visions of her sister's death fresh in her mind, she changed into warm clothes and her running shoes, tucked the perfume bottle into a pocket, then sat on the edge of the bed. She closed her eyes to concentrate hard on summoning the portal to the shadow place. Rhyn's warm power filled her as she drew on their bond as mates, and the portal opened. She stepped into the clammy, wet world of fog and darkness, pausing to focus on the portal that would lead to her sister's house. Several portals glowed, and one grew more intense as she thought hard.

Katie walked through the shadow place and through the portal, wondering how she'd explain to her sister how she suddenly appeared out of nowhere and expecting a lecture about disappearing three weeks ago.

Hannah's fiancé, an Immortal, owned a swarthy mansion in Maryland. Katie cringed at his over the top décor of gilded everything and oriented herself. She'd emerged from the shadow world into a sitting room. She walked into the hall and up a wide stairwell to the second floor.

Hannah's bedroom was quiet, the bed neatly made and her closet door open to reveal a large empty space. For once, she wished she'd paid attention when her sister told her about travel plans. Still disturbed by the nightmare, she rifled through Hannah's vanity to see if her sister left her appointment book in a drawer.

"They were in a hurry."

She whirled to see a woman in a servant's uniform Hannah insisted her household employees wear. The woman was small and pale with eyes so dull, she seemed almost lifeless.

"I think they were going to visit you in France," the woman added. "A man named Kris invited them."

Kris! What was his plan? "When did they leave?" Katie managed.

"They had a flight out yesterday afternoon. Ms. Hannah hates to travel in the morning."

"Do you know when they were coming back?"

The woman shrugged. Katie looked around, unable to tell if her sister's empty closet was indicative of a weekend trip or something more permanent. Hannah never traveled light, and there was no way of knowing what Kris was doing.

"Would you like a cup of tea?" the servant asked. "I was just preparing one for myself in the kitchen."

"I should probably get going."

"Very well, miss. If you want to wait for a few minutes, I can pull up their itinerary."

"Sure, thanks."

"Come. Have some tea while you wait."

A sense of foreboding passed through her as she reluctantly followed the servant from the bedroom into a wide hall with gaudy gilded furniture and picture frames. She paused at the top of the sweeping stairwell to look around her. The house was too quiet for her comfort, and she felt the familiar sense of being watched.

There was no one but the maid, who was halfway down the stairs. She trailed with a shiver, wanting to make sure her sister was truly safe before leaving. If the maid gave her the airline info, she could call to confirm her sister was on board.

The spacious kitchen reminded her of Ully's lab with its landscape of stainless steel. A tea kettle was already whistling when they entered, and the maid rushed across the kitchen to grab it.

Katie sat on a barstool at the breakfast bar, watching the maid pour tea into two mugs sitting beside the stove. Two mugs, as if she were expecting company or someone else was already there. Katie eased off the chair and reached into her pocket for the perfume. She needed a quiet, safe place where she could channel Rhyn's power to call forth a portal. Her mind went to the bathroom in the hall.

"I've got to run to the restroom. I'll be right back for the tea."

The maid turned, looking past her, and Katie spun away. The lanky form standing between her and the door made her gasp.

"Hello, Lunchmeat," the demon Jared said, smiling slowly. "I see you're having tea with my blood monkey."

"Who let you out of Hell?" she whispered.

"More than one way out of that place, as you discovered."

"Rhyn's here."

"If he were, I'd sense him."

He took a step closer, his blond hair and green eyes highlighting a slender face. His frame was thin to the point of gaunt. She didn't remember him being so tall in Hell, but she'd been afraid to look too hard at him when she passed his cell.

"You look well," he said, looking her up and down. He moved closer and she skirted the breakfast bar until it was between them. "Not so brave without those bars between us, are you, Lunchmeat?"

"You don't want to do this!" she exclaimed.

"Pretty sure I do. The taste of your sweet nectar before I tear you apart?" He smacked his lips, his eyes glowing. He started around the breakfast bar, and she kept pace with him on the opposite side. If she could make a break for the door … she gripped the perfume bottle harder.

"Sasha sent you," she said, willing him to talk rather than attack.

"Hell no. He'd never let me out of the zoo. The demons released us after Sasha fled."

"What'd he do?"

"Eh, Sasha killed a couple of demons he really shouldn't have. Pissed off the Dark One and the demon-leader, who freed us all to hunt him. It's coming back to bite him now."

"And my sister? Where is she?" she asked, bracing herself for the answer.

"I don't give a shit. She can't be as sweet tasting as you," he said, his gaze darkening.

"I have to warn you, I've learned some things since you saw me. I'm not the defenseless little human you saw in Hell."

"I like my dinner to fight me. Makes the final surrender so much sweeter."

She inched away, her back now to the kitchen door. The maid had set down the tea and retrieved a butcher knife from a drawer.

"Why not make this fair?" Katie asked, her gaze going to the maid. "Why don't you let me fight her? She can keep what she's got, and I'll face her barehanded."

Jared turned to see the woman on the other side of the kitchen, and Katie bolted. Panic churned within her, and she was about to cry out for Rhyn when Jared snagged her arm. She whirled and sprayed him with the perfume, wildly aiming for his face and almost gagging at the scent.

"What the hell … smells like shit!" he snapped and released her to knock the bottle away. She ran with one glance over her shoulder as she reached the bathroom. He stood in the hallway smiling, his predatory look assuring her he had no plans of letting his dinner escape him.

Katie locked herself in the bathroom, cursing Ully for the skunk perfume that clearly didn't work. She looked around for something to brace the door and ended up leaning against it. There was a moment of silence before the door buckled beneath a blow that sent her sprawling. The door held, and she scrambled back to brace it.

"Rhyn, any time!" she muttered. The door cracked in the middle beneath the second blow, and she went sailing once again. Jared kicked the fractured pieces of door out of the way. Katie pushed herself to her feet, remembering what pain a pissed-off Hell-creature could cause. She recalled the scent of her blood, what hot agony felt like as an otherworldly creature tore her apart.

She'd rather die than go through that again. God help her, she couldn't even try to off herself while trapped in the bathroom!

"Long time, no see, demon." Rhyn's voice made her heart skip a beat, and she craned her neck to see past Jared, who whirled. Jared moved away from the door into the hall to face his opponent.

"Half-breed," he hissed. "You dare challenge a full demon?"

"Unless you wanna leave my blood monkey alone."

Jared's form contorted then grew twice his size as he shifted into a creature unlike any she'd ever seen. Wings, short fur, fangs the size of her forearm ... she moved farther into the bathroom, lest she draw his attention. Suddenly, a blur of brown streaked past the bathroom, tackling the demon. She heard the sounds of fighting, grunts, growls, and gnashing of teeth. Katie inched forward, peeking out as the two creatures smashed into furniture and porcelain figurines on display in the wide foyer.

Her first instinct was to run back to the shadow world, but she had a hard time looking away from the two hideous creatures battling it out in Hannah's home. The sound of footsteps running down the hall drew her attention, and she flung herself backwards as the maid with the butcher knife tried to cut her. A piece of the broken door slashed her as she fell, and she scrambled away as the maid slashed at her again. The maid lost her balance and toppled over.

Katie scrambled up into the hall and maneuvered her bloodied arm to see the damage, suddenly aware the two demons had stopped fighting. She looked up to find both hideous beasts staring at her, drooling. Their gazes followed the drops of blood as they fell from her arm to the marble flooring. Both inched toward her, the inhuman growling filling the hall.

"Winner takes all," she said, backing away.

The maid lunged at her again, and she darted for the kitchen, followed by Jared's blood monkey, who was wailing with frustration. One of the demons launched itself down the hall after her, only for the other to tackle it and the two of them to roll down the hall in a furry mass of wings, legs, and snapping teeth.

Katie whipped around the breakfast bar, eyes roving the kitchen for the knife block or something with which to defend herself. She snatched a wooden cutting board as the maid rounded a counter with the knife raised. Katie ducked again then twisted her hips in a perfect baseball batter's swing and smacked her hard in the face. The maid dropped silently, her nose busted and blood splattered across her features.

"I have enough problems with psycho Immortal demon jackasses. You really think some stupid human with a knife scares me?" she said, furious. "Now I understand why Kris is such an ass to humans."

She shook her head to clear her anger and sat with her back to the counter, forcing herself to concentrate on the shadow world and tapping into Rhyn's power despite the sounds of demons fighting so near the kitchen. The portal opened, and she bounded through it, running to the brightest portal and through it to emerge on the snowy park behind the castle.

It was dawn, and she breathed a sigh of relief at being safe. Ully emerged from the castle, hair mussed and dressed as if for a run. From behind him, Toby tore out of the castle in a snowsuit. He dove into the snow while she stood and waited for Rhyn. Guilt made her resolve to drive him away waver.

"You've been using the repellant," Ully said. His nose crinkled as he drew near. "You ready to run?"

"Not today, Ully," she said. "Your repellant doesn't work!"

"I tested it on one of the warriors. I know it works."

She held up her bloody arm. "I just got out of a fight with a demon. It didn't work."

"It doesn't work on demons," he said. "Only on Immortals."

"What's the difference?"

"Demons are … demons, and Immortals are more closely related to angels. Completely different genealogical make-up. I can make you a demon repellant, if you want."

She gritted her teeth and wished she'd brought the cutting board with her to knock some sense into Ully. The bloodied arm was making her unusually lightheaded. She lowered it to her side and took a few deep breaths.

"Here, kitty, kitty!" Toby said in excitement. He barreled toward the forest, and she turned in time to see the black jaguar with the white eye patch seated at the edge of the park, tail flicking and intense green eyes on the approaching child.

"Toby," she called. He continued running. Alarm reignited her adrenaline. "Toby! Stop!"

Ully looked over at the child and jaguar curiously. Katie bolted for Toby, knowing the kid was too young to recognize Rhyn from any other demon-jaguar.

"Toby, if you don't stop, you're grounded for all eternity!" she shouted, running hard.

The child slowed as he neared the jaguar and turned, finally paying attention. The beast crouched, and she ran harder.

"Mama, I wanna play with Rhyn!" Toby whined. He looked at the jaguar again and took another two tiny steps, as if testing her resolve to ground him.

The jaguar launched itself at the child, and Toby's scream shattered the quiet morning as its jaw clamped on his arm.

Toby began to panic and pull, and the jaguar lowered itself farther to the ground, planting its back legs and jerking the boy towards the forest. Katie's dormant maternal instinct roared to life, and she dived at Toby, snatching his legs to keep the jaguar from dragging him fully into the forest.

With his scream echoing in her head, she staggered up and started pummeling the jaguar's face, shouting for it to let the sobbing baby angel go. The jaguar winced but kept its grip, and Toby's blood turned the snow beneath them red.

A blast of energy whipped by her, knocking her back, and the jaguar was sent flying. It smashed into a tree. Toby sagged. She looked up, shocked to see Sasha standing over them, his sharp gaze on the creature preparing itself for a second attack.

"Go back to the grass! Demons can't cross onto sacred grounds!" Sasha shouted, snatching her arm and hauling her up.

She dropped on one knee beside Toby, who was unconscious. Tears in her eyes, she whispered to him as she lifted him, tormented by the sound of his whimper. She half-stumbled, half-ran to the park area before tripping and falling flat. Toby rolled from her arms.

"I went as fast ... as I could ..." Ully gasped, reaching them. Following him was Kris, dressed in nothing but judo pants, as if Ully had dragged him straight out of bed. She crawled on her knees to Toby, heart hammering and hands shaking as she rolled him onto his back. The slash in his arm was deep, and maroon blood bubbled into the snow.

"Kris ..." she whispered, a different kind of panic rising within her.

He swept the baby angel into his arms with one quick motion and trotted back into the castle. Katie was slower to follow, feeling lightheaded once again. Ully helped her up, and they both eyed Sasha as the Dark One's servant approached.

"I hate demons," he said with another look over his shoulder. She recognized the crazed look from when he'd attacked her in Hell and inched closer to Ully.

He motioned to the castle. Ully looked at her, even more pale than usual, and she retreated to the castle, worried sick about Toby and Rhyn, even knowing the half-demon could take out half the demons in Hell if he felt like it. The only two people she cared about in this godforsaken world were both fighting for their lives.

Rhyn tossed the demon against the wall with enough power to break its back. The full-blooded demon was slow to rise, and he waited. Jared changed to his human form and held up one hand, holding his back with the other.

"Truce," he said. Rhyn growled in response but switched to his human form as well. "You know, you're not too bad for a half-breed."

"I'm half Immortal, half demon. Means I can play in both worlds, unlike you."

"I see that now. Your monkey is safe. Why don't we call it a draw for now, half-brother?"

"Only if you tell me what you're doing here," Rhyn replied.

He sensed the demon's pain behind its attempt at a chipper tone. Most who challenged him soon learned just how wild and deep his power ran. As both a demon and Immortal, he possessed the ability to wield both sources of power but not control them. At least, he hadn't been able to control them before meeting Katie. If this had been a pre-Katie battle, he'd have wiped out the state. He couldn't help but feel satisfied at besting a full demon *and* controlling his powers.

"I'm sure we'll be able to beat each other to a pulp again sometime," Jared continued. "Every demon on this mortal planet is hunting Sasha."

"Sasha? What do the demons want with Sasha?"

"The demons want revenge. We were both inmates in his zoo in Hell long enough to know how charming he was. He pissed off the wrong people."

"Not good enough," Rhyn said and started toward the injured demon. "I don't give a shit about Sasha."

"And … AND," Jared rushed on, holding up both hands, "he stole something from the Dark One, something that makes demons immune to Immortal powers. It has something to do with your blood monkey. I'm too lowly a demon to know what, but I overheard them talking about it when they came to free us from our cell block."

"The Dark One unleashed *all* of Sasha's pets?" Rhyn asked, the feeling of doom making him jittery.

"All of us."

"The demons and were-things and the Dark One's personal creations."

"Oh, my," Jared said.

"Then I've got a long list of creatures to kill, starting with you."

"Now, wait, half-brother," Jared said. "I'll admit you have the advantage here. I'm not interested in revenge like the rest of my brethren. Those demons Sasha killed really deserved it. I just wanted to eat your blood monkey because she smelled so good, I figured she'd taste even better. That's all I wanted. But I don't have to do that. I can just walk away. Or I can help you. You're going to need some allies to face what's coming your way."

Rhyn considered the words born of desperation. There was truth in everything Jared said. He knew Jared well enough after all their years in Hell together to understand the creature was too narcissistic to care about another's issues. If anything, Jared wanted just what he said: a good snack on his way to find more good snacks.

Brute force usually won any battle he fought. Recently, he'd begun thinking he'd need more if he were taking on demons, Immortals, and anything else the Dark One would throw at him. All he needed was to figure out how to win a game of strategy he didn't know how to play, before his time was up and he lost the only thing that mattered.

"Well?" Jared asked, the confidence in his voice replaced by unease.

"If you betray me, Sasha will seem like an angel," Rhyn said, straightening out of his fighting stance. "There are demons in the forest surrounding the Immortals' winter stronghold. Have you any aversion to killing your own kind?"

"None."

"I'll take you there to hunt. You'll go nowhere near my blood monkey, and if any of our demon brethren attack her, you'll defend her. Remember, you'll be the first I come for if you betray me."

"Deal."

Rhyn studied the demon, aware he could never trust such a creature fully. But, if he could get some use out of him before it came time to kill him, he might have a better chance of protecting Katie.

"Follow me."

Rhyn opened the portal to the shadow world and walked through the damp fog to the forest outside the castle. Jared limped after him and appeared beside him on the cliff edge, taking in the morning view of grey skies and green forest with a look of distaste.

"I smell two demons, and blood," the demon said, raising his head to the wind. "Angel? You have an angel here? Their blood reeks!"

Rhyn's mind went to Toby, the baby angel he'd amused by shredding pillows. Jared's senses were more acute than his, and he turned to face the direction of the castle. Something had happened while he was gone.

"Go and hunt," he said. Fire slid through his body as he contorted and changed shapes. Jared stepped back as Rhyn launched himself into the air as a hellish bird reminiscent of a pterodactyl. His long wings beat the air as he rose, and it took him a short two minutes to soar over the castle.

The stark red of blood against white snow caught his attention, and he circled the park behind the castle. There were two splashes of blood, one at the tree line and another nearer the castle. He changed forms in midair and dropped the half dozen feet to the ground, smelling Toby's blood as he landed near it. He smelled Katie's, too, and was unable to quell the surge of lust that ran through him. He entered the castle, following the scents up the back stairwell that Katie alone used to avoid the other Immortals.

The trail led him to Kris's large chamber, and he strode in without knocking. Toby was in Kris's bed, the pale baby angel stripped down to his waist and unconscious. Ully and Kris carefully wrapped one of his arms in gauze. Katie sat on Kris's couch, glassy-eyed while her own wound went untreated. Rhyn's anger stirred at the sight of her bleeding alone, and he crossed to her, snatching the first aid kit off the bed.

Kris's gaze went from emerald to amber, and he strode across the room to meet him. Rhyn nearly decked him when the blond brother shoved him back.

"Get the fuck out, Rhyn!" Kris snapped. "And don't try to tell me that black cat wasn't you! You're one twisted—"

"Kris!" Katie interjected, standing unsteadily. "It wasn't him. He was off fighting some demon that attacked me."

"You stay out of this!"

"No, Kris, I won't! You're too quick to blame everyone else! It's my fault Toby was wandering around without someone watching him, but really, Kris, who assigns a woman an Immortal kid that's not even her own and expects her to know what to do with it?"

"I'm up to here with your lip. Sit down and shut up, Katie!"

Rhyn was content to let them fight when he thought she was winning, like she normally did. He sensed Kris's agitation was increased by the ensnaring scent of Katie's blood, which was heavy in the air. At Kris's angry response, Rhyn shoved his brother out of his path.

"Talk to my mate like that again, *brother*, and I'll fuck up this castle and everyone in it before you can think of stopping me." He crossed to Katie and sat on the ottoman in front of her. She sat, dazed. Kris's gaze burned a hole in his back, but Rhyn ignored him. Instead, he focused hard on cleaning up her blood and bandaging her arm before the scent drove him too wild to control himself.

"I want you gone, Rhyn. Be out of here by nightfall," Kris said at last, his voice quiet and hard.

"You all won't live long if I go, Kris. The forest is full of demons out for Sasha's head, and the Dark One may be sending more of its creatures. At this point, I'm the only thing capable of standing between you and the monsters in the forest," Rhyn replied with calmness he didn't feel.

He felt Katie's gaze on him and looked up from the bandage, his eyes lingering on her face. Her surprise echoed what he felt from Kris. He was trying not to let the feel of Katie's skin heat his blood, but her nearness and direct gaze lit him afire.

A half-demon outcast didn't deserve anything so delicate or beautiful, but Death help him, he wanted her more than anything else in his life. He didn't even know yet if he could protect anyone's ass, except his own. He dropped his gaze to the bandage, and he finished it in a hurry. If he didn't leave soon, and she kept looking at him like that, he'd make love to her right there.

"Toby needs a healer," Ully said from the bedside.

"I know where to find one," Rhyn said, his thoughts going to the Ancient healer that had been a prisoner in Sasha's zoo in Hell across the hall from his own cell. He stood without looking at Katie. "I'll be back. Keep everyone out of the forest, Kris."

He stalked to the door, sexual frustration and anger in his blood again. He jogged through the castle and ran out into the snow, launching himself into the cold air as he changed into the bird form. For once, he was grateful for the coldness chilling his fevered skin.

For the second time in as many days, Rhyn surprised her. She wasn't expecting his ministrations—however rough and sloppy they were—or his mouthing off to Kris.

And neither was Kris. The Immortals' leader cursed and paced for a few minutes after Rhyn left before disappearing into the hallway. She rose, still wobbly, and crossed to the bed, perching on it beside Ully. The sight of Toby's near lifeless features made her feel sick to her stomach. She brushed hair away from the child's face. His sweet smell and the feel of his soft skin lingered in her senses after she'd carried him from the forest. She'd never noticed how a kid smelled, like fresh sunshine.

"You think he'll be okay?" she asked in a hushed voice.

"I don't know," Ully answered. "I think a healer can fix him. I think he's just sleeping for now."

She touched the baby angel's hand. She'd never known the type of terror that tore through her when she saw the jaguar snatch him. The image replayed itself in her mind, and guilt flooded her. It shouldn't have taken almost losing him for her to realize how vulnerable he was. He was hundreds of thousands of mortal years old, but less than half a dozen in angel years. Without Gabriel, Toby had no one but her.

"How is he?" At Sasha's voice, they both turned. A tremor of fear went through her, and Ully crept closer, as if she had half a chance of defending them. She wrapped a hand around her throat protectively.

"Fine," Ully whispered. "Sleeping."

Sasha's gaze took them both in, his eyes settling on her bandaged arm before he forced himself to look at Toby.

"I didn't know we had a baby angel in our midst. Demons don't normally attack them, unless they were trying to draw you outside the sacred grounds, Katie," he said. "They taste awful."

"I don't think you should be here," Katie said, anger rising at his considering look at Toby.

"Very well. I'm in the chamber beside yours if you need anything." While quiet, his words were meant as the threat she took them to be. She was still staring at the doorway when Kris walked through. He strode to his walk-in closet and snatched a sweater and boots.

"What the hell is going on, Kris?" she demanded.

"Later."

"No, Kris, now. Toby and I have been attacked by demons, and Sasha's wandering around the castle like he owns the place."

"I don't expect you to understand. What's clear is that your *mate* is still out of control. Sasha can help me break the bond so you don't have to deal with that anymore."

"What bond?" she asked.

"The bond between you and Rhyn. You wanted your life back, didn't you?" he asked pointedly.

"Yes, but—"

"I need Sasha's help. He's a deviant. He knows how to do things no Immortal has ever done. He brought us a vial of blood to replace you as a test subject, and he knows where we can find the information to break your bond to Rhyn."

She was silent, surprised as much by his information as she was by the turning of her stomach at the thought of losing Rhyn.

I have to do it before Gabriel comes for me.

"It won't hurt him or me, will it?" she asked.

"I don't know yet, but if it must hurt one of you, it'll be my dear little brother, who is a blight to Immortals and humans alike." His words were spoken with an unusual amount of venom. "Besides, the bond between angel and human cannot be broken, so you'll have to take care of Toby until you die."

"Why do you hate Rhyn so much?" She watched him stop lacing his boots. A haunted look crossed his face.

"I want what he took from me," he said quietly. "I can't have it, and so neither shall he."

The look on his face made her bite her tongue to keep from saying anything else. Weeks ago, when she'd been at the Sanctuary, Gabriel entrusted her with the secret of what had caused Kris to turn on Rhyn. It involved a woman, Kris's intended mate. She was working with the Dark One, and Rhyn had killed for that reason. And no one had ever told Kris. She ached to, but she doubted he'd believe her.

Kris finished tying his boots and crossed to the door, slamming it on his way out. Ully jumped beside her.

"Do you think Toby is okay to move?" she asked, afraid to be there when Kris returned. "I want to put him in my bed so he doesn't wake up scared."

"We can try it," Ully said. "I don't like being around Kris when he's in a mood."

"Me neither," she agreed.

They carefully lifted the sleeping angel and carried him up a flight of stairs to her large chamber. Katie arranged the bedding and pillows around his still form and then retrieved his stuffed animals out of his bedroom.

"Next Thursday is Thanksgiving," Ully started as they settled on either side of the bed. "Kris does a big feast here every year, and Andre used to arrange the December holiday celebration. All the Immortals who are someone are here by mid-December."

She recalled what sent her outside the castle, and her anger at Kris ratcheted up another notch. He was planning something, if he invited Hannah to the castle.

"Ully, is there any way to see if my sister is coming here? Her fiancé is an Immortal."

"Kris keeps a roster. We can have his private secretary check it. Write down the names, and I'll take it down," he offered. "I need to grab some grub, too. I can bring you dinner, if you want."

"Yes, thanks," she said and stretched for the pen and paper she kept in the nightstand drawer next to the bed. She scribbled down Hannah and Gio's names then sat back, frowning. "I guess it really is Thanksgiving next week. Doesn't seem like it's been that long since …" She trailed off, pensive.

"Time passes fast for Immortals. I guess when you stop counting hours and days and just count months or years—"

"I need to grab something. I can take this down," she said suddenly, standing. He looked surprised. "What do you want me to bring you?"

He listed a few items, none of which she heard as she continued to stare at the paper. When he finished, she nodded and hurried away. She dropped a note into the absent secretary's inbox then went to the first basement level, which housed supplies, clothing, and other essentials in the form of small department stores whose wares were free to all Immortals. She visited the small café and dropped three boxed lunches into a tote bag along with extra cocoa and marshmallows in case Toby woke up soon. She continued to the small women's boutique that stocked every kind of facial and body care product she'd ever heard of—and many she hadn't.

Two other Immortals lingered in the aisle of interest to her, and she browsed the small selection of feminine hygiene products, aware they only stocked a few brands for the few Immortal mates who were human. She made a show of reading the back of a box of tampons until the Immortals left. Only then did she venture closer to where they'd been and snag a small box smoothly from the shelf, pushing it under everything else to the bottom of the bag.

On her way back to her room, she poked her head into Kris's secretary's office. The slender Immortal glanced up from his computer.

"Saw your note," he said with a quick smile. He pulled a printout from beneath his computer and scanned it. "They should be here … tonight. I'm sending a car to the airport at about two. It's a three-hour trek, so you can expect them between five and six."

"Thanks," she said and left, feeling as if the timing couldn't be worse for her sister to show up. She wondered if Hannah knew yet about the Immortals and how Katie's tattoo hadn't been the result of a fling in Ireland as she led her sister to believe. She tucked the small box into her jeans pocket and covered the bulge with her sweater, ducking into the bathroom to hide it before rejoining Ully for their small lunch.

Chapter Three

"So this is where you're hiding out," Rhyn said.

Gabriel whipped around at the voice, lowering the weapon that emerged instinctively at the sound of a stranger in his home. Rhyn kept his distance, knowing just how jumpy an assassin could be. Gabriel was at his place in the underworld, a small cottage tucked into Death's realm, in the Everdark forest of Immortal trees whose hissing, fanlike leaves and snake-like branches moved to catch the quiet wind. Gabriel's small cottage was lit by a single candle that cast light on a collection of weapons along one wall and a few books on a bookshelf on another.

"I didn't think you could come here," the assassin said.

"The Code says I shouldn't, not that I can't. Important distinction," Rhyn replied and pulled out a chair from the table on which the candle was placed. He straddled the chair and rested his forearms on its back. "You left without saying goodbye."

Gabriel rubbed his face, and Rhyn saw the shadow of stubble the assassin never allowed to grow. Something was really wrong if Gabriel's thousands-year-old habit changed suddenly.

"I didn't have a choice," Gabriel said with some difficulty. "Death owns me now."

Rhyn understood without asking. Gabriel had always been a free man; now the human-turned Immortal was a slave.

"Welcome to my world," he said with a chuckle. "You'll find making friends is hard when everyone hates you."

"I'm beginning to see that. Didn't realize I liked having some sort of free will."

"You still have choices. Just none of them are good."

Gabriel snorted in response.

"Since I know I can drop in on you whenever I want, I promise to come back," Rhyn continued. "I need a hand finding an Ancient healer named Lankha."

"Your girl hurt again?"

"I suppose you'll be the latest to tell me she's better off without me," Rhyn said. "But no, it's not her this time. It's Toby."

Gabriel frowned and ran a hand through his hair. Rhyn watched him, concerned at finding his sole friend so affected by the recent change in his life. He sensed much more amiss than Gabriel would ever admit.

"The healers moved to the other side of the Immortal world, past Elisia and closer to Hell. I can't take you, but here." He held out his hand. Rhyn stretched to tap fists with him, and the portal information lit up his thoughts. He'd spent most his life in Hell and remembered little of the Immortal world.

"I'll come back," Rhyn promised, rising.

"Rhyn," Gabriel said quietly. "I don't think our friendship will survive what comes."

"We are both bound to our destinies, Gabriel, something you taught me. Whatever that brings, you've been my only brother and friend," Rhyn replied in the same tone.

When the assassin turned away, Rhyn stepped into the living forest. He opened the portal and stepped into the shadow world, envisioning the place Gabriel had passed to him. One of the portals glowed in response, and he strode through it, stepping into a world as sunny as Gabriel's was dark. He smelled the ocean and stood on a beach of red sand edged with small shrubs. He walked up the beach and into the shrubs, finding a path that led to a small village of red cottages. Far across the sea, he saw the black walls of Hell stretching from water to sky.

The healers' village consisted of several dozen cottages around a central square, in which many of the village's people gathered and talked or cooked meals over red flames. They grew silent when he appeared, and those nearest him scattered. He'd thought Lankha skittish when he met the healer but soon found all the healers quaking and hiding.

"Lankha!" he belted, unable to distinguish one healer from the other. They all had Lankha's flat face, no nose, bug eyes, and scrawny little bodies with feathery hands. The healers scattered like roaches in daylight. Rhyn snagged the clothing of one, and the healer yelped. "Come out, Lankha, or I eat everyone in your village, starting with this one!"

He heard whispers traded behind doors and cottages and waited.

"I'll count to three. One!"

"I'm heeeeere," one timid voice said. "What bringsss a demon to my hoooooome?"

He recognized the healer by the amount of bands winding around his arm. Each one represented a millennium, and this creature had been around longer than Rhyn's deceased brother, Andre. He released the healer whose arm he held.

"Come with me," Rhyn ordered, opening a portal. Lankha hesitated but moved forward with a look over his shoulder at the village. Rhyn waited until the healer passed him and then stepped into the shadow world behind him.

Lankha's head hung, as if he walked to his death. He trailed as Rhyn led him toward the brightest portal, and Rhyn took the healer's arm to hurry him along. They stepped into the snowy yard outside the castle. He all but dragged the healer to Kris's room, found it empty, then went to Katie's chamber. He flung the door open and shoved the healer into the room, ignoring the two surprised occupants of the chamber as he closed the door without entering.

The whiff of Katie's blood nearly undid him. He hadn't eaten in too long, and to have his mate so close … Rhyn took the stairs two at a time until he reached the roof. He launched himself off the rooftop, hungry and determined to find a demon to bleed dry. He flew to the forest and shape shifted into a jaguar as he dropped to the ground, taking off through the forest. The exercise felt good, and he ran and leapt and clambered up trees until he was panting. It was after his adrenaline tapered off that he smelled blood, and he trotted down a path in the direction of the scent.

What he found didn't surprise him. Jared, wounded and vulnerable, had been cornered by another demon in its monster shape with drool dripping off its teeth. Jared was pale and propped against a rock. Happy the demon could draw his lunch out of the forest, Rhyn pounced on the demon, cracking its neck before it could fight. He tossed the creature to the side for later and shifted into his human form.

"Nature's not so kind to the weak," Jared said with a grimace as he pushed himself up.

"You're not of any use to me like this."

"Here's where you're wrong, half-breed. The reason I'm lying here in pain has to do with my accidental ambush of Darkyn's demons," the demon replied. "Are you going to eat all of him?" He motioned to the demon's carcass a short distance from them.

"Depends on if what you have to say is worthwhile."

"Fair enough. In any case, Darkyn's demons are planning to invade the castle, where your sweet little morsel is, so they can slaughter every last annoying Immortal."

"Demons can't cross the sacred grounds."

"They have an insider. And apparently, he alone knows how to render the grounds no longer sacred."

Rhyn's thoughts went to Katie. "Did they say when?"

"They noticed me then, so no. Help a brother out, Rhyn. I'm no good to you here in this shape. I need to go to Hell for a demon healer. I'll promise to return."

"Fine." He no longer felt hungry despite the scent of blood. While he didn't care what happened to Kris, he did care about Katie and when the demons would choose to attack. He'd suspected Sasha was there for more than one reason and didn't doubt his brother had a plan.

Kris would never listen to him. The only other brother ever to extend a hand to help him was Kiki, the pragmatic half-brother who protected Asia. Rumor had it the Council hadn't agreed on anything in a few hundred years, and Rhyn began to think the brothers he hated might be the solution to the demons.

Or he could take Katie, disappear, and leave Kris and the Immortals to their fate. He preferred this idea, except that it would mean he'd be defending her from Dark One's minions and demons every minute of the rest of their lives together. Reluctantly, he accepted the fact that he needed the protection of the Immortals to keep Katie safe. If Kris didn't call the Council together, Rhyn would drag his bastard brothers kicking and screaming to the castle, dangle them over the forest of demons, and offer them a choice: him or the demons. Cynically, he suspected all but Kiki would choose the demons.

"Lankha?" Katie asked, startled to see the cowering healer in her room. She'd last seen him in Hell, where they shared a cell together. "Are you okay?"

The healer was huddled against the door, looking around with visible horror. His gaze settled on her, and he ventured forward.

"What is it?" Ully whispered.

"He's the oldest of the healers," she replied. She stood and crossed to the scared creature and took one of his soft hands. He went without resistance. She led him to the bed. "Rhyn brought you here to help our friend, Lankha."

The healer sank next to her on the bed, large eyes darting around the room as if he expected the furniture to grow fangs and chase him. His gaze finally fell to Toby, and he inched forward. Ully watched with alarm as the healer unwrapped the angel's bandage. She felt like petting the healer to calm him as she might Toby's cat but suspected it wouldn't be welcome. She grimaced when he peeled back the final layer of bandages to reveal the gouge and broken bones beneath.

The healer clucked to himself, growing more comfortable as he concentrated on his trade. Katie moved out of his way. A tap at the door made Lankha pause, and she hurried to answer it to keep the healer from being distracted.

"Madame, your sister's car has just entered the property," Kris's personal secretary said. "I thought you might wish to greet her."

Katie could think of nothing she wanted less, but she nodded. She changed quickly into dry clothing before hurrying down the back stairwell. With her arm bleeding, she couldn't risk drawing the attention of the Immortals by taking the front stairwell even to meet her sister. She went the back way—the servant's route, as Kris had so kindly informed her—to the front door.

The white Hummer limo made it up the snowy slope and slowed as it crossed the cleared cobblestone drive in front of the castle. It stopped, and two footmen went to the doors while two others opened the trunk.

Appearing refreshed and thrilled, beautiful, blond Hannah stepped from the Hummer and looked up, awe crossing her features. She was dressed in a long, white fur coat that Katie had no doubt cost more than a small house. Hannah's boots were white, her cream slacks and camel turtleneck completing her flawless look.

As usual, Katie felt a twinge of jealousy at the sight of her sister that only grew when Giovanni—Hannah's handsome fiancé—circled the car to take her arm and lead her to the stairs to the castle. Rhyn was about as uncivilized as Gio was civilized. Katie despised Gio most days, but sometimes, she wondered what a normal relationship was like. She didn't hear Kris draw abreast until the man stood at her side, staring at the gorgeous woman approaching.

"*That's* your sister?" he asked in clear astonishment. "What's this guy's name?"

"Giovanni de Medici, descendent of the Italian de Medici," his secretary answered from behind them.

"Oh. I think I've heard his name before. How did *he* get an invite here?" Both of them looked at Katie, and Kris pursed his lips.

"I was going to ask you the same about Hannah," she said with a glare. "Another of your tricks, Kris?"

"It's customary," Henri said. "Social propriety states that the immediate family of an Ancient's mate or high level Immortal—"

"You can't tell me this was an accident!"

The smallest of smiles crossed Kris's face, but he refused to answer.

"You are the biggest jackass in the world," she hissed. "You drag my sister here? Why, to keep me here?"

"You forced me to bring Rhyn here," he reminded her. "I say we're even."

"Aren't you sworn not to interfere with mortals?"

"I'm not interfering," he said with a sharp look. "Even if I don't need your blood, I'd be a fool to let you go."

"You swore an oath!"

"I take my oaths seriously, but I can't let you go for the demons to get you. They developed immunity blood the last time they had you. Consider your sister—"

"A hostage!"

"—a guest for an indefinite period of time. Besides, she's an Immortal's mate. She belongs to me anyway."

Before she could respond, Kris strode from the doorway down the path, stopping in front of the two approaching. Gio bowed deeply, but Hannah gazed up at Kris with a look of such admiration that Katie suddenly realized Hannah wasn't likely to object to staying in such a place. Kris greeted Gio, stepping aside to walk them up the path. Hannah's gaze strayed beyond Kris to catch sight of Katie. She gave an excited wave and quickened her step. For her sake, Katie tried not to look as pissed as she felt and trotted down the stairs to meet her sister. Hannah enveloped her in a warm hug that smelled of expensive perfume.

"Is this your home now?" Hannah asked, her glowing gaze going to the castle again. Well aware of Hannah's social ladder climbing aspirations, Katie couldn't help her retort.

"Don't act so surprised your little sis did something right for once."

"Who is that handsome man with Gio?" Hannah asked, gaze on Kris once again.

"The world's biggest dick," Katie replied.

"Katherine!" Hannah exclaimed. "You don't want him to hear you. Come, show me around."

Katie hesitated, then strode through the main hallways, suspecting Hannah would be too star struck to notice the looks they'd certainly receive from others.

"Where's that wonderful man of yours?" Hannah asked.

"Wonderful?" she repeated. "You mean Rhyn?"

Hannah chuckled, soon distracted as her gaze took in the entertaining parlor Katie led her to. She vaguely remembered it from her tour of the castle and was relieved to see several small groups congregated around all but one of the five fireplaces in the room. She went to the unoccupied fireplace and sat with her back to the wall, afraid of any Immortal who felt her draw enough to approach. Hannah removed her fur coat with a graceful flourish to reveal her snug clothing and perfect body. One of the servants darted forward to take her coat, and she gave a large smile before seating herself.

"So, tell me about this place," Hannah said, eyes bright.

"Where should I start?" Katie asked, uncertain what her sister knew.

"Gio told me about the Immortals. I'm still puzzling through that part. Who was the man who greeted us?"

"His name is Kris. He's sort of the leader of the Immortals. He's a manipulative, lying jackass."

"He seemed nice to me," Hannah said. Her familiar way of dismissing her opinion made Katie bite her tongue to keep from saying what she wanted.

"You staying here long?" she asked instead.

"Through the winter. I planned on going to Seychelles to escape the east coast cold, but Gio said being invited here was an honor. Then he told me about the Immortals. You landed yourself a good one, Katherine."

"I didn't *land* anything," Katie said impatiently. "We're destined to be Immortals' mates, and it's been as far from a pleasant experience as I could imagine. You just wait to see what Kris has in store for you. He'll make your life a living hell."

"You've always been a little melodramatic, Katherine. How can you still seem so negative when you're surrounded by all *this!*"

Katie clenched her jaw, realizing just how sugar-coated the Immortals' world around her would look to her sister. Gio appeared in the doorway. He caught sight of them and crossed to Hannah. He appeared more unsettled than Katie had ever seen him. His gaze was roving, and his air distracted even as he bent to give Hannah a kiss on the cheek.

"I'll catch up with you later, love," he said. "I've got some business to attend to with the other Immortals."

"Of course, my Gio," Hannah said sweetly. "I'll be with Katherine, if you need to find me."

Gio's tight smile was fleeting. Katie wondered what had called him away—news of the demons in the forest or some other awful plan by Kris? She watched him go, frowning when he turned left down the hall toward the front door rather than right to the stairwell or interior of the castle.

"Excuse me, sis," she said, rising. "Just tell one of the waiters what you want to drink."

Hannah was happy to marvel over her surroundings. Katie moved quickly through the room, refusing to meet the gaze of any of the Immortals. She emerged into the hallway in time to see a butler open the main door for Gio.

She trotted after him and stepped into the evening chill. The hidden sun was setting, and the white snow clouds glowed eerily, lit by the last rays of light. Hannah's fiancé hurried to the waiting Hummer. Hannah's Louis Vuitton luggage was lined up neatly along the path, and Katie skirted it.

"Gio!" she called. "Where are you going?"

"Katherine," he replied, turning. "You will have to forgive me. Assure Hannah this was not my idea."

"What wasn't your idea?"

"Kris asked me to bring her here. He thought she might be an Ancient's mate like you."

"Okay, so why are you leaving her?"

Gio hesitated before sighing. "He asked me to. He granted me a position directly supporting the Council, if I walked away from her forever."

"So you traded her for your ego," Katie said and crossed her arms.

"The Immortal society is not like a human's, Katherine," he scolded. "You cannot marry into a higher rung on the ladder.

You can only be granted special status by someone in a caste far above you."

"Don't you care about hurting her feelings?"

"Hannah used me to climb the social ladder, and I did not mind, because she is a beautiful, sweet girl," he said. "I, in turn, used her to climb the Immortal ladder."

Speechless, Katie couldn't help thinking Gio was as shallow as her sister. That didn't stop her from being angry at the man who would dump her sister off to deal with the hell she'd gone through.

"Leave this be, Katie." Kris's voice came from the doorway behind her. "Gio, go. Your service is eternally appreciated."

Gio bowed and got into the Hummer. The door closed, and the long vehicle pulled away. Katie faced Kris with a glare.

"What the hell are you doing, Kris?" she demanded. "Isn't it enough that I'm here?"

"I expected your sister to be as rough around the edges as you are," he said. "I'm glad she's not, and she seems to understand trading personal happiness for a social status. She's an Ancient's mate, Katie, like you. How there were two of you born into one family, I don't know."

"You can't make her stay."

"From what Gio says, she'll *want* to stay, and I doubt she'd consider mating with someone like me abhorrent."

"If you'll remember, I didn't choose which Ancient to become my mate. What if she chooses one of your brothers?" she challenged.

"We'll know soon who she chooses," he said. His gaze went to her throat. "Two Ancients' mates in the same family. Maybe you are more like Rhyn than I gave you credit for. Both of you are blemishes on your family."

He walked back into the castle, leaving her with burning cheeks. She looked up at the glowing clouds, from which snow had begun to fall again. Tears stung her cheeks. As she thought of Toby, she wondered how much of what Kris said was true. He wouldn't have been hurt if not for her, and Hannah may not have been dragged into the Immortal world if she hadn't hit the radar of Kris.

She wiped her face, determined not to abandon her sister as Gio had. She walked the short distance into the house and down the hallway, stopping when she reached the doorway. Kris wore a rare, charming smile as he sat across from Hannah, talking. Hannah's face glowed as she gazed at Kris's handsome features. Kris caught Katie's gaze and shook his head ever so slightly, warning her against coming in.

She watched for a long moment and then left, defeated and frustrated. She returned to her chamber, where Lankha still worked his magic on an unconscious Toby under Ully's watchful gaze.

The sight of Toby's blood made her feel sick, and her own blood loss made her dizzy. It was her fault he was hurt. She was an awful foster mom. Maybe Gabriel taking her to Death would make the lives of those around her easier.

Rather than join them, she paced the hall before following it to its end and ascending to the roof. The night was cold and the wind nonexistent. Snow soon covered her arms as she crossed the roof to gaze into the well-lit courtyard. Too tired to fight her tears anymore, she let them fall and stood shaking on the rooftop.

"What're you doing up here?"

She turned in time to see Rhyn drop with an audible crunch from the air to the snowy roof. Her misery increased at the physical reminder that she hadn't figured out what to do about him yet.

"Thinking," she replied.

"Dangerous."

"For you, maybe."

He drew near but stopped just out of arms' reach, alerted by her sharp tone. Embarrassed by her tears, she turned away. Mercifully, he said nothing, only stood close to her and stared into the same sky. Even at the safe distance, his body heat made her uncomfortably warm.

"You think we'll all survive this?" she asked at last.

"Probably not. As long as I take Kris down with me, I don't give a shit."

She stifled a laugh, and he gave her a sidelong glance.

"I got time if you do," he added. "You can't fuck a man once when he's outta prison and never again."

"You're on probation," she reminded him. "And your time is running short."

"Got it covered."

"Do you?"

"More or less."

"I'm not convinced."

"Seems stupid for us to stand here when we both want each other so bad," he said. "I thought we were making progress. I was good last night."

"I feel like your life and Toby's and Hannah's would be better without me in it," she said and faced him.

"I think you're afraid. Your life is shitty and you have one good thing going for you. You're the only good part of my life. I assume it's the same for you."

She said nothing at his words, surprised as always by his backhanded compliments and tormented by the knowledge that she had to do something that would hurt them both. He stepped closer until they were toe-to-toe. She craned her head back to hold his silver gaze, a tremor of desire working its way through her.

Maybe tomorrow she'd break it off. She didn't want to lose him just yet.

"I thought I made your life more difficult," she said to keep from falling into a dangerous silence.

"That, too. You're as tough as an egg dropped from a ten-story building. Really hard to rescue. Gets annoying."

"I didn't ask for this!" Her face burned at his bluntness. She was frustrated to feel more tears rise. "I'm tired of all this shit. I have no say in anything, and in the end, we're all screwed! Go back to killing things, Rhyn." She turned her back to him, hoping he'd fly off in his pterodactyl form or disappear into the depths of the forest as a jaguar.

She felt his warmth at her back instead. He draped his arms around her and pulled her against him, resting his chin on her head. She wiped her face, afraid to let herself feel pleasure in the warm body pressed against hers on such a cold night. Every time he touched her, her resolve melted. He smelled of his own musk and darkness, an alluring mix that made her blood burn.

She missed him. The sense of yearning was deep. She barely knew the man at her back, but she'd felt his absence even during the few hours in the day they weren't together. Gabriel's words and her nightmare haunted her, reminded her she couldn't let herself fall in love with him now.

"Rhyn …" She trailed off, not at all sure what she wanted to say. "Do you ever think we're better off not being together?"

"No," he said, though he shifted behind her. "Do you?"

"Yeah, sometimes."

"I think we make a good pair."

"Why?" she asked.

"No one else could put up with either of us."

She wanted to be offended by his comment but suspected he spoke the truth.

"We will make things work," he said.

"I really don't know, Rhyn."

"It doesn't matter what you think. You're already mine."

She forced herself to pull away from him. "I want to like you, Rhyn, I really do, but sometimes I don't think you know how bad things are."

"You more than like me, but you're too scared to admit it. Say whatever you want, Katie, but this is happening."

"Now you'll tell me you know how I feel because you read my mind." She leveled a glare on him.

"If I feel like it, I see every thought that crosses your mind. Like Kris saying he'd break the mating bond between us. Kris can't do it, by the way. You're stuck with me."

She stared at him, surprised. He was unfazed by the idea that traumatized her. Another thought occurred to her about her trip to the boutique earlier that day.

"What else have you read?" she asked cautiously.

"I haven't since yesterday morning. Trying to be *good*."

"Thank you," she said, relieved.

"Kiss? Breakfast tea? It ain't easy being a *good* demon."

Her emotions felt too raw to deal with him: anger, desire, regret. She didn't have the strength this night to tell him to go.

"I can't, Rhyn. I have to check on Toby," she said and moved past him before she changed her mind. "I've failed miserably in my role as a foster mom, and he nearly died because of it."

"What happened to Toby wasn't your fault." She paused at his words and turned to look at him again. "None of you knew about the demons in the forest, and you were right about what you said to Kris."

"I think I like it better when you're hard to get along with," she said with some frustration. "You're not making things easier."

"Life is anything but easy." For the first time that night, she realized he was disturbed about something. Rhyn gazed at her, considering. "I don't want to lose you, Katie."

She looked down. If she didn't find a way to push him away, she risked messing up both of their lives. She loved him, but she couldn't let him love her.

"Don't you have a checklist or something I can follow so I know what I'm supposed to be doing?" he asked.

"If there were a checklist for relationships, everyone would have a happy ending," she responded. "Do I feel whatever it is between us? Do I miss you even when I know I can call you and you'd come without question? Yes, but I don't trust you, Rhyn. It takes more than killing things, and I'm done being chewed on, mauled, and treated like crap by you Immortal idiots."

He said nothing.

"What we have is not enough for me. Do you get that?" she asked.

"What happened between last night and tonight?" His gaze had turned predatory again.

"Nothing. I just realized I can't be with someone I can't rely on, Rhyn." Her words sounded cheap, even to her ears. She turned and all but fled the rooftop, cursing herself for her weakness and the tears in her eyes.

She pushed the door open to her room and gazed at Toby. Color had returned to his face, and Lankha was curled up in a ball at the end of the bed with Ully snoring in a chair. She sat at the edge of the bed and touched Toby's soft face, not sure what to do or think about anything anymore, especially now that Hannah had been dragged into this world.

Kris watched the door to the guest bedchamber close, unusually hopeful about his discovery. He padded down the hall to his room, where Sasha awaited him.

"So I was right," Sasha said as he entered. "One more feather in my cap."

"And a trail of dead bodies you'll never make up for," Kris replied. Sasha shrugged, unconcerned. "How did you know?"

"When I tasted the sister, I saw her mind. I saw what they both were."

Kris poured himself chilled whiskey from the small refrigerator tucked in a corner. He took a sip, gaze going to the snow falling outside the window. Sasha's words reminded him that he, too, had *tasted* Katie. She'd tasted so sweet, and he prayed her sister tasted the same. She had a reason to hate him after what he'd done, and he'd been unable to apologize. He'd hoped to use Sasha's knowledge to break her bond to Rhyn and mate with her himself, despite their hostile relationship. Now, he may not have to. There was more than one Ancient's mate.

For the first time since Andre's death, things were looking better for him.

He felt the weight of his brother's death on his shoulders again. Andre had been his confidante and mentor whose guidance had helped him navigate his role as the Immortals' leader. Without him, Kris felt as if he were alone trying to solve the world's problems.

"Tell me why the forest is crawling with demons," he said and turned to Sasha. "And why their leader is demanding an audience with me to discuss you."

The smiled faded from his half-brother's face, and Sasha's gaze went to the fire. "My people figured out the right mix of Rhyn's girl's blood to give immunity to whoever has it. I was under some … pressure from the demons after some stupid misunderstanding regarding Darkyn's daughter and a few others, so I took it and came here," he said.

"Knowing your older brother would have to protect you from the most powerful demon Hell ever spat out," Kris said, anger flaring within him.

"You're sworn never to harm one who comes in good faith."

"I need to ask you something, and if you lie to me, we're done."

"Whatever you like, brother," Sasha said with too much ease.

"Were you responsible for killing Andre?"

"You forget, Kris, he was my brother, too, and I considered him a friend. He was the only neutral party among our father's sons. What he considered me, I won't even try to guess, but no, I didn't. It was rumored in Hell that Darkyn was trying to get your precious Katie. Andre was collateral damage."

Sometimes Kris hated being his father's son and resented Andre's insistence that he choose duty over all else. He'd lost his lover, Jade, that way, a sacrifice that still stung. He seemed to be the only one on the Council who truly cared about upholding the balance between good and evil, no matter what the cost. That *Rhyn* of all his brothers would be granted such an honor as an Ancient's mate made a mockery of everything. He saw firsthand how Rhyn's destructive nature took its toll on those closest to him, and the half-breed had no sense of loyalty or duty to the Council.

Even so, Rhyn's flaws stemmed from his nature of being a half-demon. Sasha had *chosen* to serve the Dark One and betray the Council and their father. Sasha may not have pulled the trigger on Andre, but someone he knew where to find their oldest brother, who had been protecting Katie when he was rendered dead-dead.

Sasha also knew the Code Kris was bound by: those who came in good faith would be given the chance to prove it. Then there were the rules their father had created about none of the brothers being permitted to kill the others, with the exception of Andre, whose sole purpose in life was to keep the Council on track and protect them. Unless Sasha posed a direct threat to the Council, Kris was forbidden from buying an assassination, despite suspecting his brother wasn't as innocent as he proclaimed.

Sasha disgusted him, but he couldn't just kill him like he wanted to.

"She looks like Lilith," Sasha said.

"I hadn't noticed," Kris said and took another sip, aware his brother was always on the prowl for some weakness to exploit. In truth, he *had* noticed that Hannah looked like the first Ancient's mate ever found, Lilith. Lilith had been intended for Kris and was pregnant with his son when Rhyn killed her and the baby both.

He took another sip. After all his sacrifices, after losing Lilith and Katie to Rhyn, he wasn't sure what he'd do if Hannah chose someone other than him as her mate.

"We aren't too different," Sasha voiced quietly. "Sometimes it only takes a small nudge to push you over the edge."

"What pushed you to the Dark One, brother?"

"A loss too great for me to bear."

Kris looked at him sharply, suspecting his brother was trying to play on his emotions. Sasha still stared into the fire.

"What did you lose?" he demanded.

"My soul mate. You stole him from me, just as Rhyn stole Lilith from you."

Surprised at the raw, bitter note in Sasha's voice, Kris studied him. "Jade?" he asked. "You were in love with Jade?"

"I was, until he became enamored with you. You don't give a shit who you fuck, but I did then. There was only one for me."

"You can have him."

"Too late. I think I burned that bridge. The demons brought Jade and Iliana to Hell."

Jade had disappeared after Kris sent him away in hopes that Katie would become his mate. He'd last seen his other trusted lieutenant, Iliana, two days ago, when he'd sent her to represent him in North America while he was away.

"Are they alive?" he asked.

"They are. The demons treat their guests well. Iliana has been a favorite among them."

Anger made Kris's face warm. Iliana was a relatively young Immortal who had been at his side for only a few decades, having caught his attention with her fighting skill and fierce loyalty. He'd promoted her to one of his lieutenants. She was tough, loyal, and beautiful.

"Our family is prone to ongoing disappointment and treason. I think we are worse to each other than the Dark One is to his enemies," Kris said, white rage buried deep within him to keep Sasha from seeing it.

"Without a doubt, brother, which is why I hope your meeting with Darkyn goes well. He's not the kind of demon you want to piss off."

Kris glanced at the clock, aware it was time for him to meet with the demon leader. He set his glass down and looked again at Sasha, who had yet to glance away from the fire. He wasn't fooled by any of his brothers, especially Sasha and Rhyn, whose treachery had been too personal for him to forget or forgive.

He threw on a jacket and left, aware Sasha couldn't leave the castle grounds without forfeiting his life and wouldn't dare disrupt the Immortals for fear of Kris's wrath. Kris could kill or have him killed in retribution for any life he took while inside the walls. Sasha wasn't that stupid, though Kris wondered what game his brother played.

The night was cold and dark as he strode across the park to the edge of the castle's grounds. A single figure already awaited him at the edge of the invisible wall that kept the demons out of the sacred grounds. More dark shadows lingered deep within the forest, watching over their leader. Darkyn was a head shorter than Kris and wider, his steady gaze and roughly hewn features reminding him of Rhyn.

Kris stopped a safe distance away on the sacred grounds, taking in the underwhelming demon leader with some surprise. He'd expected some towering monstrosity from the legendary demon who challenged the Dark One.

"You have something I want," Darkyn said with Rhyn's bluntness.

"Good evening to you, Darkyn," Kris replied. "I'm afraid my brother stays with me. I am bound to protect him."

"By Immortal Code, you must turn him over to me. He has slain a family member."

"I find it funny you demons spend your days looking for ways to break the Code then dare quote it to me. No, Darkyn, you will not have Sasha. Now, Rhyn, you can have."

"The half-breed?" Darkyn sneered. "I would rather fry myself on sacred ground. Sasha took something from the Dark One. If you will not return your brother as you are obligated, then you must return this."

Kris was quiet, pretending to consider. His opinion of Darkyn tanked. The demon was an idiot, too unaccustomed to politics or negotiating to understand how to get what it wanted without revealing what that was. There was no way in Hell Kris would give this creature the key to defeating his warriors! But then, he needed some way to keep his Immortals safe until he could determine how many demons were in the forest so he could wipe them out.

"This I will think about," he said at last. "I will speak to Sasha to determine what it is he stole, and if it is rightfully owned by the Dark One, which it must be in order for you to reclaim it."

The demon eyed him.

"If it is so, then I'll return it to you. I'll convene the Council That Was Seven for an impartial vote. This might take me a few days. I ask that, in the meantime, you refrain from attacking any Immortal traveling the road to the castle."

It was the demon's turn to consider. Kris waited.

"On the main road only," the demon agreed. "And if Sasha steps outside of sacred grounds, we will take him. No appeal of yours will work in his favor."

I hope not, Kris thought but said aloud, "I'll warn him."

Darkyn's features were too shuttered to read, and Kris didn't wait for him to second-guess anything. He returned to the castle, stopping at the sound of commotion from the direction of the forest before he reached the entrance. Rhyn's pterodactyl shape hovered over the demons at the edge of the forest, one of the creatures dangling in his talons. Kris heard the sickening sound of the demon's body breaking from the distance and watched the other demons shapeshift to charge the half-demon. Hoping they'd fix his Rhyn problem for him, he entered the castle and headed straight to the office of his personal secretary.

"Henri, summon Kiki and the others here immediately. If Tamer gives you any resistance, let me know, and I'll drag him here myself," he instructed. "And find out if Iliana made it to her destination."

Henri nodded, his fingers flying over the keyboard in front of him. Of all the thoughts on Kris's mind, Hannah and Jade were foremost. He didn't know whose mate Hannah was intended to be but hoped fate revealed it soon, or he'd help it along and claim her as his as he should've done to Katie when they met.

He'd been too good of a person a mere month before. Andre's death and Rhyn's reappearance changed everything, and Kris found himself considering alternatives he'd never have thought twice about before, like ordering Rhyn and Sasha killed despite his oath to protect his brothers and making an oath to Katie he had no intentions of keeping.

Another idea emerged from his dark thoughts, and he trotted out of the secretary's office and to Katie's chamber. Ully was sleeping soundly in his seat beside Toby's bed. Katie was huddled in a blanket before the fire, and what looked like a healer curled on the bed. Kris nudged Ully awake, motioning for the scientist to follow him out of the chamber. Ully did so sleepily.

"I have a project for you," Kris said as he walked toward the stairs. He looked back to see Ully leaning against the wall to fix his shoes. "Ully, walk!" The scientist obeyed. "Have you had a chance to test the immunity blood Sasha brought?"

"No. I was distracted by Toby. The poor little—"

"The vial is your concern now. I need confirmation before the Council meets, and I need to know if you can alter whatever it is Sasha's people did," Kris said.

"Alter it how?"

"The demons are demanding I return it to them. I want to oblige, only I want the mix to kill them. Slowly, if at all possible."

"Slowly?" Ully asked, puzzled. "Is quickly an option, if it's all I can do?"

"You're both the brightest and dumbest man I've ever met."

Ully fell silent. Kris opened the door to his lab, pushed him in, and closed it. He wiped his face with one hand and ascended, surprised to see Hannah in the hall. He forced his anger and frustration away to keep his eyes from flaring amber, then approached. She looked up at him, her sweet face glowing.

"I hope it's okay if I wander around for awhile. I'm too excited to sleep," she admitted. "And the snow makes this place look so magical!"

"It would be my pleasure to show you around," he said and held out his arm. She accepted it, and they walked down the hall. Her bouncy blond curls brushed his arm as she turned her head to take in the tapestries and look up at the murals on the ceilings.

Her draw was not as consuming as Katie's, which meant she'd have a much better chance of surviving if not every demon and Immortal was drawn to her.

"May I ask you a few questions about your family?" he asked, puzzled again as to how two Ancient's mates were born into one family.

"Of course."

"Do you have any other siblings?"

"Not at all. Katie was born about seven years after me. Our parents thought two was enough."

"Your parents, are they still alive?"

"A car accident killed them both. I basically raised Katie from the time she was ten," she said, a sad look crossing her features. "Not sure I did a good job."

"You did a wonderful job. She's a … charming woman," he forced himself to say.

Hannah laughed. "You can say it—she turned out a little rough around the edges!"

"I have to agree with you there. You two couldn't be more different."

She beamed.

"I wonder how there came to be two women destined to be Immortal mates in one family. It's unheard of. Did you ever come to know of your parents being different in any way?"

"Not at all."

Disappointed, he wasn't sure what else to ask. Ully would run blood tests on Hannah, but he doubted they'd reveal much more than Katie's had. He took in her delicate features and felt a familiar warmth stir his blood. She met his gaze and held it, her pupils dilating and a faint flush spreading across her features. He stopped walking and stood close enough for their chests to brush when she breathed in. Waiting for some sign of rejection, he lowered his head until his lips brushed hers.

"What about Gio?" she breathed.

"Do you prefer a prince or his servant?" he asked.

She hesitated only a second more and leaned into him, parting her warm lips to receive his kiss.

Chapter Four

Jade waited for Darkyn to return from his meeting with Kris. He gazed into the black flames of the fire in the hearth. This had been Sasha's study less than a few days ago. He clenched his fists, not wanting to think about Sasha or Kris or how quickly he, too, could have the tables turned on him as he had done to Sasha.

He'd decided to sleep in here last night, unable to sleep in his bedchamber with the thought of Iliana's body in the trunk beside the bed. He'd accidently hurt someone innocent, and he didn't want the reminder. He wouldn't do it again.

"It went exactly as expected," Darkyn said as he walked into the study. "Kris refused to turn over Sasha or the vial. He underestimates me."

"Kris values the Code and his duty more than he does anything," Jade said with some bitterness.

"You said there is a weakness to the castle that will render the ground no longer sacred."

"There is."

At his silence, Darkyn moved closer, his dark eyes piercing and the growl in his chest audible. Jade looked away. Until now, he'd always thought he could turn back. No one but Iliana had died, and the only person he'd betrayed was Sasha, whose death Kris might eventually reward him for by welcoming Jade back into his life and his bed.

"I will have it from you!" Darkyn said and struck him hard enough to knock his breath out as he slammed into the wall. Jade gasped for a moment and steadied himself.

"I … can make it happen," he said. "You cannot. You have to be in the castle to make it work."

"You seek to betray me as your predecessor did."

"No, Darkyn. I want my revenge against Sasha and Kris both, but there are innocent people there."

"No Immortal is innocent."

"Let me go to Sasha. I will make him our tool," Jade said, his mind working fast to find a way to keep Darkyn from destroying everyone. Darkyn studied him and then withdrew a thin collar and approached. Jade flinched as it snapped into place around his neck.

"If you do not return by dawn, this will bring you back to me, and I will show you no mercy," Darkyn warned.

"Will you consider sparing the rest of the Immortals, master?"

"You came to me to destroy those who have wronged you. I want revenge for my daughter's treatment at Sasha's hands, and I want the vial or the girl. I own you now, Jade. Do not question me again."

Darkyn strode out, and Jade watched him, torn. Sasha and Kris were his enemies, not the rest of the Immortals! He had come to Darkyn in desperation, after Sasha had invited him to his bed and then dumped him off with the demons. He'd been spared for what he knew of the Immortals, and Darkyn had taken a personal liking to him.

A violent liking to him. Jade shuddered. Demons knew no other way.

It's better to reign in Hell ...

As Kris's confidante of several hundred years, he knew most of the Immortal's secrets. He'd been unable to shake the empty hole in his heart resulting from Kris flinging him to the side to pursue a human female. Even as he thought of his last moments with Kris, he felt his anger turn to resolve.

The Immortals deserved neither mercy nor peace, especially their leader. He was doing Kris's next lover a favor. He'd use the tricks of manipulation he'd learned from Kris and Sasha both to get Sasha to do what he wanted. And then, the both of them would be gone. Forever. His revenge was all that would make him whole again.

Determined, he went to the one spot in Hell where he could cross into the shadow world. A demon guarded the tiny spot, no larger than a meter square. He opened a portal and crossed through. Long ago, before Sasha broke from the Council, he had stayed in a corner chamber overlooking the forest. Jade emerged from the shadow world into the chamber's spacious closet and stood silently, listening.

He heard movement outside the closet and eased the door open far enough to peek into the well-lit room. Sasha sat before the hearth as if deep in thought. Jade couldn't help the flash of anger he felt at the sight of such a creature comfortable and content.

"Sasha," he said, flinging open the closet door. Sasha turned to face him, covering his surprise with a smile that made Jade's skin crawl.

"Jade, my friend. How are you?" he purred.

"Seems I'm not as well off as you are. How quickly you found a safe place," Jade replied.

"My brother Kris is too good, as you know."

"He can't protect you forever, Sasha."

"I think he can and will. The fool doesn't have the backbone to kill me as he probably should."

More anger stirred as Jade bit his lip to keep from defending Kris. No matter how badly Kris had hurt him, it hadn't been for a selfish cause like Sasha's.

"That's your plan?" Jade asked. "Stay here in this room forever?"

"Simple and effective."

"You won't get tired of it here or bored? I know your appetite for women and men, Sasha. Kris won't tolerate what you do to them."

"My ... ways can be sated quietly."

Jade crossed to the window and looked out, formulating a plan to let the demons into the castle using Sasha. He debated with himself again. Once he crossed this line, he could never return.

"You're troubled," Sasha said and rose. "I can ease that tension."

"Darkyn sent me, Sasha."

"I see the collar. I assumed as much. I'd be a bigger fool than Kris to return with you, Jade."

"That's not why I'm here. He is offering you a deal," he said slowly. "If you can help him get to Kris, he'll call it even and leave you alone."

"And the Dark One?"

"Might help get you back in the Dark One's favor, but I'm here for Darkyn only."

"So, hand over Kris on a silver platter, and I'm free of those pesky demons," Sasha mused.

"You can use the vial to blackmail your way back," Jade added.

"It'll be hard to get my brother alone outside the castle where Darkyn can snatch him."

"Or you can bring the demons here."

Sasha was quiet, and Jade faced him. He expected Sasha to sense his betrayal, but Sasha's gaze glowed for a different reason.

"I'm impressed, Jade," Sasha said. "I thought you too weak to think like I do."

"You and Kris toughened me up."

"We did. Unfortunate, but I like the result. I only know of one way to let the demons in. You are certain Darkyn will consider this repayment for his whore-daughter?"

"Absolutely," Jade said without hesitation. "I haven't even changed your apartment in Hell."

Sasha considered him long and hard. Jade waited, hoping Sasha's desire to return to Hell or take out Kris overwhelmed any suspicion he had.

"Speaking of my ways …" Sasha said, his gaze turning lustful. Jade swallowed hard, still hurt from his last night with Darkyn. If this was what it took to seal the deal with Sasha …

"I have to be back by dawn," he said.

"I'll be done with you by then."

Resigned, Jade peeled off his shirt, the sense of triumph making him feel sick to his stomach.

Katie awoke to the healer's cool touch on her arm. She struggled into a sitting position, her neck achy from her spot sleeping on the floor before the fire. Lankha worked his magic with his micro suede-covered hands and gentle touch. He was almost done when the burst of coolness awoke her, and she looked down to see him smoothing the skin around her faded wound.

"How's Toby?" she asked, gaze going to the bed.

"Angel is well. Must ressssst," Lankha said. "And you must ressssst."

"This is the least bad wound I've had yet."

"Not for wound. For…" and he pointed to her stomach. She froze then looked around to ensure no one was there to overhear them.

"You're certain?" she whispered.

"Yesss."

"If you tell anyone, Rhyn will pull your arms and legs off like you're a grasshopper!"

He gasped. She felt bad for scaring him but knew the alternative—people like Kris or Sasha finding out—would doom her. She'd have to pray Rhyn didn't drop by her mind when she thought of it, or when she was trying to figure out what to do.

Her eyes went to Toby. She couldn't raise a kid in a place of demons and psychos! She stood abruptly and crossed to the bathroom, wanting to be alone. She had no luck in life!

The next time I visit the human world, I'll be leaving with two souls. Gabriel's ominous warning suddenly made sense. Her body trembling, she sat on the edge of the Jacuzzi tub, staring into space. Urgency surged within her. There was nowhere she could run from Gabriel, who had orders to bring her and the life within her to Death. Was all truly lost?

Rhyn could never know. Tears began to spill down her face as she understood the depth of Gabriel's pain. She sat in the bathroom and ran the shower to cover the sound of her crying, completely lost as to what to do.

"Katherine?" Hannah called with a loud knock.

"Just a sec! Almost done!" she belted and scrambled up to lock the door. She looked in the mirror, distraught, then scrubbed her face and turned off the shower. When she emerged, it was to the sight of a glowing, ecstatic Hannah, who sat on the edge of her bed talking to a sleepy Toby. The healer was huddled next to the fireplace, afraid to move with the presence of the newcomer. Katie's jealousy stirred again.

"Toby," Katie said, crossing to the bed. The baby angel gave a small smile that filled her with relief. He looked exhausted. "You okay?"

"I'm fine, Mama," he said with a noisy sigh. "Hungry."

"I'll get you some soup and cocoa," she said and rose. Her gaze went to Hannah, who looked so sunny, she wondered what had happened. "You wanna come, Hannah?"

"I'd love to!"

Her gush made Katie feel old and crotchety. Hannah had been a kept woman with no problems since meeting Gio, whereas Katie had always struggled to find her path. Hannah would be a basket case if she only knew the extent of Katie's issues!

She walked to the door and pulled it open for Hannah in her straw-colored pants and light pink sweater. Hannah no longer wore her engagement ring, and Katie wondered why she was so happy when she must know by now Gio wasn't coming back for her.

They entered the dining room, which was filled for brunch. Katie ignored the looks of those nearest her, and Hannah looked around, happy.

"Just need some soup to go," Katie told the host, who snapped his fingers at a servant. "And whatever you want, Hannah."

"Master Kris has ordered us to respect any wish you have, Miss Hannah. You'll find our chefs the best in the world," the host said, ignoring Katie to address her sister.

Hannah blushed, and Katie looked at her anew.

"You *slept* with him?" she asked. "That's quick even by your standards."

"Not so loud," Hannah replied with an apologetic look at the host.

"Didn't you just get dumped by one Immortal?"

"Kris explained everything to me last night, Katherine."

"Explained what? That he manipulated Gio and now you?"

Hannah looked again to the host, who pretended not to hear despite being less than two feet away. Furious, Katie left before she made more of a scene that would embarrass her sister. She was pacing the hall in front of the dining area when Hannah emerged a short time later carrying a large tote.

"I suppose he explained what he did to me, too," Katie snapped. "Or did he leave that part out?"

"He explained he's tried to do his best but doesn't always succeed, like anyone, Katherine," Hannah said. "You're making a big deal out of this. I'm an adult, and so is he."

"You're my sister. Don't you find it odd he was so quick to come on to you?"

"He believes we're meant to be."

"And what do you believe?"

"I believe …" Hannah drifted off, looking around her. "I believe I could be very comfortable living here." She smiled. Katie watched her walk down the hall toward her chambers, stunned. Hannah saw nothing but the gilded world around her; she had no idea about the dark underside to the Immortal world.

Katie had hoped to make her sister a confidante but knew it was impossible so long as Kris's claws were wrapped securely around Hannah. Gabriel, Rhyn, Hannah. Those who might've been her friends were gone. Gabriel didn't have a choice, Rhyn she was trying to protect, but Hannah … the sense of betrayal within her made her feel ill again. Of all the Immortals and creatures in the world, she felt even closer to the outcast that was her mate.

The answer became clear. She and Toby had to leave. There had to be somewhere she could go where they'd leave her alone, at least until Gabriel came for her. Her thoughts drifted to the Sanctuary, the only place she'd felt safe. When Toby was better, she'd take him and go. The convent would do a better job raising him than the Immortals. But now, she wanted a word with a certain Ancient.

Katie walked to Kris's chamber on the floor below. She heard a muffled response to her knock and walked in, not caring if he bid her enter or get lost. Kris wasn't there, but Sasha was.

She stopped in place. The door swung closed behind her, and fear trickled through her. She reminded herself she wasn't defenseless with him this time. If she called for Rhyn, he would come.

"I'm looking for Kris," she said, unable to help covering her neck with one hand.

"That makes two of us," Sasha said and rose from his seat beside the fire. He looked her up and down in approval, his gaze lingering on her neck. She silently thanked Lankha for healing her without her asking him. "You look well."

"Better than the last time we met."

"You're in one piece," he agreed and circled her with predatory slowness. She tried to keep her breathing steady even as she wanted to run screaming and hide behind Rhyn. "Something is different about you, though."

Her breath caught as she considered more Immortals than Rhyn might be able to read her mind. Sasha snatched her neck with one hand, his movement too fast for her to defend herself against.

"Don't!" she cried, squeezing her eyes closed as she waited for the pain of him tearing into her neck as he had once before. He didn't attack, simply let his cold power loose into her for a long moment before releasing her.

She opened her eyes, breathing hard. Sasha stepped back, a smile tugging up one side of his mouth.

"So simple," he said. "They can find you on the Sanctuary, too. They find you everywhere, except Hell."

"Never going back there."

"Unless …" He drifted off and crossed to the window, clasping his hands behind him.

"Unless what?"

"There's one way to break your bond with Rhyn."

"I don't believe you."

"You know no one can force the bond to break," he continued. "But if you and Rhyn voluntarily break it, you're free."

"There's nothing you say I'd ever trust. Where's Kris?" she demanded.

"You aren't worried I'll tell him your little secret?" His gaze went to her stomach.

"You'll do what you will," she said and took a step toward the door. "You almost ruined my life once. I won't stick around for you to do it again."

"Just remember, there's nowhere you can run where we can't eventually find you."

She stormed out, blood pulsing and headache growing. She wiped sweat from her brow with a shaking hand. Sasha's words echoed in her thoughts, and she tried hard to give them no credence. She didn't know what he was doing there, but he couldn't be trusted.

Even if he had one of her secrets. She felt like crying again. Now more than ever, she had to leave, before Kris and Rhyn discovered her secret and brought down what fragile supports were holding up her world. She retreated to her floor and saw Ully in the hall.

"Kris has me slaving away," Ully whispered, looking around as if Kris was around the corner. "I just wanted to check on Toby. He looks better."

"He is," she agreed. "Is Kris with you in the lab?"

"He was, but he's prepping for the Council meeting. I'm getting ready to test the immunity blood. I'm also making a special poisoned batch to give back to the demons."

She shook her head, not sharing his excitement about his experiments. She entered the bedroom quietly to see Toby awake and trying to get an uncertain Lankha to play with his stuffed animals. Toby would make an awesome older brother, she realized, unlike her flaky sister. He'd need to be if she turned out to be much worse of a mother.

Grimly, she realized he may never have the chance, if Gabriel was ordered back for her.

Rhyn watched Ully inject one of the Immortals with some concoction derived from the immunity blood Sasha brought and lowered himself into a fighting stance. The Immortal rubbed the injection spot with a grimace, stretched, and climbed inside the ring in the lowermost basement in the castle.

Rhyn didn't wait for him to settle himself but struck first with his long, oak bo, a blow that caught the Immortal by surprise. He struck again, this time drawing blood. Ully, looking exhausted, moved closer, and Rhyn waited as well.

The wound healed itself quickly. Ully nodded in approval and scribbled notes on his iPad. The Immortal launched himself at Rhyn, and the two sparred as the scientist watched intently. Rhyn enjoyed the feel of a weapon in his hand and facing a decent opponent. He restrained himself as much as possible to keep from injuring Ully's test subject. Ully blew a whistle at last and motioned the Immortal over to check his wounds.

Rhyn looked around, agitated again by the sense that something else was wrong. He left the sparring level without saying a word to Ully and followed his instincts up a flight of stairs and down a narrow hall he recognized from his visit to their father's catacombs with Kris. The door leading to his father's corpse was locked, and he tested it. Kris had managed to create a barrier around the chamber to keep Immortals from trespassing via the shadow world.

"Rhyn, the rest of the Council is meeting now in the conference room off my chambers."

He turned at Kris's voice. His eldest brother appeared less frustrated than normal.

"You're inviting me to attend?" he asked, amused.

"Unfortunately, you are a Council member."

Kris disappeared into the portal behind him. Rhyn followed. They emerged in a small conference room with one wall made of windows. Their brothers were already there, three of them sitting across the table from Sasha. Sensing the level of tension in the room, Rhyn didn't sit but leaned with his back against the wall, ready to launch across the table at whoever snapped first.

"I can guess what this is about," Kiki said. His turquoise eyes stood out against his caramel-colored Oriental features.

"Yes, tell us, brother," Tamer echoed in his husky tone. The largest of them all by half a foot, the giant was based out of Africa. "You have never once invited us here, maybe because we never agree on anything?"

"Maybe he thinks we'll steal his things," Erik, the blond Viking who watched over South America, said with a smile. "I saw a painting I may walk off with."

"I had hoped to bring everyone together to discuss the baggage Sasha has brought with him, if you'll all be reasonable," Kris said. Everyone's gaze fell to Sasha. For once, Rhyn was not the sore point.

"Hell that overcrowded they're letting murderers walk?" Tamer asked.

"They're still accepting prisoners, my dear Tamer," Sasha purred.

"Enough. Every meeting we've had has been a failure and we've not had one since Andre became dead-dead," Kris demanded.

"Our last one was about guarding your little meat-cicle, right, Rhyn?" Erik demanded. "She need more help with someone like you as a mate?"

"Why I called you all here was to finish the discussion we started at our last meeting about the immunity of two certain humans to Immortal powers," Kris interjected. "Katie, Rhyn's mate, and her sister."

"I seem to have stolen the formula that will grant Immortal or demon this same immunity. I turned it over to Kris, and now the Dark One wants me dead-dead," Sasha said.

"You have it?" Tamer sat up with interest. "I've heard the rumors through the demons in my territory. It works?"

"It appears to work. Ully is still working with it to verify," Kris replied.

"You'll grant us access to it?"

Rhyn smiled mercilessly at Kris's uneasy look. He took in his predatory brothers, well aware they were as dangerous as any of the creatures he'd spent time in Hell with. He crossed his arms, interested to know Katie's sister was as special as she was and wondering if Kris had already claimed her.

She looked like Lilith, the woman Rhyn killed when he discovered she'd plotted with the Dark One to kill the Council. His reward had been being sent to Hell, for what his brothers hoped was eternity.

"In exchange for your assistance, yes," Kris said at last. "Sasha's enemies are here in the forest. I don't know how far the Dark One will go to get Sasha or his vial of blood back, but I imagine our time is short."

"And you want us to do what exactly?" Erik asked. "I'm content to feed Sasha to the Dark One piece by piece if that means we keep the peace."

"As am I," Tamer seconded.

"Me, too," Kiki said.

"Seems practically unanimous," Sasha said, unaffected. "Except for you, Rhyn. Would you care to feed me to the Dark One in pieces?"

"I'd feed each one of you to the Dark One," Rhyn replied. "Starting with Kris."

Everyone chuckled but Kris, who levied a glare at him. He wasn't sure what they expected of him; he'd never been included in any Council meeting.

"You're no Andre, Kris," Sasha said.

Kris's eyes flared copper, then amber. "I have no intention of trying to be Andre. What I want is what Andre always tried to get us to do: to work together like the brothers we are."

"Andre lost that battle when Sasha defected and Rhyn went to Hell," Kiki stated. "We're not a team, Kris. We're barely allies."

"I don't answer to anyone," Tamer added. "I respected Andre, but now that he's gone, you're lucky I agreed to come at all. I don't need any of you, especially the headache Sasha is."

"If you want the immunity solution, then you'll work with me to protect our brother," Kris said.

No one spoke. Rhyn observed each of his brothers, sensing a silent rebellion that seemed to elude Kris, the only of them to value duty over their own interests. Kiki and Tamer exchanged a look while Sasha seemed to be the only one pleased by the arrangement.

"No deal," Erik said. "My part of the world is quiet. I don't need the solution, and I don't need the headaches."

"You took an oath to serve the Immortals, their cause, and be a member of this Council," Kris grated. "All of you, save Rhyn, who was never intended to set foot outside of Hell."

"I took an oath to my father and then to Andre," Erik retorted. "You are neither of them. In fact, I say we vote you out."

"You can't vote me out. I'm firstborn after Andre. Our father was second born, as was his father before him. It's the way things have been for millions of years!"

"What are you going to do if we refuse to follow you? You don't have it in you to kill any of us. You're sworn not to, if I remember correctly," Erik said. He rose. "Andre at least had that authority. Andre's gone, and I need none of this shit. I vote the Council split. Anyone second me?"

"I will," Tamer said.

"Very well. The Council is no more. Farewell, brothers, and stay the hell out of my part of the world."

Erik disappeared, followed by Tamer. Kris was frozen in place, as if not yet registering what had happened. Kiki rose as well, his gaze going to Sasha.

"You know they don't speak for me," Kiki said. "But I'll have to agree, Kris. You can have Sasha or you can have the Council. You're too good a man to see that on your own, so I'm telling you."

He left as well. Rhyn looked to Kris, then to Sasha, whose smile had faded.

"If I were you, I'd beat the shit out of each one of them till they did what you said," Rhyn suggested.

"I prefer a more civilized approach," Kris replied.

"Look where that got you. No one but Sasha and me left in your Council, and I doubt I was ever really a part of it."

"My own brothers want me to break the Code to feed Sasha to the wolves," Kris muttered. "Does no one take it seriously?"

"They know you don't have it in you," Rhyn said. "You can't be respected without kicking some ass. I learned that lesson when Sasha tossed me in a pit with full-blooded demons and were-things."

"Respect isn't enough for someone in your position," Sasha agreed. "They need to fear you, Kris, and thus far, none of them do."

"Except Katie. Treat them as you did her, and you'll find they fall into line."

Kris looked up at Rhyn's low voice, his gaze lingering. "I don't condone the kind of brute violence you and Sasha do, Rhyn," he said. "I won't use force against my brothers. They'll eventually remember their duty to the Code. Or they'll soon realize the threat affects us all and be back."

Rhyn pushed himself away from the wall. Kris was crushed, and Rhyn wasn't sure how his eldest surviving brother hadn't expected the rest of them to walk away. That Kris could attack his brother's mate but refuse to strong-arm his brothers into fighting demons made his anger boil.

"Keep telling yourself that. The demons are planning something, Kris, and *hoping* someone comes to your rescue is stupid," he returned.

"You're one to talk, Rhyn. I wonder if Katie *hopes* you'll rescue her every time something happens. You aren't capable of caring for someone else or keeping her safe. But, if you do as Sasha says and break the bond, I will keep her safe, I swear it," Kris said. "She'll be—"

Rhyn walked out of the room, furious at his brother. It was all he heard anymore, that Katie would be safe and happy only if he wasn't around. He forced himself to focus on something else.

The Council meeting was a bust, and there was more tension in the air than he could understand. For the first time in his life, he felt something akin to pity for Kris. The world needed a man focused on maintaining the balance between good and evil, and none of the brothers had the foresight or vision that Kris did. He was a dick, but Rhyn never wanted to be put in the position Kris was in.

Agitated, he jogged up the stairs to the level where Katie was. He'd paced in front of her chamber at some point every day for three weeks, wanting to tell her something, anything, to make her want to stay. The words never came, and he'd left frustrated each time. Hell toughened him up, yet this was one challenge he couldn't figure out. Despite telling her he wouldn't, he dropped into her thoughts to feel a little closer to her and was surprised to find she was packing to leave.

Without knocking, he strode into the chamber. She whirled to face him, moving too slow to hide the suitcase laid out on the trunk at the end of the bed in which Toby slept.

"You're leaving," he stated. "Plan on telling me?"

"You made it clear you read my mind. I didn't think I needed to tell you anything," she shot back.

"You still have five weeks."

"Four weeks and five days," she replied.

"I don't give a shit. Your time here isn't up."

"I'm not doing this anymore, Rhyn. I've got Toby to think about, and raising him where he's attacked by demons and subjected to the stupidity of the Immortal world—it's not happening. I'm fed up with aaaaall of this!"

"And you really think there's somewhere safe for you to go?" he challenged. "Where demons and Immortals can't find you?"

"The Sanctuary. I'll become a nun or whatever those women are who live there."

"A *nun?*" he echoed, horrified. "You'd go that far?"

"Is sex all you think about?"

"I only get one mate. If she becomes a nun, I'll have to start fucking—"

"Stop there. God, Rhyn. There's so much at stake, and you just …" She sighed.

"What's at stake?" he asked, sensing again there was something important she was keeping from him. A haunted look crossed her face. "Kris doesn't need your blood anymore. What makes you think he won't leave you alone?"

"He told me so. Whatever issue is between you two, it's too personal for him to forget, and he takes it out on me when you're not around," she said. "I realized he has no intention of letting me go even though he promised it. And with Hannah here, I can't leave the Immortal world with her still in it. I'm leaving *you*, Rhyn."

The words were forced, and he knew she was in love with him as much as she did. He watched as she tossed more clothing into her suitcase, certain what he wanted to say would only make her pack faster. So he stopped to think and pace. Lankha was huddled in a corner with his hands over his head. Katie had been crying earlier. Her eyes were red-rimmed.

Something was really wrong, and he couldn't help but think it was more than him this time. She'd been acting squirrelly the past two days. No matter what, she'd be safer at the Sanctuary than at the castle, now that the Council was in disarray and the demons were plotting in the forest.

"I'll take you there," he said at last.

She paused and looked at him hard. "Really?"

"Yes, really."

"Just like that?"

"Just like that."

"Why?" she asked suspiciously.

"If you feel safer there …"

"And you'll just let me go," she said, anger sparkling in her eyes. He couldn't figure out what the hell the puny human in front of him wanted.

"Things here are about to go to shit," he said.

"How?"

"The Council disbanded. Sasha's plotting something, and the demons are going to flood this place soon."

"Are you serious?" She paled at his words.

"You better go soon," he advised. "I'll follow."

"Rhyn, if you're serious, then I can't leave without Hannah."

"She treats you like shit, along with that Gio ass."

"She's with Kris now," she said. "But she's my sister. That may mean nothing to you Immortals—"

"It doesn't."

"—but to us lesser beings, family means something!"

"Which is why you're doing your damndest to convince us both you're leaving me," he said and crossed his arms.

"Can't you tell the Council not to disband?" she asked, visibly flustered.

"Me? Not the way it works, blood monkey."

"Then what're you going to do?"

"I'm going to watch the world fall apart."

Her features darkened, and she turned away, saying, "I thought you had some level of honor or decency."

"You're the only one."

"I'm taking my sister and going to the Sanctuary, where I'll raise our child without you."

"I told you, I don't claim Toby. That little thing is yours."

"You're such a jackass! What was I thinking … it never would've worked anyway!" she snapped. Fury turned her face bright red. She flung a shoe at him hard, then a second. He deflected the first, but the second slapped his cheek. A knock at the door distracted his response, which wouldn't bode well for either of them. She breezed by him and paused at the door to say, "Rhyn, I'm not talking about Toby," before she wrenched it open.

Her meaning didn't click, and he turned to see who had interrupted them.

"We have to find Sasha," Kris said, ignoring her to push his way into the chamber. "Katie, take Toby and the healer to the basement with the warriors."

"What's wrong?" Rhyn asked.

"I'm not sure."

"Where's Hannah?" Katie demanded.

"I'll send her down. Go."

Katie motioned to the healer, who scampered from his corner to the bed. She hurried to Toby and lifted the sleeping angel carefully before she and Lankha left. Rhyn joined Kris in the hallway and waited until Katie was out of earshot.

"Let me guess. The demons have crossed sacred ground," he said dryly.

"And how do you know this?"

"I heard them plotting. You really think Sasha came here to throw himself on your mercy without some sort of back-up plan?"

"I'm doing what I'm obligated to do. Of course I suspected him of something," Kris snapped. "I didn't know what."

Rhyn trotted to a window. The peaceful, snowy park was now swarmed with Immortals and demons fighting. Sasha hadn't lost time in acting after the ill-fated Council meeting!

"How can he make something unsacred?" he puzzled aloud.

"The ground is sacred because our father is buried here. Even in death, he holds power."

"He moved our father's body?" Rhyn asked with a laugh. "Hope he chucked it off a cliff."

"I've sent Immortals after it. Laugh all you will, Rhyn, but this is my home, and the refuge of our Immortal brethren. I don't intend to lose it. If you give a shit about anything, you'll get your ass out there and fight."

Furious, Kris stalked away. Rhyn watched him, aware he was much more useful in another way. Kris's Immortals appeared to outnumber the demons two to one for now, and Katie would call for him if she needed help. He opened a portal and crossed into the shadow world and then through a portal into a Japanese-style palatial estate overlooking Tokyo.

"Kiki!" he called, ignoring the startled servants scampering away from him.

"You just can't give me a break, Rhyn," Kiki grumbled. He trotted down a set of black lacquered stairs, an iPad tucked under one arm. "Did Kris send you?"

"Not exactly."

"Then get out of my house."

Rhyn snatched his brother by the front of his shirt and slammed him into the ground. The iPad skittered across the floor.

"I'm not Kris, Kiki. If there's any part of you that thinks I won't snap your neck like a twig in a hurricane—"

"Fuck, Rhyn! What're you doing?"

Rhyn planted one foot at the base of Kiki's neck and wrenched his head back. Kiki strained to breathe.

"I'm doing what Kris won't. I'm not bound by those rules of his. Sasha needs to fry, and the Council needs to remain intact, or all Immortals die. I don't particularly want the world to go to shit before I get a chance to enjoy my time away from Hell," Rhyn said calmly. "Now, you can send your soldiers to the castle where the demons are staging an attack, and rejoin the Council, or I can bury you here in your front yard. Make your choice."

Kiki wheezed for a long moment, then said, "Yes, fine. Let me go, you dick."

Rhyn obliged and stepped back. Kiki glared at him, but Rhyn knew this brother to be the easiest of the three to sway. He was about to address Kiki again when Katie's angry words hit him.

She hadn't been talking about Toby.

"What?" Kiki eyed him warily. "I already agreed. Don't look at me like I'm your dinner. I take it you're going to see Erik next."

"Yeah," he managed. "Erik."

Holy fuck. There was a hatchling growing within her.

Chapter Five

The demons couldn't get near Sasha so long as he had the coffin holding his father. Jade watched from the brush nearby. Sasha sat on top of the sarcophagus and looked around, smug in how safe he was sitting on top of the coffin. The forest was full of demons. Most had attacked the castle while Darkyn's personal guard went after Sasha. Jade hadn't wanted to come; he'd asked a personal favor of Darkyn not to come. Darkyn had laughed and dragged him.

Jade's insides still churned at the sight of the demons and Immortals fighting. Technically, this was Sasha's doing, for he had dragged the coffin out of the protected crypt and left the Immortals exposed. This fact did little to assuage Jade's guilt when he saw the slaughter around the place he'd once called home.

"Where's your master, fools?" Sasha shouted to the forest.

"I'm here," Darkyn's voice boomed from a good hundred meters away, the nearest the demon could come.

"What of our deal?" Sasha demanded. "I gave you Kris and the Immortals."

Darkyn's chuckle filled the air around them, and Jade watched Sasha's face turn from expectant to furious.

"So that bitch Jade betrayed me," Sasha muttered. "No matter. I can sit here all day, Darkyn, and you can't come near me."

The sounds of fighting from the direction of the castle made Jade sweat. He hadn't wanted all the Immortals to die, just the ones that hurt him. He shifted in the brush, wishing he could've found a better way to draw out Kris and Sasha than by sacrificing everyone.

"I can't, but Jade can," Darkyn said, unconcerned.

"Jade's a coward and a fool!"

"He tricked you, didn't he?"

Sasha sneered in response. He rose and began to pace, the first sign of his anxiety. Jade's hands were sweaty as he drew a machete. He'd crossed the line. There was no going back.

"Jade, kill him and bring me the vial," Darkyn ordered.

Jade closed his eyes, drew a deep breath, and stepped from the forest. Sasha was armed with two daggers and lowered himself into a fighting stance. Jade had trained under Kris, the greatest of the Immortal warriors, and knew Sasha to be a lazy fighter. His first few blows were deflected, but the third slashed Sasha's arm.

"Wait, Jade," Sasha said, surprised. "We can make a deal, you and I."

"You have nothing I want."

"I am still an Ancient. I will make you my mate."

"I saw how Ancients' mates work. You get no choice, Sasha!" Jade snapped, the hurt caused by Kris's rejection renewed. He slashed again. Sasha's guard fell quickly, and Jade hacked at the Ancient with all his fury until Sasha lay in a bloodied heap.

His whole body shaking, he tried to calm himself and withdrew, wanting to wipe away the taint of Sasha's blood from his clothing and skin.

"The vial, Jade!" Darkyn barked. "We are watching. If you try to take it, your death will be the most horrible I devise yet."

Jade hesitated, not wanting to go near Sasha's body. He knelt beside the Ancient and set the machete on top of the sarcophagus. Sasha was far too chopped up to be alive. Jade rifled through his pockets, part of him praying he didn't find the vial. He'd been responsible for enough Immortal deaths this night; he couldn't stomach more.

Jade's hand brushed the glass in Sasha's pocket. Sasha had the vial. The fool had really believed he could bargain with Darkyn and the Dark One! Or maybe he was desperate to return to the only place that would accept him and all his sick ways.

Jade pretended to continue to search, mind racing. It was one thing to feed Kris and the Immortals here to the demons, another thing to give the demons a tool they could use to destroy all Immortals, if not humanity, too. He'd thought he crossed the only line that mattered by selling out the Immortals but found there was another he wasn't ready for.

He left the vial in Sasha's pocket and rose.

"It's not here," he said.

"Not there," Darkyn repeated. Jade bristled for an attack, even knowing the demons couldn't draw near. "Where else would it be?"

"Kris has a scientist named Ully who would've likely been given the vial. Maybe this..." he kicked Sasha's body, "wasn't as stupid as we thought."

"Or Kris locked it away because he knew better than to trust that piece of shit," the demon leader added. "Take the bodies and throw them into the sea, where no one will find them. We will find this Ully and take him to Hell for interrogation."

"Yes, master."

"And Jade?"

Tensing, Jade turned to face the direction of the demon's voice.

"Welcome to Hell, your new home."

Jade said nothing, conflicted. He heard the demons withdraw from the forest around them toward the castle. Suspecting some of them remained, he gave no indication he'd found the vial as he carefully lifted Sasha's body and laid it on the sarcophagus. He stepped back to look at father and son, dead-dead together.

Very fitting.

He opened a portal, mind racing with how to keep the demons from getting the vial. Darkyn had said to dump them in the sea. He lugged the coffin through the portal into the shadow world and then paused to think.

Sanctuary. All of them were located in the middle of a sea. If he tossed Sasha's body close enough to one of them, the vial would be safe.

He concentrated on which Sanctuary he wanted, the farthest from the castle, and lifted Sasha's body. He crossed to the glowing portal and threw Sasha's body through it, satisfied when he heard a splash. He turned back to the coffin, not nearly as concerned about the dead-dead Immortal he'd never met but who'd fathered at least two fucked-up sons—three, if he counted Rhyn.

The Immortal should've died in Hell, where he probably belonged. Jade focused on another part of the ocean, Challenger Deep, the deepest part of the Pacific Ocean. Maybe the depth of the sea would crush this Immortal's perfectly preserved body. If nothing else, the father of the Council would never again be found.

He lugged the coffin to the new portal and shoved it through. He didn't stay to hear the splash this time but walked through the shadow world toward the only portal that glowed black, the portal to Hell.

While feeling vindicated that Kris might already be dead, he couldn't help the growing guilt at hurting so many other Immortals. Nursing a cratered heart, he stepped into Hell, well aware he had nowhere else to go.

Katie paced her corner of the gymnasium, where she had been herded with the rest of the Immortal mates. Toby was awake and sitting, fascinated by Lankha's soft hands. She glanced at them again and looked toward the door.

It had been an hour, and Hannah hadn't appeared. She didn't know if there was a second gym where other Immortal mates were, but Kris had said Hannah would be down. She waited another few minutes and then headed to the bathrooms. Women were packed even in the luxurious bathrooms with their sitting areas decorated with couches and a gilded fountain. She crossed to a stall and closed the door, focusing on a portal to the shadow world. She envisioned Kris's chamber on one of the upper floors and emerged from the shadow world into the chamber.

The door was open, and she ducked down as a furry shape rushed by.

Some of the demons had made it into the castle. She drew a deep breath, terrified of running into one of those creatures alone, then crept to the door. When she heard nothing in the hallway, she eased out of the safety of his room.

Hannah hadn't been there long enough to learn the castle. She knew Kris's chamber, the guest chamber, Katie's chamber, and the dining hall. Katie trotted to the chamber next to Kris's, knowing the guest chambers were near but not sure which was which. She pushed the door open to the next chamber and ducked inside.

"Hannah?"

Silence from the room, footsteps from the hallway. She darted to the other side of the bed and dropped to her stomach, peering under the bed through the door. A massive creature with black fur and fangs paused in front of the open door, sniffing the air. She held her breath. Her heart pounded as it swung its head to face the room.

It jerked suddenly and bolted down the hallway with a snarl. She heard the clash of bodies and waited for the sound to fade before rising again. She peeked out to see two creatures at each other's throats and frowned, wondering why demons were fighting one another. With the creatures too distracted to notice her, Katie drew a breath and darted across the hall, shoving the door of the guest bedroom open.

"Hannah!" she hissed.

"Katie?"

The sound of her sister's voice brought a waterfall of relief. Hannah peeked from the bathroom door, her normally neat hair mussed and her eyes red from crying. Katie closed the door to the bedroom behind her. She'd barely left it when it slammed open, and two furry forms barreled into the room, snarling and fighting. Hannah screamed. Katie covered her head as they trounced over her and rolled to the other side of the chamber, fighting.

She rose and ran into the bathroom, jostling Hannah out of the way as she slammed and locked the door.

"Katie!" Hannah exclaimed, her face a mask of terror. "I was taking a bath earlier and I heard sounds in the hallway. When I—"

"Hannah!" she snapped. "Look for anything to brace the door!"

Hannah looked around, lost. Katie's gaze swept over her, and she was grateful to see her sister unharmed. She closed her eyes to summon the portal when the door bucked. Hannah cried out and scampered to the far side of the bathroom. Katie rushed to the door, trying to brace it. The sound of snarling came from the other side, and she closed her eyes as the demon struck the door again. She sailed across the bathroom and landed on Hannah. The demon crouched in the door, then roared in pain and whirled.

The other demon had clamped its teeth around its leg and dragged it out of the doorway. Katie hauled Hannah to her feet and pulled her through the doorway, across the bedroom, and into the hall. Another demon down the hall caught sight of them and charged. She led them into Kris's room again and slammed the door, vaguely pissed at the Ancient for having the only door that locked in the whole castle. The door bucked but held.

Her gaze went around the chamber and settled on the alcohol in the corner. She crossed to it, took a deep swig, then flung it against the door. The glass carafe exploded. She threw another and pulled the final from the fridge. As if reading her intentions, Hannah forced herself out of her shock and hurried to the low-burning hearth. She snatched the lighter on the mantle and ran to the door, standing close until the alcohol lit and spread.

Fire licked across the wooden door. The door bucked again before all went quiet. Hannah stood close to her, and Katie stared at the door, willing their fire to keep the demons at bay. For a long moment, she thought their simple plan worked, and she closed her eyes to concentrate on the portal.

The door exploded open in flames, wood, and black fur. Hannah dragged her down as fiery splinters sailed over them. The two fanged figures battled until one lifted the other and cracked its back over its knee. It slammed the creature onto a broken piece of burning word. The dying creature let out an otherworldly roar of pain as it burned. It went limp.

The remaining creature turned to them. It contorted into a human form, and Katie cursed.

"Lunchmeat," Jared said with a toothy smile. "You brought a snack to our little party."

"Hannah, you have to trust me when I tell you jumping out that window is a better death than what this thing will do to you!" Katie said, dragging her sister toward the window.

"Easy, Lunchmeat. I came to help, at your half-breed's request," Jared said, holding up his hands. "I smelled you from outside the castle. Oh, the sweet smell of—"

A roar in the hallway made him whirl.

"Come with me, morsels," he said. "I'm your only ticket out of here."

Katie hesitated. Jared morphed again into a massive creature. It beckoned for them to follow with one paw and knocked the burning door out of the way. She trailed it, wanting nothing more than two minutes of relative peace so she could summon a portal. Hannah clung to her arm as they entered the hallway.

Jared launched himself at the demon barreling toward them. Katie gasped and flattened herself against the wall as they soared past them. She grabbed Hannah's hand and bolted for the back stairwell at the far end of the hall. Steadying herself against the walls of the winding stairs, she ran as fast as she could without stumbling, aware of what likely followed them. Barks and roars from further down the stairs made her stop and grip the railing.

"This way!" Hannah cried, pointing to the doorway they'd just passed to one of the mid-level floors. Katie followed her into another hallway on the floor where the castle's serving staff lived. This hall was smaller and narrower. Hannah stopped at an intersection, and Katie took her hand again, continuing down the hall toward the second stairwell.

Her breathing as loud and ragged as Hannah's, Katie paused for a deep breath inside the larger stairwell. Hannah draped an arm over her, gasping for breath. Katie heard nothing pursuing them and closed her eyes, focusing hard. Rhyn's energy filled her. She visualized the portal and the basement. As soon as the portal appeared, she dragged Hannah through it, racing to the glowing door on the other side.

Only when they both emerged into the basement did she stop to catch her breath. Hannah dropped to the floor beside her, and Lankha inched away while Toby smiled.

"Master Kris has ordered an evacuation," Henri, Kris's secretary, said as he approached. "He said you'd know where to go, Katherine."

She nodded, sucking in air.

"How did you do that?" Hannah asked, turning to her. "We were somewhere else …"

"I'll explain later," Katie promised. "I'm not waiting for any demons to find us. Lankha, pick up Toby."

She closed her eyes and focused again.

They crossed unimpeded through the portal and onto the island Sanctuary, one of four such sites bridging the mortal and immortal worlds. Sanctuaries were managed by a convent of women who cared for the lost and injured. Katie didn't recognize the woman who greeted them and ushered them into the small fortress on an undeclared—hidden by magic—island in the Caribbean. She led them into a courtyard lined on all four sides with lopsided doors.

"Master Kris said you were coming. We have several refugees here already," the woman in the long brown robe said. "We're assigning quarters as soon as they arrive and providing a hot meal afterwards. Ladies, you are in these two rooms." She pointed to two doors. "The healer can stay there, and the angel—"

"With me," Katie said.

"Then you can take the larger of the two rooms. I'll wait while you look around your quarters."

Katie knew from experience there wasn't much to see. Lankha was nearly buckling under the weight of Toby. She opened the door to her tiny room, taking in the two twin beds with sagging metal frames. Lankha set Toby down on one before they joined Hannah in the courtyard.

"Is it normally this ... exciting around here?" Hannah asked as they walked to the cafeteria.

"Seems to be so far," Katie admitted. "Nice of Kris to abandon you upstairs like that."

"I'm sure he didn't mean for that to happen," Hannah said, sounding unconvinced. Katie glanced at her troubled sister, unable to help the guilt she felt at Hannah's look.

"He means well. He said he sent someone to find you," she forced herself to say. "He's kinda got a whole bunch of people to worry about."

"I know, Katherine. I'm not upset at him. I just wasn't expecting to be confronted with … what were those things?"

"Demons."

"Not what you want to see when you've just taken the most heavenly bath."

"Probably not."

"You did really good back there," Hannah said, turning her winning smile on Katie. "I'm impressed, little sis."

Despite her anger at her sister, Katie felt the warm smile affect her. Hannah used that smile to charm everyone from waiters to potential boyfriends, but it was nice to have her sister smile at her rather than remark about how disappointed she was.

"You think Kris is okay?" Hannah asked, her smile fading. "I feel like we ran off and left him."

"You don't want to be there to see how bad things get," Katie advised.

"You don't worry about Rhyn?"

Katie hesitated, her hand going to the tattoo at her neck. "I do, but I know he's the scariest thing out there. I don't think anything can hurt him."

She found herself hoping Gabriel made it here before Rhyn did. She'd been so pissed at him, she'd told him what she'd planned to keep from him. A sense of desperation almost took her strength away. She dropped to her knee and pretended to retie her shoe.

Gabriel was coming for her and the life growing within her. She could barely fathom what that meant. She didn't understand much of the Immortal world, but she knew Death always won. In Gabriel's mind, he'd already killed her, or he wouldn't have looked at her with regret instead of pity.

"Hannah, I need to lie down," she said and rose unsteadily. "Go eat and I'll see you later."

She turned without waiting for her sister to respond and made her way to her room. Her emotions crippled her, and she flung herself on the bed, sobbing.

Rhyn slammed Tamer to the ground one last time, too incensed to notice his half-brother was trying desperately to tap out. Kiki grabbed his arm and yanked to get his attention.

"Enough, Rhyn!" he shouted.

Rhyn blinked and stepped back. Tamer was still for a long moment, until Kiki shoved a foot beneath his belly and rolled him over. The large man gasped for air, his eye swollen already.

"Can we count you in?" Kiki asked.

Tamer nodded. Kiki extended a hand and pulled him up. Rhyn paced, eyeing Erik, whose bloodied nose had finally stopped bleeding. His tactics would never earn anything but scorn from Kris, but they worked.

"I'll send my men," Tamer grunted. "Tell Kris—next time he wants something—to call instead of sending this animal."

"Enough from both of you," Kiki said. "I think we need to get a few things straight before we go."

Rhyn ceased pacing, and Erik frowned.

"One, what do we want to do about Sasha?"

"Kill him," Tamer said without hesitation.

"Yep," Erik agreed.

"Let Darkyn have him," Rhyn growled.

"The consensus is that Sasha dug his own grave," Kiki said. "Two, what are we going to do when Kris chooses the Code and his oath over our unanimous vote to kill Sasha?"

Three pairs of eyes went to Rhyn, who stood ready to take on any of them that mentioned leaving the Council.

"We fucking live with it," Tamer said with a scowl. "Even though Sasha is going to kill us all."

"Very well," Kiki said. "Next, how soon can you all have your men to the castle to kill some demons? Mine are on the way."

"As are mine," Erik said.

"I'll send them now," Tamer said.

"Best Council meeting ever," Kiki declared. "Rhyn, to the castle?"

Rhyn gave a nod, hands clenching at the thought of facing off against some demons. Kiki tucked his iPad under his arm and opened a portal through which all three went before Rhyn followed. They emerged into the castle, and he sensed the demons before he'd even set foot into the hallway outside of Kris's conference room. A blow sent him smashing into a wall, and he morphed instantly, diving at the demons chasing his brothers as they retreated through the burnt doorway of Kris's chambers to search for weapons. He tore through the demons and panted as he waited for his brothers.

"I see Kris on the park," Kiki called from the window. "Never seen so many demons!"

Tamer emerged from Kris's chamber into the hallway first, armed with a scythe and a bo, while Erik followed with a long sword. Kiki trailed with nothing more than his iPad and a long knife. Rhyn snorted at him as Kiki strapped the iPad around his body.

They charged through the hall toward the stairs and descended to the main floor. Rhyn was the first to engage any demon in his way while Tamer and Erik beheaded every creature that crossed their paths. Rhyn led them down the main floor and out the front door, slamming into one of Kris's Immortals by accident.

"Rhyn, you idiot!" Tamer shouted.

Rhyn righted himself, unconcerned, and barreled toward the demons. Kris's two-to-one advantage had dwindled, and Darkyn didn't hesitate to unleash every demon he could. Kris and a few of his Immortals were surrounded in the middle of the park while demons darted from the forest to attack pockets of Immortals. The snow was drenched with blood, like an Immortal snow cone. Kris, he knew, was the best Immortal warrior ever known.

Rhyn tackled one of the demons who took down Kris's wingman and slashed its throat open. He fought with unrestrained fury, not wanting to stop and think of the most ridiculous thought ever to cross his mind. That he, a half-demon, half-Immortal who had spent the better part of his years in Hell, was looking at becoming the first of his brothers to father a hatchling …

Confusion and rage blinded him, and he threw himself into the battle, not noticing the nicks and bruises his opponents inflicted upon him. He focused on the taste of their warm blood and on tearing them limb from limb.

In his blood-filled haze, he heard one of his brothers shout, and the demons shift their focus from Kris's small group—which Rhyn defended—to the warriors pouring out of portals onto the small battlefield. He fought until the yard was lit only by the castle's outer lighting, then onward to dawn, free after so long restraining himself around the Immortals and humans.

Stability. It was a word Andre had used that Rhyn never understood. For once, Rhyn knew some sort of stability within himself, no doubt because of his bond to Katie.

He tore apart a demon and stood breathless, seeking his next opponent, only to see the body-strewn park was empty of living demons in the early morning light. He panted, agitated by the snowfall and not having anything else to kill. Everywhere around him, the Council's Immortals were finishing off the few demons remaining.

"Rhyn?" Kiki asked uneasily as the half-demon approached.

"You'll have a sword to the throat if you don't transform," Kris snapped.

Rhyn growled but shifted to his human shape. His skin and clothing was soaked with demon blood, and Kiki gave him a long look.

"Where's Katie?" Rhyn demanded.

"They're fine. I evacuated the castle," Kris said. His white hair was streaked red with blood, his roving gaze tired. "Kiki, I owe you. Whatever you said to bring the others back, thank you."

"You can thank Rhyn for beating some sense into us," Kiki replied.

Rhyn met his eldest brother's gaze, not expecting any words of appreciation and not disappointed. Kris turned away and maneuvered through the piles of dead-dead Immortals and demons toward Tamer.

"Kiki, I need a count of living and dead-dead Immortals!" he ordered.

Irritation flashed across Kiki's face, and Rhyn raised an eyebrow in warning.

"Fine," he grated.

"The Council needs to come with me," Kris added. "That includes you, Rhyn."

"You can leave Rhyn out," Erik said.

"I'll sit outside the door to make sure no one leaves," Rhyn suggested. The dangerous note in his voice drew Kris's attention. Kris looked at each of the brothers then back at him, as if forced to acknowledge what—or who—had compelled them back. He said nothing of his thoughts but strode into the castle.

Rhyn didn't want to follow. He wanted to track any remaining demons in the forest and kill them, too. He trailed his brothers. Kris didn't go far, just far enough to be out of earshot of the Immortals.

"We need to find Sasha," he said grimly.

"And kill him," Erik added, earning a sharp look.

"He took the vial of blood he brought with him," Kris said. "The next time the demons attack, they may be immune to death by our hands. Kiki, Rhyn, check our father's crypt. You two come with me."

Tamer grumbled but obeyed, and Rhyn shook out his tense body.

"The last thing I want to do is go down there," Kiki said. "You're not pissed about the display, are you?"

Rhyn eyed him and started down the hall, not caring what his brother thought of anything at the moment. He trotted through the body-littered floor to the back stairwell. Kiki followed him through to the basements, and Rhyn stopped in front of the door to his father's crypt. The door hung by a single hinge. He saw before entering that the sarcophagus was gone.

He explored the crypt, gaze going to the display of his mother on one wall. He felt the sense of foreboding again, the unseen danger toward Katie. His eyes traveled to where his father had lain.

The son of a demon and an Immortal had turned out too fucked up for anyone to tolerate. He doubted Katie would be anything like a demon mother, and yet, he could see the both of them ending up as his father and mother did: dead-dead before their child was six. He wondered what a half-human son would be like, and his thoughts went to Gabriel, who started out human before turning Immortal. Bitterly, he realized he didn't know who had the best chance of killing them: the Dark One, the demons, or one of his brothers.

She'd be better off without you. He'd wanted to continue denying the words of his brothers. Gazing at his dismembered mother, he couldn't help thinking they were right. Everyone who had ever been close to him died horribly. His chest grew tight at the thought of Katie's fate if she stayed with him. Now, there was something else to consider. His gaze went to the statue of him.

"There's nothing here," Kiki said with a frown. "C'mon."

And still Darkyn pursued her in her nightmares. Katie jerked awake from the latest one where she and Toby were running from the unseen demon down a sandy beach. The first light of day filtered in through the small square window above her bed. The creaky bed protested as she sat, and she tried hard not to make more noise and wake Toby. She slid her feet into plain sandals provided by the convent along with her plain sweats and T-shirt. The Caribbean air was heavy, the ocean chill warmer than the weather at the castle. She wasn't hungry but walked toward the cafeteria so she wouldn't be alone with her thoughts.

A breakfast buffet lined one end of the cafeteria, with brown-robed women moving in between the food and the kitchen. Two Immortal mates were already eating, and she looked over the food with disinterest. The makeshift bar in the corner, however, drew her attention.

"Excuse me."

She turned to see Helga, the woman who had greeted them when they arrived.

"We had an Immortal wash up on our shores last night. He's alive but a frightful mess, and we haven't been able to identify him. I thought I'd ask before you sat down for breakfast."

"I doubt I'll be much help," she said. "I'm rather new to this world."

"The ladies eating didn't know him either. I have to keep checking though," the woman said with a level of determination that made Katie smile.

"I'll come with you," she said. "I take it this guy is unconscious?"

"Yes. Our healer did what we could. We think he might be an Ancient, but he's so weak and his face has been so damaged, we can't tell."

Katie stopped in place, her chest growing tight. Helga turned to look at her curiously, and she forced herself forward.

"You don't normally allow Ancients inside the walls," she said. "You made an exception?"

"He was mostly dead when we fished him out of the bay. When he's strong enough, we can send him outside the walls."

Katie couldn't help the sense of panic growing within her. She rubbed her scarred arm and glanced up at the sky, which had begun to lighten. Helga led her to the men's wing of the Sanctuary and opened a door to a room smaller than Katie's.

Sasha's face was a mottled mess that made him resemble Frankenstein's monster, with newly sewn stitches holding together the edges of swollen red gashes. She took in the bandages around his chest and arms. He looked as if he'd survived a run-in with a blender.

"He is an Ancient," she said. "Sasha."

Helga gasped. "The first to betray the Council and serve the Dark One?"

"The *only* to betray the council and serve the Dark One!" Katie shot back in irritation. Rhyn had done neither of those things, despite the legend he had! The distinction was lost on Helga, whose look of horror made Katie pity the woman.

"He cannot be here," Helga said. "But by the Code, I cannot throw him outside the walls when he is so injured."

Katie hesitated to speak her mind, her gaze taking in Sasha's beat-up body. It wasn't a coincidence he was there. She debated with herself about his intentions. Would he go to this extent to be granted admittance, even though he might not survive long enough to get whatever it was he came for? What had he come for? Her or Hannah? Refuge from the demons?

"Was he carrying anything?" she asked. "Or was there anything in his pockets?"

"I'm not sure. If he was, it would be in the trunk under his bed."

Katie inched forward, terrified he'd leap off the bed to attack her. She eased the small trunk out from under his bed and carried it into the hallway. She set it down and opened it. His shredded clothing had been laundered and folded. Pulling it out, she sucked in a breath and withdrew a familiar vial of blood. She stared at the discovery in her hands. With the castle flooded by demons, she didn't know where she could take the vial to keep it from Sasha when he woke.

Whatever Sasha's plan had been, it must've backfired. He'd never risk losing something so valuable! Without replacing the clothing, she tucked the vial into her pocket and rose.

"Is there an Immortal named Ully here?" she asked.

"Not that I recall," Helga said. "There are four Sanctuaries. The Ancient Kris probably contacted the other three, because we only have about forty Immortal refugees here now. We're the smallest Sanctuary by far."

"You need to toss him outside the walls, fast," Katie said. "Or you're risking the lives of everyone here."

Helga appeared aghast, then torn. Katie strode back to her room, mind racing. Rhyn might come if she called him. Or he might not after her accidental slip-up. Either way, she feared seeing him again before she had her it's-not-me-it's-you speech ready. She opened her door and glanced over at Toby then did a double-take. The youth sitting on Toby's bed wasn't Toby.

"Who are you?" she demanded, startled.

"Toby, Mama," he said with a snicker. The kid on the bed was closer to twelve than five, and near her height. She stared at him hard, recognizing the brown eyes but not the lean face and body.

"Today must be your birthday," Helga said from the doorway.

"Yes, ma'am."

"Someone care to explain?" Katie asked.

"Angels jump from age to age. They mature slowest of all Immortals, but when they hit certain points in angel years, they jump to the next human stage of maturity," Helga said. "It's fascinating. We raised an angel here for several hundred millennia. You wake up one day and find he's turned from child to man overnight."

Just when she thought she understood the rules of the Immortals, they changed.

"A hungry man," Toby added.

"I forgot your cocoa and marshmallows in my suitcase at the castle," she said. "I'll bring them back with your toys next time I go there."

"I'm not six anymore, Mama. I'm going to breakfast."

She stood out of his way, barely able to care for a child and at a loss as to what to do with a boy on the verge of becoming a teenager. As if unaccustomed to his longer legs, Toby tripped twice on his way to the door, stabilized himself, then started forward more cautiously.

Katie waited until he was gone then shook her head, tired of Immortal surprises. Her hand went to her pocket, where the vial was.

"I need to get this someplace safe before Sasha wakes up," she said. "Another Sanctuary maybe, so I can find my friend Ully?"

"Your mate can help you, can't he?" Helga asked with a glance at her neck.

"He's sort of busy fighting demons."

"Then I can help you get to the Indian Ocean Sanctuary."

"I feel like I should take my sister and Toby with me. If you throw Sasha out, can you keep him from entering?"

"No, we cannot. It's an informality that the Ancients respect about visiting us," Helga said. "But, we can try to keep him asleep. You came with a healer, didn't you?"

"Yes, Lankha."

"I'll have this Lankha keep the Ancient in a deep sleep until you return."

Katie hesitated again, afraid to leave her sister after the demons invaded the castle. The vial had to go to Ully, though, and at some point, she'd have to face Rhyn. For the first time since meeting him, she almost preferred to deal with Kris.

"If anything happens …" There was nothing anyone could do, least of all her. She couldn't bring herself to voice the words out loud. Helga gave her a warm smile.

"We've crossed this bridge before," she assured her. "Your family will be safe here. Come, I will show you a picture to where you must take the portal through the shadow world."

An hour later, Katie stood in a similar-looking fortress several times the size of the Caribbean Sanctuary. The courtyard was packed with women in brown robes and Immortals. Large shade trees and bamboo cabanas provided seating and protection from the sun. The Immortals were grouped beneath the trees, and none of them appeared the worse for wear from their escape.

She wandered the courtyard, looking for any sign of Ully or anyone she recognized. The fortress around the courtyard was four stories tall and lined with wooden doors indicating guest rooms. Several were open, and she saw much more comfortable accommodations and beds than at the small Sanctuary. The cafeteria was four times the size of the one she was used to, and she lingered in the doorway, finally catching the attention of a convent member.

"I'm looking for an Immortal named Ully. I don't know his last name or anything," she said as the woman approached.

"You'll have to check the register. We haven't been able to record everyone's names yet, but what we have is in the guestbook in the office, down that hall, last door on the right," the woman replied, pointing to a hallway behind her.

Katie moved quickly in the direction she indicated and found a line in front of the guestbook as Immortals wrote their names. When she reached it, she scanned all the names on each page, disappointed at not finding his anywhere.

She began to wonder if he made it out of the castle.

Gabriel stared at the portal in front of him. He dreaded stepping through it. The results of his trip to the mortal world would forever alter his life, and that of his only friend. He would've been content to stay in his cottage for another hundred years or never again visit the mortal world. Death, however, had different plans.

You're going soft.

He hated those words, because he was the biggest and strongest of all Death's assassins. That he came from the mortal world rather than the Immortal one had left a taint on him that no amount of success could get rid of. He suspected Death always thought him weaker despite service that had been, until now, flawless.

He gathered the tools of the trade, weapons for killing quickly this time, and stepped through the portal to the shadow world. If he tried, he'd be able to locate his target and track her as she moved until she was dead-dead. Instead, he emerged from the shadow world into the center of the Caribbean Sanctuary. He knew she wasn't there, and the longer she stayed away, the more time he had to think about what to do. He went to a dark corner in the cafeteria to wait.

She'd be safe, as long as she stayed away.

Chapter Six

Katie emerged from the shadow world with her heart pounding. Ully's lab was a disaster, with glass covering the floor and counters flipped on end. The door was closed but lopsided in its frame while half the lights overhead were burnt out. She heard no signs of demons fighting from outside the room.

"Ully?" she called, picking her way through the broken glass and fallen instruments. A sound came from the back of the large room, and she made her way there. A small door—possibly leading to a bathroom or closet—was closed and blocked by one of Ully's science toys the size of a copy machine. The sound came from behind it, as if someone were trying to open the door.

Hesitating only a moment, she shoved the machine. It screeched across the floor a few inches. With a deep breath, she shoved again, enough for the door to crack open.

"Ully, is that you?" she called, ready to run if a demon tried to lunge at her.

"Katie!" Ully sounded relieved. "I'm stuck in here!"

"Are you ok, Ully?" she asked, surprised.

"Alive. Did you bring Rhyn?"

"It's just me." Ully sighed in disappointment, and she rolled her eyes. "I can leave you in there!"

"It's probably safer," he agreed.

"You're worse than some damsel in distress. Aren't you supposed to be protecting the weak, puny human?"

He said nothing but pushed at the door. She shoved the machine again until the space was wide enough for him to squeeze through. The scientist's glasses were missing, his expression growing sorrowful as he looked around at his destroyed lab.

"I brought you something to cheer you up," she said and dug the vial of blood out of her pocket. "I found it on Sasha."

"You sure it was Sasha?"

"Pretty sure."

"Let me see something," he said, striding to where his desk was. He pushed the wreckage around and dug his notebook out of the mess. Katie watched as he walked through the lab, collecting undestroyed pieces of equipment and tools. One counter was still standing next to the refrigerator tucked in a corner, and he swept the broken glass from the top to create a little work space. She looked around the area where his desk had been and spotted a perfume bottle similar to the one he'd give her before.

"What do you think is wrong with it?" she asked as she bent to retrieve the bottle. *Demon* was scribbled on the side. She sniffed at it and sneezed at the familiar skunk scent before shoving it in her pocket.

"I don't think anything is wrong with it, but I want to make sure," he explained.

"Good thing Sasha washed up on shore at the Sanctuary or the demons would have this one," she said. "I guess it wouldn't matter if you succeeded in altering it like Kris said."

"Altering it?"

"Did you get hit on the head or something? Kris told you to make a toxic version he could trade back to the demons."

"I do have a headache," he said, distracted. "You say Sasha washed up somewhere?"

"Really weird, Ully. I don't know what he's doing. The women at the Sanctuary said they pulled him out of the water, and he looks awful."

"Which Sanctuary?"

She looked up at the uncharacteristic demand. Ully appeared to be prepping his tools for whatever tests he wanted to run. The vial sat on the counter next to his notebook, and she watched him pick up a syringe. She'd never noticed how long his nails were or the sinewy strength in his forearms. Suddenly, she wondered just how well demons could shapeshift and why they'd lock Ully in the closet instead of killing him.

"I'm feeling really sick, Ully. Do you have any food?" she asked. She sagged against a counter, hoping he believed her. She reached for the perfume in her pocket. For once, she hoped Ully's oddball experiment didn't let her down.

"Sure," he said, the dark note in his voice gone. "This won't take long. I should have something in the fridge and then we can go get some real food."

Having spent many afternoons with him in the lab, she knew he kept only serums and instruments in the refrigerator. He made his way to the appliance, and she darted for the vial, snatching it off the counter then running through the mess to the door. The demon that was Ully gave a half-bark, half-roar before he smashed through the lab toward her. He snatched one arm and she sprayed him with the perfume.

The demon coughed and batted at his face.

Thank you, Ully, thank you!

Uncertain whether or not the battle still waged between demons and Immortals, she braced herself to be attacked as she flew past every doorway towards the back stairwell. Bodies blocked her descent to the basements where the warriors were, and she struck off down a narrow corridor that dead-ended in another set of stairs leading to a door hanging from one hinge.

She heard no signs of the demon pursing but trotted down the stairs, hoping to find another way into the dungeons where the Immortal warriors lived. It took all her strength to shove the hefty door wide enough for her to enter the dark chamber beyond that was lit by a single torch.

It looked like a crypt. The altar in the center was empty while seven statues kept watch over it. The air was heavy and her attention was drawn to the life-like statues. The tallest looked a great deal like Andre, the deceased Immortal she'd met a short time before he was killed. The second looked like Kris might've in his younger days, when his face still glowed with hope. Sasha's wore a genuine smile. She vaguely recognized the other three and knelt beside the statue of Rhyn, who was no older than Toby had been the day before.

Even at such a young age, Rhyn's features were troubled and somber, as if he knew what kind of a life awaited him. She sat back with a frown, unable to feel anything but pity for the half-demon child who knew no acceptance anywhere in life. She touched her stomach with a flutter of panic. The idea of bringing a new life into such a horrific world made her feel sick. No child of hers would end up like Rhyn—tormented, rejected, and abused!

"What're you doing here?"

She whipped around to see Kris standing in the doorway, holding the door open as if debating whether to enter.

"Is that really you?" she asked suspiciously. She rose to keep the altar between them.

"What kind of stupid question is that?"

"Tell me something only you and I would know," she ordered.

"I slept with your sister."

"God, Kris, did you have to go there?"

"You delusional or do you have a reason to think I'm someone else?" he asked and entered fully.

"I ran into someone I thought was Ully in the lab. Turned out to be a demon. I didn't know they could shapeshift into someone else's form."

"Only a very few of them can assume the form of another human. Demons are born with predetermined forms that are unique to the demon. A few can assume forms, but they're rare," he said. "You say there was one in Ully's lab?"

"Yes."

"We'll have to scrub this place from top to bottom to make sure no one else pops up somewhere they shouldn't be. Like you being here."

"I was more concerned with hiding than with where I went," she said, agitated by his accusing look. "What is this place?"

"It was our father's crypt, until yesterday, when Sasha stole our father's body."

Her gaze went to the altar, and she shivered. The Council That Was Seven had been immortalized safeguarding their father in death. It was creepy. Who kept a dead man on a shrine in the basement?

"The statues are beautiful," she managed. "It's hard to imagine Rhyn as a child."

"He was cast out of the Immortal world fairly young. None of us know—or care—where he went, except Andre, who saw something in him that—to this day—never materialized."

Her face grew red at his easy dismissal of his youngest brother. Her gaze settled on the statue of Rhyn, whose large eyes held an ominous look too old for his chubby little face.

"How can you be like this, Kris?" she asked, unable to stop the angry words. "You take great precautions to safeguard Toby, and yet, you rejected your own brother?"

"Someone like you could never understand."

"You're right, Kris, I can't understand how you could turn your back on the person who needed you most and justify it with your shortsighted arrogance. I pray to God Hannah doesn't choose you as a mate!"

"I believe she already has," he said, irritation in his voice. "Rhyn was a lost cause from the beginning. Our own father wanted him dead. I'm sworn to protect Toby, and I've done my duty in protecting Sasha, who is also my brother, according to the Code and the oaths I swore to my father and the Council!"

"You chose the wrong side, Kris. If you had half a brain, you'd have helped Rhyn and killed Sasha."

"I do what I am obligated to do, and that's all that should concern you," he said through gritted teeth. "I won't have some stupid mortal telling me how to do things!"

With all the insults and arrogance, she couldn't take her mind off the statue of Rhyn and her sister being at the mercy of such a man.

"I'm going to tell you a secret someone told me, Kris," she said, facing him. "Do you know why Rhyn killed Lilith?"

He stared at her.

"Yes, I know the story," she said. "It was revealed to me by someone you trust when I was at the Sanctuary a few weeks ago. Lilith was trying to destroy the Council. She was a plant by the Dark One who lured you and probably the rest of your brothers into bed. Rhyn killed her to protect you, Kris. You owe him your life. He's the most flawed of anyone I've ever met, but he's a more honorable man than you'll ever be!"

He crossed the distance between them in three strides and slapped her hard. Pain flared through her. She touched the blood that bubbled at the side of her mouth.

"Get the fuck out of here," he hissed.

She reached into her pocket and withdrew the vial, shoving it at him.

"I may be a stupid mortal, but I know right from wrong," she said in a trembling voice. "Sasha's at the Caribbean Sanctuary. Go rescue him again, so he can kill more of the Immortals, like those you sacrificed to protect him the first time!"

She fled, her ears ringing and cheek burning from his strike. She'd never understand a man like Kris, who saw the world only in black and white! The image of baby Rhyn and Kris's words distracted her as she hurried through the hall back to the stairs. She couldn't imagine what he'd been through: thrown out at such an age with a father who wanted him dead and brothers who hated him. He wasn't the kind to pity himself. She doubted he saw anything wrong with the treatment he was accustomed to.

Soon enough, nothing would matter, not when Gabriel came for her.

For the first time since arriving over three weeks ago, she missed her cavernous chamber. She wondered if twelve-year-old boys played with stuffed animals. Toby had tons of them in his small bedchamber off hers. She found herself ascending the servants' stairwell at a run, in case the Ully-demon was still stalking her, until she reached her floor, which appeared blessedly free of any signs of battle and death. She pushed her door open and scanned the room before entering and closing it fast.

She'd never liked her room, but she found some comfort in its familiarity. One of Toby's stuffed animals had fallen to the floor when she carried him to the basement before the demon attacks. She retrieved it and hugged it, not at all certain what the new Toby would and wouldn't want that the old Toby had loved. The bag she'd started to pack still gaped open, half-full on the trunk at the base of her bed.

"Hey."

She turned at the familiar voice, pleased and surprised to see Megan, the Immortal warrior who befriended her and showed her around when she arrived to the castle several weeks before. Megan's dark eyes were glowing though her clothing was covered in blood.

"You shouldn't be alone up here yet," Megan warned. "Bad guys in the castle still. We're sweeping the castle now."

"So it's over?"

"Mostly. The Council sent in their warriors to help Kris. We lost quite a few of our friends," she said with a frown. "Defeated the demons, except for a few hiding out here."

"I'm so sorry, Megan," she said softly.

"It's what we train for. Doesn't make it easier but …" Megan shrugged. "C'mon. We cleared out the basements. You can stay in your old room."

"I'd like that," Katie said. "Let me grab a few more things." She packed hurriedly and grabbed another of Toby's stuffed animals before meeting the female warrior in the hallway. Megan spoke with a gentle British lilt, and her dark eyes took in everything as they walked.

"How many are lost?" Katie asked as they walked.

"About half of Kris's warriors. Not sure about the others. Your mate can fight like a monster. Never seen anything like that before. He was shapeshifting like a maniac and just tearing demons' heads off. He kept up at it all night."

"I imagine." She suspected she knew what made Rhyn fight like a demon. For once, it wasn't his half-demon blood.

"He brought the Council back together," Megan said in a whisper. "At least, that's what some of Ancient Erik's warriors said. Ancient Kris would never admit to that."

"What do you mean, brought the Council together?"

"They split before the demon battle, and Rhyn rounded up all the brothers. The guy I spoke to said he beat the ever-living shit out of them all at once, until they agreed to come back and do what Kris says."

A laugh bubbled up. Katie tried to suppress it, not wanting to offend her friend, but it escaped. Megan looked at her curiously.

"Sorry. I guess I can see him doing that," she explained. She doubted it happened as the rumor mill said, but if Rhyn of all people had brought the Council together … She was impressed. He'd saved the Immortals that shunned him. She was pleased by the news, despite knowing none of his brothers remotely deserved to be saved.

"They went hunting for Sasha," Megan added. "I hope they find him."

Katie said nothing. She wanted to return to the Sanctuary, though not before she found out what happened to Ully. They descended to the warrior's barracks level of the basements. For the first time in three weeks, she felt safe and relieved as she looked around the tiny room that had been hers when she first arrived. The barracks area was heavily guarded, but she was struck by the lack of activity in the part of the castle that normally hummed with life.

"You know where everything is," Megan said at the doorway. "I gotta keep looking for demons or any other Immortal survivors."

"Have you seen Ully by chance?" Katie asked.

"Not yet. We're trying to get a handle on who went to which Sanctuary and where else Immortals scattered to. We should know by nightfall."

"Thanks."

Megan closed the door behind her, and Katie sank down onto the bed.

Rhyn finished his task of clearing Kris's floor of dead bodies. He tossed the last one out the window. Kris was glaring up at him, he knew without looking. But he wasn't about to walk up and down the stairwell or traipse through the shadow world a million times to accomplish the same goal.

A pyre had been built in the middle of the cobblestone courtyard to burn the bodies of the demons before nightfall, when they'd come back alive. He wiped his bloodied hands on his shirt and trotted down the hall. He'd sensed Katie's appearance in the castle a short time ago and had avoided going directly to her, for fear he wasn't quite ready to say what he needed to. With nothing left to occupy him, he strode to the familiar room where they'd shared the fateful night weeks before. Katie looked up from her spot seated on the bed as he entered, her face troubled.

"You're a mess," she said in disapproval. He glanced down to see how bad his clothing looked. It was soaked through and dried with blood and his exposed skin was tinted red.

"Rough night," he said, sitting on the bed across from her. "Really rough night."

"So I hear."

They gazed at each other for a long, quiet minute.

"This room has a lot of memories," she spoke at last and looked around.

"Yeah," he agreed, glance going to her stomach. He'd never had a thought more foreign than that of what grew within her.

"Not all good," she said and crossed her arms self-consciously. "Megan said you brought the Council together."

"They just needed a little encouragement," he said with a shrug.

"It was a very good thing for you to do."

"Sometimes I get things right."

"You're a better person than I am. I would've let them all go down in flames for how they treated you," she said.

The awkward quiet fell again. He didn't want her storming out as usual when he said something wrong.

"Is it a boy or a girl?" he asked at last.

"You don't know anything about this do, you?"

"I assume one day it hatches."

"Hatches?" she echoed, astonished.

"Demons hatch."

"I'm not a demon!"

"It'll be a boy."

"It could be a girl."

"It can't be. Girls can't fight and they just make life really difficult," he snapped. He'd never felt like panicking in his life but in that moment, he almost did. He stood and paced.

"Look, I'll make this easy on you," she said. "I'll go live with Hannah, out of your hair, and you can run around killing things and beating up your brothers. We'll both be … happy."

"We'll see," he said. His thoughts went to his father's crypt.

"We'll see what?"

"I'm thinking," he growled. "You still intend to leave me. I still don't want to lose you, but all I do is cause you trouble." She looked down, and he noticed for the first time one of her cheeks was red. "What happened to your cheek?"

"Nothing. Just pissing people off today. Did you hear I found Sasha?" She hurried to change the subject. "Rather, he magically appeared at the Sanctuary."

"He happen to be carrying a clear coffin?"

"No, but he had the vial of blood. I brought it to Kris."

That explains her cheek, he thought darkly, not caring one bit about Sasha or the vial. Katie couldn't stay with her sister if her sister chose Kris, or she'd be subjected to the same treatment he was. His gaze went to her neck, his resolve solidifying at the sight of her exhausted features and red cheek. He had one chance to make a safe life for her and their … hatchling. He found himself wishing again that Andre was alive. Instead, he found himself mulling over the advice from another brother.

"What's wrong?" she asked as he paced.

"Maybe you're right. We should split," he forced himself to say. "Sasha told me how to break our mating. I think you have a better chance of being accepted by the Immortals if you're not my mate."

She looked surprised. "Rhyn, what are you saying?"

"I'm saying, I release you of our bond."

"You *what?*"

"I don't know exactly how to do it, but from this day forward, I'll no longer claim you as my mate. You should be safe now."

He couldn't read the look on her face. Her emotions were flying and intense. He started to leave, and she stood.

"Rhyn, wait!" she said. "I didn't want to leave you because of the Immortals or any of that. There's something else I need to—"

"Katie, if I do this, I know you'll survive. If I stay with you, I don't know if you will. And now there's the hatchling to think about," he said. "I'd rather lose you as my mate than lose you forever. So, it's done. I'll always take care of you both, but I won't endanger you anymore."

With regret heavy in his stomach, he left. She didn't try to stop him. He strode through the halls and stairwells until he broke free of the castle. He would go to the Sanctuary and bring Sasha back to Kris. He'd serve on the Council and force it to stay together. He'd rebuild the Immortal empire and use his half-demon skills to protect them all. He'd sacrifice himself to the balance of good and evil by taking on the enforcer role Andre's death had left open.

Most importantly, he'd protect Katie by building a world that was safe for her and watching over her from a distance. Kris had sworn to protect her if Rhyn un-mated her. If Kris were willing to protect a twisted bastard like Sasha because of a stupid oath, he'd do the same for Katie. Maybe then, she'd know peace. No one would hurt her or hunt her just to get to him. He'd find a way to deal with the loss that ate a hole through his body. What mattered was that she was safe, and he no longer caused her pain.

Rage pounded through his body and he threw himself into the air, relishing the pain the shapeshifting brought.

"We found something while scouting the forest." The Immortal on the other side of his door was too excited to wait until he entered to shout the news.

"Come in," Kris ordered from his spot at the conference table. It was otherwise empty, and he'd escaped for a break from the death burning in the courtyards and any interaction with others, especially a certain mortal who'd managed to reopen an old wound. He looked up as the scout entered. Snow had begun to fall again and clung to the scout's clothing. "What is it?"

"Darkyn's preparing for another attack in the forest."

"How many demons?"

"More than we have Immortals."

Kris rose to find his brothers.

"Kris," the scout continued. "There's something else. The demons are heading to the mortal village. We heard them say they have orders to kill everyone."

Kris was silent, surprised at Darkyn's audacity. Immortals and demons fought among themselves, for mortals were too weak and temporary to bother with. It was an understanding as old as the Dark One, who had stopped his demons once before when they launched attacks on humans. While Kris would love to sacrifice a certain infuriating mortal to further his cause, he wouldn't even sacrifice her, let alone allow Darkyn's to wipe out a village. Any bleed over of their battle into the mortal world was unacceptable.

He strode into the hall, calling, "Kiki!"

His brother poked his head from the burnt-out remains of Kris's own chamber.

"Scout, tell him. I'm going to find my brothers."

The scout bobbed his head. Kris opened a portal to the Indian Ocean Sanctuary, where Erik had gone to seek out Ully. The vial was in his pocket, and he strode into the Sanctuary, eyes roving for Erik or Ully.

The largest of the Sanctuaries, it was packed with the majority of the Immortals who had been present in the castle. His eyes took in the different people as he sought out Hannah before realizing she had likely gone to the Caribbean with her sister. Katie's words stung despite his attempt to ignore them. Someone had lied to her about Lilith, who had died defenseless and alone. Andre never approved of Lilith, either, but he'd never accused her of evil. An unbound Immortal's mate had no protection from demon or Immortal Code. He'd learned this the hard way when Andre refused to do more than send Rhyn to Hell for killing Lilith. Had she been his mate, Andre would've made Rhyn dead-dead.

Kris wasn't about to lose Hannah the same way. While Lilith's tattoo—and therefore, her bond to him—had never fully materialized, he'd find a way to ensure Hannah's did.

Frustrated at not finding either of the men he sought, he created a portal to the Caribbean Sanctuary and emerged outside the walls. He beat on the door then entered unbidden. A small woman in a brown robe rushed to remind him of the rules.

"I know, good lady," he said. "I will not be here long. By chance, have you seen—"

"Kris?"

He looked up at the sweet voice, his anger melting at the sight of Hannah's pretty face. She smiled uncertainly. He excused himself to cross to her. She appeared healthy, and her blue eyes were bright.

"I am glad to see you well," he said. "Did Toby make it safely?"

"Yes, of course. Katherine brought us here."

"I see. I gave orders that everyone was to rendezvous elsewhere, but I am happy you're safe."

"I have something to show you," she said and took his hand, pulling him toward the guest rooms lining the small courtyard.

"Hannah, I must—"

"It'll be quick."

He allowed her to pull him into her small room and close the door behind him. He waited while she rolled up her sleeve in excitement, then displayed the blood-red tattoo there. Inside an intricate pattern of Immortal writing was the word *K R I S*. His throat tightened at the sight of something he'd waited his whole life to see. No matter what lies Katie had been told, he couldn't believe what was said about Lilith. The evidence Lilith wasn't meant for him was clear. Immortals only had one shot at their mates, and Andre had tried to warn him Lilith was not his intended. His dead-dead brother was right, or Hannah wouldn't bear Kris's name.

He caressed the tattoo with a thumb and smiled, feeling genuine happiness for the first time since Andre's death. Hannah's face glowed, and she threw her arms around him. He held her close and breathed in her scent.

"Katherine was gone before I could show her. She'll be so thrilled to welcome you to our family!" she exclaimed.

Kris knew the opposite to be true but said nothing, enjoying the moment of peace. There was a tap at the door. He pulled loose from her to answer it, not surprised to see another of the convent members there, probably to tell him the same thing the first did.

"Master Kris," the woman said, "we have your brother, Sasha, here. He's in a deep sleep, but his presence here is causing much unease among us."

"Hannah, I promise to come back soon. I must handle this," he said, turning back to give his mate a kiss on the cheek.

"You'll return today?" she asked hopefully. "Or can we go back to the castle?"

"I have to make sure the demons are gone before you come back," he said. "I will visit again soon, my Hannah."

She beamed another brilliant smile, and it took all his willpower to leave her to see one of his least favorite people. He rejoined the awaiting convent member in the courtyard outside Hannah's room and trailed her through the Sanctuary. A familiar shape in the dark corner of the cafeteria caught his attention as he passed, and he paused to raise a hand in greeting.

"Gabriel?"

The death dealer emerged. He looked ... different, though Kris couldn't pinpoint why. His eyes were colder, his face more somber. At Tamer's height and built like a tank, there had never been anything soft about Death's assassin, but he seemed more distant than usual.

"You here for me?" He gave the typical greeting.

"No," Gabriel said.

"For Sasha maybe?"

"No."

"It would ease a lot of my issues if you were," Kris admitted. "Walk with me. You're here to watch over Toby, as usual?"

"Of sorts."

Kris gave him a sidelong look. Gabriel had been a friend to all the Council members, though he suspected the assassin favored Rhyn the most.

"I hadn't seen you in a couple of days. Demons attacked us after Sasha did something with our father's body. I don't know what he intended. He was safe at the castle," Kris said as they walked.

"People are often victims of their own natures."

"Do you ever find it difficult to follow the Code when it seems so wrong to do so?"

"Not until recently."

Gabriel's ominous words made Kris uneasy. The assassin had been an even greater stickler to the Code than he was. Kris had come close to breaking the Immortal rules or his own oaths to his father. To his knowledge, Gabriel never had, and the assassin was not one who would ever allow emotion to cloud his decisions.

"I guess there comes a time where even the best of us are tempted," he reasoned.

"Unfortunately, it seems that way. A good man once told me sometimes all the choices we have are bad."

"Wise words from a wise man," Kris said. They reached Sasha's room, and the convent member pushed the door open to reveal Sasha's torn-up body. "What I can't figure out is why he came here."

"His name isn't on my list. He doesn't have a contract out on him yet," Gabriel said.

Kris took in his mutilated brother's body. He thought of what the Council wanted him to do and of what Sasha had done. Killing in cold blood was forbidden. He'd have to figure out what to do with the wounded man. He could buy an assassination, but part of him preferred the idea of handling family matters within the family.

"When he's well enough, we'll move him," he told the anxious woman in brown. She frowned in response. "I'll post two Immortal guards to ensure he doesn't do anything stupid."

She nodded, relief on her face, and he turned away from his injured brother. He'd send someone to take Hannah to a different sanctuary, unwilling to risk his newfound mate to one as unpredictable as Sasha.

For her sake, he had to find a way to live with Katie, or their differences would turn into a family feud. He couldn't bring himself to include Rhyn in the picture and hoped Katie came to her senses one day and dumped the half-demon before the worst happened, and she ended up extending the bloodline of the loose cannon that was her mate.

"How long are you here for, Gabe?" he asked.

"As long as it takes."

"You're here on business."

"I am."

"Good luck to you," Kris said. "You'd have my eternal gratitude if you could find a place for Rhyn in the underworld."

"Not here for him."

"Maybe next time. I'm returning to the castle. I'll send Immortals to watch over Sasha."

His thoughts on preventing demons from killing innocent humans, he missed the resentful look that crossed Gabriel's face.

"You will find him and bring the vial or the girl to me, or I will spend eternity tormenting you!"

Darkyn's angry words echoed in Jade's mind. His body was bloodied from Darkyn's whip. The cold early winter wind dried the tears on his face and made his cheeks stiff. Limping, Jade returned to the site where he'd killed Sasha. Sasha's blood was hidden beneath fresh snowfall. He stopped to lean against a tree to rest, unable to shake his own surprise at discovering Sasha wasn't dead.

He'd chopped him to pieces; he shouldn't have survived! And the vial never should've found its way back here!

It was Katie again. His fury rose once more. She'd been the reason Kris turned his back on him, and she'd been the one to bring the vial to the demon she thought was Ully. If he found her, he might find the vial.

His mind foggy with pain, Jade began to humor thoughts he'd previously rejected. They appeared more reasonable in his current state. If he killed her, Kris would finally see the folly of his ways. He'd have to deliver the vial to Darkyn first. Maybe there was a chance he could leave Hell and come back to Kris. After all, Kris hadn't died in the attack, and Jade could blame it all on Sasha.

A new idea struck, and he looked down at his bloodied body. He would go to Kris and tell him just that—that Sasha had done this all, and he, Jade, had tried to help but been nearly killed by the demons!

It would work. It *must* work! Darkyn was too cruel a master to betray.

Jade shook his head, feeling as if madness born of desperation were creeping into his mind with the pain. He straightened and limped toward the castle. No one challenged him, for the Immortals had no idea what he'd done. He passed through them tensely, many of them as bloody or bruised as he was. He saw only warriors on the main floor of the castle and ascended with increasing pain to the floor where Kris would be.

Kris's chamber was a burnt-out hull, and he lingered for a moment, regret in his belly. He'd spent many wonderful nights in the now crispy bed. He went next door to the conference room and opened it.

Kris looked up, surprise crossing his face. Kiki, the Ancient from Asia, sat beside Kris at the small conference table and looked him over with a frown. Jade's words stuck in his throat at the sight of Kris's beautiful emerald eyes. Emerald was the color of Kris thinking, and Jade's favorite hue.

"My god, Jade, where have you been?" Kris managed at last, standing.

"I needed some space," Jade replied. "When I came back, the demons were attacking. I chased them into the forest and ended up surrounded. Barely made it back."

"We lost half of Kris's warriors and quite a few of mine," Kiki said. "You're a lucky man."

"Kiki, can you leave us alone?" Kris asked. Kiki obeyed and left, closing the door behind him. Jade's heart started to soar. His one love wanted to be alone with him!

"I would hug you in greeting, but I'm down to one of my last sets of clothing," Kris said somewhat ruefully. He moved to the edge of the table nearest Jade and crossed his arms as he leaned against it. "You need a healer, my friend."

"I've seen better days," Jade agreed. "I am sorry I wasn't here when you needed me."

"We survived. Barely. Waiting to see what Darkyn intends by sending his remaining warriors to the human village."

"He would do that?"

"Seems that way. Kiki's men are at the village now to protect it."

Jade was quiet, struck by the importance of such a move. Darkyn had said nothing of this to him! It was one thing for the demons and Immortals to fight, but to attack the innocent humans was madness. *He* would never go so far.

"I am happy to see you. I was worried," Kris said in a soft voice. Jade's pulse leapt at the words. "A lot has changed in so short a time. The Council is working together for once, and Sasha tricked us into thinking he was returning to the Council, disappeared and washed up at the Caribbean Sanctuary. Our father's body was stolen."

"I saw Sasha take the body into the forest," Jade said carefully. "He was shouting at the demons. Said he'd done what they told him and given them you and the castle so they'd leave him alone."

Kris's gaze darkened, and he stood, pacing to the window. He stared into the dark night, watching the snow fall.

"I guess they changed their mind. They slashed him up good, but he's still alive," Kris said. "I wonder how they got him away from the coffin. He should've known to stay put."

"I don't know. He did say something about the Sanctuary," Jade said, seeking some lie to keep Kris's suspicions from turning to him. "It's all I heard. I was fighting the demons."

"In any case, I'm pleased to see you again, my friend," Kris said. He seemed to shake his dark mood, and Jade relaxed. "I have more good news for you."

"We need good news!"

"I found my mate."

Jade drew a sharp breath. "Katie?"

"No, her sister. There were two Ancient's mates born into her family. I discovered this when her sister arrived here."

Jade saw his chance of returning to his ex-lover's side disappear. The pain returned, and he realized he hadn't noticed its temporary reprieve until it clutched his chest again. His thoughts turned to Katie. He'd give anything for the vial and the feel of her blood on his hands! She'd brought him nothing but pain, and now her family had taken Kris from him. His whole life was in shambles because of her.

"You need some rest and a shower. The guest room is open. Please, go take care of yourself," Kris said, not unkindly.

Jade couldn't bring himself to ask about the vial for fear of giving himself away. His battered body felt heavy, and his emotions grew chaotic. He stared at the ground in front of him, heartsick.

"Is Katie all right?" he forced himself to ask. "Was she pleased to know her sister was joining our … family?"

"Not exactly. She and her mate have become even larger thorns in my side. I'm sending her back to the Sanctuary in the morning."

Jade looked up again, interested as much in the sudden anger in Kris's voice as he was in the knowledge that Katie was in the castle.

"But, that's for a different time," Kris said with a small smile. "Go and rest."

"Thank you, I will." His voice sounded mechanical to his own ears. Jade opened the door to leave when Kris's voice stopped him.

"Jade, you know I'll always care about you."

"It's too late for that," he said and walked out. He went to the guestroom next door and closed the door. The chamber seemed … foreign to him. It would be his last night with the Immortals, for no one would forgive him once he followed through with the plans forming in his mind.

Kris waited until the guest bedroom door closed before he motioned to one of the Immortals posted on either end of the hallway. With a sinking heart, he realized he'd lost the Jade who'd been his friend and lover for a few hundred years. Something was drastically altered about his friend, and the thin collar around his neck told Kris everything he needed to know. What he didn't know was what happened to his other lieutenant, Iliana. If Sasha was telling the truth, the chances of her being alive weren't good.

"Post six guards in this hallway. No one leaves this floor unless it's me. Understood?"

The Immortal nodded and trotted away to gather more. Kris waited until five Immortals were present in the hall before he retreated to his conference room. Once more, he caught himself thinking of Andre and missing his brother's—and best friend's—guidance.

Andre was dead-dead. He had to do what Andre would have done.

Kris crossed to his burnt-out bedchamber and dug through a trunk in the closet. He withdrew a dagger he'd purposely buried there, never intending to follow in the footsteps of Andre's enforcer role. It was the dagger used to kill Rhyn's mother, and the same one Andre would've used to kill Sasha for breaking his sacred oaths and trying to kill his brothers.

It was the same one he'd use to kill Jade and Sasha.

Kris closed his eyes. He didn't want this role. It wasn't in his nature. As much as he didn't want to admit it, this was a role for Rhyn, who had brought the Council back. He gave his youngest brother no credit for understanding either the importance of the Council or the good intentions behind bringing the Council back together, but Rhyn knew how to use brute violence when it was needed.

"You going hunting?"

He whirled to face the man of whom he thought.

"For me?" Rhyn asked with a cunning smile. "You're the best Immortal warrior there is. It'd be an honor to kill you."

"Believe it or not, I was thinking of killing someone else," Kris replied, rising. He tucked the dagger into his belt and shoved Rhyn out of his way as he exited the closet.

"It's gotta be Sasha."

Kris said nothing.

"I came to tell you something else."

"I take it more bad news?" Kris said. "It's my day for that shit."

"I think you'll take this as good news, knowing how much you like to see me suffer."

"Then tell all."

"I let Katie go."

Kris turned, surprised. "I didn't think you were smart enough."

"It's the only way to keep you and the other Immortals from treating her like shit."

"You really did this?"

"I did."

"So you're going back to Hell?"

"No, brother, sorry to disappoint you," Rhyn said dryly. "I'm staying here. With you and the Council. It's where I'm supposed to be, isn't it?"

"I don't understand," Kris said with a frown. "You're leaving her but staying here."

"I'm going to make sure you and the Council do what it must to protect her and everyone else like her."

Kris looked at his condemned brother anew, not sure how to take Rhyn's newfound intent and resolve. Rhyn's gaze fell to the dagger Andre had carried.

"You don't have the heart or stomach for what that entails."

Kris's face felt warm, but he knew Rhyn was right for once.

"Andre and I were more alike than you know," Rhyn added.

"You were nothing alike. What he did was for the good of Immortals and humans alike," Kris said.

"Right, because killing in cold blood isn't something a Council member does."

"It's not something I do," Kris retorted.

"I will. Whomever you want, and whomever you don't want, I won't."

"You'll take orders from me?"

"On this. On everything else, probably not. But, I'll keep the Council together to protect Katie and our hatchling."

Kris stared at him. "Humans don't hatch," he whispered, not sure what else to say.

"I don't give a shit how it works."

"Dear god, Rhyn!" he said and shook his head. Now he understood Rhyn's powerful motivator, and he was both impressed and horrified.

"And she wants to become a nun at a Sanctuary," Rhyn added. "Good place for her, Toby, and the hatchling. I only ask one thing of you, Kris, in exchange for doing your dirty work."

"I'm all ears at this point."

"You take care of her like you said you would after the Council meeting. No more of the shitty treatment you've been giving her. She's no longer my mate. Treat her like she's the sister of your mate."

Kris hesitated. He'd never had a conversation with Rhyn where the two of them didn't behave like testosterone-plagued teenagers. He didn't want to agree to Rhyn's terms, but the side of him willing to take in a creature like Sasha emerged again. At the end of the day, he'd try to do what was right. If Katie wanted to go to the convent, he'd be the last to argue with her. It'd keep her out of his hair, safe, and the powerful force that was Rhyn working for him.

"We have a deal," he said. He withdrew the sheathed dagger and tossed it to Rhyn. "I still can't believe … I shouldn't be surprised. You fuck up everything."

"I know," Rhyn said, unaffected. "Who do I kill first?"

Katie stood in the back doorway to the castle, hoping Rhyn returned soon. Snow fell from the sky to be either burned by the pyre or to cover the red mess that was the rest of the park. Immortals lined the perimeter of the park shoulder to shoulder and roved the interior of the castle. Kris had assigned her a babysitter and ordered her to spray herself down with the skunk spray so she wouldn't draw any unwanted attention.

Something tickled her neck, and she looked down to see the first of the letters of her tattoo flutter to the ground. They fell delicately one by one, like feathers. She grabbed at one of them, then let it fall. It was what needed to happen. He had to let her go, but the sense of yearning and pain was too strong for her to sleep.

She sank down with her back to the door, not caring about the cold day or the snow that seeped through her clothes to chill her. She stared at the blood-colored letters as the snow buried them. She'd tried opening a portal soon after Rhyn left to return to the Sanctuary but failed. Though there was a wall of Immortals between her and the forest, she felt the demon watching her, waiting for its opening, now that she was no longer protected. Again she found herself hoping Gabriel took her soon.

Darkyn. He wasn't like the other demons. None of them had gotten into her head.

"You're like bait out here." Kris's voice made her tense. "Go to your chamber. I'll have you taken back to the Sanctuary tomorrow."

"I want to go back today," she replied.

"Not until I find Ully and test the vial you brought me. If it's not the immunity blood, then Ully will need you here in his lab."

She rolled her eyes, once again a test subject to the great overlord of the Immortals. She rose and shook out the chill.

"Besides, you should be resting," he said with a forced note of kindness. She looked up at him questioningly. To her surprise, he walked with her toward the stairs. "I understand you want to go to the convent."

"Rhyn told you?"

"He told me many things, such as he'd let you go."

"Convent would be nice," she whispered. Her chest was clenched so tight, she felt physical pain. "Safe place for us."

"I'll arrange it as soon as I can."

"Thanks, Kris." She left him at the base of the stairs and ascended alone. It was as it should be. Rhyn wasn't coming back for her, yet her heart felt as if it'd fall out of her chest. She hadn't been certain about the kind of life she'd have with him, but she was certain she didn't want a life without him. At least she wouldn't be around long enough to find out.

She entered the chilly chamber. Her Immortal guard poked his head in every corner and door and looked under the bed before he left her in peace.

How she hated this room!

Her suitcase was on the trunk. Tears rose as she realized she was about to leave for good. She didn't want to sleep for fear of the demon from her nightmares—or Gabriel—coming for her. Dragging a blanket to the warm fire in the hearth, she wrapped herself in it and sat.

She dozed and awoke to the sound of something bumping her door. The fire was lower but still burning. She hadn't slept too long. The bump sounded again, as if someone ran into it. Frowning, she rose to see if her Immortal guard was nodding off at his post. As she neared the door, she heard the sounds of scuffling.

Her heart slowed, and she stepped back, imagining the Immortal fighting off some demon that had stayed hidden until dark. Before she could search the room for something to use as a weapon or run, the door wrenched open.

Jade stood before her, blood spattered across his otherwise clean clothes. She gasped, not expecting Kris's traitorous lieutenant but knowing his presence was an awful omen. His bloodied knife was out at his side, his dark gaze blazing.

"I will ask you this once," he said. "Where is the vial the demons seek?"

"Good God, Jade, are you working with them?"

He strode to her and snatched her arm, squeezing until it hurt.

"I don't know!" she cried. "I gave it to Kris!"

His face mottled with anger, he released her with a curse and paced. She noticed his limp.

"What happened to you, Jade?" she whispered.

"Shut up! Everything that's gone wrong has been because of you!" he returned. "If you hadn't appeared, Kris …" He stopped suddenly. "Where's your mating tattoo? Is Rhyn dead?"

"Not hardly," she said and turned away. "Sounds like he did the same to me as Kris did to you."

Jade was silent. She wondered if Kris would check on her then dismissed the idea he'd seek her out for any reason. Her guards changed every eight hours, and this one would've started his shift at midnight. Two hours ago, according to the clock on the mantle. If she called for Rhyn, he wouldn't come. Desolation absorbed her into her thoughts, until Jade spoke again.

"Demons. They'll take more than your soul."

She looked at him to see the haunted look that crossed his face.

Rhyn.

Jade was lost in his thoughts for a few minutes, staring without seeing. Rhyn didn't come. Crushed, she realized she had six hours to keep Jade busy in the hopes he didn't kill her. By the wild look in his eyes, she doubted she'd make it one. Jade shook his head, as if tormented by his own thoughts.

"I can ask him for it," she ventured.

"Like I'd trust you."

"If it's what you came for, then what choice do you have?"

"I've got you if I can't get the vial," Jade said. "Darkyn said—"

"Darkyn?"

"You know him?"

"Only from my nightmares. He's been tracking me for weeks."

"So you'll take him from me, too, will you?"

"I've never taken anyone from you!" she said, baffled. Fury she didn't understand crossed his face. He raised the knife, lowered it, raised, lowered. His gaze burned into her, and she held her breath, awaiting his decision of whether or not to leave her alive.

"I've crossed that line," he muttered to himself and moved forward. He snatched her arm and sheathed his knife. Hauling her to the bed, he shook out a pillow from its case and draped the case over her head like a hood.

"What line?" she asked.

"The one where I kill innocents to get what I want."

He opened a portal so fast, the shadow world sucked her breath out. He dragged her through it, and she dug her heels in. It was worthless—he was too strong. She pulled off the hood just as they emerged in a place she'd never thought she'd see again. The black fortress and dark skies made her heart drop to her feet. There was no Rhyn to rescue her this time. She was going to die.

He made his way through the fortress to a bedroom and slammed the door behind them. She stood in the middle of the chamber, quaking and praying he wasn't the sadistic bastard Sasha was.

Jade ignored her and crossed to a trunk in the corner. She watched in horror as he pulled out a crumpled woman's body, even more shocked to realize she recognized the woman's face when Jade set her on the bed. She had been one of Kris's lieutenants, Iliana. The woman's hair was red with blood, and her face clammy, but she appeared to be alive.

"What're you doing, Jade?" she whispered, inching closer.

"It is called a proof of life," he said and withdrew a knife. "Darkyn wants you alive, if I can't get the vial. Kris will need to be convinced to turn it over to me."

He lifted Iliana's hand, and Katie realized what he intended.

"Jade, no!"

Chapter Seven

"I didn't expect to see you here," Rhyn said, taking in Gabriel's muscular form as he fought the sparring dummies behind the Sanctuary. He assumed Gabe brought the dummies with him; he'd never seen them before. Nearby were more of the assassin's belongings: a few books in a large crate full of dark clothes. "You moving in here?"

"Maybe," Gabriel grunted and continued his merciless beating of the dummy. "What're you doing here?"

"Kris gave me one of Andre's old jobs."

Gabriel stopped and looked at him, taking in the dagger at his belt. Sweat coated his exposed chest, and he wiped his brow with his forearm. Considering how much Gabriel couldn't tolerate sunlight, Rhyn was surprised to see him during daylight at all, let alone without his shades.

"Makes sense," he said at last. "You've got the guts to do what he won't."

Again, Rhyn heard the uneven note in Gabriel's voice. His friend was troubled, and he didn't know why.

"You here for Sasha?" Gabe asked.

"Yes, though Kris said I have to wait for him to wake up and give him a chance to defend himself," Rhyn replied. "Fucking rules."

"How's Katie?"

It was midmorning on this side of the world, and Rhyn squinted up at the sky. He purposely didn't think of her, even though she was the reason he'd chosen this path. He felt the loss of their bond like he'd felt the isolation of Hell. He hated it.

"Fine," he said. It was the assassin's turn to give him a hard look. "How long do you think Sasha will be before he wakes up? I don't want to stay long." *And risk seeing her again.*

"I don't think he'll wake up soon. The healer's been working with him constantly. Seems to be in some sort of coma."

"Lucky bastard," Rhyn grumbled.

"Everything okay?"

"As good as it is for you."

Gabriel gave him a ghost of a smile.

"I didn't think you'd be allowed away from your mistress," Rhyn said as he sat on a boulder near Gabriel's crate of clothes.

"She ordered me up for a job, but I'm considering not going back."

"Life's a bitch."

"It's worse than that, Rhyn. I think sometimes I should've moved into the cell beside yours in Hell. At least there you know what kind of shit you'll go through."

Rhyn listened, sensing his friend was more than troubled: he was deeply disturbed. Gabriel began to beat up the dummy again. Rhyn watched, not wanting to leave for fear of being alone. For the first time in his life, he felt and thought too much, and he wanted to keep himself occupied with the world around him rather than the pain within him. He grabbed one of the Immortal books, fingering the soft, leather-like cover and transparent pages.

"You know, Gabe, even though we're no longer bound, I can still control my power. Maybe I just had to reach a certain age," he said.

Gabriel froze mid-strike at his words and lowered the bo. "What did you do, Rhyn?"

"The right thing for once. Sasha told me how to un-mate her, and I did it."

"Are you mad?"

Rhyn looked up from the book. Gabriel looked truly confused.

"I don't want to talk about it. Just found it interesting that I'm not having issues blowing things up," he said. "You know why?"

"No," Gabriel said after a long pause. "Unless … you gave up your bond but she didn't give up hers."

"Didn't know it worked that way."

"Because no one ever does that, Rhyn. It's madness."

"I don't want to talk about it!" he all but shouted. He dropped the book, anger rising. Gabriel returned to his dummy, beating it with renewed strength. Rhyn rested back on the boulder and closed his eyes to the rhythmic sounds of waves and Gabriel trying to kill the practice dummy. He tried to ignore his thoughts and didn't hear Kris's approach until his eldest brother spoke.

"Rhyn, now."

He twisted his head to see Kris standing outside of a portal. Unconcerned with what his brother might want, he rested back again.

"It's about Katie."

His heart almost stopped at the grim note in Kris's voice. Gabriel turned at the words, and Rhyn rose. Kris gave no explanation, simply strode into the shadow world. Rhyn trailed. They entered Kris's conference room, where Jade paced on the far side. The object sitting in the middle of the table made his blood run cold.

It was a severed hand, a woman's hand by its small size. Fury flooded him, and he started toward Jade. Kris caught him and shoved him back into the wall with his forearm across Rhyn's throat.

"We don't know where she is, brother, and we never will if you kill him!" he hissed.

"I can make him talk!"

"No! You know I will not break my oath to you. Let me handle this."

Rhyn wanted to change into his demon shape and rip Jade's head off. But Kris was right; this was time to think, not act. Gritting his teeth loudly enough for Kris to grimace, he nodded.

"Tell Rhyn what you told me, Jade," Kris said with calmness that made Rhyn's blood boil more.

"You didn't need to bring the half-breed here. Darkyn wants the untainted vial. I will trade you her for the vial."

"You were behind the demons attacking us," Rhyn snarled.

"That was Sasha."

"Fucking liar!"

"Rhyn! Shut it, or you'll wait in the hall!" Kris snapped. "I don't have the vial, Jade."

"Katie gave it to you," Jade said.

"It'll do you no good. Ully modified it."

"We have Ully in Hell."

Rhyn paced furiously. His gaze fell to the hand, and he stopped suddenly, puzzlement easing his anger. Katie didn't have fingernail polish on when he last saw her. He wasn't sure he ever saw her with it on at all.

"I want both of them back," Kris demanded. Jade faltered and wiped his mouth. "Go and talk to whoever you have to and make this happen."

"Darkyn doesn't negotiate, Kris," Jade said.

"Neither do I. You're wasting my time," Kris said coldly. "Go find your master and come back when you have an answer."

Jade's face skewed, and he whipped open a portal, storming out. Rhyn moved to the table.

"It's not hers," he said, relief pouring through him.

"It's Iliana," Kris said. "We hadn't seen her in a few days. I can't imagine Jade would …"

Rhyn saw the pained look that crossed Kris's face. He wasn't about to comfort a man he tolerated but didn't like. He could, however, pity the woman whose hand was cut off.

"He does have Katie," Kris said. Rhyn looked up, anger stirring again. "He didn't take her hand, which means Darkyn probably wants her alive. If they can't figure out what Sasha did about the vial, they'll need her and Ully."

"I'll go to Hell and get them both."

"You wouldn't survive. Jade said if they don't get what they want, they'd unleash their demons on the human village. Darkyn's smarter than I thought."

"I'm not going to leave her there to the demons!"

"I'm the brain, you're the brawn. You don't think, Rhyn," Kris said. "For now, your former mate is safe. That probably won't last."

I doomed her. He couldn't help the thought, and he dwelled on Gabriel's words. He broke her ability to use his power while retaining her calming effect on him. He'd left her defenseless when he meant to leave her in peace. She probably couldn't call forth a portal. How did he undo what he'd done when he wasn't sure how she became his mate in the first place?

"If you don't figure it out in sixty seconds, I'm going to Hell," he said and began pacing again.

Jade walked into Darkyn's open chamber to find the demon arming himself for battle.

"Master," he said with a bow of his head. "I tried to get the vial from Kris. He's demanding we return Ully."

"If we return the scientist, we won't know if it's tainted."

"Didn't Sasha's lab figure it out?"

"He slaughtered everyone before he left. No one knows but those who are dead-dead."

Jade paced. There had to be a way to get the vial and keep the girl. He wanted her dead, but he couldn't risk Darkyn's anger before he had it. And if Darkyn knew the human was meters down the hall …

"No doubt, you delivered my message to Kris that if I don't get what I want, I'm taking out the human village," Darkyn said. "I plan on doing it anyway. I want that vial or the girl, Jade."

"I'm not sure how to get it. I've got nothing to offer him."

"Didn't Sasha have one of Kris's Immortals? The demons passed her around. Give her back. And do it quick. I'm losing patience with you, my pet."

Darkyn strode past him, and Jade bowed his head again. He wiped his face and walked slowly down the hall. He didn't even know if Iliana had survived what he did to her. He hadn't thought he'd need her, or he would've taken the hand of someone else. He pushed the door open to his chamber and saw Katie on the bed with an unconscious Iliana. The woman had wrapped Iliana's hand and elevated it, though the blonde's wheezing led him to believe she wouldn't last long.

"You have to get her help, Jade," the human whispered. "Isn't there some part of you that wants to make this right?"

"It's too late for that. I've crossed all the lines."

"What lines? You hurt her, but you can fix it. It'll be like you didn't do anything to her at all."

"She's not the only one I hurt," he said. "The Immortals in the castle."

"Sasha did that."

"I made him."

A look of horror crossed her face, and his anger boiled.

"This is all because of you!" he shouted. "You made me do this! You made me hurt them." He strode toward her, determined to beat some sense into her. She scrambled over Iliana's body.

"I believe you, Jade!" she said as she fled. "Sasha didn't have to do what he did. He had a choice, and he made it. You can still make things right!"

He shoved her against the wall, and she hunkered down.

"You can make this right, Jade. Just get her somewhere safe. Leave me here for the demons to guard, if you want. She's an innocent."

Her words fed at the small piece of him that didn't want to live in Hell forever, that still thought he could go back to the Immortals and his old life. He released her and turned to look at Iliana.

"Take her to a Sanctuary," Katie said softly. "There's an Ancient healer at the Caribbean Sanctuary. I know because I came from there. He could fix her fast."

"I can make things right," he repeated.

"Yes, Jade."

A knock at the door jarred him, and he whirled to see the demon that entered. It froze, looking from him to the woman on the bed before his eyes settled on Katie. Recognition passed over his face. Terror of Darkyn finding out made Jade snap, and he withdrew his machete. The demon was too surprised to react, and Jade hacked him down until the black walls were sprayed with demon blood.

Chest heaving, he dropped the machete from his hand as he realized what he'd done. Darkyn would know he killed a demon. They'd do the same to him that they did to Sasha.

"Sanctuary, Jade."

He turned at her voice and saw the girl shaking with her eyes averted from the mess. He snatched up his machete and crossed to the bed to grab and sling Iliana over his shoulder. He motioned Katie forward with his machete, then stopped her to drape the pillowcase over her head as he had when she entered Hell with him.

Darkyn followed Jade as the madman hauled his two prisoners toward the portal to the shadow world. So far, everything was going as planned. Jade and Sasha would soon be out of his way, and his gamble on the hidden honor of Rhyn had paid off. Feeding Sasha information about the only way to break the bond—without telling him the breakage was only temporary—rendered the girl he'd been tracking for weeks vulnerable. The window of her weakness was short, only a week in mortals' time, but long enough for him to act. If he took down the Council, too, he would be all the more content.

Satisfied he'd outsmarted everyone, he waited for Jade to hack apart the demon warrior guarding the portal and then disappear into the shadow world on his way to where Sasha was, the one piece of information Darkyn didn't have. He'd have the girl soon, and he'd create an army unlike any that preceded him.

He leapt through the portal before it closed in time to see which one Jade chose. Darkyn pursued and peered through it with a slow smile, recognizing the place from Katie's dream.

Katie had never been so relieved to feel the chill of the shadow world! She stumbled but pressed herself to keep up, in case he left her there and she was trapped. When she emerged, she dropped to her knees, crippled once again by the sensation that hadn't bothered her when she was bound to Rhyn.

She whipped the pillowcase off her head and vomited, her insides burning hot then turning cold. Jade had led them onto a beach. She couldn't see the Sanctuary through her blurry eyes, just the blue of water and the tan sand beneath her hands. When her body adjusted, she sat back.

Jade was marching up the beach, Iliana flopping over his shoulder like a ragdoll. He seemed to have forgotten about her, and Katie stood unsteadily, hoping he'd brought them to the Sanctuary—and safety.

She stumbled through the deep sand until her calves ached and her breathing was hard. When she reached the top of the beach, she paused to catch her breath before hurrying after

Jade, whose determined walk soon outdistanced her. The Caribbean air was heavy and her body was soon covered with sweat. The outer wall of the Sanctuary appeared over a rise. Jade stopped and crouched, all but flinging Iliana's body down. She drew near, both hopeful and dreading what he intended to do.

"Stay here," he ordered. "I want to kill Sasha first."

The madman had lost it. She said nothing to dissuade him. He darted up the hill and disappeared from view over the top. Carefully, she rolled Iliana onto her back and propped up her injured arm again. Blood was everywhere, and Katie peeled off her sweater to wrap around Iliana's severed wrist. There were no trees for shade, and Iliana's labored breathing worried her.

She feared leaving the injured woman, in case Jade lurked on the other side of the hill or there were animals that might drag her away. Yet she wasn't sure how else to get help. A group of boulders nearby offered some escape from the sun. Katie rose, hefted Iliana beneath the shoulders, and dragged the woman over to the shade. She lowered her and sagged against the boulder.

"Sasha and Jade will soon be out of the way, leaving just us."

She recognized the familiar voice and froze. Her nightmares returned and for a moment, she wondered if this was one of them. She turned to face the creature who'd been stalking her in her dreams.

He stood a head taller than her and thick, his eyes colder than Gabriel's, and his heavy, lopsided features set off by neatly trimmed dark hair. She'd heard his name before.

"Darkyn," she whispered.

"Katie."

"What do you want?"

"A new breed of demon warrior, one that cannot be defeated by Immortals," he said and glanced at her stomach.

"You want more than my blood?" she asked, confused.

"Much more. I want your daughter."

She stared at him.

"Part demon, part Immortal, part human who's immune to magic? Incredible." He shook his head, and his eyes glowed. "And you, un-mated by the half-breed, are ripe for the picking."

She didn't want to remember she was utterly alone in facing him. He radiated the kind of quiet power Gabriel did. She wanted nothing to do with anything from Hell, especially this creature.

"Who do you think told Sasha how your mating could be undone?" he went on. "Or who let him have the vial or who knew how to use Jade to get to Kris? I knew you were in Hell in Jade's chamber."

"You couldn't have known Rhyn would leave me."

"I took a chance, and it paid off. I helped strip away his chances of staying with you. He's wild, like his mother, with an Immortal's honor."

Coldness slid through her. Rhyn had been as manipulated as poor Jade, who was now crazy with guilt and anger. Rhyn had quit on her in the hopes she'd be safe, only to leave her more vulnerable than ever.

Exactly where Darkyn wanted her.

"Darkyn." Gabriel's voice startled her, and dread settled deeper into her stomach. "She's on my list."

Darkyn looked from her to the assassin. Her tears rose at the sight of both creatures, one who wanted to drag her to Hell and the other who wanted her dead.

"Normally I respect Death's wishes," Darkyn said. "But this time, I cannot, assassin."

"You cannot obstruct Death," Gabriel warned. "This is one Code even a demon can't break."

"If I may interject," Katie voiced. "I understand my fate is either bad or really bad. But Gabriel, can you please help Iliana? Then you can argue all you want over who gets to kill me."

Gabriel glanced at Iliana's still form.

"You can save her or I can kill her," Darkyn offered. Gabriel moved forward and touched his hand briefly to Katie's head. She felt nothing.

"She's marked as Death's," he said. "You cannot take her to Hell."

"My master may disagree," Darkyn said, dark eyes flashing. "I'm certain we can work this out between us, assassin. I have something you want and will trade her for it."

"You have nothing I want."

"The key to your newfound chains."

Gabriel went silent and still, and Katie looked up at him. His face was emotionless, but the impact of Darkyn's words was unmistakable.

"Gabriel, help Iliana," she urged. "Deal with this shit when you get back."

He moved woodenly to lift the body at her feet and walked away, disappearing into a portal.

"What do you mean by that?" she asked.

"He sold his Immortal soul to Death so she wouldn't kill Rhyn."

"How do you know this?"

"Death bragged about her latest acquisition. It wasn't hard to figure out why he did it after so long refusing to become Death's slave," Darkyn answered. His honesty terrified her; he knew he wasn't going to lose and didn't care what she knew before he took her to Hell.

She'd never guessed the depth of Gabriel's friendship with Rhyn. The assassin she'd come to accept as a fixture in her unusual life was suddenly more: he was Rhyn's guardian angel as well as Toby's, and her friend. She felt his pain once more at taking away everything Rhyn had and pitied the assassin, despite her predicament.

Her gaze went to the sky, where the demon bird had appeared in her dream. Rhyn wasn't there. Her soul felt empty, and tears rose. Her fate would be decided by a demon and an assassin, and she'd never see her Rhyn again.

"He's not coming back," Rhyn warned as they waited for Jade to reappear in the conference room.

"Give him time," Kris said again, though he'd begun to look more concerned.

It'd been an hour. It felt like five hundred years in Hell. He was about to rise and open a portal to Hell—Kris be damned!—when an Immortal knocked and opened the door.

"A lady from the Caribbean Sanctuary has come with news," the Immortal said. "May I show her in?"

"Don't ask, just do it," Rhyn snapped, earning him an irritated look from his oldest brother. He issued a challenging look in return. They'd spent the hour in the conference room without fighting or threatening to kill each other. He wasn't sure what that meant, but it seemed to be a good thing. For now.

A small woman in convent browns entered and curtseyed. Kris pushed him aside to offer her a chair.

"Daniela," he greeted her, and Rhyn recognized the leader of the Sanctuary that had taken care of Katie weeks before.

"Master Kris," she said. Her gaze went to Rhyn. "Master Rhyn. Your Immortals caught a man who claims to be an Immortal as well. He's bloodied and half-mad. He attacked them to get to the Ancient Sasha."

"Jade," Kris muttered. "Is everyone in the convent safe?"

"Yes, but I have to object to Immortal business being carried out in the Sanctuary. Since your castle was attacked, we've had an Ancient wash up on our shores, Death's assassin sitting in our hall, and now this. It is not at all customary to how the Sanctuary is meant to be used," she said sternly.

"My apologies," Kris said. "If you will permit one more intrusion, we will go and retrieve both the madman and the Ancient." She frowned and looked between the two of them before responding.

"I will allow it."

"I am grateful."

Rhyn glared at his brother. Kris was gracious and gentle with this woman, who he could very easily treat like he did his Immortals and brothers. Kris opened a portal. He allowed Daniela to enter first and then followed. Rhyn trailed and emerged again into the balmy, bright island day. The portal opened in the courtyard, and Kris's gaze went immediately to the rooms lining the women's wing. Daniela's little legs moved fast, and she was across the courtyard while Kris stared toward the room where Rhyn assumed his mate was.

"Come on, lover boy," Rhyn said and slapped his brother's arm.

Daniela led them to the men's wing, where one sweaty, bloodied Immortal was standing outside of Sasha's room while the other stood guard over Jade, who was hogtied in the middle of the small courtyard around which the men's wing was situated.

The whites of Jade's eyes were visible before they drew near enough to hear his muffled shouts. Rhyn stood over him, his hand ready to grab the dagger at his belt and plunge it into the traitor's neck. Fury rose within him again as he took in the Immortal who had betrayed them and taken Katie. As if sensing what he intended to do, Kris took his arm.

"Not yet."

Rhyn looked away from Jade and stepped back before he snapped and was banned eternally from the Sanctuary. Daniela's lips were pursed and her frown deep.

"We need to talk to him for a moment before we leave," Kris said. "He's taken a human hostage, and we need to know where she is."

Daniela crossed her arms and gave a stiff nod. Rhyn snorted at her defiant stance and Kris's respectful bow and leaned down to grab the rope binding Jade's ankles. He dragged the Immortal over the grass and concrete into the vacant room beside Sasha's. Kris entered and closed the door. Rhyn planted a knee in Jade's chest and sliced his gag free.

A torrent of nonsense escaped from Jade, a mix of words that made no sense. Rhyn slapped him hard enough for him to fall silent.

"Rhyn, just move," Kris said impatiently. Rhyn knelt on one side of Jade, close enough to reach him when warranted. "Jade, I want you to tell me where Katie is."

"In Hell, dead-dead, I cut off her arm and I brought to Kris—"

Rhyn slapped him.

"I don't know."

Rhyn slapped him again.

"She's outside!" Jade shouted.

"Outside where?" Kris demanded.

"Darkyn said the girl or the vial. He said to trade her for it. I brought her with me."

"Here?"

"Iliana, I have to get her help then everything will be okay. If I get her help, she said everything would be okay, and everyone would understand Sasha killed the Immortals."

Rhyn looked at Kris, puzzled by the nonsense.

"Was she right, Kris? Will everything be okay?" Jade asked imploringly. "I never meant for any of this." At their silence, Jade's face went red and his eyes blazed. He thrashed, knocking Kris back. "The whore lied to me! I should've killed her! She swore this would—"

Rhyn snatched a pillow from the bed and covered Jade's head to drown out the madness.

"I see why he was gagged," Kris said. "Did any of this make sense to you?"

"Fucked-up crazy talk," Rhyn responded. "He's wearing a collar. Can't read his mind with that on."

Jade's shouts turned to screams, and Kris motioned Rhyn out of the room. Daniela stood where they left her, frowning fiercely. Even with the door closed, Jade's madness and the sounds of his body thrashing against the wall were audible in the small courtyard.

"Almost done, good lady," Kris said before she could kick them out. "I promise you."

"I'm going to Hell to get her," Rhyn said and started away.

"No, Rhyn. Just wait a minute. It makes no sense she'd be there, and if she is, the demons have her, or Jade wouldn't be here alone."

"He's not alone." Gabriel's voice was quiet. The death dealer emerged from the hall running between the two wings, the trembling form of Lankha held under one arm like a bag of cement. "He brought them both with him."

"Katie's here?" Rhyn seized on his words.

"For now," Gabriel said and looked away. His reaction fueled the sense of doom that had been growing since Jade appeared with Iliana's hand.

"Where? Is she okay?"

"This…" Gabriel lifted Lankha's trembling body, "is for Iliana. I left her outside the walls because I didn't want Toby to see."

"I'll grab Jade and meet you there," Kris said, striding to the door. "Thank God Iliana is all right!"

The sounds of madness had subsided during their conversation. Rhyn thought nothing of it until Kris opened the door. Jade had freed himself during his thrashing and launched out of the door, machete in hand as he flung himself on Kris. The weapon fell once, and Kris's blood sprayed them both.

Rhyn reacted out of instinct. He flew to his brother's side, snatched Jade, and snapped his neck. The Immortal crumpled. Kris appeared surprised and furious. The machete had sliced through his collarbone, and blood spurted from the wound into the courtyard's grass. He reached for the weapon with a shaking hand. Rhyn hauled him over his shoulder in a fireman's carry.

"I want all of you out," Daniela whispered, horrified.

"That shit works on Kris but not on me," Rhyn snapped. "Gabe, give me the healer, and get Iliana. Daniela, go get a room ready for Iliana and send Toby and Hannah to the cafeteria. Keep them busy for a while."

Gabriel crossed to him and held out the healer. Rhyn took the small creature under one arm. He didn't wait for the shocked leader of the Sanctuary to respond but took Kris into one of the empty rooms and laid him out on the bed.

"Never thought you'd defend me," Kris managed through teeth clenched in pain. "Thought you'd be the first to turn on me."

"You're a shitty brother, and you're an even shittier judge of character," Rhyn replied. He set the healer down. "Heal him, or I eat your village."

"You're such a dick," Kris muttered. His face was white with pain, and Rhyn looked over his brother. He'd lost a lot of blood. If anyone could fix him, an Ancient healer could.

"I thought Lankha would be too busy," Gabriel said. "I brought her here."

Rhyn moved to the doorway and watched him set Iliana down gently on the floor beside the healer. The woman was unconscious, her severed wrist wrapped in Katie's sweater.

Katie's sweater. It was her favorite one, and she'd been wearing it when he last saw her. She really was on the island.

"I have to go," Gabriel said. He started toward the courtyard. "I'll come back in a little bit."

"Where are you going, Gabe?" Rhyn asked, following him. Gabriel stiffened, and Rhyn's suspicion ignited.

"I have to go."

Gabriel disappeared, and Rhyn gazed at the spot where he'd been. The assassin had been acting strange for quite a while. That he was troubled was no secret, though Rhyn didn't understand why, aside from being a slave to Death.

I don't think our friendship will survive what comes.

She ordered me up for a job, but I'm considering not going back.

Katie was the job. Rhyn's realization paralyzed him for a long moment. He whirled and strode into the room, pushing the healer aside to kneel over Iliana. He rested his hand on her head and rifled through the half-dead woman's memories.

Jade locking her in a trunk, Katie screaming at him not to cut off her hand while she writhed on the bed, Katie sobbing and bandaging her after, blurred memories, the vision of ocean and sand, nothing.

She was somewhere on the island. With a curse, he rose and ran to the courtyard, changing into his demon bird. Beating his wings so hard they hurt, he rose into the sky and soared around the small island, finally spotting three lone figures in small valley not too far from the Sanctuary. He dropped fast and changed shapes too soon, landing hard on the ground near them.

All three whirled, and Katie's eyes lit up. It was the demon leader, Darkyn, who caught his initial attention. He didn't expect to see Darkyn here.

"What the fuck are you doing here?" he asked before his eyes went to Gabriel.

"Half-breed," Darkyn sneered. "Negotiating with Gabriel over who gets your former mate."

"There's no negotiation," Gabriel said in a hard voice. "She's on the list. She goes with me."

"No, Gabriel," Rhyn said. "She can't be on your list and if she is, the hatchling isn't."

"Death ordered both dead-dead."

"Brother, I'll kill you both if either of you tries to take her," he said. "You have a contract on her, Gabe?" The assassin nodded. "Let me guess, Darkyn, the Dark One ordered this."

"We'll just say he doesn't disagree with me."

Rhyn's heart dropped to his feet, and he looked at Katie. He'd meant to make her safe and left her to the worst fate imaginable. He'd never wanted to lose her, and he wasn't about to back down now. He leveled his gaze on Gabriel.

"All right." He drew a knife from his boot. "I'm challenging you, assassin, demon. You can have her when I'm dead."

"Rhyn, no!" she cried.

"I can handle it," he said.

"Rhyn—" She started forward, and Gabriel held out an arm to block her. Katie planted both her hands on his arm to push it away. Gabriel resisted, and she glared up at him. "Back off, Gabriel. It's not like I can run anywhere!"

"Two minutes," Gabriel warned. "By Immortal Code, Darkyn and I are obligated to accept his challenge."

Rhyn watched her approach, his gaze dropping from his foes to her sweet face. Her eyes glowed with emotions he'd been waiting for weeks to see. He wanted to sweep her away for one last intimate moment before his death but doubted the assassin and demon would wait.

"This is the stupidest thing you've ever done," she said.

"Letting you go was the stupidest thing. I'm doing something right for once," he replied, glancing at Darkyn as the demon shifted.

"They'll kill you," she whispered.

"If they do, go with Gabriel. Death's a bitch, but she's better than Hell."

"This isn't right," she whispered. Her eyes watered, and he marveled once again at how a half-demon fuck-up had almost ended up with such a beautiful creature. He cupped one soft cheek and rubbed away a hot tear with his thumb.

"I'm not dead yet," he said, amused and touched by her tears. She wrapped her arms around him, and he pulled her close. Her small body molded against his.

"Can't we just run away, right now? Turn into a bird and carry me with you?" she asked, desperation in her voice.

"Even if we did, they'd both come after us."

"You can go. I'd rather know you're safe than live without you."

"No, Katie," he said, his world clear for the first time in his life. "I know where I belong, and it's right here with you. I have to make things right. I couldn't live if I lost you."

"Katie," Gabriel called.

"Rhyn, I love you," she said.

"I know." He forced himself to withdraw. He gave her one last, long look and pushed her hair from her face. With a kiss on her forehead, he stepped away. Gabriel drew a long sword, and Darkyn pulled two free. Gabriel motioned her over to the rocky area.

"Bring it, my friends," Rhyn replied. He moved a short distance away to more level ground and lowered himself into a fighting stance. He'd never faced a full-blooded demon and assassin at the same time before. Gabriel bent to whisper something to Katie and then moved in front of him. Rhyn lowered his machete and held his hand out. The assassin took it, and Rhyn gave him a quick hug.

"To our destinies, brother," he said for Gabriel's ears only.

"Forgive me, Rhyn."

"Sometimes all we have are shitty choices. I don't fault you," he replied. A tormented look crossed Gabriel's face, but he nodded once. Rhyn shook his arms out and looked at Darkyn. "See you in Hell, demon."

"Look forward to it," Darkyn said.

Rhyn lowered himself into a fighting stance and faced off against the two.

Horrified, Katie watched the battle from her dreams as it began. Unlike the nightmares, this time it was real and agonizingly slow. She'd cheered Rhyn's sudden appearance but then quickly understood what it meant: only one of them was going to walk away from this. She wasn't sure what she expected, but it wasn't for him to fight for her, especially when she was already damned.

I love you, you fool!

The men battled with speed and agility that left her breathless. Her eyes stayed on Rhyn, and she'd never been as awed as she was watching him fight a flawless battle against the full-blooded demon and the assassin. The scary, confusing world she'd entered weeks before crystallized and grew clear as she watched the lethal battle. She belonged with Rhyn. Nothing else mattered

Break the bond, and Death will save you both. Rhyn will die-dead otherwise. Gabriel had whispered the words from her dream before facing off against Rhyn. She tried to decipher his meaning as she watched them fight, terrified to take her eyes off Rhyn.

Rhyn landed a blow on the demon, who snarled in response. She gasped. *He can do this! He can beat them!* A few minutes later, Rhyn went down under Gabriel's blow, rolled, then bounded up, but not before Darkyn slashed his side.

"Rhyn!" she cried. Rhyn gave a throaty chuckle and launched himself back into the battle. Though his side was soaked with blood, he showed no sign of slowing. He couldn't outlast them. He'd landed one blow on Darkyn and none on Gabriel.

Break the bond, and Death will free you both. She knew what it meant in her dream but was terrified of following her footsteps. Katie tried to concentrate on the words, wanting to help Rhyn before it was too late. She forced herself to close her eyes to the battle and repeated the phrase over and over, searching for another meaning.

"Not the time for riddles, Gabriel!" she muttered. Rhyn had broken their bond. Unless, like her dream …*I have to break it, too*. Her eyes flew open, and she stared at the men battling. What words had Rhyn used? "I release you of our bond, Rhyn."

She opened her eyes, expecting a miracle to occur and the battle to be won. Nothing happened. "I release you of our bond, Rhyn."

Nothing. Darkyn turned on Gabriel and slashed his back. Rhyn blocked a second blow that might've taken the assassin's head off and shoved Darkyn before whirling to meet Gabriel's blow. Darkyn changed into his demon form and tackled Rhyn, who threw him off.

He wasn't going to make it. If he died, it was because of her, and either Death or Hell would claim her.

"I can't live with that, Rhyn," she whispered.

Death would free them. *Her* death, as in her dream. There was no other choice. Her attention turned to a different direction, the way they'd come from the beach. She hesitated only a second more before she started running. She left the sounds of the battle behind her, her thoughts on Rhyn and nothing else.

The distance back to the beach seemed much longer than it had in her dream. Terror drove her to ignore the pain in her lungs and legs. She made it to the sand before forced to slow to a walk by the ankle-deep, loose sand. Agonizing over how much time Rhyn had, she finally reached the water-soaked sand and sucked in ragged breaths as she knelt for a moment of rest.

"Death will free us both." Her hand went to her stomach, and her eyes watered.

Trust my Gabriel, human, a woman's voice whispered into her mind. *This is the only way.*

Heart hammering, she rose, took a deep breath, and waded into the warm water. Waves licked at her ankles, her thighs, her chest. She started to chicken out when one went over her head and filled her mouth with salt water. Katie stood on her tiptoes and looked up, taking one last look at the blue sky before she held her breath and ducked beneath the water. She swam as far from the beach as she could, expelled her breath, then drew in a mouthful of water.

Chapter Eight

Rhyn's power rippled through him, the shockwave knocking down Gabriel before he could deliver the death blow. Darkyn fell as well, and the walls around the Sanctuary tumbled in the distance. He sat up, bloodied and lightheaded, unable to quell the power roiling through him. He spit blood and pushed himself to his feet. Gabriel and Darkyn rose, their attention going west toward the ocean. He didn't remember his power being so strong. He couldn't catch his balance and steadied himself against a rock.

"Ready when you are," he called to his opponents.

Darkyn growled from deep within his chest before returning to his human form. Gabriel sheathed his weapon. Confused, Rhyn joined them and followed their gazes. He saw nothing but a distant beach and the ocean. He glanced to the rocks where Katie had been, only to find she was gone. He looked back at the beach without seeing her.

His heart felt as if it stopped. His powers were back in full force, without her to steady his control. She'd broken their bond. He didn't have to ask how.

"Gabriel," he said.

Gabriel turned to him. He reached into his pocket and withdrew a small black pouch, pouring its contents—two green gems holding the dust of human souls—into his palm. He dropped them onto the ground and crushed them with his heel. His job was done.

"Gabriel!" Rhyn's voice turned raw with emotion.

"Next time," Darkyn said, agitated. "I kill you both." He opened a portal and disappeared.

Rhyn's head spun with power and emotion. He dropped to his knees, unable to battle both influences for his balance. Pain rippled through him and another wave of power radiated off him, turning the boulders nearby into powder. Gabriel knelt beside him.

"You have to trust me, Rhyn," the assassin said. "I have to go, before she comes. Don't do anything stupid."

The words registered slowly. Rhyn sagged to the ground and watched Gabriel walk away and then disappear. Sorrow and rage pierced him to the core. He could think of nothing but Katie and his ultimate failure.

"Not looking so good, half-breed." Another form knelt beside him, this one with blond hair. "I had no idea you were *that* half-breed, the brother of the Ancients." The demon righted him and tried to heft him but stopped.

Rhyn blinked himself out of his stupor enough to steady himself. Jared squatted in front of him, looking more bruised than the last time he saw him.

"Now that we're friends, I thought you might let me have a taste of your monkey."

"She's dead," Rhyn whispered. He felt as if he stood outside his body, watching the world around him.

"And the body …"

Rhyn grabbed him and smashed him to the ground. He staggered back, unable to control the power within him. Jared lay still for a moment before sitting up.

"That's some serious power," he said. His eyes began to glow again. "We make a good team, don't you think? We could do a lot together."

"Leave me be."

"For now, I will, but I'll be back to talk. I still owe you a favor. I overheard something you might want to know."

Rhyn flopped onto his back and covered his eyes with one arm. He was alone, roasting in the sun for a long moment before he sensed Kris approach. He lowered his arm enough to see his determined brother, unsteady on his feet with one arm in a sling.

"What happened, Rhyn?" Kris asked, sitting heavily on the ground beside him.

"You're alive."

"I owe you one."

"Kill me," Rhyn said.

"What?"

"You owe me. Kill me!" Rhyn snapped.

"I can hardly walk let alone lift a weapon. At one time, I would've probably agreed," Kris admitted. "What happened here? Where's Gabriel?"

"Took Katie to Death."

Kris was quiet for a moment. Then he said, "Not sure how to break it to Hannah. That would explain why the walls around the Sanctuary are in ruins."

Rhyn saw enough to see that what his brother said was true. He could look straight into the courtyard of the men's wing, and the furious Daniela standing in the middle staring at him.

"I can't control it, Kris. Stuff just happens."

"I see. And Gabriel won't come back."

"Better not." Even as he spoke the words, he knew he'd never completely disregard his friend. He had one, now that Katie was gone. Even thinking of her made him feel as though his insides were burning and dying.

"Come to the Sanctuary. I'll figure something out," Kris said. He struggled to rise.

"I'm staying here."

"Fine. I'll send Toby out to check on you. He's yours now, Rhyn."

"I don't want a fucking angel dogging me everywhere."

"No choice. You were her mate, and Toby was hers."

Rhyn said nothing more, aware it was all he might ever have to remind him of the mortal intended to be his mate. If he had it to do over again, he never would've un-bound her. He would've taken her and run away somewhere safe where no one would ever find them, as he initially wanted to do. In all his years in Hell, he'd never known this kind of pain.

It was too late. He'd failed. He'd lost the only thing that'd ever mattered, and the only person who ever truly loved him. He threw his head back and roared with fury and pain until his throat was raw

The waves had pulled her under before darkness took her. She awoke with a jerk and looked around at the tiny cottage, lit only by a candle. The bookshelf was empty and weapons lined the opposite wall. Her heart beat like a hummingbird's wings as she took in the one-room cabin. The windows were open and the sky beyond the trees dark. She didn't notice Gabriel in the corner until he spoke.

"Took you long enough."

She jumped at the sound of his voice.

"What happened?" she asked. "I don't think I like this place."

"Welcome to my home."

"Your home? I'm in … Deathland or whatever you call it?"

"Sort of."

"Is Rhyn okay?" she ventured and braced herself for the answer.

"He is."

"Oh, thank God!" she said with a deep sigh.

"Are you well enough to travel?"

"Travel where?"

"At any time, I expect a furious Death to knock on my door. I told you about the loophole, and she won't like that."

"What loophole?" she asked uneasily.

"When someone sacrifices himself for someone else, the assassination contract is void."

"But I'm still dead, aren't I?"

"Eh, tough to say," he said.

"What the hell does that mean, Gabriel?"

"It means, if Death finds you, probably. But if I can get you to the mortal world and back to a Sanctuary, then she'll have to reissue the contract," he explained.

"And then you come to kill me again?" she asked with a frown.

"Nope. Consider not killing you my resignation."

She gazed at him, sensing the importance of what he'd done. Gabriel rose and began pulling weapons from the wall and planting them on his body.

"You sacrificed your soul for Rhyn and your life for me," she said. "You're incredible, Gabriel."

"No offense, but I did both for Rhyn. I barely know you, but he's all I've got."

"Me, too."

"She's okay, too," he said. "Rhyn's gonna flip out when he finds out it's a girl." He glanced at her, his face softening. His eyes went to her stomach.

"Does he know we're okay?"

"No one does or can until I get you back. Death and Darkyn will have every assassin they own roaming the shadow world. We'll take the back way."

"I hope you're good at what you do," she said with some discomfort as he continued to load his body with weapons. She doubted *the back way* was more dangerous than a short cut.

"The best."

"What happens to you after we get to the Sanctuary?"

"Don't know and don't care."

She rose and tested her legs. She felt weak, but she was alive. *Sorta*. Her heart ached for Rhyn. Even though she stood in Death's realm with a slim chance of ever seeing the blue sky again, her life had never seemed so clear to her. She'd faced Hell, and now Death. There was nothing else to fear.

"C'mon," Gabriel said and whipped the door open. "This won't be easy."

"I'm ready, Gabriel," she said, in awe of his determination and dedication. At the quiet resolution in her voice, he turned to face her. "Take me back to Rhyn."

"I will. I swear it."

I'm coming, Rhyn.

RHYN'S REDEMPTION

Book III

Chapter One

Death was waiting for Gabriel when he dozed off. He'd planned on staying awake and moving so she wouldn't catch up to them, but even he needed a short nap after three straight days of grueling travel in the underworld.

He found himself on the Caribbean Sanctuary, in the small chamber with the Oracle book. Sea breeze swept through the small windows of the room, and he took a step towards the lectern on which the open book rested. The pages displayed had a few words written on them rather than the constantly shifting writing that normally scrawled itself across the pages. He felt himself compelled towards the book even as his fight-or-flight instinct reared up.

You know what they say about the inner ring of Hell, Gabe. Death's words were written on both pages of the Oracle's book.

"Why did you bring me here?" he asked the air around him.

I can't talk to you directly, or I am obligated to take you with me, Death's words appeared in the book.

"This isn't the time for your games," Gabriel said. "I know what happens if you catch us. What I don't know is why you'd try to talk to me. You know where we are?"

I'd know if I wanted to. The underworld is mine.

"As I thought," he said with a frown. "No matter. I'm taking her out of the underworld."

You know I can't let you.

"But you're not here to stop me."

If she escapes, it won't be with your help.

The words chilled him from the inside out. There was one way he'd leave Katie, and that was if he was dead-dead. Gabriel looked around the small room, irritated with Death.

"Come out," he ordered her. "I've known you longer than any creature still in existence. This is a dream. You can talk to me here."

"There was a time when you feared me then a time when I thought you almost loved me," Death said, materializing from the shadows. "Is this what happens when your weak human emotions fade? You betray me?"

"I have to do this. If you have to stop me ... it won't change how I felt about you."

"You could've ruled the underworld at my side, Gabriel."

"What we are—*were*—is of no concern now," he said slowly. The words were harder to say than he expected. He'd gone from Death's favorite – and the only death-dealer serving voluntarily – to just another of her assassins obligated to serve her, after he traded his soul for his best friend's life. Death had done her best over the years to force his human emotions out of him. But she was right. He had loved her for so long, until he realized even he was a pawn in her games.

"Very well, Gabriel," she said. "Then I must warn you. If I find either of you, I am obligated by rules much older than the Immortal Code to do what I must."

"I understand. Is that all you came to tell me?"

"No. I came to tell you that you saw something I didn't."

He said nothing, aware the creature before him wasn't capable of communicating a truth in a way most others could understand. Death was from a time before time. He would never understand what she saw when she looked out over humanity and saw its Past, Present, Future, and the soul of each human that ever lived. The size of her vision rendered her unique interpretations puzzling, even to him.

"You saw something I almost missed," she added. "Maybe I was more interested in detailing your human weakness than in understanding what your instincts told you. Deities don't need instincts. We simply *know*. But even I cannot know all."

"You're not pursuing us, because I was right about something," he said. "What was I right about? We've spent millennia arguing. Not once have you uttered those words."

"I didn't utter them now," she pointed out. "Let's just say, I may have misjudged more than your affection for me."

"Rhyn."

"Perhaps. Though I will say, I haven't yet made my final determination. He has a test he must pass. I didn't expect him to get so far, and he may not pass at all. In any case, I have a much larger problem. I interfered when I shouldn't have," she said. "And now, it might be too late to make things right."

"You did take an unusual interest in Rhyn," Gabe said. "His soul should've been just one more jewel for your collection, considering how many souls you deal with and relationships you break a part." *Including ours.* These words he kept to himself.

"It was not Rhyn that drew my attention, Gabriel. It was your interest in him."

"You're blaming me." He looked away, at the blue sky visible through the window.

"I interfered. You have until he passes or fails the final trial."

Gabriel cursed under his breath. He had no way of knowing what kind of test a deity like Death could create, but it wasn't likely to be good. While he had full faith in Rhyn, he also knew better than to trust the petite woman in white standing in his dream.

"If he fails, we're dead-dead," he guessed. "If he passes …"

"We'll see."

"You can't check the Oracle?" He motioned to the book.

"I cannot. My Sight has been stunted, no doubt as punishment for my tampering in Fate's court."

"I know I'm doomed. What about Katie?"

Death shrugged with a knowing smile that told him more than if she spoke. Gabriel gazed out the window of the small room, thinking.

"How long do I have?" he asked at last.

"Until the seventh day after she drowned herself, assuming Darkyn doesn't catch you first."

"Four days left. I take it you won't come to my rescue if he does."

Another smile.

"Why seven days?" he asked.

"There are some rules older than time. I've broken several already, but this one is entirely out of my ability to influence."

From their years together, he knew the cryptic response was the best he'd get. Gabriel's gaze swept around the room again, and he looked out at the blue sky. He'd never again visit this room or see the mortal world. This much he knew the moment he chose to help Rhyn and Katie over his promise to Death. The dream sky wasn't even real, and he missed it already.

"It's too late for either of us to turn back," Death said.

"I wasn't considering it. I'll keep her alive until Rhyn passes his test." Gabriel approached her until he towered over her. Memories of their nights together made him sensitive to the warmth of her skin, the tension between them. "This will all be worth it to hear you say you were wrong about something, and I was right."

"You may not get that chance, even if I was wrong," she said. "Watch yourself, Gabriel."

The resignation in her tone sounded like a farewell. Gabe studied her, uncertain what could stop Death from doing anything she pleased. She was not only letting him go when she shouldn't, but she was telling him just how much time he had to get Katie out of the underworld. Gabriel knew something was wrong if Death was turning her back on the duty of collecting souls, a duty she normally took such joy in. She'd been unwilling to do that for *him* when their relationship had been at its peak.

"Send me back," he said.

Gabriel snapped awake. It was still dark, and the moons of the underworld hadn't moved far across the sky. He sat, uneasy with the dream exchange with Death. A small fire burned between him and Katie, whose pale features and shadowed eyes were showing the effects of both her pregnancy and the toll the underworld took on mortals.

"You need to sleep," he told her.

"I was guarding you while you dozed."

He snorted.

"I don't feel so hot, Gabe."

"I know. Just a few more days. Get some rest."

"This place is creepy. I don't think I can sleep with bugs the size of my hand just waiting for me to fall asleep so they can crawl all over me."

"If you're asleep, you won't feel them," he said.

"That's not the point, Gabe."

As much as he respected the tough little human, he found that she was driving him crazy. He'd spent his life relatively alone, crossing between the underworld and human world as needed. Death had been far from co-dependent, and he'd had free rein. Until two days ago, when he crossed into the underworld with Katie slung across his shoulder. He'd forgotten what it was to have someone completely dependent on him. He didn't feel up to the task, not when failure meant breaking the man he viewed as his brother.

"I'm never doing this again," he said.

"You've told me that twice. It's not like I want to be here, either."

"Sleep, Katie," he said in a kinder voice. "I'm going to scout around for a bit."

"Do you think we'll make it out of here?"

"I hope you do. I have no faith I will."

"I'm sorry for snapping at you about the bugs, Gabe. I'm just exhausted."

"I'm normally much more patient." Gabe looked her over then offered what smile he could muster. "Too much on my mind."

"You're afraid, too," she said, studying him. "Gabe, if we don't make it for some reason, I want you to know how much I appreciate everything you've done."

"I did it for a man I see as my brother."

"You keep saying that," she said and rolled her eyes. "But I think you kinda like me, too."

"You're growing on me," he allowed. "Much like fungus."

Katie chuckled, and he was almost relieved at the sight of her smile. Her features had grown paler and gaunter under his watch. He feared the underworld would sink her spirit, too. One of them had to have some sort of hope they'd make it out alive.

"Please, Katie, try to get some rest. We've barely had any down time since arriving, and you need it," he said again. "I've gotta make sure nothing has found us yet."

"You need rest, too, Gabe."

"I'll rest when you're safe."

Another small smile crossed her face, and she sat down. Gabe left her, knowing even if she did sleep, it wouldn't be long. Death may have ignored their presence in her domain for three days, but something had made her reach out to him now. He knew they'd have problems at some point and only hoped he could get Katie out of the underworld, before his own fate was sealed.

Rhyn approached the boundaries of his newest prison – the one meant to keep everyone else on the Caribbean Sanctuary safe from the magic he couldn't control. The ocean's calming rhythm and flavorful breeze made the beach more bearable. Tents had sprung up two nights before, and the two people who could keep his powers from spinning out of control remained at the center of the beach. He was far enough away from the Sanctuary's fortress not to cause a threat to those there, so long as the two people buffering him stayed close.

He raised his head to the sky then held out his arm across what he'd figured out was the boundary of his buffers' influence. Magic jolted through him like electricity, flinging him onto his back. His power spun through him, but it was nothing compared to what he would feel without the two buffers.

"Again?" a youth's voice asked.

Rhyn lay still and folded his hands beneath his head, staring at the sky. He heard the angel, Toby, drop beside him, the glow of his Nintendo 3DS bright in the night. As one of Rhyn's buffers, Toby was as trapped on the beach as he was.

"It's gotta hurt," Toby said.

Nothing hurts anymore, Rhyn thought.

"Kris wants to assign Hannah as my new mom," the angel continued. "I don't want her as my mom."

"Why do you give a shit?" Rhyn asked.

"I want Katie."

Rhyn's jaw clenched, and he fought the raw feeling inside him, the one that betrayed him every time he tried to convince himself he'd survived worse. For the first time in his life, he'd thought he found his calling: protecting people as defenseless as his mate, Katie. And then, she'd died, and any purpose his life had died with her. Now, he just wanted to die-dead.

"Auntie Hannah says she'd be my mom for all time, so I wouldn't have to have any other moms." The angel sounded troubled. "Rhyn, can I stay with you?"

"No."

"I know, I know, Kris says I'm an angel and angels are supposed to protect humans and you're anything but human but I still want to stay with you. Please, Rhyn?"

"No."

Toby sighed loudly and turned off the glowing 3DS. Instead of leaving like Rhyn wished he would, the angel lay down beside him.

"How long are we staying on the beach?" Toby asked.

"Until Kris figures out how to send me back to Hell," Rhyn said, suspecting this was what his brother intended to do. He couldn't be trusted free. As hard as he tried, he had no control over his power without the buffers. Kris and his mate, Hannah —Rhyn's other buffer—weren't about to live the rest of Immortality on the beach with him.

"You could kidnap us both and take us wherever you want to go," Toby offered. "Then you'd be stable and you could leave the beach."

"Right, because I have somewhere to go."

"You can go see Death and ask her for Katie back."

"It doesn't work that way for mortals."

"If you hadn't un-bonded her, it'd work."

"Look, you little shit, why don't you –"

"Gods, Rhyn, don't talk to him like that," the eldest surviving brother of the seven brothers, Kris, snapped as he approached. "Did you ask him, Toby?"

"He said no, like you said," Toby said, disappointment heavy in his voice.

Rhyn ground his teeth, fury bubbling within him. He wanted them all gone, so he could spend the remainder of his long life laying here alone, waiting for Death or one of her assassins.

"Go back to the tents," Kris instructed the young angel.

Toby went without another word, and Rhyn drew a deep breath to settle his emotions.

"You haven't been sleeping," Kris said and squatted beside him.

Rhyn glanced at him, taking in the arm in a sling. Kris was healing from an attacker Rhyn had saved him from, the day Katie killed herself. Rhyn had lost his mate the same day he earned some small piece of respect from his brother.

"Is your offer still on the table?" Kris asked.

"What offer?"

"The one where you become the Council's assassin."

"You seem to forget I can't go anywhere without your mate and the damn angel," Rhyn said in irritation.

"Where I want you to go, I don't care if anyone survives," Kris said. "I have an idea. The two of them can walk you through the shadow world and you can jump through the portal."

"You don't intend for me to return."

"It would be a noble death for a good cause, if it came to that."

"What is it?" Rhyn asked.

"I want my castle back," Kris said. "Scouts are reporting it's overrun with demons and Darkyn has adopted it as his terra headquarters for his trips here from Hell. Go in and wipe out the demons."

Rhyn's thoughts drifted to the castle. He felt the urge to destroy it, not save it. After all, it was where he and Katie spent the few good moments they'd had, where he'd found something worth living for. And where everything had gone wrong.

"I can wipe out everything," he mused.

"I'd be happy with the demons gone," Kris said. "I want the castle. It was our father's."

"When do I leave?"

"In the morning. Pre-dawn."

"Alrighty."

Kris rose but didn't leave. "Rhyn, if you come back, we can try to find some way for you to live as normal a life as possible," he said slowly. "I'm converting a room at this Sanctuary into a lab, for when we find Ully."

"We both know this is a suicide mission."

Kris was silent for a long moment. Then he said, "I'll tell Toby to leave you alone so you can get some sleep tonight."

Rhyn listened to his brother pad away in the soft sand. He'd spent thousands of years in Hell wishing to be dead-dead. Tomorrow, he'd have his chance.

The ocean's cold breeze swept over him, and his thoughts turned from his dead mate to his best friend, Gabriel, who had tried to kill him then disappeared. He'd lost them both, the only good parts of his life. He'd left Hell only to fuck up his life worse than before.

His eyes closed. He hadn't been able to sleep in two days but fell fast into a deep, peaceful slumber. Katie awaited him in his dreams, looking as she had the day he lost her. They stood in the spot where he'd fought his friend, Gabriel, and the demon lord, Darkyn. She wore a sweater that made her light eyes glow. Her hair whipped in the wind chilling his body.

When his eldest brother died, he'd felt pain and anger, but he'd never felt the crippling ache he did standing on the rocks near the ocean staring at Katie.

"'Bout time you showed up," she said, crossing her arms. "I've been waiting for you for two nights."

"Maybe you should've told me your plan before drowning yourself," he snapped.

"Seriously? You're going to lecture *me*? Who un-bonded who?"

"I get no rest, even in my sleep."

"You're about to get all the rest you want. An eternity full. Are you really going to let your jackass brother send you on a suicide mission?"

"I am," Rhyn said. "I'm done fucking up my life and everyone else's."

"What if I told you I'm not dead?"

"Bullshit."

"Oh, because you Immortal jackasses know it all, right?" She raised an eyebrow. "You're doing exactly what Kris wants you to, Rhyn, going to your death like a lamb."

"I'm better off as demon fodder. I was doomed when I was born a half-demon."

"You can't believe that," she said, her features turning from irritation to concern. Katie approached him and stopped within arm's reach, gazing up at him. "Rhyn, you're better than this."

Gods, but he could smell her sweet scent! Her large eyes seemed to see right through him. He feared reaching out, in case she slid through his fingers like smoke. He'd lost her in life; he wasn't going to risk losing her in his dreams. He could imagine closing the distance between them, sweeping her up into his arms, and making love to her on the beach.

The way he should've done, before she'd walked into the ocean and killed herself to protect him from a fate he deserved.

"You should've let them kill me," he said in a hoarse voice. "I could die peacefully knowing you were safe, but I'm not worth saving."

"You're the only Immortal I've met worth saving."

"Stupid little human."

She rolled her eyes at him.

"How's Death?" he baited. "Gabe says she's a bitch."

"I haven't met her yet."

"Rhyn."

He snapped awake at the voice. The dream seemed so short, but the sky had begun to lighten on the horizon. The dream faded as he sat up. Toby stood nearby, his young face solemn. The angel looked ready for a journey with his backpack and sturdy boots. Beside him stood Hannah.

"I'm ready," Rhyn said and rose. He rubbed his stubble-roughed jaw.

"We appreciate this, Rhyn," Hannah said.

"Voluntarily going to my death? You're welcome."

"That's not what I meant."

At her hushed tone, Rhyn turned. Hannah held one of the lanterns donated to their exiled party by the Sanctuary. The blond woman was pale and gaunt.

"The Immortals need a home," she said. "They can't live scattered around the world."

"Right."

"You're not the only one hurting, Rhyn."

Out of respect for Katie, he bit back the bitter words at the tip of his tongue. He stalked past her, waiting for the moment he could release the pent up fury and magic. He'd make a crater of the castle and the surrounding countryside!

"You can't leave me here," Toby said, running to keep up. "You need me if you want to survive."

"I don't."

"But when Katie comes back, she – "

"Enough!" Rhyn said and gripped both the angel's shoulders. He shook the youth. "She's dead-dead! Get over it."

"But Rhyn – "

Rhyn released him and walked away again, towards the tent where Kris was staying. Kris stood outside, waiting for him. He held out a familiar dagger. Rhyn hesitated then took it. It had been their eldest brother's before his murder, and their father's before that. The ancient dagger was heavy and cold in Rhyn's hands. It was the symbol of the enforcer of the Council That Was Seven, the only of the seven brothers sanctioned to kill in cold blood on behalf of the Council and Immortals.

"You'll need this when I'm gone," Rhyn said.

"We'll see," Kris said. "If you survive, it's yours. If not, I'll find it when I return to the castle."

Fashioned by Death herself, the dagger was immune even to magic as strong as Rhyn's. He tucked it into his belt. Rhyn ignored Hannah's approach, and Toby shuffled his feet.

"I wish there was another way," Kris said.

"You've wanted me dead for thousands of years," Rhyn pointed out.

"That was before you saved my life."

"It wasn't the first time."

Kris frowned and opened his mouth to speak when Toby gave an exasperated sigh.

"Let's get this over with," Rhyn said.

Hannah looked less than pleased, but Toby's face brightened. Kris opened the portal to the shadow world and held out his hand to his mate. Hannah took his and one of Toby's hands, and Toby slid his small hand into Rhyn's.

The feeling of the angel's soft, cold hand in his own reminded Rhyn of the first thing he'd touched in Hell that hadn't been stone. Gabriel had brought him a book with a worn, leather-like cover, and he'd lost himself dwelling on the sensation of buttery leather under his fingertips after the hazy nightmare that had been his existence in Hell.

The sense returned, and Rhyn looked down. Toby's hand was all that felt *real* after the past three days.

"Is that it?" the angel asked in a hushed voice.

Rhyn looked up at the brightest of the portals lining the otherworldly landing between worlds. He released Toby's hand.

"Rhyn," Kris said. "Be careful. I mean that. We'll figure out something."

Rhyn glanced back to see both Kris and his mate frowning as they watched him. He didn't understand both their concern and eagerness to get rid of him, but felt familiar coldness settle into his chest. There had been two other people in the entirety of the universe that cared for him, and the two people with him now were not the same.

Adrenaline shot through him as he faced the portal. The only other thing that made him feel alive was killing and destroying – the demon side of him that always won out. He salivated at the thought of demon blood and walked to the portal.

"Toby!" Hannah cried.

A streak tore past him just as he reached the portal. The angel moved with inhuman speed as he sprinted and dived through the portal ahead of Rhyn, disappearing.

"Shit! Rhyn you—"

Surprise and then alarm filled Rhyn. He'd walk happily to his own death, but angels were sacred creatures among the Immortals. He ignored Kris and plunged through the portal.

Kris had opened it near the cliff. On the other side of the world from the Caribbean Sanctuary, the French Alps were dark and cold, and it was sleeting. Rhyn slipped in the muddy snow beneath him and looked around for the angel. His plan of blowing up everything hadn't included an innocent like Toby being hurt.

"Toby!" he shouted, furious at the angel.

He neither saw nor heard anything else around him. Too fast, he felt the buffers' effect on his powers lessen, and magic exploded through him. He dropped to the ground, unable to stabilize the raging power within him or release it to destroy everything around him as he planned. He gritted his teeth to keep it contained, silently cursing both the angel and Kris for not just letting him die-dead, like he deserved. Agony tore through him as will combated magic, and he seized on the ground, helpless.

Katie!

Chapter Two

Katie followed her instincts through the dreamscape until she climbed the last rocks and saw Rhyn curled in a ball just on the other side of a small ridge on the Sanctuary. Her heart leapt, and she hurried to him. In her last dream, he'd been there one moment then disappeared, just when she reached out for him. She couldn't help wondering if these dreams were more than dreams. This wouldn't be the first time she lived out reality in a dream.

"Rhyn? What's wrong?" she asked, pausing near him.

His teeth were grinding loudly enough for her to hear, and his face was ashen and drawn in a look of pain. He couldn't answer – that much she discerned at the rippling muscles of his clenched jaw.

She knelt beside him and touched his arm tentatively, waiting for him to disappear again.

Instantly the grinding of his teeth stopped, and his ragged breathing began to slow. He uncurled, and she withdrew her hand before he disappeared from the dream again. Even so, she wasn't able to shake the warmth of his magic flying up her arm and through her, reminding her of what it was like being near him when she was alive. Even the skin of a half-demon was smooth and warm. She used to resent the way his touch made her feel like she belonged to him, until she'd walked into the Caribbean knowing he might never touch her again.

"What … did you do?" he rasped.

"Thank God!" she exclaimed when he didn't disappear. "What are you doing? Did you do what Kris said?"

"Toby," he managed. "He went through the portal."

"So that coward of a brother of yours sent a kid to face a bunch of demons?" she demanded. She wanted Kris dead in that moment, even if the arrogant Immortal was her sister's husband.

"Toby went before we could stop him."

"Oh," she said. "Is he okay?"

"Trying not to blow him up. I can't control it."

Katie watched him stand with effort. The strain on his face was clear, and a tremor of fear crept through her.

"You can do it," she said.

"I've never been able to."

"Rhyn, you can. I know you can. How else can you protect him and everyone else?"

He looked at her hard. She saw the resignation to his own death in his silver eyes.

"I didn't drown myself so you could give up!" she snapped, growing upset.

"I'm not *giving up*. I can't fucking control it!"

"You are the strongest person I know. If anyone can do this, you can," she told him. "And I forbid you from killing Toby! He's annoying and mouthy, but he's just a boy. Or an angel or something. I can't imagine killing an angel is any better than killing a little boy."

Rhyn said nothing. She watched him pace, his long, muscular legs drawing her eyes. A familiar ache filled her, one that made her want to launch herself into his arms and never leave the dream world. It was better than traveling the underworld with Gabriel or fighting with Kris for an ounce of respect.

At the same time, she knew whatever Rhyn faced outside the dreamscape was as bad as what awaited her, if not worse. She didn't know how either of them could make it back to each other, but they had to.

"Gabe says hi," she whispered.

Rhyn met her gaze. She never imagined him being defeated by anything, and she felt pain at the look on his face.

"I couldn't even protect my own mate. I can't protect anyone else," he said.

"You must find a way. Find Toby," she said. "Please."

"Find Toby, blow myself up," he said. "I can do that."

"Rhyn – " she objected and reached out to touch him.

He disappeared again, and her hand met air. Katie muttered a few curses and looked around. When he wasn't there, she was alone on the dream island, until Gabriel awoke her. Fortunately, Death's assassin didn't wait long to shake her.

Katie awoke from the dreamland and sat up groggily. It was dark. The dual moons of the underworld were high overhead, another sign she hadn't slept more than an hour or two. The trees overhead hissed as the branches moved like snakes in a soft breeze.

Gabriel held out a hand and pulled her up, silent despite his size and small armory of weapons.

"More circles again today?" she complained. "I'm so sick of this jungle."

"Concentric circles throw off the creatures pursuing us," he reminded her. "Unless you want them to catch you."

"Maybe they'll feed me something other than gummies."

"Eat these. Don't feed the trees." The words had become his mantra over the past three days.

She took them and shivered in the chilly night. Food and sleep had become luxuries during their travel. Gabriel handed her the food and water gummy cubes she'd first had in Hell. While they took away the fatigue and gave her energy, she could think of nothing but chocolate sundaes and pickles. Together, maybe with caramel sauce. She considered throwing the tasteless food cubes to the trees he warned her against feeding every day.

Lost in the food fantasy, she didn't see Gabriel disappear into the jungle. Katie blinked and looked around, still uneasy with the snakelike branches that moved of their own volition overhead. She didn't know what kind of creatures followed or what other critters would live in the Immortal jungle, but she wanted nothing to do with such a weird place.

"C'mon," Gabriel said with some urgency, reappearing to her right.

"Gabriel, what are we doing, walking in circles?" she asked as she obeyed.

"Buying us some time."

"Time for what? I thought we had to reach a Sanctuary. Can't we just go through the shadow world?"

"No."

She waited for more to his explanation. He said nothing but followed a trail she couldn't see. A startled bird with three wings darted with a squawk from a tree overhead. Gabe had become edgier over the past day, and she couldn't help but wonder what had happened. Whatever it was, it hadn't been when he was around her. Although exhausting, their journey had been relatively peaceful.

"So the people pursuing us. What are they?" she asked, looking up.

"Assassins like me."

"An army of Gabriels."

"And demons."

"And they hate circles as much as I do?"

Gabriel glanced over his shoulder at her with a look of tired amusement. She waded through the brush of the possessed jungle, unwilling to admit just how scared she was. She'd seen demons and what they could do, and the size and strength of Gabriel was enough to warn her she never wanted to meet another of him.

Looking back, she couldn't help but think they were being followed. The sense was unlike any other: the hairs on the back of her neck stood up, and someone's warm breath brushed the back of one ear. She saw nothing other than the trees in the dark and started forward again.

"Gabe, can I ask you something?"

"Go for it."

"Is your boss a girl?" she asked.

"My boss?" he asked, turning fast enough for her to run into him. "Why do you ask?" He'd gone still, like a panther about to launch itself.

"Before I became somewhat-dead, I heard a woman tell me to trust you. She called you *my Gabriel*. Then she told me to kill myself."

"You're saying Death spoke to you?"

"I think so, yeah. Is that bad?" she asked.

Gabriel frowned, appeared pensive then struck off again without another word.

"Gabe, is that bad?" She scrambled after him.

"I don't know what it means. Death can take on any form she wants, though, so I don't know if it was Death or not," he said. "She's a conniving, self-serving, arrogant creature. Heartless, too."

"Wow," she said, taken aback. "I've never heard you speak bad about anyone. You have a thing for her?"

"Not anymore."

"But you really were, um, with her?"

"For thousands of years. And then I wizened up and realized I'm just another gem in her collection." Gabe's bitterness was quiet but evident. "I think I might've entertained her until she grew tired of me."

"Her loss," Katie said. "Any normal woman would know you're a catch."

"Death is far from normal."

"She's an Immortal or demon or what?"

"She's almost as old as time itself and older even than the Ancients. I think she was a goddess at one point," Gabe answered. "She found me when I was a youth, after I'd seen the slaughter of my family at the hands of demons. I watched her take their souls." His voice took on a hushed note.

"And she let you live?"

"She can't take a soul whose time has not yet come, and she was in the mortal world. She offered me a job instead, to work for her."

"And you took it."

"I did. But she never let me forget I was once a human. She always resented my human *weaknesses*."

"So you started working for her, and then you guys became … romantic," Katie said. "Then, what? She got tired of your humanness and dumped you?"

Gabe was quiet for a long moment, leading them through the jungle in thoughtful silence. Katie felt the strange sense of something following again and moved closer to him.

"I guess you can say I ceased to fascinate her one day," he said at last. "I was her only voluntary assassin. I traded her my soul for the life of a friend."

"Wow, Gabe. You're friend must've meant a lot to you."

"And to you. You did the same," he said with dark humor. "She wanted to kill the one person who always believed in me."

"Rhyn?"

"Yes. We both saw something in him that she didn't. He's fortunate to have someone like you, who would give her life for him. You are exactly what he needs to balance his nature," Gabe continued. "I ended up Death's plaything because she pursued me. She was beautiful, and I had eternity alone ahead of me. Made sense at the time. What drew you to Rhyn?"

Katie didn't answer for a moment, pensive. Gabe glanced back at her then slowed, as if sensing she was growing tired.

"At first, I think it was knowing he was a black sheep like me. My sister always treated me like I was a blight on the family name. She tried to help me in her own way, I guess, which was better than what Rhyn's brothers did to him. I wanted to believe he could make it in the Immortal world, because if he could, I could, too," she started. "And then I saw how good his heart is. He's a train wreck, but he's honorable and capable of such good. Kris pulled me into this world and assumed I'd do what I was told like a good little human. But when I told Rhyn I wanted to leave him, he asked for another chance. It's like he woke up then and realized he wasn't in Hell anymore or trapped by his brothers' expectations."

"He had a reason to be more than what people told him he was," Gabe said.

"He did. He wanted to make the world safer for me, for our …" Katie's throat tightened. She cleared it. "He realized he doesn't have to be in the shadows anymore. And the way he looked at me that last day…" she drifted off again, this time recalling the intensity of emotion on Rhyn's face the last time she'd seen him in the mortal realm. "I almost believed we had half a chance."

"You have more than half a chance," Gabe said with a chuckle. "You saw in him what I've always seen and no one else has. He would do for me what I did for him. Trading my soul to Death was not an easy decision, but I never would've done it for anyone else."

"I probably wouldn't have walked into the ocean for anyone else," she said. "I am only sorry for you, Gabe. I don't think Rhyn or I can save you."

"I'm not sure I can save you. We'll deal with one soul at a time."

Katie's gaze flickered from the snake-like movement of lively jungle trees to Gabe's back. Gabe's words terrified her. If the strongest man she'd ever met couldn't save her, what hope did she have?

"I do know you need to be back soon, within a few days," Gabe continued. "I'm not sure your mortal body will hold up much longer down here."

Her fate was uncertain, but his was sealed. She saw it on his face every time he looked at her. Where he'd once looked almost noble with his chiseled features and air of command, he now looked haggard. When she gave herself too much time to think, she began to understand the depth of the despair he must've been feeling. After all, her own soul – and that of her daughter's—was just as likely to be lost if she didn't escape.

"How will I know if Death takes my soul?" she asked. "Does it hurt?"

"It doesn't seem to," he answered. "You'll be made dead-dead first and then she'll take your soul."

"So the soul is a physical thing?"

He turned, and she stopped. With the tip of one dagger, he tugged a necklace free from the shirt hiding it. On it was two small green gems.

"Death has a twisted sense of humor, worse than mine," he said. "These are what souls look like. She let me keep my mother and brother's."

Katie stared at the necklace, horrified by the idea of looking at a soul and fascinated by the fact they looked like emeralds. Gabe turned away and started through the forest again.

"They're beautiful," she managed at last. "And creepy. She makes necklaces out of them?"

"She makes whatever she wants out of them. Most of them go in the bottom of the Lake of Souls, where they can find their loved ones and be in peace."

The idea of emeralds swimming around in a lake was too much for Katie. She felt nauseous again at her overwhelming situation and stopped, leaning against a tree. What she would give for a sip of real water!

"You ok?" Gabe asked, returning through the forest to her side.

"Just don't feel good," she said. "And, Gabe, I feel like someone's following us."

"I would sense it if so."

"I've felt it since we started out again. Maybe I'm immune to magic here, too."

Gabriel went still like he did when he was stretching his senses to test their surroundings. She held her breath.

"I sense something, but magic is blocking it. C'mon. We need to leave the forest," he said, shifting after a long moment. "We should move as fast as you can."

Her hopes rose as he started forward at a faster pace, until she realized he hadn't yet abandoned his pursuit of concentric circles. By the time dawn came, she was breathless from keeping up with him, and the jungle looked as if it'd never end.

The snakelike branches overhead were creepier when she could see them in daylight, and the few birds and insects she saw made her shudder. The sense of being followed didn't leave even in the full light of day.

Gabriel stopped at midmorning, and she sagged against a tree, exhausted. The large death-dealer's gaze went from their surroundings to her face. She wondered if she looked as tired as she felt.

"Start eating one every couple of hours," he said, holding out a handful of the food and water cubes.

She grimaced and took them. Gabriel peeled off his heavy jacket as she chewed and watched him. His hands absently traveled over all the places on his body where weapons were hidden and he pulled free a dagger with a jagged edge.

"Stay here," he said and moved into the jungle. "I'm going to circle back to see what might be there. Rest for a few minutes."

Katie bit back a plea for him not to leave her in such a creepy place. She sat on a thick log. He disappeared into the shadows of the jungle, and she pulled her knees to her chest, listening. He was silent while the branches overhead hissed and rasped against one another and the cries of distant birds drifted to her. She inched away from a plant whose slender stalk was maneuvering through several other plants to position its leaves in direct sunlight.

She'd long suppressed fear, knowing there was one way to Rhyn, and it was with Gabriel. Unless Rhyn got himself killed first. Then she wasn't sure what she'd do. One hand went to her stomach, where their child grew. Her emotions started to surge again, but she pushed them down with her fear and steadied her breathing.

She had no idea how to be a single mother in the real world, let alone in a world as unforgiving as the Immortal one. She'd proven she couldn't raise Toby without a bottle of vodka permanently glued to her hand. Rhyn had been exiled for his mixed origins, and she'd never been especially welcomed by anyone but Gabe and Toby. If something happened to Rhyn or if she couldn't leave here …

Panicking made her already surging hormones worse. She felt nauseous.

The snap of a branch pulled her from her misery. She twisted to face the direction from which it had come, expecting to see Gabriel. Nothing was there. The jungle around her fell suddenly still, and the possessed branches stopped in place, as if watching her.

"Gabe?" She rose.

Another snap of branches from a different direction. Katie whirled in time to see the shadow of someone – or something – disappearing behind a thick tree.

"Gabe, if that's not you, you better be about to kill that thing," she called. She pulled free the small knife the death-dealer gave her.

Snap. She turned, expecting to see another shadow disappear. Instead, someone stood before her, close enough to touch her. Katie yelped and leapt back at the familiar form.

"*Andre?*" she breathed, adrenaline surging fast enough for her to lose focus. She stared at the dark features and glowing turquoise eyes of the eldest of Rhyn's brothers, who had died weeks before. Andre showed no emotion, didn't even seem to see her. He was like a statue, only she *felt* the warmth of his body and the tingle of magic in the air.

"C'mon," Gabriel said from behind her.

"Gabe!" she cried, facing him. "He's here!"

"Who?" Gabriel asked.

"Andre. He's …" She turned as she spoke to see the figure had vanished. "You didn't see him?"

"I saw the demon I killed," Gabriel replied and knelt to retrieve his jacked. He wiped the bloodied dagger on the ground. "You're seeing dead-dead Immortals?"

"I did. I think. But it's not possible."

"Your pupils are dilated. Did you eat one of the plants?"

"Gabe, he was right here."

"Must be the effects of the underworld on you," the death-dealer said and rose. "Somewhat-dead mortals aren't supposed to be here." He peeled off the necklace he wore around his neck and gazed at it briefly before handing it to her.

Katie took it and eyed it, not sure she could handle wearing the souls of others around her neck.

"They should keep you anchored in time, too, since your world's time means nothing here."

"They look like emeralds."

"You want to know their names?"

She felt nauseous again. As if reading it in her features, he smiled.

"Those are the most precious things in the world to me. If you lose it, I'll kill you. Quickly, though, because I do kinda like you," he said with dark humor. "If you talk to them, they'll talk back."

"Oh, god!"

"I'm joking about that. Not about the quick death, though."

"You have the worst timing for your jokes." Katie swallowed hard and finally put it on, feeling even more nauseous about the idea of wearing souls around her neck. "Gabe, does it ever strike you as odd that Death hasn't found us? Isn't this where she lives? Why hasn't she tracked us down?"

Gabe looked away and started walking again. Katie saw his shoulders hunch. When he didn't respond, she asked,

"Has she tracked us down?"

"Pretty sure she has," Gabe answered. "But … something is off. She might be trying to fix it."

"What do you mean? Isn't she a god? Goddess, I mean."

"She's bound by rules older than she is. She may have interfered somewhere she shouldn't have. There are Immortal Codes too old for even me to know and some that only the deities know. I think she violated one of those."

"Maybe she cares for you more than you thought," Katie said thoughtfully.

"Hardly. She's not capable of acting anyone's interest but her own. And, if I don't try to get you out of here, she'll still take you and your baby's souls."

"Then why would she have done something against her nature?"

Gabe glanced at her, his frustration at Death on his face.

"Ah, ok. It's a sore subject," Katie said. "But, maybe she did something for you?"

"She never does something without getting something in return."

"If Rhyn can learn to overcome his nature, she can to."

"You've never met her."

"I hope I never do, but not because I'm not curious. More because I'm not ready to die."

"Speaking of dying, do you still sense someone following?" he asked.

"Yeah," she replied after a pause.

His pace quickened. She looked around, waiting for Andre or a demon to leap from her surroundings. Nothing did, and she trailed Gabriel once again.

Chapter Three

The demon lord, Darkyn, circled the shape-shifting demon, looking for any signs its true nature hadn't been completely screened by the combination of its own skill and the injections. Demons that could take on the forms of whatever human they pleased were rare, and Darkyn had hand-selected the one before him for this mission. Impressed, he stood back and motioned the cowering Immortal in the corner forward. The Immortal scientist, Ully, crept towards them, the chains around his feet rattling with each step.

"The transformation is complete?" Darkyn asked.

"Yes," came the hushed answer.

"Certainly looks convincing. I see why Andre recruited you. And the immunity blood?"

"It'll render him near-invincible for several days."

"Define *several* for my demon."

"Four, maybe five. He can test for it by cutting himself. When he no longer heals instantly, the shots are wearing off," Ully explained.

"And there is nothing hidden in these injections that will alert your kind?" Darkyn asked again.

Ully shook his head and looked down. "It'll work like it should."

"You're a smart creature, Ully. If I suspect you've betrayed me, I'll turn my new super-demons on your Immortals. Four days is long enough to wipe all of them out."

"Except Rhyn," Ully whispered.

"Rhyn," Darkyn dwelled on the name of the half-breed. "He's about to lead my demons to the underworld. With the Immortals in disarray and Death's ... mistake, I can own the underworld before Rhyn can control his power enough to stop me."

"He won't do it," Ully whispered. "He won't betray his brothers."

"The Immortal side of him is weak. He'll do whatever it takes to get his mate back, and I intend to plant the idea in his head." Darkyn turned his attention to the shapeshifter. "You will kill any demon or Immortal in your path. They must believe you are who we made you to be. Understood?" Darkyn ordered.

"Yes, my lord," the shapeshifter answered.

"You are to find your way to the underworld. When you are there, you will plant this in the ground." He handed the demon a small pouch that contained the concentrated magic of Hell. One pouch wasn't enough to break through Death's weakened barriers, but three would. "Your name is Gabriel. You will find the death-dealer you resemble and assume his place until the sign is given in the sky for you to attack."

"Yes, my lord."

"Go. Await my messenger. Once Rhyn enters the underworld, you will follow him," he said, looking over his creation with satisfaction.

The super-demon opened a portal and disappeared.

Darkyn held out his hand. An hour glass with streaming black sand appeared in his palm. He'd lost three days already. Four was cutting it close. Once the bond between the half-breed and its human re-emerged a mere seven days after it was severed, Rhyn could channel his power again. Death was waiting for that day, and Darkyn had to beat her at her game. That meant making it into the underworld in four days.

He glanced at the demon guards in the corner and motioned for them to leave. A moment later, a thin figure entered the room. The last of the shapeshifters created, this one was a mirror image of the mad scientist, Ully.

The Immortal cowering in the corner gasped. Darkyn circled the super demon in satisfaction.

"You have your instructions," he said to the demon.

"Yes, my lord."

"This is for the underworld, and this you will know when to use," Darkyn said. He handed the shapeshifter a pouch identical to the one he'd given the other shapeshifting demon and a small talisman on a chain. "Go. Remind Jared what happens if he disobeys me."

"Yes, my lord." The Ully demon left.

"And now, Immortal, we wait," Darkyn said to the mad scientist. "I want you to see the underworld fall and the Immortals destroyed as you die. Unless you'd like to take Sasha's place in my lab."

"Sasha was a traitor. I'm not," Ully said in a quiet voice.

"When I take over Death's domain and her army of souls, I'll be invincible. By my side is the only place anyone will be safe."

Ully shook his head again.

"Very well." Darkyn suspected twisted Immortals like Sasha were rare. One of the brothers on the Council That Was Seven, Sasha had been strategically placed to provide Darkyn more information than he'd hoped for. Sasha's only flaw had been his madness, which ultimately resulted in his death. Sasha had identified Ully, who was hand-selected by Andre. While Darkyn didn't know the full details of how Andre had gotten Death to release the once-dead human, he did know Andre and Death wouldn't have done something so important if Ully wasn't the brilliant scientist he was.

It was unfortunate that Ully would be killed as soon as the three shapeshifting demons reached the underworld, but Darkyn didn't believe in loose ends.

"Guards!" he called to the demons waiting outside the door. "Take Ully away."

The Council's scientist hunched as the demons took his arms and withdrew him from the chamber.

Darkyn glanced at the sand in the hourglass. He had one more chain of events to set in motion.

Rhyn uncurled from his position on the cold, wet ground. He hadn't meant to fall asleep and didn't expect ever to wake up, not with the magic tearing him apart. He looked around, disoriented. The magic in his blood had stabilized as it did when Hannah and the angel were around, yet he didn't see them. His thoughts drifted to the second night of the strange dream.

Had a dead woman touched him and somehow calmed his magic?

"I'm sorry, Rhyn." Toby emerged from the early morning shadows of the forest.

"Go home, Toby."

"I can't open a portal."

Rhyn pushed himself up. He was freezing and drenched. He tested his power and found it wasn't just calm – it was bound. He couldn't access its depths, couldn't call upon a portal to send the damn angel home. Couldn't destroy this awful place.

"Did you do this?" he demanded. "Bind my magic?"

"I can't do that."

"You're saying we're stuck here?"

Toby shrugged and then shivered. Rhyn looked him over, noticing the angel was as wet as he was.

"What was your plan?" Rhyn snapped. "Just dive through the portal and then what?"

"What was *your* plan?" the angel shot back.

"Destroy everything. It's what I do best."

"Katie wouldn't approve."

Rhyn bit back his response and looked around. No matter what he wanted to say or do, he was stuck with the angel in the forest.

"I'm cold," Toby complained.

"You should've thought of that before you jumped."

"Hungry, too."

"C'mon," Rhyn muttered.

He stalked off into the forest, away from the castle and cliff. Toby clambered through the brush and trees after him, the angel's footsteps loud where Rhyn's were silent. Rhyn found a deer path and followed it until he reached a snowy meadow. Crossing it, he continued to look for a place to stash the angel where the kid wouldn't freeze to death. After another hour of walking, he found a small pocket in the roots of a massive tree.

"Are there bears in there?" Toby asked as they stopped.

"Better than demons. Go."

The angel looked up at him doubtfully then picked his way across roots to the pocket in the tree trunk. Rhyn scavenged for what dry wood he could find and took the armful back to the tree. Toby was huddled in the small cave, shaking with cold. Rhyn focused the little bit of magic he had remaining on the wood. Fire sprang up. With it, Rhyn felt a stitch of the seam binding his power snap. More magic leaked into his body, warming him.

"Ever skin a demon?" he asked Toby.

Toby looked surprised.

"What'd you think we'd be eating?"

"I don't want to eat a demon."

"Oh, that's right. You didn't plan ahead when you jeopardized my suicide mission," Rhyn said. "If I'm doing the hunting, you're eating demons."

The place where Katie touched him in his dream stung. Rhyn moved out of the drizzle, close to the fire, and peeled off his shirt. There was a welt resembling a bee sting where she'd touched him. He frowned.

"I'll eat tree bark. But I'm feeling sleepy now," Toby said suddenly in a rushed tone. "You should go hunt." The angel ducked into the cave, clutching his backpack to his chest.

Rhyn looked around, wondering what spooked the kid. He sensed nothing and pulled his shirt back on. The angel was still shivering despite the fire. He needed dry clothes and probably, human food. There was one place where Rhyn could find them.

"Stay here," he said. He went back to the deer trail and jogged through the forest to keep his body warm, making it to the castle in an hour.

Rhyn crept carefully through the demon scouts positioned throughout the forest surrounding the castle. The demons wore the Dark One's uniform of all black with waterproof cloaks and hoods. The demon side of him rendered his presence similar enough to a full-demon's that the others wouldn't be alarmed. He sized up each demon he passed, until he found one who appeared to be his size. The creature didn't hear his soft step, and the snapping of the demon's neck was the only other sound in the falling rain.

Rhyn stripped and changed into the demon's warm clothes. He pulled up the hood and strode into the forest, towards the castle. Beneath the hood, he took in the numbers of demons present. There weren't as many as he expected but far more than he could fight without his magic. He entered the castle, and his step slowed as memories he'd buried wriggled free.

He went straight to the basement, where the body of their father had been kept. The key to keeping the demon's away, it had been stolen by Sasha, the brother who betrayed the rest of them. Rhyn pushed off the hood as he entered what had been the most sacred chamber of the Immortals.

The coffin was gone, but the mutilated body of his demoness mother remained on the far wall. Rhyn stood before it as he had less than a week before. This time, he felt something towards the decapitated creature: hatred. She'd made him what he was, a disaster no one could fix except for a dead human.

"The preferred fate for any demon," a woman's voice said.

He tensed, guessing who it was without turning. He felt Death's cool presence, the same coolness that preceded Gabriel's visits.

"And half-demon," Death added.

"I welcome it," Rhyn replied, facing the small woman with flowing white hair and gown. "What the fuck do you want?"

"I came to see what was worthy of the attention of my best assassin," Death said and looked him over. "I see nothing but Gabriel's human weakness for a creature he should've let die-dead."

"Funny - he was right about you. You're the cold bitch he said you were."

She frowned, a ripple of something else crossing her pale features.

"Don't like that, do you," Rhyn said. "I'll ask you again. What do you want?"

"I came to warn you. You cannot destroy this place or start a war with me before four days have passed."

"Why not?"

"You simply cannot."

"I don't give a shit about your agenda. Tell me why it matters to *me*."

"I can make you dead-dead right now," she reminded him.

"I won't fight you," Rhyn replied. He flung open his arms, giving her his whole body as a target. "Kill me. Do me, you, and everyone else a favor!"

She stared at him.

"I got nothing to lose."

"There's Toby," she said.

"He means more to you than me."

"Gabe."

"You mean the assassin you sent to kill my mate? Not sure we can be friends after that."

"Katie."

"Already dead. And you can have my brothers right now. I'll give you the order I prefer you to kill them in," Rhyn said.

"There are factors at play I cannot share with you," Death said. "You would risk destroying this world and every human in it?"

Rhyn smiled.

"Of course. You're a half-demon. It is not in your nature to care for anything beyond you," she said, frown deepening.

"You took everything I cared about," he growled. "If I can destroy everything to spite you, I will."

"I am not your enemy!"

"I don't care." His anger growing at the petite woman who'd taken Andre, Katie and Gabe from him, Rhyn stalked towards the door.

"Then I will grant you a favor."

He stopped at her words, surprised.

"One favor from a deity of unimaginable power," she said. "In exchange for four days."

"Katie," he said instantly.

"Done," she replied just as fast.

Rhyn turned to face her. "Alive, not her body or pieces of her or anything twisted."

"She will be as she was before she walked into the ocean."

Speechless, Rhyn's heart flip-flopped at the prospect of seeing his mate again.

"Do we have a deal?" Death asked.

"Yes," he forced himself to say. "But if you trick me, if the fourth day comes and Katie isn't alive, I'll wipe out everything and hunt you down."

"Agreed."

Part of him rejoiced while another part of him thought the boon was too easily won from the creature before him. There had to be a catch. Death wouldn't agree to anything so easily. He found himself wishing for the advice of Andre or Kris, men smart where he was brash. She said nothing else and Rhyn turned away, striding out of the chamber.

Sensing demons in the upcoming halls, he replaced his hood and stepped from the stairwell leading to the basement into the hall on the main floor. Half a dozen demons paced the corridor, three dressed as scouts like he was. Rhyn made his way through his half-brethren, once again getting an idea of how many were there. He wasn't about to believe Death until he saw Katie for himself. A minute after midnight on the fourth day, if Katie wasn't standing beside him, he'd need the knowledge of where to set off the atomic bomb within him.

He ascended two floors to the hallway where Kris's supplies had been stocked. He recalled how hard it could be taking care of a helpless creature like Katie or Toby. He strode to the chamber that had served as a department store full of clothing to Kris's Immortals. Not surprised to find the chamber ransacked, he sifted through the remaining clothing on the floor. He guessed Toby's size and stuffed a bag with a few items before going to the food supplies. Demons didn't eat human food, and the storage area was virtually untouched. Rhyn grabbed several cans and packages of foodstuffs then left.

The forest was growing dark when he reached the tree to find the angel sitting in front of a dead fire, shaking with cold.

"You couldn't add wood to the fire?" Rhyn asked, irritated by the helpless creature.

"I tried," Toby chattered.

Rhyn started the fire again and sat beside Toby. He handed him the bag of clothing and food. Toby withdrew the clothing skeptically.

"Are these women's clothes?"

Rhyn looked at the articles of clothing the angel held up, unconcerned.

"The coat is pink and there are purple hearts on the sweater," Toby said. "I think I'd rather freeze to death."

"It'd make my life easier."

The angel sighed, dumped out the food and sorted through it. He held out a can finally and Rhyn took it.

"Can't open it," Toby said.

Rhyn ripped it open with his teeth and handed it back.

"So what's the plan?" the angel asked. "Are we raiding the castle?"

"Soon," Rhyn replied, dwelling on his conversation with Death.

"Thank you, Rhyn. I expected you to abandon me. Kris says you don't know how to care for anyone else and Hannah said -"

"Fuck them."

"Yeah, fuck them. They were mean to Mama," Toby said. "Can I tell Kris to go fuck himself when I see him again?"

"I'd be disappointed if you didn't."

"I know you don't want me here, but I'm glad I came. I like you best of all, Rhyn. Maybe I should call you Dad. Or Pops or Father."

"What?" Rhyn demanded.

"You're Mama's mate. Do you like Pops better?"

"If you call me any of those things, I'll hang you upside down from this tree and watch you starve."

"You should get used to it, though, Pops. What'll you do when your daughter is born?"

"Daughter?" Rhyn echoed. "Katie's …" *dead*. At least, she was for another four days. If Death kept her word, Katie would be back. "How do you know Katie will be alive in four days?"

"Really, Rhyn? You think she's dead?" Toby asked and rolled his eyes. "She's alive now. I told Kris and Hannah the same thing. No one listens to me."

"I'm listening now."

"I'm her guardian," the angel said. He puffed himself up, the scrawny body of a juvenile who hadn't thought to carry more wood to a dying fire. "If she was dead-dead, I'd have to have a new human, but I don't. Kris wanted me to *choose* a new one, but I—"

"Where is she?"

"Probably stuck in the Immortal underworld," Toby said with a shrug. "She's not in the mortal world. I'm sure Gabriel will take care of her. He knows his way around the underworld. I'm old enough to start to access the angel memories. But I don't know if this has ever happened before."

"He'd have to defy Death to keep a human alive in her domain," Rhyn said, considering. The histories of humanity— and Immortals— were passed down from angel-to-angel in the form of memories. He'd heard them mentioned before but didn't know much about angels. "No wonder the bitch agreed to my terms."

"Who?"

"Death. She told me I couldn't destroy the world for four days and offered me Katie's life in exchange."

Toby snorted a laugh. "Uncle Kris is right. You are more brawn than brains, Pops."

"Shut up and go to sleep."

"But I'm not done –"

Rhyn snatched the open can of food and flung it into the forest. Toby stared at him then took his pink coat and crawled deeper into the little cave. Rhyn stretched out on his back next to the fire, his mind puzzling over the angel's words. However much he tried to focus on what it was Death had agreed to, he couldn't escape his mixed emotions or one errant thought.

Daughter.

He was doomed any way he looked at things.

Chapter Four

Katie had barely closed her eyes when Gabriel shook her awake.

"We need to move," he whispered. "Quickly."

She pushed herself up, reaching into a pocket for a food and water cube. Gabriel took her arm and pulled her to her feet. She nearly choked on the cubes and swallowed them whole, struggling to keep up with the death-dealer as he darted into the forest.

"Did someone find us?" she asked.

"Yes. Not sure how, but we're going straight out of the forest."

"Thank god!" she said. "I'm so sick of the forest."

"Couldn't agree more. As fast as you can, Katie. Things are looking bad."

The forest was soon filled with the sound of pursuers. Katie needed no further encouragement. She pulled her arm free and ran behind Gabriel as he kept to the invisible path. A shadow caught her attention. She glanced over and froze, tripping.

Andre ran beside them a short distance away. He stopped when she did, never looking at her.

"Gabe!" she said and pointed.

He hauled her up with a glance in the direction she indicated.

"I see —"

"Katie, quiet!" the assassin ordered, body bristling with tension. "Follow this path until you reach a stream. Follow the stream towards the smaller moon. I'll catch up with you. Whatever you do, don't leave the stream."

"Where are you going?"

"I've gotta take care of whatever found us." He tucked another dagger into her pocket. "Kill anything that gets near you. And don't feed the trees."

"What is it with you and the damn —"

"Run. Now."

His shove almost drove her to her knees again. She steadied herself and looked up in time to see him disappear into the jungle. Fear made her heart pound. The strange path he'd been following appeared ahead of her, revealing itself only a few steps at a time. She started at a walk and quickened to a jog, making sure the path wouldn't close and trip her. The path kept up with her, and she ran.

The phantom of Andre appeared to her right again, keeping pace with her. She slowed to draw a heavy knife. It slowed with her. She sped up, and so did the creature. Katie stopped fast. The shadow Immortal stopped with her. This time, it faced her and pointed into another direction. It beckoned for her to follow and turned around, starting off in the direction he indicated.

Katie hesitated then continued onto the path Gabriel had told her to follow. She didn't know what the creature was. He looked like Andre, but Andre was dead-dead, which meant the creature following them was something else.

Shivering, she began to run again on the trail. She heard the fast moving stream long before she reached it and paused to catch her breath on its bank. The water looked … black in the moonlight. She took a step back and looked up towards the moons. As Gabriel indicated, one moon was lower than the other. In the distance, she heard the sounds of both fighting and pursuit.

Still breathless, Katie forced herself onward along the stream's rocky bank. The sounds of fighting grew faint and then disappeared. The stream wound through the jungle until it reached a small waterfall that fed into a massive lake whose black surface reflected the stars and moon. Katie slid down the hill beside the waterfall to the lake's edge, uncertain what to do. Gabriel hadn't mentioned the stream ending or the lake.

Andre appeared before her suddenly, and she stopped. The phantom looked at her then past her. Katie glanced back without seeing anything. The phantom had moved when her gaze returned to where he had been. He stood a short distance away, pointed to a small hollow in a tree then took up a protective position several feet away, watching the way she'd come.

There was no way she was sleeping tonight, even if she didn't feel any threat from the phantom. She definitely didn't feel safe without Gabriel there. She hesitated before going to where the ghost indicated, not wanting to continue without Gabe. Popping a food cube, Katie huddled in the hollow of the tree and waited.

Rhyn was alone on the island sanctuary in his dreams and awoke to the feeling that his magic had slipped even more from its binding. His body was hot from the inside out despite the cold rain falling in the forest. The fire had died overnight. He pushed the waterproof cloak off him.

Toby was gone.

Rhyn rose and crossed to the small cave, peering into its depths. Toby's backpack was there along with his pink coat. Rhyn straightened, angry at himself for not hearing the boy leave. A flash of purple caught his eye through the trees, and he loped through the forest. Toby's purple sweater, streaked with foul-smelling angel blood, was strung across a low branch.

"He's in Hell, with our kind." Darkyn's quiet voice made Rhyn tense. The demon lord materialized from the surrounding trees.

"What do you want with Toby?" Rhyn demanded.

"It has a name? Interesting. The angel is a guest. As long as you do what I want, he'll remain unharmed."

"You're the second *thing* that's tried to use the angel to bargain with me. Take him. Eat him."

"I'll call your bluff," Darkyn said. "You don't bring something food and clothing if you don't care if it dies. If you want it – *Toby* - to live, come to the castle this evening after dark falls. We have matters to discuss. Bring Kris. If you want the angel to die then stay right here."

Rhyn clenched his fists. Darkyn said nothing else and walked away, disappearing into the morning shadows of the forest. Rhyn felt fevered. His power was leaking out of his body, killing the plants around him. He grappled to control what he could, aware he would soon not have that option.

He didn't have three more days' worth of control. The idea he'd likely explode before Death delivered Katie made him feel fear, an emotion he hated and hadn't felt until responsible for the life of someone he cared about.

Testing his magic, he realized he could call forth a portal. He needed an ally, but it wasn't Kris. He had no intention of bringing Kris to meet Darkyn, not when he didn't know what Darkyn wanted. His thoughts went to Gabriel, the best friend he hoped he hadn't lost completely. Gabe wouldn't try to negotiate with Darkyn if things went bad.

Rhyn opened a portal and walked through the cool shadow place. The shadow world felt ... strange this time. He looked around, unsettled by the sensation that someone else was there. The black portal to Hell throbbed then dimmed, as if someone and come through. But he didn't see anyone else in the shadow world. Shaking his head, he continued to his destination. He emerged through a portal leading to Death's corner of the underworld. It was a place no demon or Immortal was allowed to go, and he'd thought it impossible to get there, until he'd tried. He'd visited Gabriel once before.

While not large, the Immortal underworld was separated by several different domains, two of which – Hell and Death's domain - were contained within shields no one could enter. At least, no normal Immortal or demon could enter. As a creature of both worlds, Rhyn could enter Hell, and he'd found by visiting Gabe that he was able to enter Death's domain, too.

It was clear and cool outside of Gabe's small cottage in the middle of a possessed jungle. Rhyn felt the sense that someone else was there once more and looked around. Assuming the feeling has something to do with his magic, Rhyn shook it off once more. He opened the front door without knocking, already sensing it was empty. Gabe had left in a hurry. The wardrobe near his bed was open and his walls were missing many of the weapons Rhyn had seen last time.

Frowning, Rhyn pulled a dagger from the wall and tucked it into his belt. He'd never tried tracking anyone through the Immortal underworld before; if Gabriel didn't want to be found, Rhyn wasn't going to find him in the death-dealer's backyard. Sweat dripped down his face in the still air of the cottage.

He called another portal and strode through it to the house of the one brother he'd come to almost trust. Kiki's feet were propped on a cast iron table while he gazed intently at the screen of his trusty iPad.

"Rhyn," the Immortal with Asian features snapped up at Rhyn's appearance. "I did what you wanted. Kris said –"

"I'm not here for Kris," Rhyn said.

"You aren't dead-dead."

"No shit."

"No, I mean, you aren't out of control. How is that?"

"I don't know. But I know it won't last long. Kiki, I need… help," Rhyn forced the words out.

"Kris would've helped you. Why did you come all the way here?"

Rhyn shrugged.

"It's been three days! You and Kris couldn't get along for three days?" Kiki demanded and frowned. "Your war with Kris needs to end now. You two will destroy – "

"Don't care, Kiki."

"You should care. You couldn't just tell him what you did?"

Rhyn eyed him. "What do you mean?"

"After I left the Sanctuary, I guess you could say I had a visitor who told me about Lilith and why you killed her. How she was working with the Dark One to try to drag Kris and the rest of us down to Hell," Kiki explained.

"Who told you that? Death?"

"Death? I don't rate the attention of that creature. It was a dream. Andre told me everything. He also told me you never told Kris, and Kris has believed the worst about you for thousands of years. It's a long time to bear a grudge, brother, if it's true. Is it?"

"I don't care about any of that right now," Rhyn said impatiently.

"Answer the question, Rhyn."

"Yes, it is. Now, if we could – "

"You're like two little – "

"I can beat the shit out of you again to make you help me."

"Fine," Kiki said and crossed his arms. "What do you need from me?"

"I need help rescuing Toby from Darkyn."

"You surprise me, Rhyn. When did you start thinking for – did you say *Darkyn*?"

Rhyn nodded.

"The demon lord Darkyn."

"There's only one, Kiki."

Kiki considered him for a long moment. Then he said, "On one condition. You must tell Kris about Lilith. I'm sick of this war between you two. We need you both on the Council."

"You sound like Andre," Rhyn said and scowled, wondering how a long-dead woman and a newly dead woman could still cause him such grief.

"Yes or no."

"Yes."

"Let's go. Wait," Kiki said as Rhyn opened a portal. "Do you have a plan?"

"You."

Kiki sighed. "Nevermind. Wait here. Ully was working on something awhile ago. I was supposed to field test it for him."

Rhyn crossed his arms, irritated. Kiki trotted from the patio into the house perched on a hill overlooking Tokyo. He returned ten minutes later with a small briefcase, a jacket and a hard case for his iPad. Rhyn opened the portal, and the two strode through it, back to the massive tree where Rhyn had lost Toby in the cold, wet French Alps.

"You should've told me it was raining," Kiki grumbled. "How far are we from the castle?"

"An hour jogging. Their scouts don't start until about half a mile from the castle," Rhyn answered. He watched Kiki set the briefcase down and open it. "What is it?"

"Another of Ully's experiments. Hopefully it's better than his demon skunk spray."

Rhyn's gaze went to Toby's backpack. The cold rain felt good against his hot skin, and he stripped down to his T-shirt in the frigid weather to buffer the heat and magic growing within his body.

"This is supposed to incapacitate a demon," Kiki said and loaded a handgun with a small dart. "I need to test it."

"I'll bring you a demon," Rhyn said, turning.

A sting bit the arm opposite the one Katie had touched in his dream. He whirled and glared at Kiki, who waited expectantly.

"Tell me if it does something," Kiki said.

Rhyn yanked the dart free and looked from it to the small welt forming on his arm. It matched the welt on his other arm. He gazed at his other arm for a long moment then strode to Toby's bag. Snatching it, he unzipped it and dumped its contents onto the ground. Alongside Toby's 3DS, a pair of clean underwear and socks, and gamers magazine was a small shaving bag. Rhyn opened it, surprised to find a syringe and two small bottles, one empty and one filled with wine-colored solution.

"What is it?" Kiki asked.

"That little shit."

"Is this Toby's?"

You need me if you want to survive. Toby had said before they left the Sanctuary. Rhyn unscrewed the lid of the full bottle, recognizing the scent of Katie's blood at once. It made his body roar to life, and he realized just how hungry he was. He'd foregone food after her death, hoping to starve himself.

"Weird," Kiki said and took it. "The other bottle's empty. Did he inject himself?"

"No, he injected me," Rhyn replied. "How did he know to do this?"

"I don't know what this -"

Kiki's voice stopped suddenly as blackness swept over Rhyn.

Chapter Five

Toby huddled against the black stone wall of his cell in Hell. He wished he'd thought to bring his backpack with his 3DS and magazines until he remembered why it was better he left it: Rhyn needed the other dosage of Immunity blood if the half-demon wanted to make it to the seventh day after Katie's death.

"Are you ok?" Ully called from the cell across the narrow hallway.

"I don't like it here," Toby said. "It's really boring."

"Yeah, I wish I had my portable lab set with me," Ully agreed. "Or maybe, just my anti-demon skunk spray."

"It didn't work very well."

"It was a work in progress. But I'd like to piss off someone like Darkyn right now."

"He'd kill you, Ully."

"He'll kill me anyway."

Toby frowned, worried as much about his human charge as his Immortal friends. Even if he wasn't with Katie, he could sense her. She was in some kind of danger, which meant he was the worst guardian angel in the history of guardian angels.

"I'm such a failure," he said with a sigh.

"You're just a baby," Ully said with a chuckle.

"No, I'm not just a baby! I'm almost full grown. I should've done a better job."

"It's not your fault, Toby."

Toby was silent, knowing a normal Immortal could never understand. He didn't yet have the full power of a real guardian angel, but he should've been able to do more than … nothing. Angels were placed with human mothers so they could understand the creatures they were meant to take care of. Human mothers raised them as their own, yet none of his human mothers had gone to the extent Katie did to try to protect him. Her circumstances were unique among all the humans he'd met, even if she wasn't the greatest mother he'd had. She still tried.

"Maybe I can go work for Death," he said glumly. "Isn't that where angels who fail go?"

"That's what I hear," Ully said. "You'd rather kill humans than protect them?"

"Not really."

"I brought you a friend," a third voice said.

Toby looked up as the familiar demon named Jared passed his cell, trailed by two demons carrying a body with another familiar face.

"Gabriel!" he exclaimed, bounding to his cell door. "Gabriel!"

His long time friend, the assassin, was bloodied and unconscious. The demons tossed Gabriel's body into a dark cell two down from Ully's before they left.

"Hello, my Immortal Twinkies," Jared said, his slender form pausing in the hallway between them. A slow smile slid across his face, revealing pointed teeth.

"I remember you," Toby said. "You're Rhyn's friend."

"Friend, no. Formerly indebted to him for my life, yes."

"What're you doing here in Hell?"

"There's a saying, better to serve in Hell than get your head split open somewhere else."

"That doesn't sound right," Toby said.

"He's messing with you," Ully said.

"Maybe you can help us leave!" Toby said, his excitement growing.

"I'll get right on that," Jared said and rolled his eyes. "Or I could stay right here and watch Darkyn pull you limb from limb. That's my idea of a good time."

"He can't leave, Toby," Ully added. "He's stuck here unless Darkyn lets him go. I heard the demons talking about it when I was in the lab. Jared is a glorified prisoner."

"That's not entirely accurate," the demon said with some irritation. "I'm allowed to roam the fortress."

"When you're escorted, you can. I have more freedom than you when I'm not in this cell."

"I'll be happy when Darkyn orders your death. I plan on eating every part of you, down to your bones," Jared snapped and bared his teeth.

"Ully has skunk blood, and I'm an angel. You'd gag to death first," Toby said and giggled at the look that crossed the demon's face. "I can almost pull a portal, with someone's help. I could get all of us out of here."

"You're too little," Jared said. "Immortals can't portal out of here anyway. Only demons can."

"I'm not a normal Immortal," Toby cried. "I'm an angel! I can do whatever I have to save my human."

"That is true," Ully said. "But I think you have the same limits as other Immortals?"

"Maybe," Toby muttered.

Though scowling, Jared was listening. He hadn't left them, and Toby's hopes rose again. Rhyn had liked this demon for some reason, and because of that, Toby trusted the flawed half-demon as much as he did Gabriel.

"You're not strong enough to take us all with you," Jared said at last. "And I won't be left behind."

"I can take me and Ully and you and Gabe," Toby replied. "It'll be hard, but I can do it, with Ully's help."

"That's four. You'd be pushing it with five."

"Five?" Toby asked. "Why would I need to take five of us?"

Ully sighed. "Because Darkyn replaced Gabe and someone else with shapeshifting demons."

"There's another Immortal down here?"

"Not Immortal, human," Jared answered. "You couldn't take us all, and I'm certain I'd be the one who's left behind. Humans take priority to you angels. No, sweetmeats, I won't help you escape." With that, the demon left.

"Ully, who is it?" Toby asked. He gripped the bars of his cell and pressed his face against them, trying to see into the neighboring cells.

"Fuck!" Gabriel's furious curse made Toby jump.

Toby looked his direction the best he could through the bars of his cell and saw the walls around the dark cell shake.

"Gabe!" he called. "Are you okay?"

"Toby? What're you doing in Hell?"

"Darkyn found me."

The death-dealer issued another string of curses.

"Where's Mama?"

"Stuck in the Immortal underworld."

"Gabe, she can't stay there! Death will find her!"

"Katie's alive?" Ully asked. "That's why Darkyn had me clone you, so he could get to her."

"Clone?" Gabriel echoed.

"Shapeshifter demon."

"And he's with her now."

"She's safe, I think. Darkyn wants her as a hostage, just in case," Ully whispered.

"Gabe, what're you saying?" Toby asked, listening with increasing panic. "Mama's been caught by a demon? Why?"

"I don't know, but we need to get out of here," Gabriel answered.

"A human in the Immortal world doesn't stand much of a chance," Ully said.

"You think I don't know that?" Gabe snarled. "I defied Death to rescue her. Played right into Darkyn's hands. I'm a fucking fool!"

"You couldn't have known," Ully said. "But if she stays with the demon, who knows what Darkyn's plan is. And if she runs …"

"She's dead-dead," Gabe finished.

"Gabe, get us out of here! I have to help her!" Toby shouted. "Where's Rhyn? He'll save us!"

"Calm down, Toby," the death-dealer said. "Right now, there's nothing we can do. Let me think in peace."

Toby's heart somersaulted in his breast, and he tried hard to reach the depths of the powers that would be his when he was just a little older. He couldn't. He was trapped, useless, unable to help the woman he was assigned to guard. Tears of frustration blurred his vision. Ully smiled gently at him from across the hall.

"We'll think of something, Toby," the mad scientist said. "Okay? Don't panic. We'll figure something out."

The phantom stayed with Katie throughout the night and into the first light of morning. Katie didn't sleep, not with the creepy phantom and no sign of Gabriel. She huddled in the hollow of the tree by the lake, praying for Gabe to reappear.

Find Rhyn now. The same voice that got her into this mess and told her to drown herself had given her this reminder twice. Katie sensed she wasn't safe where she was, but she didn't want to travel without Gabriel.

Midmorning warmed the world around her, and she rose finally. The phantom disappeared. Katie turned towards the lake and drew a deep breath. She would find her way back to Rhyn.

"This way," Gabriel's voice startled her.

She turned to see him motion her towards the jungle surrounding the lake. His clothing was torn, and blood stained his skin. He appeared to have been running; his boots were covered in mud that had splashed to his thighs, and his face was flushed.

"Gabe!" she exclaimed. "Are you okay?"

"I'll survive," he replied. "C'mon. We're not out of danger yet."

"I did as you said and kept to the stream. I saw him again."

"Who?"

"Andre."

"Andre's dead-dead."

She sighed and followed him, almost too exhausted to argue. The odd sense of someone following – a sign she now knew was the phantom trailing them - returned. Andre's specter appeared to her right, keeping pace silently with her.

"You don't see him?" she tried one last time.

"No."

The specter pointed back towards the lake. Katie slowed and watched Gabriel continue onward. She'd liked Andre above any of the Council members, but his insistence that she go in the direction opposite of which she was headed puzzled her. If he was dead-dead, what creature wanted her to go elsewhere and why? If he wasn't dead-dead, why didn't he speak to her?

"Gabe, where do Immortals go when they die?" she asked.

"Same place as mortals."

"Then what's the difference between mortals and Immortals?"

"Mortals can be killed by anyone. Immortals can only be killed by other Immortals or demons. It's part of the Immortal Code."

"How many rules are in the Immortal Code?"

"More than I can count."

"Hundreds? Thousands?" she prodded.

"More."

"Then how do you know if you're breaking them?"

"Immortals have an eternity to learn the rules," he pointed out.

"Do demons have Immortal Codes?"

"Why do you ask?" he asked and turned suddenly.

"Just curious."

Gabe studied her then allowed a small smile to cross his features. It was a hollow smile, and she wondered if Death was on his mind again.

"Yes, they do," he said and turned to begin walking away. "There are ten."

"And the Immortals have thousands," she said. She swiped at a branch that snaked in front of her. "Do demons have to *pretend* to respect a human's free will like Immortals do?"

"No. Mortals are like … candy to demons. Demons don't need them, but they taste good."

Katie almost laughed at the oddity of his words. He didn't seem to be joking, but she couldn't see his face to tell one way or another.

"And some rules are too old even for the Ancients to know," she repeated his words from earlier.

"That's correct."

They subsided into silence, and the gravity of her situation hedged in on her again. She liked talking to Gabe. He took her mind off her own issues and the creepy forest. And the phantom keeping pace with them. Katie looked over at Andre again. The phantom seemed content, neither interfering nor trying to communicate with her.

"So … is it possible for a dead-dead Immortal to come back to life?" she asked.

Andre shook his head even before Gabriel spoke.

"Not that I know of," the assassin said. "Though I guess if Death doesn't find their soul like she can't find yours, they can just … linger."

"That'd be interesting. But you said she does know where we are."

Gabe's step faltered, and he tripped for the first time since he'd led them into the forest. Katie's gaze went from Andre to the death-dealer.

"I wonder what she's planning," Gabe said.

"If she'd tell anyone, it'd be you."

"She'd never give me the time of the day. She barely even makes time for Darkyn."

"Why would she? Darkyn isn't a deity, right?"

"He is not, but he is a warrior worthy of her attention in battle. The Immortals always say, at least they understand Darkyn. No one can predict Death. No one even sees her, unless they die-dead."

"It must be a lonely existence for her," she said, puzzled as to why he'd speak more highly of Darkyn than he had of Death.

"Loneliness is not something a deity can feel. Only humans and Immortals."

"I'm sure she felt something for you, Gabriel. A woman doesn't take a man to her bed for thousands of years and not feel something for him."

"Interesting idea."

Katie frowned. In the course of a day, Gabe had gone from emotional to unaffected when discussing Death. He was distracted, and she felt like she was talking to someone completely different. Blaming herself for taking his mind off of their survival, she fell silent and followed him.

Briars and branches caught her pant legs, and she found herself slowing to push more and more of the jungle's flora out of the way. Gabe, too, began to struggle with the bramble, and she noticed the jungle no longer laid their path before him. Instead of clearing away to allow them passage, it stayed where it was, obstructing them.

"Gabe, are you sure this is the right way?" she asked finally, tired of wrestling with branches.

"I'm more likely to know than you, mortal." There was frustration in his voice as well, and he was sweating hard ahead of her.

"Where are we going anyway?"

"Death's palace."

"Are you serious?" she demanded. "Why? Won't she – "

"She has a portal in her palace. It's the only way out."

"But I thought -"

"It *should* be this way. Unless Death is fucking with me."

Or you're lost. The familiar voice – Death's voice – made Katie stop. She watched Gabe hack down another slithering branch. The Andre phantom stood nearby. He pointed in a different direction once more.

"Maybe it's that way?" Katie asked, pointing in the same direction.

Gabe cast an irritated look over his shoulder but looked where she indicated. He lowered the sword he was using to hack through the brush and started in that direction. Katie watched as the forest cleared a path for him, the way it had before.

"I'm starting to worry about you, Gabe," she said. "I thought you knew your way around here."

"It's Death," he said. "She can do whatever she wants in her domain." He breezed past her.

Katie drew a deep breath before following. Gabe was more than distracted. Something was wrong, but she had no idea of knowing what. At least he'd told her their destination.

She followed quietly for the rest of the day. The phantom and the strange exchange with Gabe troubled her. She didn't know her way around the Immortal underworld; she could only hope they were headed in the right direction again. Straight to Death. If what Gabe said was true, he was taking her to the only way out of the underworld. And yet, she feared what that would mean. Was she supposed to reason with Death? Plead for her life? Sneak into Death's palace, when Death already knew where they were and where they went?

Fatigue kept most of the thoughts from gaining traction, and they melted away like much of her dreams did. Gabe stopped at sunset, as darkness settled into the jungle. Katie watched him set up a small fire.

"Aren't you going to scout around first like you do every night?" she asked. "Or are we safe?"

His movements paused then continued. "We're safe."

The Andre phantom stood behind Gabriel, pointing again for her to leave.

"You're certain?" she asked.

"I know the Immortal world better than you, mortal."

"You didn't sense the demons earlier. I had to tell you."

Gabriel glanced at her and straightened. He handed her more food and water cubes then motioned for her to seat herself by the fire.

"You need rest," he said. "I'll be back."

Katie rolled her eyes at the gummy cubes before popping several into her mouth. The Andre phantom settled on the opposite side of the fire from her, mirroring her cross-legged position.

"You gonna say anything?" she challenged.

It didn't, though it did motion to her belt. She looked down at the knife Gabriel had given her. Uncertain, she offered it to the phantom, who shook its head. He motioned to the knife then looked around them.

"You think I'm in danger?" she asked.

It nodded.

"Andre, are you really dead? Or a ghost?"

A faint smile, the first sign of human emotion, crossed its face. It pointed to her other hand – the one holding food cubes - then to the trees.

"Oh, no. Gabe said not to," she said, frowning.

"Gabe said not to what?" the death-dealer asked as he stepped back into the small camp.

"Nothing."

"Who were you talking to?"

"Andre."

The assassin shook his head and crouched near her, warming his hands by the fire.

"Gabe, how much farther do we have?" she asked again with a sigh.

"Not far. I saw the palace when I climbed a tree. Maybe a day or so."

"I really miss Rhyn right now," she murmured. "He'd have a way of keeping my mind off of things. I think the demon side of him makes him a better Immortal than people like Kris."

"Demons are superior to Immortals," Gabe agreed. "Maybe the half-breed's demon blood hasn't weakened him as much as it could."

Katie looked at him, expecting him to be joking. He didn't seem to be. She finally allowed herself to admit something about the man helping to save her life: He was acting really strange. Katie stretched out by the fire, exhausted. Gabe leaned across her to grab the bag with his weapons' polishing supplies. A necklace with two emeralds – identical to the one he'd given her to wear – dangled above her.

"I thought you only had one of those," she said and pointed to his neck as he straightened.

He froze again and looked at her hard then shrugged.

"Whose souls are on that one?" she asked.

"My family's."

"Interesting. Can I have it?"

Gabriel gave her a harried look, one that said his patience was at an end. He withdrew a dagger and sliced it free of his neck then tossed it to her. She caught it. He rifled through his bag and prepared a dagger to sharpen.

"You're not going to threaten me about losing this one?" she asked after a pause.

"Don't lose it," he said.

She studied him, not understanding why the necklace with his family's souls was worth killing her for one day and not a concern the next. The one he'd given her was tucked safely against her skin.

"I think you should get some sleep," he added. "We might have to fight our way into the palace tomorrow."

Katie almost protested his abrupt dismissal then rolled so her back was to the fire. Something was really off about Gabe. She fingered the gems on the new necklace. Although they were the same shape, they were lighter, like comparing plastic beads to glass ones. The leather-like necklace itself contained the stiffness of something new, rather than the well-worn suppleness of the one around her neck.

It felt fake. Her sense of danger grew more heightened at the thought that something had happened between the time Gabe originally gave her his necklace and now.

Ully. She recalled how a demon in Kris's castle had taken on Ully's appearance, down to his goofy grin. The guise had been almost perfect, except for Ully's hands, which had been bony with sharpened nails rather than Ully's human hands. She was about to roll over and check Gabriel's hands when she recalled he always wore gloves.

"Gabe?" she said.

He sighed in frustration.

"Do you think my son will have Rhyn's powers?"

"He might have some of them. I don't know what your human blood will do, dilute or enhance his abilities."

She squeezed her eyes closed at his response. The real Gabriel had been the one to tell her that the child she carried was a girl.

"I guess we have to wait and see," she forced herself to say and added silently, *I hope you're safe, Gabriel, wherever you are.*

Part of her desperately tried to make excuses for Gabe. Maybe he was fatigued or Death had done something to him. She debated what to do. She knew where Gabe was allegedly taking her, but she couldn't outrun or fight a demon or an assassin or anything else chasing her through the underworld. She'd need help.

She squinted into the jungle, trying to see Andre again. This time, he wasn't there.

Chapter Six

Rhyn grunted and rolled onto his stomach. The stone floor beneath him was cool but not cool enough to soothe the hot fury of his magic. The effects of whatever Toby had injected into him were almost gone.

"My plan didn't exactly work," Kiki's tone was frustrated.

"What happened?" Rhyn squinted towards the sound of his brother's voice, struggling to balance the sensations within him. Kiki was chained to the wall while Rhyn was sprawled on the floor of the small room.

"Ully's dart worked a little too well. You went down like an elephant."

"Where are we?"

"The dungeon."

Light filtered in from somewhere, and Rhyn tried to make sense of his surroundings.

"How long was I out?" he asked.

Kiki didn't have a chance to answer before the wooden door to their prison creaked open. Rhyn's head spun as he was hauled up and dragged into a well-lit hallway. Light and shadows wreaked havoc on his sense of place and time until he hit the cool stone floor again.

"Still no control," Darkyn said, his voice seeming to come from everywhere. "At least try, half-breed. You made it to the castle by nightfall. I'd planned for some sort of onslaught, not to find you slung over the shoulder of your brother – the *wrong* brother, though I guess that's the most I can expect out of a half-breed."

A tingle of alarm went through Rhyn, but his head was too heavy for him to process it. Instead, he focused hard on containing the power within him. When he felt he wouldn't explode, he looked around. Darkyn had claimed Kris's library and stood near a pane of windows overlooking the snowy Alps. The morning light was too bright for his eyes, and he turned to face shelves of antique books.

Toby. The angel needed him. Rhyn focused hard on the demon lord then on putting one foot, then the other, beneath his shaking body. He rose despite his whirling equilibrium.

"So I made it," he said. "You have to let Toby go."

"I said I'd let him live, not let him go."

"Fucking Kiki." Rhyn grabbed the arm where his brother had shot him. It throbbed still. "What do you want, Darkyn?"

"I happened to overhear your little talk with Death in the sacred chamber."

Rhyn eyed him.

"I know you spent most of your life in the same place I did, Hell. Which makes me think you don't know that what she promised you cannot be."

"She swore it."

"And you trust her?" the demon-lord challenged.

Rhyn said nothing, aware the creature before him couldn't be trusted anymore than Death.

"If Death frees a mortal from the underworld, she violates a code even older than she is. I don't know what the consequences will be," Darkyn explained. "But I know her well enough to know she won't make a deal that breaks bad for her."

"What are you saying?"

"She set you up. She bought herself the time she needed. She won't need to break the Immortal Codes and return your mate to you, because in the next three days, you'll be out of her hair."

"She's counting on you to wipe me out," Rhyn said, his stomach sinking. He'd suspected Death's promise was made too easily, but it had seemed too clear to be anything but what she'd said. Yet Darkyn's words made too much sense. Gabe had told Rhyn enough about Death's double-talk for him to know the deity always seemed to shape things to benefit her.

"I imagine she has a few options. Kris isn't your biggest fan, either. You have fewer allies than I, half-breed."

"All I want is Katie back," Rhyn said.

"Go get her."

"As if it's that easy."

"Why isn't it? You've been to Hell. You can go to the underworld. You can find Death and force her to give you what you want," Darkyn said. "You have the power."

"Power I can't control."

"You're on your feet right now and the walls are still standing."

Rhyn glanced around, not noticing his head had cleared and his magic was contained until Darkyn pointed it out. Anger at Death – not power – made his blood boil.

"You are half-demon. Death can only contain your Immortal powers in her domain, just like I can only contain your demon powers in Hell."

"What do you gain by having me go to the underworld?" Rhyn asked, ignoring the bait.

"How much do you want your mate back?" Darkyn countered. "There's only one way to do it. You can stay here as my prisoner until Death gets what she wants and one of us kills you. Or, you can find her and make her give you back your mate. Only Death knows where Katie's soul is. Make a choice."

"Obviously, I'll find my mate."

"Good. Then go."

"Just like that?" Rhyn asked skeptically.

"Just like that."

"I'm taking Kiki."

"I won't stop you."

Rhyn couldn't help feeling as if Darkyn was playing him as Death had. Yet Darkyn asked for nothing in exchange for freeing him.

Save Toby. The words were faint but firm in the same tone Katie had taken with him in the dreamland. Rhyn ignored them, instead fixating on how to track Death in the underworld. He stumbled with his first step but was soon running hard through the castle, his mind on finding Death to regain Katie. He found himself outside the door where Kiki was being kept prisoner. For the first time since leaving Darkyn, Rhyn realized no one had tried to stop him yet. No demons stood in front of Kiki's door and Darkyn hadn't ordered the castle after him.

Darkyn was serious about letting them go. Wrenching open the door, Rhyn strode into the chamber. Kiki sprang up from his seat in the corner.

"Toby's in Hell. You need to go save him," Rhyn ordered.

"I can't travel to Hell, Rhyn."

"I'll drop you off."

"Gods, Rhyn, take a minute to think before you act. What's gotten into you anyway? We have some time to think about this," Kiki said, peering at him closely.

"I'm going to find Death and take Katie back."

Kiki started to chuckle and then frowned. "You can't be serious."

"I am."

"Let's talk to Kris. I can't just go to Hell without a plan, and maybe he can – "

"No, Kiki. I'm doing this on my own. You want me to drop you off in Hell or not?"

"I want to see Kris first."

Rhyn turned on his heel and left.

"Rhyn, wait!" Kiki called after him. "You can't offset the balance of the entire universe for one woman."

"She's my mate, Kiki."

"You'll destroy everything, Rhyn, and for what? The two seconds you have with your mate before the Dark One unleashes demons across the mortal realm?"

He's right, Katie's soft voice said.

"No," Rhyn growled.

"Andre never would've brought you to the Council if he didn't see the good in you," Kiki called as Rhyn walked. "All you have to do is –"

" - nothing and let Kris send me to Hell again?"

"There is a higher purpose to our own suffering. Maybe this is what Hell should've taught you."

"As if you know suffering!" Rhyn said. He spun, surprised his pragmatic brother would compare an existence in Hell to one of luxury and freedom.

"Every man, woman, and creature knows suffering, Rhyn," Kiki said. A shadow crossed his features, one Rhyn didn't expect to see.

"Nothing compares to Hell."

"Lost love?" Kiki offered. "If you loved her enough to destroy the world for her, then you know the pain Kris has been through twice. Hell cannot hold a candle to that kind of pain. Every one of your brothers has felt it at some time. It's what reminds us of why we fight for humanity, and it's what makes us who we are. But you have to move on, Rhyn. It's the way the world works. Katie is dead-dead. There's an ounce of honor in you. Andre saw it, and I see it. Kris gave you the position of enforcer. Take your place with us on the Council. We can deal with Death without breaking down her front door and pissing her off."

"It doesn't have to be this way," Rhyn replied. "Not for me, not with the power I have. Besides, Death promised to return Katie to me after four days and lied."

Rhyn opened a portal and left Kiki in the hallway. He paused in the middle of the cool shadow world gazing at the portals. He thought of Hell, and the portal glowed blacker than night. He thought of Kris, and the portal for the Sanctuary lit up. He thought of the Immortal underworld—Death's domain—and the portal turned gray.

Rhyn stepped into Death's domain.

At the Sanctuary, Kris was just getting ready to return to his tent when Kiki burst onto the beach, looking as if he were being chased by demons. The portal closed behind his half-brother, and Kiki lowered the knife in his hand, facing Kris.

Kris crossed his arms, recalling the last message he'd received from his spies. They'd been certain of two demon shapeshifters infiltrating his organization. While no one knew who they'd replaced, one thing was clear: he couldn't assume people were who he thought they were.

"What's wrong, Kiki?" he asked.

"What's not wrong?" Kiki snapped in response. "Rhyn's gone ape-shit crazy and decided to kill Death. Toby's in Hell, and Darkyn is planning something big, but I don't know what."

"C'mon, we'll talk," Kris said and motioned for him to follow as he walked to the tent he shared with Hannah on the beach. His nerves had been shot since Rhyn left and the Immortals stumbled upon the message about the shapeshifters. Even the Sanctuary didn't feel safe anymore.

Kiki poured himself a glass of whiskey and tossed it back. Kris watched him for any telltale signs he was a demon. So far, every move was very Kiki.

"I thought Rhyn was going to kill Darkyn," Kris started. "What happened? And why were you there?"

He listened as Kiki explained Rhyn's visit, ending with the half-demon's resolve to destroy the boundary between Death's domain and the Immortal underworld in the hopes of getting

Katie back. When Kiki finished, Kris poured himself a glass of whiskey while he thought.

"That puts me in a difficult spot," he said at last. "I don't know if Rhyn could kill Death, but if he disrupted the balance between worlds …"

"He's done that since he was born," Kiki pointed out. "He's just taking it to the next level."

"He's a menace to everything."

"If Katie hadn't died …"

"She balanced him, even though there wasn't a day that passed where I didn't want to strangle her. And I thought he'd started to accept a role on the Council, even if it was the one of the enforcer."

"Can Hannah's blood be used like Katie's?"

"I don't know. Even if it could, only Ully knew what Ully was doing in the lab," Kris said in frustration. "I told him for years to take notes so our other scientists can pick up wherever he left off."

"Whatever Darkyn is planning, it has to do with Rhyn. He let us go. There were no guards when Rhyn came for me and no demons to stop us," Kiki mused.

"Maybe he's gunning for Death's seat and using Rhyn to get to her."

"Andre always said Death was more dangerous than the Dark One, because he understood what the Dark One wanted."

"Andre never factored Darkyn into the equation," Kris said. "Still, Rhyn can't kill Death. I'm not sure what good Rhyn is to Darkyn. Maybe Rhyn going on this crazy journey keeps him out of Darkyn's hair."

"Darkyn let us go. I'm convinced of that," Kiki replied. "There's no other reason why, unless Rhyn is doing what Darkyn wants him to. If Andre was still alive …"

"He's not!" Kris snapped. "As much as my brothers wish I were him, I am not. You just have to deal with it."

"Sorry, Kris. Andre had a way with people, even Rhyn. Without him or Katie, we can't fix whatever it is Rhyn is going to do."

"We're assuming he will do something," Kris said. "What if this business with Katie changed him? What if he understands the greater good now?"

"Rhyn does understand, but he can't control what he is. Even if he wanted to do good, he'd fail. He's too weak to control his impulses, Kris."

"Do you believe that?" Kris returned. He rose and paced. He flexed his injured arm and recalled how he'd be dead at the hands of a traitor if Rhyn hadn't saved him. There had been no hesitation, no second guessing when Rhyn snapped Jade's neck.

Over and over, Kris had tried to convince himself he'd do the same for his half-brother. Over and over, he finally admitted he wouldn't. He'd let Rhyn die, just as he sent Rhyn on what he thought was a suicide mission expelling demons from the castle. He'd talked it over with Hannah, and they agreed it was the only option they had.

Yet it hadn't sat well with him, despite what he knew about Rhyn.

"I don't know. He pulled the Council together after we split. It wasn't for us, I'm certain, but for Katie. I don't think he has a reason to try anymore," Kiki said at last.

"Something doesn't feel right," Kris voiced. "I sent out a party to search for our father's remains so we can have a safe place for the Council and Immortals again." Instead of the supportive response he expected, Kiki was quiet. Kris faced him. "You think this was a bad idea?"

"I think the era of us having a safe haven is over. I think … " Kiki paused. "Kris, I think the era of the Council as a whole is over. I think we are all meant to go our separate ways."

Kris heard what Kiki didn't say, that only Andre had been able to keep the Council together after their father's death. The six headstrong brothers of the Council That Was Seven had respected Andre, who was an adult when the rest of the brothers were born. Even before their father's death, Andre had taken on the duty to raise and mentor them all.

"Our father – and Andre – would've wanted us to stay together," Kris said in a hushed tone, wounded by his brother's inference.

"We'd be safer if we could manage the wars within our boundaries. To quote Tamer, there's too much bureaucracy."

"No, Kiki, we wouldn't. We'd be easier to pick off by the demons! This isn't up for debate right now. Just because Rhyn isn't here to beat you all into submission doesn't mean the Council can break up."

"We know you won't do it," Kiki said. "Listen, Kris, I'm not trying to be an ass, but logistically and in practicality, there's no reason for us to maintain the Council."

"We're not talking about this now, Kiki."

"Alright, but know that Tamer's planning on bringing it up next meeting."

"Let's focus on Rhyn," Kris said with barely controlled anger.

"We have two options that I can see. Do nothing, and wait to see what happens, or go after him," Kiki replied.

"Go after him," Kris repeated. "And leave Darkyn here to do whatever else he's doing?"

"When Rhyn left, he said something that's been bothering me. He said Death promised him to bring Katie back."

"Death talked to Rhyn?"

"It's what I made out of his nonsense. Death can't bring a mortal back from the dead – it would break every Immortal Code there is. I may be wrong, but what if …"

Kris didn't hear Kiki's words. Instead he mulled over the notion that Death had sought out Rhyn. Their eldest brother, Andre, had spoken long ago about talking to Death on several occasions. Whatever passed between them, Andre had never trusted the deity. Their father as well had been a distant acquaintance to the elusive deity. Death had visited the leaders of the Council – and Rhyn.

The Council had broken under Kris's leadership and been kept together only by Rhyn. No one gave the half-demon credit for anything but brute force, and yet, none of them knew him after his years in Hell. He'd returned coarse and violent, the opposite of the man Kris was. But he hadn't run away, even when openly scorned by those around him. Rhyn hadn't backed down when defending a woman they all were bound by Immortal Code to protect. Rhyn was the reason the Immortals had survived Darkyn's attack at the castle.

At that moment, Kris couldn't help resenting both Rhyn and Death or hoping Death's visit to Rhyn hadn't been her way of showing support for Andre's successor.

"Kris," Kiki snapped. "What do you think?"

Kris felt as if he'd glimpsed his fate – and it wasn't good. He shook out his shoulders, trying to focus on whatever it was Kiki had been talking about.

"Run that by me again," Kris said.

Kiki frowned. "I think Katie is alive."

"Not possible. We saw her die."

"There was no body."

"Gabe can take mortals and Immortals straight to the underworld, bodies and all," Kris said.

"You got a better explanation? If Death told Rhyn she would give him Katie back, then Katie can't be dead."

"If that's true, why would Death promise to bring her back?"

"That's what I can't figure out," Kiki admitted. "But I know where he's going."

"You can't be serious about following him. It's forbidden for us to travel uninvited into Death's domain."

"Two things, Kris. One, Rhyn can get us into Hell, where Toby is. Two, I'd rather not piss of Death. If we can talk Rhyn off the ledge, maybe she won't crush us all," Kiki said.

"You want me to help you save Rhyn from himself," Kris said, crossing his arms.

"Maybe we should give him a second chance."

"Really, Kiki? Have you forgotten what he did?"

"No, but I don't think he's the same Rhyn we sent to Hell. I think he deserves a chance to make things right."

Kris wanted to think that Kiki was the demon trying to drag him into Hell for nefarious purposes. It was almost easier to swallow than reaching out to help the brother he'd held as his enemy for so long. And who might've been more able to hold the Council together than Kris.

Kiki was waiting for him to speak. "If you can't do it for Rhyn, do it for Toby. We need Rhyn to get him out of Hell."

"Ok," Kris said slowly. "Give me a couple of hours then we'll leave."

Kiki nodded without leaving the tent. "What's wrong, Kris?"

"Nothing," Kris said and turned away. "Go rest up for a couple hours."

"You can do that to Tamer or Erik but not me. I see it on your face. Something's bothering you."

"It doesn't matter, Kiki. I'll do what I'm supposed to. It's what I've resigned myself to do."

"Try not to act so happy about protecting us all from demons."

"It's not that," Kris said with an irritated glance towards his brother. "Kiki, I know none of you have faith in me. I'm trying to do what's right, and you fight me all the way."

Kiki was quiet for a moment. Kris sighed and sat down, rubbing his face. His body had not yet healed from the beating Jade gave him.

"I'll admit, we're skeptical. Andre was Andre. No one questioned him," Kiki said at last. "He was the backbone for all of us. I think we all feel his absence."

"No one more than me. I've got to deal with losing him and trying to manage you all."

"Look, Kris, don't take our resistance personally. Anyone who tried to step into Andre's shoes would receive the same treatment. It's too soon after his death."

"Rhyn pulled you all together. I couldn't do it after you all walked out," Kris said. "Andre's memory may live on, but I'm the one who inherited his responsibilities."

"Give it time. One man – even Andre – couldn't solve the world's problems. You just have to wait it out. And hope we all come to our senses before the end of the world," Kiki said with a small smile.

"That's not good enough. I have a duty to fulfill, an obligation to my Immortals," Kris said, pensive. "And I don't feel adequate compared to Andre."

"You're more than adequate, Kris. All of us look up to you. You don't have Andre's legacy as the family protector, but you'll find your way. You've lost your spark. Is this why?"

"Mostly. And part of it is Jade," Kris whispered.

"You have a penchant for betrayers, that's for sure."

"What the fuck does that mean?"

"Lilith, Jade, I'm just hoping Hannah isn't among them," Kiki said.

"Lilith?"

Kiki's features shuttered and went stoic. "Never mind that one. Bad joke."

"Lilith would never betray me, and neither would Hannah," Kris snapped. "You know better, Kiki."

"Maybe. In any case, whatever you felt for Jade, you have to figure out how to get over it. You have your mate. I've been waiting for mine for a lifetime. Unlike you and Rhyn, I'd welcome a partner to share eternity and this disaster of a world with."

"I'm appreciative. But sometimes I look at Hannah and see Katie," Kris said, recalling how he'd taken Katie's blood by force soon after she went to the castle. He'd never forgive himself for that, even if Rhyn's mate deserved little more respect than the half-demon himself. "Hannah is lovely – and my duty. Jade was …"

"Dead-dead the moment he betrayed you. I may sound like Rhyn, but if someone turns on one of my brothers, I want that person dead-dead," Kiki said flatly.

"Thanks," Kris said, managing a smile. "You're about as effective at pep talks as Rhyn."

"Don't get me started," Kiki said. "Go see Hannah and take a nap. This will all blow over soon, and things will go back to normal." He slapped Kris on the arm. "Ok?"

"Thanks," Kris said again. His response was enough to satisfy Kiki, who left the tent.

Kris lingered, deep in thought, until Hannah sought him out. She still looked pale. He smiled at her, understanding what it was to mourn the loss of a sibling. As much as he missed Jade, he was glad he at least had Hannah to fall back on. She had Katie's beauty – without the abrasive personality.

"How're you feeling?" he asked, holding out a hand to her.

"Better." She took it and squeezed. "Was that Kiki I saw leaving?"

"Yeah. Apparently Rhyn has gone on some rampage to kill Death. Kiki wants us to go to the underworld and stop him."

"Oh, no, Kris, you can't!"

"It's against Immortal Code," he said. "But if he pisses off Death, we'll have her and the Dark One after us. One deity for an enemy is bad enough."

"She's too powerful for him to kill. She'd probably laugh at him and he'll come crawling back to you," Hannah said.

Kris let out a surprised laugh at the image in his mind of Rhyn being sent packing like a misbehaving puppy.

"Really, Kris, I don't think you should go without me," Hannah pressed. "If Darkyn is serious about killing us, he'll come back. I'm safer with you."

"I won't be gone long. You're safe here," he assured his beautiful mate. "Kiki thinks this is the only way we'll get Toby back, too."

"What did Rhyn do to Toby?"

"Let him get snatched by Darkyn. I guess Toby is in Hell. Kiki thinks we can break him out, if Rhyn will take us there."

Hannah's pretty eyes grew dark. Kris kissed her on the forehead, not wanting his mate to worry, even if he didn't know what would happen once he and Kiki left for the underworld.

"How will you get out of Hell?" she asked. "If you need Rhyn to get in, do you need him to get out?"

"Hopefully he doesn't ditch us," he said with forced lightness. "You're too precious to me to worry. I'll be back in a day or so, I promise."

"You don't know that. I heard the Immortal underworld is an awful place. What if Death decides to keep you or Rhyn drops you in Hell forever? What will I do? I'd rather die with you."

"You'll be treated well among the Immortals for the rest of your life."

Hannah raised an eyebrow.

"We take care of our own," he said.

"Except for Rhyn."

"He's a half-demon. He doesn't belong in either world. I've gotta get ready to go. Please, don't worry, Hannah," Kris said. "It's late. Go get some rest."

"You won't change your mind."

"No."

She hesitated then kissed him on the cheek and turned to go. Kris watched her, unable to shake the uncanny sense it was the last time he'd see her.

Chapter Seven

"Rhyn, what if this is the only time we ever have together?"

Rhyn shook his head, uncertain how he'd ended up on the dream beach when he'd just walked through the portal from the castle in the Alps to Death's underworld. He faced his dead mate. Her blue eyes were large, and she looked tired.

"It won't be," he said. "I'm coming to get you."

Instead of looking cheered at his words, she looked unconvinced.

"You're welcome," he said, bristling.

"I'd be happy to see you," Katie replied. "But, Rhyn, what if you can't save me? What if this is all we have?"

"Why do you say that? It can't be. It won't be."

"Let's pretend like it is, just for now."

"I don't want to pretend." He searched her features with his gaze, not understanding her strange insistence that she was really dead. She was troubled. This much he could see, though he couldn't tell why.

"Do you ever wonder what would've happened, if we'd both been able to live?" she asked.

"No."

"You don't think about where we'd live or how we'd fit in with the other Immortals?"

"I don't like this game," he said.

"I don't think both of us will make it out of the underworld. It makes me think about all the things I wish I'd done before I died. I wanted to backpack through Europe and go on a cruise somewhere warm. I wanted to make love with you on the beach under the full moon. Without worrying about demons or Kris or anything."

"Katie." Rhyn took her hands tentatively, growing more confident when she didn't disappear. "I will get you out, and you can do those things. *We* can do those things together. I swear it."

"I hope so, Rhyn." She hugged him hard.

Rhyn wrapped his arms around her, marveling at how real her body felt in the dream. Her hair tickled his face, and he rested his chin on her head. They held each other for a long moment. His thoughts grew dark as he thought about what it would take to save her. He'd have to risk the wrath of Death.

"Rhyn, will you promise me something?" she asked, propping her chin on his chest to look up at him. "Will you promise to protect Hannah, Toby and everyone else, even if it means losing me?"

"No." His grip tightened instinctively around her.

"You're a good man, Rhyn. You've done so much to help me and your brothers. You must do this one last thing for me."

"It won't come to that," he said hoarsely. "I'd destroy everything to get you back."

"I know you would, and I'm asking you not to. I'm asking you to protect what's left of good in the world."

Her words fell heavily, as if she knew she was already doomed to her fate in the underworld. Rhyn said nothing for a long moment.

"I chose to sacrifice my life so that you'd have the chance to do this, Rhyn. Don't make my choice a bad one," she told him.

"It was a bad one," he said with a snort.

"Sometimes all we have are shitty choices," Katie said. "Promise me!"

"If it'll shut you up, fine."

"Thank you." She took his hand. They walked towards the beach that had formed his prison for three days in the real world. She faced him. "I want to kiss you one last time, but I'm not ready for you to disappear again."

Heat surged through his body, but he hesitated. She really believed this was the last time they'd be together.

"Is this place even real?" he asked.

"Does it matter?"

Rhyn smiled faintly, admiring the woman before him. She was foolishly stubborn and lippy – and he loved that about her. She was the first creature ever to see beyond his half-demon curse. She'd stayed strong in Hell, through confrontations with demons and Immortals alike, through his own failures. She hadn't just survived; she'd found some part of him to believe in.

The idea of caring for her overwhelmed him again. He'd never had a reason to try to control his power or to focus on anything other than surviving. That a simple little mortal could show him just how little his Immortal and demon powers really meant humbled him. If he found his way, it would be because of her.

Her distress and sorrow were, buried but he still saw them. She was trying to be brave, asking him for one last moment of comfort before what she thought was the end. He owed her that, and so much more.

"No, it doesn't," he said softly. He reached out to her. His hands trailed down her soft cheek and tangled in her wayward curls. With his index finger, he drew a line from her chin, down her neck, between her breasts and rested his hand on her belly, where the hatchling grew.

A different kind of sorrow filled him, one he recognized as regret. If he failed, he'd never see the little girl Katie carried. Their hatchling would be as stubborn as her mother, and he could almost imagine huge eyes as blue and clear as Katie's peering out at him from a sweet, curly-headed demon child's face. He wished he'd told Katie how terrified – but thrilled – he'd been when she told him about the hatchling. He wished he knew one fucking thing about raising a child or being a mate. Every one of his brothers could've managed these things, but his nature left him better apt at destroying than nurturing.

At least he could kill anything that came near his mate and child, if he had the chance. He'd been reluctant to accept any role with the Immortals, fearing his own broken nature was too weak.

"I'm sorry, Katie," he said.

"You have nothing to be sorry about."

"I didn't protect you. You shouldn't have had to make the choice you did."

She took his hand, squeezed it and then wrapped her arms around him. "I don't regret it, Rhyn. You've had the deck stacked against you. The least I could do was give you a second chance."

"You're the only one who would."

"The Immortals need you. They're too fucking stupid to know it, but Kris can't manage Hannah let alone the Council," she added. "You have so much to give, Rhyn. You just have to believe you can."

"I'd trade everything for you."

"But you won't, because you promised me," she reminded him. "Besides, you have to show up Kris and the rest of them." A peaceful quiet settled over them until she spoke again. "Do you like the name Hazel?"

He shrugged.

"If we would've lived through this, I'd name our baby Hazel."

"*When* we get through this," he corrected her.

"*If* we get through this, we get to spend our lives together. I don't know anything about you, Rhyn," Katie said. "What the hell happened to you to make you as you are?"

"I've always been broken."

"I don't mean broken. I mean, how are you not a traitor like Sasha or a cold jerk like Kris? How did you spend so long in Hell and still try to follow parts of the Code? How did you and Gabriel become friends?"

"Gabriel is more of a brother to me than my own brothers. I don't know why I am the way I am. I don't even know much of the Immortal Code, just the few key parts Andre used to lecture me about. Loyalty to my brothers, my mate, the Immortals, humanity. Respect for Death and her domain. Other variations of those."

"Then start from the beginning. Tell me your story."

Rhyn hesitated, unable to shake the disturbing sense that Katie's interest came from her resolve that this was the last time they'd see each other.

"I was born, wandered the Immortal world for the first few years. I met Gabe, and he took me to Andre, who raised me for a few years, before my brothers decided I was better off in Hell," he summarized. "That's it."

"There's more to you than that."

"If you say so."

"Gabe has been your guardian angel," she added. "I'm happy he found you."

"Me, too."

"I think he's in trouble, Rhyn."

"What do you mean?"

"Something's not right. I guess he can take better care of himself than Toby," she said. "Have you found Toby yet?"

"I have an idea where he is."

"You have to protect him, Rhyn. He's too young to get himself out of things."

Rhyn glanced from the rolling teal waves to his mate. Her words about Gabe were troubling, and he couldn't determine if she was purposely vague or really didn't know. Her pretty face was puzzled, and he frowned. She was beyond tired. Whatever was happening to her in the underworld, it wasn't good. Anger filled him. As much as he wanted to stay in the dream world in case it really was the last time he saw her, he couldn't help her while stuck in the dream.

He closed his eyes, trying to wake himself up. He was losing time to find her. When he opened his eyes, he was still on the beach.

"I gotta get outta here," he said.

"Why?" she asked.

"I have to find you."

"I'm right here."

"No, the *real* you. I have to find you before it's too late," he said impatiently.

"What if – "

"We have forever to talk things out," he said. "But I don't have forever to find you." Rhyn trotted away from the beach as he spoke. Katie scrambled after him.

"Rhyn, wait!"

"Katie, I can't. I'm running out of time."

"Be careful, Rhyn." Her soft, forlorn words sounded like a farewell.

"This is killing me," he muttered. He strode to her, wrapped his arms around her, and kissed her. She yielded more easily in the dream than she ever had in real life. Her soft, warm lips welcomed him hungrily, and he lost himself in her sweet musk, warm skin and honeyed taste. He didn't want to leave; he wanted to spend the rest of his life making love to her on the beach. He wanted to feel his skin pressed against hers and for her to run her fingers through his hair before scraping her nails down his back. He wanted to take her every way he could imagine, until they lay spent and panting on the beach, until nothing but their entwined bodies and souls remained of their world.

If he stayed, he'd lose her forever.

Struggling against the demands of his roaring blood, Rhyn closed his eyes, sought his magic and willed himself awake.

The phantom Andre was squatting beside her when Katie awoke. She jerked, surprised at how close he was. He was real enough for her to feel his body heat, even if he was invisible to everyone but her and moved without a sound. The fact that Gabe was sleeping a short distance away didn't seem to faze the ghost. Instead, it pointed to something it had written in the dirt beside her.

Demon.

Katie pushed herself up. She raised an eyebrow at the word. Andre pointed to the death-dealer.

"You think Gabriel is a demon?" Katie whispered.

Andre nodded. She frowned.

"Or are *you* a demon?" she challenged.

The specter shook its head and rose, moving away without disturbing the flora on the jungle floor.

"Because I should trust a creepy ghost that looks like someone I once knew over the Immortal who rescued me from Death."

Gabriel snapped awake at her words. Andre didn't bother to disappear, as if no longer worried the Immortal might see him. The death-dealer looked lost for a moment then rose and strapped on his weapons. Katie ate her food and water cubes, waiting for Gabriel. She fingered the second necklace he'd given her, not convinced Andre was wrong. The beads felt like plastic, and something about Gabe had changed.

This Gabriel really did look like the Gabriel she knew. She looked hard at his hands before he pulled on his black gloves.

The shapeshifter demon that took on Ully's form hadn't fully been able to disguise its arms and hands.

Gabriel's hands looked like they were his.

"Gabe, what happens in three days?" she asked.

"We'll find out when the time comes."

"What happens if I feed the trees?"

"Come again?"

"Can I feed them?"

"I don't give a shit." He turned his back to her to start walking, and she was grateful he didn't see her reaction.

Andre took up his position flanking her, and she shot him a look. She couldn't imagine why a demon would want to pose as Gabriel – and insist on guiding her through the underworld. Her limited experience with demons was that they all wanted to kill her or drag her to Hell or to Darkyn. This one had taken over Gabriel's mission.

Then again, she didn't know what Gabe's destination had been. Katie looked behind her, wondering what she was missing. Her eyes went to the slithering tree branches overhead. She couldn't survive on her own in the underworld. That much had been made clear to her by Gabe. And escaping a demon on her own didn't seem like a smart option.

She counted the food and water cubes she had remaining. A few of each remained, long enough to get her through the day, but not long enough for more than one day.

"Gabe, I need more of these," she called, holding up a food cube.

The death-dealer faced her then pulled a satchel over his head. He handed it to her. She took it and opened it. There were two small pouches of cubes and nothing else.

"C'mon," Gabriel said and started off into the jungle.

Katie followed, her eyes on Andre. The phantom motioned for her to follow him instead and waved her towards the direction she recognized as leading back to the lake. She slowed her step and pointed at Gabriel with a questioning look.

Andre's eyes fell to her body. Katie pointed to the dagger, and Andre shook his head. She indicated the satchel next. He nodded. She frowned and pulled out the contents: food and water cubes, holding them up for him. The phantom pointed to the pouch with the food cubes.

Don't feed the trees, Gabriel had told her when they set out.

Katie dumped a few of the cubes into her hand with another look at Andre. She drew a deep breath and tossed the cubes after Gabriel. She stopped walking as the cubes hit the ground behind him.

Nothing happened.

She sighed, wondering why she was paying attention to a dead-dead Immortal in the first place. Maybe Gabriel was right. Maybe the underworld was having some effect on her. She'd been fatigued since arriving, but she'd explained it away with the fact she'd had little sleep and an unexpected pregnancy.

She reached the place where the food cubes had landed, bending to pick them up in case she needed them later. The cubes were gone. Swiping at lively bushes, she inched forward, searching for the cubes.

The ground beneath her rumbled suddenly, and she straightened, balancing herself against a tree. Gabriel stopped ahead of her and Andre motioned her quickly away from the spot.

"What is that?" she asked as the tremors grew stronger.

"I don't know. I don't sense any magic," the death-dealer said with a frown. "Do you?"

"No. Nothing."

Andre's motioning grew frantic, and Katie looked down. A small crack had begun to form where the food cubes fell. The crack grew fast, flying down the trail towards Gabriel. The sound of the earth tearing grew louder. The trees on either side of her expanded, quickly doubling and then quadrupling in size. Afraid of being crushed between them, Katie darted off the trail towards Andre, who ran ahead of her. She heard Gabriel shout something that was lost in the roar of the ground splitting apart.

Andre ran hard for a creature that was already dead. Katie chased him, terrified of looking back when the awful sounds seemed so close. Only when the ground stopped trembling did Andre stop. Katie doubled over, breathless.

"What the … hell just … happened?" she gasped and turned.

The two trees whose girth had been small enough for her wrap her arms around had expanded in width and height, reaching towards the gray sky of the underworld. Katie craned her neck, unable to see the tops of the trees. Their trunks had grown outward from the trail until they were as wide as a football field. Their massive roots ruptured the ground that had been the trail, creating a ravine she could see even from their safe distance.

"Don't feed the trees." She repeated Gabriel's warning, stunned. She shuddered and glanced at the phantom. "Where is he?"

Andre shrugged. Katie heard nothing outside of the rasping trees. Gabriel was gone. Andre motioned her to follow him, and she drew a few more heavy breaths before following.

"We're going towards the lake," she said.

He nodded.

"Are you getting us out of here?"

He shrugged again.

"Do you have a plan?"

Andre shook his head.

"Wait, so I just ditched my guide to follow you and you don't know where you're going?" Katie demanded. "Was that supposed to be a rescue?"

The phantom ignored her and continued to walk.

"Rhyn's rescues look like well-planned military campaigns compared to this," she muttered. Her thoughts went to him and her latest dream. He claimed to be coming for her. She didn't think she'd ever leave the underworld, especially now that she didn't have Gabriel.

Katie looked over her shoulder again towards the massive trees. She didn't know what happened with Gabriel, but she hoped he was safe, wherever he was. Her fate, she was certain, was sealed.

Chapter Eight

Rhyn awoke from the island dreamscape in the shadow world. He rose, uncertain what happened but recalling his urgency. He crossed through the glowing black portal into the one place he'd hoped never to see again: Hell. Unwilling to get stuck in the cell where he'd spent many lifetimes, he chose to open the portal into the office of the Council's betrayer, Sasha. The office was as he remembered it, down to the black flames in the hearth.

His half-demon blood would render him cloaked among the demons, as it had in the castle. Rhyn shuddered, recalling just how bad Hell could be.

The room even smelled like Sasha. Rhyn cursed his dead half-brother silently and left, traveling the black stone halls of the fortress in Hell where he'd spent most of his life. He reached the door before the block of cells where Sasha had collected his favorite creatures in Hell to create his own twisted, private zoo. They'd referred to the sick Immortal as the zookeeper, a creature as deserving of a cell as any.

Shaking his head, Rhyn realized how sweaty his palms were as he stood before the door leading to the zoo. Sasha's mages had sat in the antechamber, repairing any damage the inmates did to their cells or preparing some magical torture that Sasha wanted.

It was the last place in the universe he wanted to be. Rhyn's body felt wooden, and his heart flew. He opened the door to the antechamber and stopped, surprised at who sat within.

"Jared?"

"Rhyn!" The full demon dropped the book in his hands and lurched to his feet.

"Darkyn made you the jailer," Rhyn growled. "You better not—"

"Wait!" Jared barked. "I didn't do anything. To any of them, as much as I wanted to eat the human. So succulent and sweet-smelling, like barbecued –"

Rhyn drew his knife as Jared's feature lit up.

"But I didn't," the demon rushed on. "I'm as much of a prisoner as they are. I can go here and I can go out on the block."

"You're a prisoner."

"Yes."

"Prove it."

Jared motioned him away from the door. Rhyn stepped aside warily. The full-demon tried to walk through, only to be thrown to the ground by an invisible shield.

"Darkyn wouldn't let me stay in the mortal realm. I came here and hid out," Jared explained. "I knew these *things* were your friends." He motioned dismissively towards the cell block.

"Is the angel here?" Rhyn asked.

"Yes. And the man in black who used to visit you. Smells like a human, acts like an Immortal."

"Gabe?"

"Sure."

Rhyn moved to the door leading to the block, unable to help the small tremble of his hand. Not only had he spent too long in this very place, he'd seen Katie hurt here and barely escaped alive with her.

"And the girl."

"What girl?" Rhyn asked, freezing.

"I don't know it's name. It was with Lunchmeat at the Immortal stronghold," Jared said, using his nickname for Katie. "Can you get us out of here?"

"Why would I do anything for you?"

"As a reward, for not eating any of your friends."

Rhyn considered how he might use the demon, as he had once before. He didn't answer, pushing the door open to the cell block. Nearly all the cells were empty.

"Where is everyone?" he asked.

"Darkyn incorporated them into his army. He sent most to the Immortal stronghold," Jared said. "Miss your old friends?"

"Not in the slightest. You put Gabe in my old cell," he said, stopping in front of it. He sensed the death-dealer's presence without being able to see into the dark room.

"Rhyn!" Toby's gleeful shout jarred him. "I knew you'd come! I knew Jared would help."

Jared bared his teeth in response. Rhyn stopped in front of Toby's cell and saw the young angel bouncing around.

"Oh, thank gods," Ully said from the cell across from Toby. "Rhyn, Darkyn created two shapeshifter demons. You must find them before they - "

"Rhyn," Gabriel's ragged voice drew his attention.

Rhyn stepped closer to his old cell, hating it and the fact his friend was trapped in it.

"I'm sorry, Rhyn," the death-dealer said. "I failed you and Katie both."

"What're you talking about?"

"The fucking demons got me. I don't know what they want with Katie, but it's been almost two days. I was leading her through the underworld."

"She's not dead," Rhyn said and drew an even breath, trying to calm the side of him that was screaming for him to find her as fast as he could. Two days with demons ... he'd seen what happened to her here, in Hell, over a similar period of time. Sasha was twisted, but Darkyn was merciless.

"Yes, she's alive, or was when I left her," Gabe said.

"Where were you when this happened?" Rhyn asked. "How did you get Katie away from Death?"

"I told you, she's not dead!" Toby shouted. "No one listens to me!"

"The underworld," Gabe answered. "Toby's right. She found a loophole. As long as Death doesn't find her and we can get her back to a Sanctuary, she'll live."

"Darkyn was right," Rhyn said.

"About what?"

"Death offered to return Katie to me after a few days. Darkyn said she wouldn't do it, and he was right. She doesn't have Katie."

"It would break every Immortal Code – some older than Death – if she returned a mortal to the mortal world," Gabe said. "If she finds Katie, she'll never let her go."

Rhyn felt like the fool he was.

"Tell the demon to let me out," Gabe said. "We need to go."

"Jared, free Gabe," Rhyn ordered.

"Only if – " the demon started.

"Yes, fine. We'll come back for you."

Jared returned to the antechamber.

"Ully, Toby, you're staying here until we get back," Rhyn said.

"What?" the two responded simultaneously.

"You're safe here. And, you're out of my way."

"Rhyn, no!" Toby whined.

"You need my help!" Ully added.

"Then I'll come back for you. Right now, Gabe and I are going to the underworld. You'll slow us down," Rhyn said.

"Rhyn, I can help you," Toby pleaded. "Katie is my human. I can find her for you."

"I'm not looking for her. I'm going to find Death."

The cell block fell silent. Even Jared looked at him in surprise. Rhyn took the talisman dangling from the demon's hand and pressed it against the wall of the cell holding Gabe.

"You can't go after Death," Gabe said quietly as he stepped from the cell. The death-dealer was more unkempt than Rhyn had ever seen him. His clothing was ripped and his face unshaven. "Do you know what she'll do to you?"

"You don't have to go, Gabe," Rhyn said. "You can stay here or I'll take you to the Sanctuary. I just need you to tell me where she is. She's after Katie. We find Death before she finds my mate."

Gabe took a deep breath. "I know the underworld better than you. I'll take you to where she might be."

"Rhyn, you need to know something," Ully said. "One of the shapeshifters took on Gabriel's shape. I think Darkyn knew Katie was with Gabe, and they wanted to replace him."

"Why? Gabe, where were you going?" Rhyn asked.

"There's a secret portal in the underworld, similar to the one here in Hell that allows Immortals to come in and out. It's how I could visit you when you were in Sasha's zoo," Gabe explained. "I couldn't take Katie through the shadow world place, because Death and Darkyn had assassins waiting for me to step foot in there. The secret portal is in Death's palace."

"Wow," Toby breathed. "You were taking her straight to Death."

"Not straight," Gabe said. "I was taking a route no one else could track."

"And the demons grabbed you and replaced you with a shapeshifter," Rhyn said. "But why?"

"Because your bond will reappear seven days after you broke it." Toby's voice was a whisper. "I'm not supposed to tell you that."

Rhyn stopped in front of the dejected angel's cell.

"I dreamt where Death told me about the seven days … " Gabe drifted off and shook his head, as if to clear a bad memory. "You're saying Rhyn didn't break the bond?"

"I'm saying, the mate of an Ancient or any Immortal is preordained. No one can break that bond, not even Death," Toby answered. "But since no one ever listens to me and I've failed at my duty as a guardian – "

"Stop whining, Toby," Rhyn snapped. "Why seven days?"

"I don't know."

"Angels have a shared consciousness with all other angels. It's how they pass on memories and human history," Gabe said. "If Toby can't find that answer, it's not something any of the angels know. Or he's too young to tap into it fully."

"I know I'm a failure," Toby said, blinking back tears.

"Darkyn said the shapeshifters only had to be effective for a few days," Ully added.

"Whatever he's planning has to be done by the time your bond returns," Gabe said.

Rhyn frowned. Toby, Darkyn, and Death knew about the seven days. He felt a flutter of hope where he'd felt desperation before. In seven days, his bond to Katie would return. She'd no longer be vulnerable in the Immortal underworld. She could move between worlds as he could, and he'd no longer be at risk of destroying everything he came into contact with.

Death wanted him to wait until the bond returned. Darkyn wanted him to act before then. Rhyn didn't understand the battle the two were locked in, but one thing was clear: Katie would need him before the seven days was up.

"Ully, you said there were two shapeshifters?" he asked. "Who is the second?"

"Hannah," Ully said and motioned to a cell farther down. "He replaced her before Gabriel."

"Really?" Toby asked, pressing his face against the cell door. "I didn't even notice."

"That's because I used the Immunity blood to enhance their talents," Ully said. "No one can tell the physical difference until the injections wear off."

"Darkyn replaces Gabe to get to Katie. Why replace Hannah?" Gabe asked.

"To influence Kris," Rhyn said. "Gabe, we can talk on the way."

"Rhyn, don't leave me here," Toby said again.

"You'll be fine. Jared, move Hannah in with Toby. If you touch one hair on any of them, I'll -"

"I understand, half-breed," Jared said. "I don't want to be here when Darkyn gets back."

"We'll come back before then."

Rhyn left the cell block to Toby's protests and walked with Gabe through the antechamber and into the hallway on the other side. Gabe's gaze was dark, his air brooding. Rhyn opened a portal, and they crossed through to Gabe's cabin in the underworld.

"I left her near a stream," Gabe said, looking around. "But I don't know where the demons would've taken her."

"We're not going after Katie," Rhyn said again.

"Death will crush us and hopefully, any demons in her domain."

"If we find her, we can stop her before she takes Katie. We don't know what the demons are doing, but we know Death is looking for Katie."

"She'll find Katie before us, if she hasn't already," Gabe agreed. "But seriously, Rhyn, no one bargains with Death and wins."

"I'll deal with that when we find her. Take us to Death."

Gabe sighed before striking off into the jungle. His walk turned to a trot and then a run. Rhyn ran after him, feeling alive as they raced through the enchanted forest towards a fate he wasn't entirely certain how to handle yet.

They ran until daylight then slowed. Gabe followed a trail Rhyn couldn't see that led them to a stream. The assassin stopped and knelt to splash water on his face.

Rhyn looked around, wishing he could sense his mate. She was alone in the underworld with a demon, a thought that made him incensed with the urge to find her.

"This stream leads to the Lake of Souls then beyond to Death's fortress," Gabe said and stood. "I told her to keep to the stream. The demon probably picked her up between here and the Lake."

Rhyn paced. He still felt the need to find Death, that if he found her, she'd lead him to Katie. They could wander the underworld for millennia without finding Katie, but Death … Death would know where she was.

"The underworld sucks much of our power out, like Hell," the death-dealer said. "You should sit down and rest, Rhyn."

"I don't have time."

"You have two days. We can find Death in two days."

"It won't matter if Darkyn gets to Katie first."

"Or if Death changes her mind."

"Changes her mind?"

"Two days ago, I had a dream where she told me you had four days to pass some sort of test. I don't need to tell you what happens if you don't pass."

"I can guess that bitch is pretty unforgiving," Rhyn said. "And I imagine, if I don't pass, she'll take Katie."

Gabriel met his gaze, and Rhyn ceased pacing. Sensing his urgency, Gabriel stood.

"Let me check on something," he said, striding away. "There are signs when Death is in her fortress. I might be able to see the trees in their defensive positions from here."

Rhyn watched his only friend trot into the jungle. He resumed pacing, surprised when Gabe reappeared quickly. The death-dealer motioned for them to start walking along the stream. Rhyn sprung forward, anxious to be moving again.

"What do you plan on doing when you find Death?" Gabriel asked.

"Whatever it takes."

"That's a dangerous mindset to have when you go into a meeting with her."

"I have no choice. I want my mate back, and I will destroy anyone in my path."

"You know the Council needs you," Gabriel said. "Kris can't keep everyone together. He needs your … charm."

"I don't give a shit, Gabe."

"You should, Rhyn. If you get Katie back and the world goes to shit, all you've done is given her an Immortality of hell on earth."

"I can do both. I can protect her and the rest of humanity. I think … no, I know that's what I'm meant to do. I never knew that until I found Katie and I started to realize –"

"- you can use your demon powers for good."

"I wouldn't call killing things *good*," Rhyn said. "But I'd only kill things that threatened those who couldn't protect themselves."

"You'd do what Andre did."

"I suppose."

"And your father. Almost like you're making up for your mother killing him and then Andre killing her," Gabe said. "You'd almost be making things right, assuming you chose this role."

. "All I care about is finding Katie, kicking Death's ass and then going home, wherever Katie wants that to be. Whatever happens then - happens." Rhyn said with a glance over his shoulder

"What if Death has her already, Rhyn?" Gabe asked. "What if you do succeed in forcing Death's hand and she brings Katie back from the dead? You'd tear the fabric of the universe and invite the demons to take control. She's all that stands between us and them."

"Gods, Gabe. You've spent too much time with Death. When did you learn to think?"

"Would you do it? Would you kill Death or risk destroying the worlds for Katie?"

Rhyn froze. The voice was Gabriel's, but the assassin's argument was unlike Gabe, who would know exactly what Rhyn would do after their conversation in Hell. In fact, the whole conversation seemed … off.

"Why?" he asked.

"I want to know what you're getting us into."

"You already know that." He turned.

Gabriel was gone. No one followed him, let alone spoke to him. Rhyn looked around uneasily, wondering who—or what—he'd been speaking to. He started back to the spot where they'd stopped for water. A few minutes later, Gabriel reappeared.

"Follow the stream. We should reach the fortress in the morning. It looks like she's there," Gabe reported.

Rhyn stared at him, looking for any sign the death-dealer wasn't his friend.

"What, Rhyn?" Gabe asked.

"I just had a five minute talk with you. But you weren't here."

Gabe frowned.

"Something about this place is fucked up."

"It wasn't just my voice? You saw me?" Gabe asked.

"Like I do now."

A troubled look crossed the death-dealer's features.

"What is it?" Rhyn asked, suspicion rising.

"Katie said something similar about seeing someone who wasn't there. From now on, we don't separate."

"Agreed. Let's walk." Rhyn sensed there was more to Gabriel's thought, but he wasn't about to stand around talking when Katie was out there somewhere, being stalked by Death.

"What did the other me ask you?"

"If I'd kill Death to get Katie back."

"And you said?"

"I turned around to look at you, and you were gone," Rhyn said.

"That's probably a good thing. The last thing you want is Death's spies telling her you're coming to kill her."

Gabe sounded more relieved than Rhyn thought the encounter warranted. He looked closely at his friend, wondering what might be bothering him.

"Let's get going," Gabe said, avoiding his gaze.

"Lead on."

Chapter Nine

Kris glanced up, expecting Kiki to enter his tent; however, it was one of his Immortal messengers who approached. The messenger held out a small thumb drive with what Kris hoped contained a report identifying the two shapeshifter demons. He left, and Kris plugged the thumb drive into his small PDA. A single file was on the drive, and he opened it.

It was blank. Puzzled, he pulled the drive free of his PDA and reinserted it. The single file within was still empty. Kris tossed it on a table.

"You're a difficult creature to find."

He lowered the PDA at the voice. The temperature of his tent seemed to drop by ten degrees. Rather than feel privileged by her visit, he felt his sense of foreboding grew stronger. The petite woman who materialized out of the shadows wasn't what he expected. Her flawless features were unremarkable, her large eyes turning colors faster than his. She wore white and smiled, more like a nursemaid than the woman whose job was to collect souls.

"It's a pleasure, my lady," he said, at once thrilled and uneasy that she'd finally acknowledged the leader of the Council That Was Seven.

"You're getting ready to raid my underworld," Death said, her glance falling to the rucksack beside his feet.

"Raid is a bit of an overstatement."

"Trespass?"

He wasn't sure what to say. Andre had never spoken well of Death, but the woman in his tent seemed harmless. It was enough that she came to see him.

"It's not a good idea," she chided him. "Though lately, I'm surrounded by fools with bad ideas."

"Is that why you're here?" he asked. "To talk about my potential trespass?"

"As troubling as I find the latest trend of people entering my domain uninvited, I feel able to handle it. What I came to discuss with you was a dream you had."

Kris drew a sharp breath, unaware that the deity could enter his dreams.

"The one where you died," she added.

"I haven't had that dream," he said.

"Maybe you don't remember it."

"I would remember a dream where I died."

"Humor me, Kris. Let's pretend you had a dream where you died," Death said. "It was a noble death for a good cause."

The eerily familiar words – the same he'd spoken to Rhyn before sending him on the suicide mission – sapped Kris's enthusiasm at Death's visit.

"You will go down as legend among your people," she continued. "That would please you, wouldn't it? Your legacy has been of concern to you."

"No one wants a bad one," he said carefully. "My reputation is important."

"Which is why you hope to keep the Council together."

"I hope to keep the Council together because it will do the most good."

"Of course. It has nothing to do with living in Andre's shadow your whole life and now having the chance to prove yourself," she said with a faint smile. "Only you can't do what Andre did, what Rhyn can do."

"I've done it so far." He bristled at the mention of Rhyn in the same sentence as Andre. One half-brother had been noble, courageous, honorable, willing to sacrifice himself for their cause. Rhyn was the opposite.

"Andre has only been dead-dead for what? A few weeks? And the Council has broken up at least once."

"What are you saying?" Kris crossed his arms, looking hard at the deity.

"I think I said it."

"You want me to let the Council break apart."

"That's not quite what I'm saying. I know you understand that great sacrifice is sometimes warranted for a greater good. And what you might be learning is that the greater good also sometimes requires doing what might be called evil," she said.

"Evil cannot be done in the name of good."

"You buy assassinations from my death-dealers. Maybe your definition of evil is different than mine."

"I don't have time for philosophy," he said, growing irritated with her word play. "Are you here for any other purpose than to discuss my definition of good and evil?"

"I guess not. Except ... " She trailed off, gazing around the tent.

"Except what?" he asked after a long pause.

"Several weeks ago, you bought two assignations from Gabriel. Do you remember?"

Kris blinked, trying to figure out what the deity wanted. He thought for a moment, remembering. He'd paid in advance for two assignations after he began to suspect there was a traitor in his organization. The second had been for Katie, in case she couldn't be reasoned with. She was a risk for revealing the Immortal society to the human world or alerting the demons as to where Kris's strongholds were.

"You remember," Death said, reading his features. "You paid for two deaths. Gabe came to collect, and those two lives ... disappeared. They're in my underworld right now, running from me."

"One was for Katie. But who was the second? Rhyn killed Jade when he attacked me. He was the traitor operating beneath my nose."

"What a broken heart will make a person do."

"So he wasn't the second," Kris said, ignoring her mocking reference to his former lover, Jade.

"Rhyn's daughter was the second."

"Rhyn's ... " Kris's thoughts flew from Katie to another woman, Lilith, who long ago had been pregnant with his own son. She—and the child—had died at Rhyn's hands, which was the catalyst for Andre sending Rhyn to Hell.

Death's words made the air in the room feel heavy. Kris sat down at the table.

"Think about that when you enter my domain," Death said.

"I settled an old debt and didn't even know it."

"That's one way of looking at things," she said. "Kris, what if I said you could have anything in the world from me? A favor. A wish granted. Whatever you want to call it. What would you ask for?"

Her bizarre changes of subject made him understand why Andre hadn't liked dealing with her. Was there hidden meaning in her words? Or was she a bored deity there to mess with him?

"I don't have time for this," he said and rose.

"Answer me, Kris. What is your deepest desire?"

"To be more powerful, so I can wipe out my enemies and force my brothers to stay in the Council."

"I can't help you there."

As suddenly as she appeared, Death was gone. Anger rising, Kris looked around to make sure she really was gone then cursed. He no longer felt slighted by her exclusion. Instead, he was grateful he hadn't had to deal with her before.

"Kris, I—"

"What, Kiki?" he snarled.

Kiki froze halfway through the doorway, frowning. Kris breathed a sigh, wondering how one tiny woman could make him tense enough he wanted to raze the beach.

"Sorry, Kiki," he said. "I'm ready if you are."

"It's okay."

"Did you have something for me?"

"It's nothing. I'll open a portal." Kiki left, and Kris felt he'd frustrated the one brother willing to help him.

Instead of following, Kris dwelt a moment longer on Death's words. He hadn't realized Katie was dead because of him. He hadn't believed her death inevitable, and only bought contracts on those he perceived as potential threats. He had every right to feel vindicated after losing his own potential mate and son so long ago. As much as he'd loved Lilith, Andre had told him she wasn't meant to be his mate and encouraged him to focus on his duty rather than the woman.

Kris's memories stirred stronger than he liked. He remembered Lilith, a beautiful Immortal whose laugh had filled him with happiness. Their love had been intense and brief, lasting less than a human year in total. One day, she was just ... gone. Slaughtered by Rhyn, who had taken her head the same way his brothers took the head of Rhyn's demoness mother.

Even if Lilith wasn't meant to be his mate, she didn't deserve such a brutal death. She didn't deserve death at all. Instead of mourning a son, Kris could've spent the past few thousand years raising a successor.

Yet he didn't feel vindicated. He'd unknowingly killed a woman and her child. Was this what Death meant about doing evil for the greater good? It couldn't be. Katie had stabilized Rhyn, allowed the half-demon to use his power and join the rest of the Immortals. Without her, Rhyn was a hazard to everything and everyone. Maybe Death meant he would have to kill Rhyn to keep the peace. Not attacking one of their brothers had been Andre's sacred rule. Perhaps this had been the evil of which Death spoke.

The alternative – that Death might see Rhyn as a viable leader for the Council – was inconceivable. No self-serving, reckless, half-evil being could be entrusted with the fate of humanity!

Baffled by the deity's bizarre visit, Kris pushed the memories out of his mind. He had to find Rhyn. He picked up his rucksack and joined Kiki outside the tent. Kiki stood before a portal on the dark beach. Of all the things Death had told Kris, she hadn't seemed in the least concerned about trespassers in her domain.

"Rough night?" Kiki asked as they stepped into the shadow world.

"Let's get this over with. We're going to find Rhyn. Then what?" Kris asked. "We try to talk some sense into him? Kill him?"

"Kill?" Kiki snorted. "We wouldn't have a chance."

"We would if we had Andre's dagger. It was fashioned by Death. He'd die-dead if we – "

"You're serious." Kiki stopped walking.

"Come on, Kiki," Kris said, continuing onward. "I'm sure it won't come to that."

"You don't sound convinced."

"I'll do whatever I must to protect the Council and Immortals. If Rhyn tries to kill Death or something stupid … "

"Rhyn is the only one who has half a chance of keeping the Council together," Kiki replied. "If you're serious about not splitting, you need him."

His words were an echo of Death's assertion. They struck Kris bone-deep. Kiki's doubt was apparent for the second time that day. Kris watched Kiki pass him and disappear through the portal to the underworld. Kris stepped through, distracted from his dark thoughts by the new world. They stood on a small rise overlooking a jungle-like forest edged in the distance by an ocean of black water.

"So this is the underworld," Kiki said. "Where the fuck do we start?"

Kris caught a glimpse of what looked like a shopping mall west of them. His gaze lingered. As far as he knew, no Immortal voluntarily came to Death's underworld.

"That way," he said, pointing. "I don't know what it is, but it's a place to start."

"Do you feel that?"

"Feel what?"

"Feels like our power is gone. I tried to open a portal and couldn't."

Kris attempted to summon a portal. Nothing happened.

"You think Death knows we're here?" Kiki asked.

"It wouldn't surprise me."

"At some point, we'll have to ask her to help us out of here."

Kris didn't answer, not wanting to think of how that conversation would go with the deity. He tested his power again. Kiki was right; they had none.

"Kris?"

Both of them spun at Hannah's timid voice. Kiki was the first to regain himself.

"What the fuck are you doing here?" he demanded.

Hannah looked to Kris, her blue eyes watering. "I overheard you talking. You're coming to save Katie. I'm going, too."

"Hannah, you shouldn't have followed us," Kris said. "I have no powers here. I can't send you back, and I can't guarantee any of us will live through this."

"She's my sister."

Kris pursed his lips, wanting to release the curses coiled on his tongue. He looked her over. She'd at least worn sturdy shoes, long pants and shirt. She was in decent shape, slender and toned from Pilates and the gym.

"If you have any problem keeping up, you have to tell me," he said.

"Seriously, Kris?" Kiki demanded. "She can't –"

"What alternative do we have?"

Kiki shook his head and stalked off into the brush. Kris held out his hand to Hannah, unable to shake the small part of him that was grateful he had one ally, even if she shouldn't have come.

In Hell, Hannah had been crying since Toby started to tell her the truth. He was an angel, and he wasn't her real nephew. Oh, and they were in Hell. From there, things had gone downhill, and Toby no longer knew what to say.

"But Rhyn is coming back for us," he told her again. "You shouldn't worry."

"What … is wrong with this world?" she sobbed.

"Mama took it a little better. She didn't cry. She just drank a lot of vodka."

"Katie knew?"

"Yeah. She's immune to us."

"Why didn't she tell me?" Hannah demanded, looking up at Toby through tear-swollen eyes.

"I don't know," he mumbled. "She tried to tell you she didn't remember me."

"Not remembering and getting sent to Hell are two different things!"

Baffled, Toby shrugged and moved to the bars of his cell, looking to Ully for help. Ully rolled his eyes.

"Hannah, try to be a bit calmer, in case that creepy demon comes back," he said.

"Demon?" she echoed and burst into a new round of crying. "What did I do to deserve this?"

"Rhyn's coming back," Toby said helplessly. "He's a half-demon. They're not that bad. Well, he's not. The rest of them will eat you."

"Katie married a half-demon? Is she going to Hell?"

"She's already been."

Toby felt almost as distraught at having to stay in the cell while his human was lost in the underworld. Not that he didn't trust Rhyn or Gabe, just that, he might be able to find her first. He knew about Death's domain from the angel memories.

"Hey, Toby," Ully said in a quieter voice. "I've been playing with this. I think I got it." He held out a hand that contained a small talisman. As Toby watched, Ully stuck his hand out of the cell and placed it on the wall.

His cell door clicked open. Toby bounced to his feet.

"Me, too!" he exclaimed.

"Ok, but let me talk to the demon first. We have to get past him to leave Hell."

Toby held his breath as Ully disappeared through the door to where Jared sat. When the mad scientist wasn't sent sailing back through the door, Toby sat down to put on his shoes. He glanced at Hannah. She was in no shape to walk, but she'd have to. He couldn't help thinking his mama had been a little tougher when she found out about the Immortals.

Ully returned a couple of minutes later. He strode to Toby's cell and dangled the talisman before it. Toby's door opened.

"C'mon, Auntie Hannah!" Toby cried.

"No, she has to stay," Ully said quickly. "Jared won't let us all go. Just two of us. Um, no offense, but I think you and I should go."

"Agreed." Toby stepped out of the cell and closed it. "We'll be back, Auntie Hannah. Promise."

Hannah was crying too hard to pay attention. Ully led them into the antechamber, where Jared stood to one side with his arms crossed. Toby crowded Ully, not liking the way the demon's eyes gleamed.

"I see you left me the cupcake," it said. "Good choice, Immortal. If you don't return … "

Toby shuddered, and Ully's step quickened. They exited the jailer's room into a long hallway, and Ully turned to him.

"Can you get us out of here?" the mad scientist asked.

"Um, I'm checking." Toby closed his eyes, focusing hard on searching the memories of all the angels that came before him. To his delight, one of his predecessors had known of the secret portal leading to and from Hell. "Okay, follow me."

Ully obeyed. They crept through the hallways, avoiding any that seemed crowded. Toby followed the directions he saw in his memories and led them to a small chamber near the center of the fortress. They entered and closed the door, seeing the open portal hovering in the middle. He took Ully's hand, and they stepped into it.

"We're going to Mama?" Toby asked as they walked towards a glowing portal.

"Yeah. We'll probably get in trouble for this. Can you find her?"

"We'll have to see."

"Do you have any more angel superpowers?"

"Not yet," Toby said with a sigh. He ran ahead of Ully through the place between worlds and the portal to the underworld. "Hurry, Ully!" He let out a whoop as he emerged into the underworld. "We're here, Ully."

"Eh, I kinda prefer the other world," the scientist said, looking around.

Toby darted into the jungle, knowing they had little time, and that he had to find his human before anything else bad happened to her. He didn't know where the demon with her wanted to take her, but he knew where anyone leaving the underworld would go to escape.

"Toby, wait!" Ully called.

Toby slowed until he caught up then darted ahead again.

"Do you know where you're going?" Ully demanded and snatched his shoulder.

"Ow," Toby muttered. Ully's fingers dug into his shoulder. The Immortal didn't look as if he had that amount of strength in him. "I sense her this way."

"I think we have a better chance if we go to Death's fortress."

"No. Because then we can't beat Death to her."

"But if Death already has her, then —"

"Then it's too late. We have to go this way," Toby said and pulled away. "Trust me."

When Ully didn't follow, Toby turned to beckon him forward. The scientist looked in the direction of where Toby's angel memories told him the fortress was. Grudgingly, the Immortal followed him.

"Come *on*, Ully. If you keep dragging your feet, we won't make it."

"Alright. What's so important about finding her anyway?"

"I'm her angel. It's what I do."

"Then you probably should've tried harder not to get thrown into Hell. You were of no help to anyone there."

Toby didn't answer, unwilling to admit just how much Ully's words stung. He led them deeper into the jungle. The branches hurried to create a path for him, and he smiled at them. According to his angel memories, the trees were more than trees in Death's underworld. They were *alive*.

"Thank you, trees," he said as he walked. "Angel memories say …" He turned to see Ully several meters away, suspended in the air and battling branches that tried to grab his arms. "Trees! Stop!"

Ully was dropped to the ground at Toby's command. He hurried back to the Immortal, worried he'd be hurt. Ully was unconscious.

"What's gotten into you?" Toby asked the trees. "He's my friend! Leave him alone."

The branches around him darted around then fell still, as if watching. Toby knelt beside Ully and grunted as he rolled the Immortal onto his back. Disappointed to have their journey paused already, he looked around then back at Ully.

Something about the trees' reaction to Ully bothered him. They'd cleared a path for him then tried to obstruct the Immortal. It didn't make much sense. Toby rose and walked to the nearest tree, placing his hands against it. There were no angel memories about how trees communicated, but he willed it to speak to him anyway.

It didn't. Frustrated he couldn't help Katie while Ully was out, Toby started off again into the jungle, looking at each tree until he found one he thought he could climb. He leapt to the lowest branch, which slithered in his grip before it wrapped around him. Toby gasped as the branch picked him up then waited.

"Up, above the tree line," Toby said, stretching towards the next one.

The branch obliged him and passed him upwards to another, which stretched him as far up as it could reach. Then dropped him. Toby yelped as he fell. Another branch caught him and lifted him upwards again.

Finally, he broke through the thatch of branches and leaves blocking most of the sun. The day was darkening. In the distance, he saw the massive fortress that was Death's, and he saw the Lake of Souls he'd seen in angel memories. He saw birds but couldn't see through the jungle to where Katie might be. The branch holding him swayed in a heavy wind that smelled of rain. Toby clutched it and twisted in the branch's grip, until he could see the dark storm clouds moving slowly across the sky.

"Toby?" Ully sounded disoriented.

"Down, tree," Toby ordered.

The tree dropped, caught, and dropped him again, catching him half a second before he hit the ground. He landed on his back at Ully's feet. The scientist knelt beside him, one hand on his head.

"Not sure I like this place," Ully said.

"It's not bad. You ok?"

"I think so."

"I'm not sure why the trees attached you." Toby stood and dusted himself off then hauled Ully up by his arm.

"Bad luck maybe."

"I'm searching the angel memories to see why. Maybe they don't like Immortals. In a couple of years, I won't have so many problems searching the memories. It'll be instantaneous, like that!" he said and snapped his fingers.

Ully flinched. "Don't worry about it, Toby."

"No, I need to know why. It might mean Mama is in more danger than I thought."

"Really, it's fine Toby."

"Though I think if trees didn't like humans, Mama would be dead, and if they didn't like Immortals, Gabe couldn't stay here either," Toby reasoned. "That leaves demons. Maybe trees don't like demons."

"What're you saying?"

Toby grinned. "Maybe you're so ugly, they thought you were a demon!"

"That's not funny, Toby." Ully's face was graver than Toby had seen it, and his wiry body was tense.

"Just joking, Ully."

"Let's walk."

Toby shook his head and started forward again, wondering when Ully had lost his sense of humor. He led them in the direction where he sensed Katie, until night and clouds rendered the jungle too dark. Ully stopped when the first drops of rain fell, and Toby retreated as the Immortal seated himself on a fallen tree.

"It's just rain, Ully. I know where we're going," Toby said. "I don't think we should stop."

"I'm so fucking hungry, I could eat an angel," Ully snapped.

Toby looked him over again. Ully was frowning. Even in Hell, the scientist had maintained his cheerful visage. Toby sat near him, at the base of a tree whose branches moved closer to cover him from rain. The trees left Ully in the rain.

Toby leaned back, wishing he knew how to start a fire like Rhyn. He closed his eyes to search the angel memories for information about the under-worldly trees. Uneasily, he found the memories he sought. They confirmed what he'd already figured out: trees didn't like demons.

Ully cursed as he moved to seek cover from the downpour. Safe beneath his jungle roof, Toby watched him. The brave, cheerful Ully that sat with him in Hell seemed lost in the underworld, and Toby began to suspect there was another reason their jailer, Jared, had freed them.

Unable to sleep without knowing the truth, Toby huddled beneath the jungle leaves and stretched his senses until he found Katie. He couldn't put her in more danger, if there was something wrong with Ully. She was close enough for him to find when he needed to. If he kept some distance between him and Katie, he could figure out what was wrong with Ully without endangering her more.

Chapter Ten

Andre continued without any sign of slowing, until Katie stopped. Her head spun and she felt sick again. She was too tired to continue. The phantom appeared before her, pointing. She shook her head and slumped against a tree.

"You may have endless energy as a dead man, but I don't," she told him. "I need a break, Andre."

The phantom shook his head in silent objection. Katie ignored him and cradled her forehead in her hands. She ate another food cube and sighed. When she looked up, Andre was gone. Since they'd left the demon-Gabriel, Andre had disappeared twice before, but not for long. She rested her head against the tree behind her and waited.

The moons appeared through the branches in the jungle, almost alone in the dark sky except for a wisp of clouds floating beneath them. She watched the clouds pass. More came, quickly blocking the moons and stealing most of the light from the jungle. Katie sat up and blinked until her eyes adjusted to the new level of darkness. The sky took on an eerie silver glow, like it did in Maryland the night before a hard snow.

Andre didn't return. Katie waited longer, until the chill of the night dried the sweat that'd covered her since they began running earlier.

"Andre?" she whispered into the darkness.

He didn't appear. Unease filled her, and she wondered if the phantom would leave her there alone, even knowing she was helpless without it. Katie ate a water cube and rose, starting off in the direction Andre had been headed. She walked for half an hour, until rain began to trickle through the jungle overhead. Andre didn't reappear.

He'd left her there. She cursed herself for insisting on resting and paused, looking up at the cloudy sky visible through the overhead canopy.

The rain was cold, and she was alone without as much as a jacket. Katie shivered and tried to quell the panic within her. She wore the same clothes she'd been wearing several days ago, when she walked into the ocean. Before that, she didn't think it was possible for her life to get worse. Then she's come here.

Pain streaked through her, the kind of pain with no physical source. Katie began to cry, unable to see an end to her ordeal that would mean she – or her baby – lived. She hugged her stomach and sobbed for the loss of Rhyn, her own life, their child's.

Life isn't supposed to hurt this much, she thought and sank to the ground. Her thoughts went to Rhyn then Hannah then the past few weeks as she sought to figure out where she'd gone wrong. She was alone and soon, she and her baby would be dead.

A strange sound pierced her sorrow. She ignored it, not wanting to exert the effort needed to leave the dark place where she'd fallen.

The sound came again, the cry of someone who was hurt. Katie wiped her eyes. She was drenched with rain and curled against the large root of a tree. The birds of the jungle made screaming sounds, but this was different. This was human.

"Hello?" she said. "Is someone there?"

"Please help me!" came the faint response.

Katie started in the direction of the woman's voice. She stumbled over fallen, slick wood and brambles she couldn't see. Whatever magic that had cleared a path for her was gone. She struggled through the jungle before calling out,

"Can you hear me? I can't see much. You'll have to say something, so I can find you."

"I'm here. You sound close."

Katie angled herself towards the voice once again. The woman was close. She continued and then stopped suddenly, nearly tripping over the small form in her path. She looked at the woman closely in the limited light to make sure it wasn't a demon or some other kind of under-worldly creature out to eat her. The woman looked human enough. Her features were hard to make out in the dark, but she at least had two arms and two legs.

"What's wrong?" Katie asked and knelt beside her as much out of exhaustion as curiosity.

"I tripped in the rain. I think my foot is stuck in a root."

"Are you from here?"

"I don't think so. I'm from Maine."

Katie hesitated before shuffling forward on her knees. She carefully touched the woman's leg then patted it as she followed it down to the thick roots wrapped around her ankles. Unable to see exactly how she was stuck, Katie used her cold fingers to fumble around the root and the woman's sneakers.

"It's really jammed in there," she said at last.

"I slipped. Couldn't see anything in this rain," the woman said. "I think I could cut it away. I've tried taking off my shoe and maneuvering my foot every which way."

"I can try to saw through it," Katie said and pulled out the knife Gabriel had given her. She paused. "Can I ask you something first?"

"Sure."

"What are you doing here?"

"I'm not sure. I was at home when someone broke in. I heard someone screaming then something hot went straight through me. Everything went black, and I woke up here," the woman explained.

"So you died."

Silence.

"Sorry. I mean, it sounds like you died," Katie said quickly. "But what do I know? It's my first time here, too. What's your name?"

"Deidre."

"I'm Katie. If I go through your shoe or something, just yell," she said and began sawing at the root.

"You think we're dead," Deidre said in a quiet voice.

"If we aren't, we will be soon. I don't think I'll make it out of here."

"Me neither, I guess. I don't know how. Didn't know dying was like this."

Katie's throat tightened, and the knife slipped. She drew a shaky breath and glanced around for Andre again. The damned phantom had lured her away from Gabriel and left her to her fate. She was a fool.

Anger filled her, and she began to saw in earnest, unwilling to let another innocent person die in the darkness of the underworld.

"Maybe we can find a way out," she said. "I know I want to go home. I *must* make it home."

"I have no family living. I have nothing to go home to," Deidre said. "Do you?"

"Sorta," Katie replied. "It's a long story. I have a mate waiting for me, if he hasn't gone off and killed himself." Her knife slipped again, this time slicing her hand. "Dammit!"

"We need more light," Deidre said.

"Maybe the storm will clear up."

Deidre shifted with a grunt. Katie sat back on her haunches, not sure what to do when she couldn't see what she was trying to cut. Deidre was shaking as hard as Katie was, and Katie crept closer for body heat.

"I'll stay with you until we can see well enough to cut you free," she said.

"If you were going somewhere, you can go. I might be dead anyway," Deidre said with a sigh.

Something within Katie snapped at the despair in Deidre's voice. It was the type of helpless self-pity she'd felt since entering the Immortal's world. Katie glared at the jungle around them.

"No. I'm staying here. We'll cut you free. I'm sick of this shit."

"Pardon?"

"I'm done playing the victim here. I've lost everything because I listened to stupid Immortals who thought they knew more than me," Katie nearly shouted in frustration. "If Death wants me, she can come get me, but I'm not leaving you here to deal with what I've dealt with the past few weeks!"

"I have no idea what you're talking about."

"By morning, we'll probably be surrounded by shapeshifting demons and assassins out to get us. I'm tired of playing this game. I'm not going to be helpless anymore." Katie stood and threw her head back. "Fuck you, Death! I'm not afraid of you like everyone else is! I bet you get off on fucking with us little people, don't you?" Her head felt ready to explode with anger, and adrenaline warmed her from the inside out.

Deidre was quiet for a moment. Then she chuckled. "Rough turn, eh?"

"I don't know what's worse: running from the one *thing* that should help us or facing the guy I know wants to do bad things to us," Katie snapped. "You can't trust the good guys, because they'll use you for science experiments, and the bad guys put you in Hell."

"I guess we just have to do the best we can," Deidre said.

"There's a difference between free will and having the deck stacked against you. Humans need someone to protect them from these reckless Immortals, not to mention the demons."

"Sounds like a lot of responsibility."

"Rhyn could do it. He's my ... I guess *was* my mate," Katie said, melancholy descending over her with the rain. "All he needed was someone to believe in him and make him realize he was worth saving. And, well, probably Gabe and a few allies, instead of the assholes he's surrounded by."

"If he can't deal with that kind of adversity, how could he deal with something greater, like protecting us little humans?" Deidre asked.

Katie glanced towards her, surprised by the question from someone who barely seemed able to cope with the fact she was probably dead.

"He never had a reason to try," she replied.

"And he does now?"

"Yes," Katie said. "He does."

"Sounds complicated."

"Sometimes all we have are bad choices, and we still have to choose," Katie whispered. "Sorry for going off. I'm frustrated."

"I got that from the rant," Deidre said with a tinkling chuckle.

"Enough about me," Katie said. She sat heavily, inching towards the other woman for warmth. "We've got some time before morning. What's your story?"

"There's not much to me," Deidre said. "I was born and raised in the same place. I lived a sheltered life. Never left. That's about it."

"There's more to you than that. There's more to everyone than where they grew up," Katie urged.

Deidre hesitated. "I don't remember my parents. Sometimes I don't think I ever had any. No siblings, no friends. I was ... different. Always different. Scared most people away. Probably a good thing, because I've always had a rather ornery streak."

"You sound like Rhyn."

"Your mate?"

"Yeah."

"Hmmm. Anyway, I took over the this huge corporation at a young age. I kept too busy to get out much. Not that I had much of a role. I just did the crappy job while watching everyone else make mistakes. When you inherit a job like that, you don't have as much say in the way things go as you'd like," Deidre said with some distaste. "You see, I'm a dull person."

"You don't sound dull," Katie replied, suspecting Deidre was the daughter of some billionaire with a corporation spanning the world. "You sound … wanting. You never wondered what other people did, since you were always working?"

"Sometimes."

"Never wanted to try to make friends or anything?"

"Never cared for people too much. I was happy alone," Deidre said.

"Assume this is the last day of your life, since it might really be for both of us. What one thing would you have done if you knew it was your last day?" Katie asked. She settled next to the trapped woman, trying hard to keep her mind off how cold she was. She was grateful for company, even if Deidre seemed as lost as she was.

"I would've told him I loved him."

"So there was someone!"

"Long ago, yes. I drove him away. We were from … different sides of the tracks. I had everything, he had nothing," Deidre said. "I wouldn't give it all up, and he wanted no part of the soulless corporation I manage. I made him leave me."

"Sounds rough," Katie said. Deidre sounded accepting of her decision, but Katie couldn't help wondering how long it had taken her to come to peace with sacrificing love for the demands of her job.

"What about you? What would you have done if you knew it was the last day?"

"Exactly what I did," Katie said. "Though in hindsight, it doesn't seem like anything is really ever enough. I could've said so much more than I did or maybe, just did something in addition."

"At least you have the peace of knowing you did something."

"Yeah, I do. And no regrets about what I did, though the few days I've spent here make me wonder if there was an easier way."

"If we knew all of life's secrets, we might be bored," Deidre said. "Since I'm here, I guess it's a good thing I didn't take a chance on him."

"Everyone should find that person that makes them feel alive and have a chance with him," Katie said and rested her head against a wet branch. "I wish I'd been more willing to take that chance, too. Might've had more time with him before ending up here."

"He deserved better than me."

"Everyone deserves a chance at happiness, Deidre. Even rich girls running empires."

Deidre said nothing. Rain fell steadily, until Katie's skin was too numbed to feel it. She heard Deidre's breathing grow deeper as the woman fell asleep. Aware there could be demons or other creatures in the dark, Katie roused herself to keep watch, as Gabriel had kept watch over her.

Her thoughts returned to Rhyn, and she recalled how he'd fought the last day they'd been on the Sanctuary. She'd never seen anything like it, a combination of power, agility and fire. He'd been willing to kill his only friend on her behalf, and the memory was both gratifying and sorrowful. He'd done it for her. He'd do it for others. It was who he was, if he gave himself the chance to realize it. The man who spent lifetimes in Hell out of a sense of family loyalty would be just as loyal to any he was charged to protect.

The night was long and cold. Deidre slept, and Katie drifted between a fitful doze and her thoughts. Dawn crept across the jungle, peering first from the tangled branches overhead then inching through the trees. As soon as she could see well enough,

Katie crawled to Deidre's feet. The woman continued to sleep, and Katie looked her over. She looked like any other college student in cargo pants and a light sweater. Deidre's long, flaxen hair was in a messy braid, and her skin was pale.

Katie's gaze dropped to Deidre's hands. They looked normal, but so had Gabriel's. Andre had warned her about the Gabriel-demon. She looked around, wanting to believe the phantom would reappear if it sensed she was in danger. The Gabriel-demon had appeared distant, as if uncomfortable acting out its role. Deidre had been open and warm towards her, like a real human.

Katie touched the roots ensnaring the sleeping woman's ankle. The mess baffled her, as if the roots themselves had reached out to grab Deidre's ankles instead of her slipping and stumbling into them. The gnarly roots were twisted and thick, wrapped too tightly for her to pry them apart.

She started to saw at them with the knife. The wood was thick and wet. She shifted closer, gasping when the root healed the cuts she'd just made. Furious at the latest trick from the Immortal underworld, Katie sawed furiously at the root, until her arm ached. She'd barely made a dent when she switched arms.

The cut healed itself in seconds.

"Shit!" she shouted and flung the knife into the nearby brush. "This placed is cursed!"

Deidre awoke and looked at her then at her ankles. Katie was caught by the other woman's eyes. They were large and turquoise, like the shallows surrounding the Caribbean Sanctuary.

"It's not working. The trees keep repairing the damage I'm doing," Katie said. "I'm not sure what to do."

Deidre grunted and visibly tugged at her feet.

"Damned magic ..." Katie drifted off, looking at the roots anew. "Magic."

"Ugh."

"Here, eat these. I've got an idea," Katie said. She handed the pale woman a food and water cube and popped two of her own. Standing, she waded into the brush where she'd thrown the knife. It glinted in the morning light. Katie swiped it, glad the trees didn't have a taste for metal as well as Immortal sustenance.

"What's your idea?" Deidre called after her.

"It probably won't work. If you're with me long, you'll find I have the worst luck ever. But it's worth a try," Katie answered then muttered, "Not like I got anything else to lose." She made her way back to Deidre with the knife and knelt.

Katie pulled up the sleeve of her soaked sweater and nicked her arm. She set down the knife and squeezed out a few drops of blood, watching as they landed on the roots. Then she sat back and held her breath.

"What are you doing?" Deidre asked.

Katie was quiet, willing the tree roots to be vulnerable to her immunity blood. She hacked at the root again and paused. The area where she'd dripped blood stayed cut while the area around it healed.

"I'm getting you out of here," she said, thrilled. With a grimace, she sliced the palm of her hand and smeared the blood on the root.

"You're insane," Deidre breathed. "How are you doing that?"

"I don't know. It's my curse and sometimes, my blessing. I'm immune to young magic," Katie explained. "I assume this tree isn't that old."

"Doesn't it hurt?"

Katie nodded and sawed at the root, dripped more blood, then sawed again. She forced herself to continue even as she grew tired. Sticky blood covered the hilt of the dagger, her pants, the root, Deidre's shoe and pants leg. Katie kept on, uncertain what might happen if she stopped for a break.

"You don't even know me," Deidre said, her surprise clear.

"I'm going to be like Rhyn. I'm going to take care of you, because it's the honorable thing to do," Katie said.

"Maybe you should become the protector of humanity."

"Not a job I want. I'd be happy living with Rhyn in some cave like hermits. We could raise our …" Katie's hands faltered with her voice. She cleared her throat and focused hard on cutting her newfound ally free.

"I hope we're not dead," Deidre said. "You deserve better."

"Rhyn deserves better. I think I got what was coming to me for being as selfish as my bitchy sister."

The roots around Deidre's left foot snapped free. Katie shoved it aside before it could change its mind and started on the roots around her right foot. Deidre moved her foot with a look of pain. She rubbed her ankle, and Katie cut her arm again.

By midmorning, Deidre was free. Katie grimaced as she wrapped the dismembered sleeves of her sweater around her wounds. Blood soaked the sweater quickly, and she held it over her head. Even before she stood, she felt woozy. Deidre tested herself and limped a few feet. Katie steadied her breathing to keep from dropping to her knees.

"Where were you headed when you found me?" Deidre asked.

"I'm not sure. I had a guide, but he … they left me," Katie said. "I was told to walk in an eastern direction."

"I came from the east. There's a fortress that way."

"Then that's where we're going."

"Seriously?"

"Yes. I think that's where Death is. I think that's my way out," Katie said, not fully convinced but unwilling to admit it. She had no other option. "You in?"

Deidre smiled faintly and nodded.

"Is it far?"

"Maybe a day away."

Katie's mind went to Gabe's words about needing to leave before the seventh day. It was day six. She wasn't sure they'd make his timeline—or even why it still mattered that she reached wherever he was taking her. There had to be something to what he told her, and she wished once more he'd told her why.

She was done being at the mercy of Immortals. The first Immortal, Death, she'd tell that would probably be the last, but she was done with this game.

Chapter Eleven

The entire fortress was empty. Rhyn ducked his head into a salon the size of half Kris's castle. He and Gabe had reached the gleaming marble palace at the center of the underworld just after dawn only to find it unguarded and missing its key occupant.

"This is just weird," Gabe said again from down the hall. "She's planning something."

"A trap for her least favorite demon and assassin?"

"Trust me, if she wasn't curious about you, you'd be dead-dead. She probably finds all this entertaining."

Rhyn heard the note of pain in the death-dealer's voice. In a week's time, Gabe had gone from quietly confident to troubled to lost. The death-dealer was struggling with himself, a feeling Rhyn knew well.

"If she's not here, where is she?" he asked.

"Out tormenting others."

"In the underworld?"

"Yeah." Gabriel fell quiet for a moment, looking around with a frown. Death's palace felt much like Hell had to Rhyn. Something about it tugged at his power.

"At the stream ... " Rhyn started, watching Gabe carefully.

The death-dealer grimaced. "That was her. Toying with you. Testing you."

"Could she be fighting demons?"

"Her guards are gone, which means they're off tracking demons. Death is unpredictable, but if I were to guess, she's somewhere in the underworld."

"Hiding?"

"No. Toying with someone else."

"Not Katie. She'd have to kill her," Rhyn said.

"Not us, not Katie, not the demons. That leaves other Immortals. Looks like we're not the only ones here."

Rhyn thought of Kiki, suspecting his brother went to Kris. He wondered who Kris sent after him to make sure he didn't follow through on his threat to confront Death.

"We only have today," he said. "Let's find them."

"You go. I'll wait here for her. She always comes home," Gabe said.

"Gabe, it's not safe for you here."

"My fate is sealed, Rhyn. I've got nothing to lose now. If she comes back, I can distract her, give you until midnight."

Rhyn looked hard at his friend, sensing what the death-dealer didn't say. He'd known Gabe was likely going to suffer worse than any of them, once he faced Death's wrath. There was regret mixed in with Gabriel's resignation. They'd known each other long enough for Rhyn to suspect Death would finally succeed in what she'd been doing to Gabe all these years: She was about to win the battle to crush his soul.

"There's always hope, Gabe," Rhyn said. "I'll find a way to help you. I swear it."

"I'm beyond help, Rhyn. I've always believed you could be all that Kris and Andre and your father were not. Your half-demon nature makes you better prepared than all of them combined. I think that's your fate, to follow in your father's footsteps."

"Kris might disagree. Oh, and probably every other Immortal out there."

"Katie knows it. I know it. I'm ready for my fate. Do what you were born to do, Rhyn, and don't think twice about me."

"I spent years in Hell for a brother who hates me. I'll do whatever it takes to free my only friend from Death, Gabe," Rhyn said firmly. He slapped Gabe on the arm. "You need to shave. You look like shit."

The death-dealer smiled faintly. Rhyn trotted away from him, out of the palace and into the jungle. He suspected freeing Katie from Death would be easier than freeing Gabe from Death. There was more at stake for her if she lost Gabe.

Thunder cracked overhead. Rhyn had ignored the rain, accustomed to being miserable. Hell was either broiling or freezing, and the Alps were just as cold. The underworld's chilled rain didn't compare.

He looked up instinctively, sensing something different about this thunder. It didn't sound like the rumbling thunder he'd heard in the mortal world. It sounded like an explosion in the sky. The jungle canopy blocked his view, so he leapt up to catch the branch of the nearest tree. He scaled the tree quickly, stopping only when he broke through the layers of leaves. More tiny explosions came, and he twisted to see what they were.

A portal had opened overhead, back towards what Gabe had called the Lake of Souls. Demons fell from the sky, some changing into their winged forms while others simply fell. It was too far for them to survive if they fell, and he estimated half of them were likely dead on impact.

The other half numbered in the hundreds. The winged demons hovered around the portal and then took off in separate directions, swooping low above the jungle.

Rhyn scampered down the tree and fell far enough to knock his breath out. Demons flew overhead, unable to see through the canopy. He froze, watching them circle then leave, and stood, catching his breath. Fear penetrated him, colder than the rain. Katie was vulnerable. Gabe was vulnerable.

Death alone could drive the invaders from her world.

As Darkyn had said, the underworld tempered his Immortal magic, but Rhyn felt the demon power broiling behind the constraints, seeking a way out of him. He was sticking to his plan, though he no longer had time to find Death. He was going to try to make her come to him. She'd know where Katie was, and Rhyn could find her before more demons closed in.

He knelt on the ground and closed his eyes, seeking out the writhing darkness of his demon side. If the demons had the power to transform and fly, he could access his demon powers, too, even if the Immortal side of him was bound by Death's underworld.

"Berries," Toby commanded the tree before him.

The tree obliged and lowered one of the low hanging branches to Toby's level. He plucked a few of the red, tart berries and popped them in his mouth.

"How'd you do that?" Ully asked.

Toby hunched his shoulders. He'd wandered far enough away from camp that he'd hoped to get some food before running from Ully, who was still sleeping. The angel memories convinced him that Ully's strange comments and the trees attempt to combat him indicated Ully really was a demon. Toby turned slowly to face the scientist, whose hands and body had begun to transform back into its demon form. The Ully-demon hadn't yet realized it.

"Angel memories. This is where old angels go before they die," Toby said. He huddled deeper into his coat, more than the rain chilling him. The Ully-demon still wore Ully's face, but the rest of his body had grown bony and taller. Toby couldn't help wondering when Ully had been swapped for a demon, but it had to have been before they left Hell.

It now made sense how Ully had been able to free them and talk Jared into letting them go. Toby had been too excited to find their escape too easy at the time, but now, he realized it was … weird. He'd failed again. He couldn't even escape on his own.

"This way," he said and started towards Death's palace.

Thunder cracked overhead, and Toby looked up. Ully ran into him as the angel stopped, and they both stared at the sky. He thought he saw something in the sky, but the trees blocked it.

"Let's keep going," Ully said.

"I want to see what it is," Toby said. He approached a tree. "Branch! Up!"

The tree lowered a branch to him, and he wrapped his arms around it. It was warm and writhing, and one small branch wrapped around him to keep him secure as it shifted him upwards. Toby broke through the treetops and gasped.

Demons flew towards him.

"Down, down, down!" he squawked. "Down!"

The branch lowered him so fast, his stomach turned. Toby scampered off the branch and stared upwards, wondering how Death could allow the demons into her domain. He looked around wildly, expecting them to leap from his surroundings.

"What's wrong?" Ully asked. By his darkened gaze, he knew.

"Tree!" Toby shouted. "Help!"

The Ully-demon launched towards him. The tree snatched Toby and lifted him to safety, and Toby dangled far enough over Ully's head that the demon couldn't reach him. As he watched, the Ully-demon transformed into its natural form, a creature of wings, talons, and teeth longer than Toby's fingers.

"Throw me!" Toby whispered, clawing at the tree as the demon shook out his wings. "Now!"

The tree obeyed. Toby bit back a yell as he was launched over the treetops into the sky, in the direction of the Lake of Souls. Another tree branch caught him, and he struggled to orient himself. He heard the sounds of pursuit but was stuck upside down. A blur of wings and darkness caught his attention.

"Throw me!" he cried again.

He flew through the air, drawing the attention of nearby demons in midflight. He saw them shift directions and dart towards him just before he dipped beneath the jungle canopy again.

"Don't let them through!"

The branches flung upwards, snatching the legs and wings of the demons. Toby heard a demon shriek as its wings were torn from its body. The tree lowered Toby to the ground. He looked up once more, turned and ran through the jungle, leaving the trees to fight off the demons.

Katie was close. Toby could sense her. He ignored the branches whipping his face and the brambles tripping him. Instead, he just ran, the screams of demons in his ears.

Even the thunder of the underworld sounded weird. Katie glanced towards the sky, silently cursing the rain. She made her way over a fallen log and waited for Deidre before continuing.

"I hope we're going the right way still," she said. "I'm not good at directions."

"The jungle looks the same everywhere," Deidre agreed. "But I think this is right. It's still easterly. I think."

More thunder boomed. Katie wondered what other kinds of storms the underworld might have. Would it rain something other than black water? With her luck, it'd rain bugs, like the beetle nest she skirted.

"Watch out. These things will probably take a leg off," she said, pointing to the nest.

Deidre paused beside the bubbling nest of beetles the size of her hand. Katie watched as she picked up one, peered at it and then flung it. Deidre giggled.

"We call those beetle bombs where I'm from," she admitted. "I guess that's the kind of thing you do when you're bored."

Katie smiled, amused despite the rain, thunder and bugs. The woman was as unique as she'd claimed to be, at once easily entertained and melancholy. Katie couldn't quite keep up with Deidre's odd mixture of emotions, but she pitied the woman, who seemed more lost in her own world than anything.

The sound of something screaming wiped the smile from Deidre's face. Katie turned to face the direction from which the sound came. It wasn't a bird, and it wasn't human. The single voice was joined by several, and Katie grabbed Deidre's hand.

"We have to keep going," she said, hurrying forward. "I don't know what that is, but it's close."

"Demons," Deidre whispered.

"Don't let all my talk scare you. Let's just um, run for awhile!" Katie said and took off.

Deidre was close on her heels. They navigated the jungle as fast as they could, catching themselves against trees as they slid through slippery piles of leaves and over fallen branches. Katie ran until she was breathless. Deidre kept on running, and Katie pushed her body forward.

Suddenly, someone launched from the trees. Deidre stopped. Katie smashed into her and knocked them both to the ground. Katie rolled and pushed herself up, missing the look exchanged between Deidre and the newcomer.

"Toby!" Katie exclaimed. "What're you doing here?"

The young angel's face was streaked with blood from where branches had struck him. He was pale and terrified – and staring in shock at Deidre.

"Toby," Katie said again, stepping forward. Her eyes went to his hands. He didn't have demon hands. "It's okay. She's a friend."

"Mama," he managed and flung himself into her arms. Katie grunted and caught him, hugging him to her.

"Toby, what're you doing here?"

"Mama, there are demons everywhere. They opened a portal in the sky and are just flying and flying, hundreds of them!" Toby's voice rose in panic.

"How did you get here?" she demanded.

"I wanted to protect you. Rhyn and Gabe came to find you, but I knew I could find you faster, so I came with a shapeshifter."

Katie bit back the words she wanted to say. Toby was too small to protect anyone, and she couldn't help feeling panic stir again at the thought that now he – and Deidre – were now as vulnerable as she was to the demons. The thought of Rhyn being close made her body warm from the inside out. Maybe, if she could find him …the cry of a demon overhead drew her attention.

"I don't understand," she murmured. "I thought Death wouldn't let the demons into this place."

"Something's wrong," Toby said. "Darkyn did something. He replaced Gabe and Ully and Hannah with demons."

"Hannah? Is she okay, Toby?"

"Yeah. She's in Hell. She's fine."

"Jesus. Hannah's in Hell," Katie mused, doubting her sister was remotely *fine*. "Explains why Gabe went crazy on me. You said Rhyn and Gabe are here, too?"

"Somewhere. They were coming to find you and make Death give you back to Rhyn."

The trees overhead rustled, and Toby yanked away, staring. Katie saw shadows but nothing else. Even so, she doubted these were the freaky underworld birds.

"C'mon," she said, snatching Toby's hand. "We have to get somewhere safe."

"Death's palace. Follow me," Toby said. He cast another puzzled look at Deidre and ran forward.

Katie followed, trailed closely by Deidre. The sounds of their escape were nothing compared to the sounds of what followed. Katie cast a look over her shoulder and saw several demons had dropped into the jungle and transformed into panther-like forms. She stopped and reached into the pouch slung across her chest.

"What are you doing?" Deidre demanded.

"Go! Run with Toby!" Katie said and pushed her. "I'm going to feed the trees."

She pulled two food cubes free and flung one towards the demons then dropped one where she stood. Turning, she grabbed Deidre's arm and ran hard. As before, nothing happened at first then the earth roared as it split apart. The ground trembled, throwing both of them down.

Toby hauled Katie up and tugged her forward. Katie pulled free and grabbed Deidre just as the earth beneath her collapsed. Katie slammed to the ground, holding Deidre as tightly as she could.

"Toby!" she shouted. "Stay back!"

The angel ignored her and dropped beside her, wringing his hands helplessly. The blond woman dangled over the widening chasm, clutching Katie's hand. She braced her feet against the side of the chasm and walked upward, until Toby could grab her belt. The angel pulled hard, and Katie pushed Deidre on top of the angel, who yelped.

"We must run!" Katie said, rising. The ground still rumbled, the trees surrounding both food cubes expanding fast and tearing up the ground in several directions as they did. She looked around, irritated to find she'd caused a chasm to form between them and the direction they'd been running.

Deidre and Toby stood. Katie started forward, only for the rumbling ground to drive her to her knees. Horrified, she saw the chasm form a rough circle around them, trapping them on a small island surrounded by football field wide trees and chasms too wide to jump.

Deidre landed on her back beside her, and Katie pulled Toby against her. They huddled on the ground, waiting for the trees to crush them or the demons to snatch them. The ground continued to rumble. Slowly, the sounds died down then fell silent. Katie peered apprehensively out at the world.

Their small island was untouched. The trees and jungle beyond were decimated by chasms and fallen trees.

"So that's what happens when you feed the trees," Toby said in part wonder, part horror. "I'm glad I didn't try it."

"Shit," Katie muttered and stood, walking to the edge of the island. "Demons are gone, but we're fucked when they come back."

"Wow," Deidre breathed. "I haven't felt a rush like that in eons."

"You should be grateful Katie didn't let your slow ass fall," Toby said.

"Toby!" Katie chided him. "You are in so much trouble for being here."

"I'm your angel. I'm supposed to help you, but all I do is screw up," Toby said in frustration. "I'm the worst angel in the history of the world."

"You're young. I'm sure your time will come," Deidre said.

"Exactly. In the meantime, you're grounded," Katie said. "No marshmallows or video games or whatever it is kids like. Why are you wearing a pink coat?"

Toby rolled his eyes in response and crossed his arms. Katie shook her head. The angel was visibly upset and completely disheveled. She softened, sensing his distress.

"It's ok, Toby. You're doing better than I am," she offered. "You always knew I was the worst mother in the world."

"Yeah. But I'm the worst angel in the world."

"Then we're meant for each other," she told him. "Now, let's get the hell out of here." She held out her hand. Toby smiled grudgingly and took it. Katie led them around the island, trying to find some part of the chasm that was narrow enough to jump or a log they could roll across the gaping ravine.

"Why don't we just ask the trees?" Toby complained at last.

"What do you mean?"

"I mean, ask the trees." Toby sighed loudly and stepped away from her. "Tree! Lift us over the ravine!"

Katie stared at him, suspecting he'd lost his mind. To her surprise, a branch wrapped around her body. She yelped, shoving at it then went still as it plucked her from the ground and moved her across the ravine, dropping her off in the jungle again.

The tree deposited Deidre and Toby in a heap, and Toby sprung up, pleased with himself. Katie looked at the tree in uneasy mistrust. The trees of her world were alive, but this was something else.

"This way," Toby said and started into the jungle.

"Determined little guy, isn't he?" Deidre said, amused again. "He cares about you deeply if he came here by choice."

"He's bat-shit crazy, which is where I'll be soon if we don't find a way out of here," Katie replied. "You ok?"

"Fine. You?"

"Good enough. This place is making me dizzy, though." Katie rubbed her forehead. She needed sleep and real food. Her hand went instinctively to her stomach, and she couldn't help wondering if the food and water cubes were good for the baby. "We need to find Rhyn. I think this place is doing bad things to me."

"Because you're not dead!" Toby called over his shoulder. "Mortals can't come here unless they're dead. Or, it'll kill you."

"Let me guess. That happens tonight, if I don't get to wherever it is Gabe was taking me."

Toby was wrestling with a bush and didn't respond. Katie breathed deeply and pushed forward, wanting very much to stop and sleep but suspecting she'd never awaken if she did. She didn't have enough food cubes to drive off more than one more demon attack. They'd have to find Rhyn and Gabe fast.

Rhyn had come for her. The thought thrilled her. She didn't doubt he would try, and she hoped he hadn't done something like violate the obscure Immortal Codes he tried to follow just to get to her.

Chapter Twelve

Kris and Kiki both looked towards the sky when the thunder began. They'd both given their jackets to Hannah, whose step was growing slower the farther they went into the jungle. Kiki muttered but didn't openly bitch, probably knowing Kris had no patience for anyone insulting his mate.

"How far was the place you saw?" Kris addressed Kiki with a worried look towards Hannah.

"It didn't seem far. I would've thought we'd be there by now."

"Can you check again?"

Kiki gave him a fiery look but moved to the nearest tree. Kris watched him scale the large tree and disappear beyond the canopy of leaves.

"I hope it's close," Hannah said. She sagged against a tree.

Kris sat beside her. Hannah's skin had gone from pale to gray, and her features looked gaunt. He couldn't help thinking Katie wouldn't survive a week down here if Hannah was suffering so badly after a day. He touched Hannah's hair, revolted when a handful came off in his hand.

Hannah looked down at it then at him. Her blue eyes had turned dark, and Kris shook the hair off his hands. He tried to smile reassuringly.

"It's just the underworld. When we're home, it'll grow back. Don't worry, love."

She didn't look convinced. Kris moved away her, his anxiety and concern growing. They'd come there to rescue one human and might just lose two. He paced and gazed up the tree, unable to see Kiki. He heard Hannah stir and glanced towards her. She rose from her seat.

"Kris, I think I – " She was cut off by a shout.

Kris looked up in time to see Kiki crash through the canopy and plummet towards the ground. Kris gasped and sprung forward. A streak of black crossed his vision as a flying demon snatched Kiki out of the air.

"Kiki!" he bellowed. Instinctively, he reached for his power, only to find it bound by the magic of the underworld. He was as helpless as a stupid human. "Hannah, wait here. I'll – "

Hannah was gone. Kris spun in time to see her disappear around a large tree, deeper into the jungle. Kris looked between the two before taking off after Hannah.

"Hannah!" he shouted. "Hannah, stop! We'll leave here together – don't worry about your body!"

"Kris!" Kiki's yell was pain-filled.

Kris stopped, torn.

Duty before all else. It had been Andre's mantra, and Kris had always done what he thought Andre would've wanted. He'd lost Lilith when Rhyn killed her and their son. He'd given up Jade, the man who held his soul, to take Katie as a mate, only to have Rhyn interfere again. Paralyzed by indecision, Kris struggled to determine which Andre would've wanted him to do: save his brother or his mate. Of the two, Hannah was weaker, but Kiki was his *brother*.

"I can't lose her," he said, sweating with fear. Kris started forward again, pursuing Hannah. He ran as fast as he could through the unfriendly forest, cursing Death for stripping his power.

Hannah's blond hair flashed through the trees. As fast as Kris ran, he couldn't catch her. He grew more baffled when she seemed to pull ahead of him without any sign of the exhaustion she'd showed when they stopped. Desperation could motivate, and so could fear for her sister. He pushed himself harder to catch her.

Thunder boomed overhead. Forms he assumed were demons swooped above the canopy, casting shadows. He caught glimpses of fur and wings through leaves and ran until his chest was heaving. Hannah remained ahead of him, though he realized he was beginning to gain on her. He had to reach her before the demons did and swept her away, as they had Kiki.

Suddenly, Hannah stopped. Kris barreled towards her. He glimpsed movement before he burst into the small clearing. It wasn't until he leapt over the final hurdle – a massive fallen tree – did he see what stopped her. One moment she stood with her back to him. The next, she was on the ground, Rhyn's dagger dripping with blood.

A similar scene flashed before Kris. One from long ago, when another blond woman had fallen to the devil that was his brother.

"*No!*" His scream was inhuman even to his ears.

Rhyn looked up, and Kris charged him. He knocked Rhyn to the ground, wrestling the dagger free, and lashed out. Instinct and fury blinded him. He felt the dagger sink into flesh and struck again, only to find himself flying backwards through the air. Rhyn shouted something at him, but Kris couldn't hear him, not with the memory of both Lilith and Hannah dying.

"I should've done this years ago!" he shouted at the half-demon. "You never should've been born, Rhyn! You should've been strangled the moment you hatched!"

"What the fuck, Kris! It's not— "

Kris launched at him again. Rhyn spun and flung him away again. Kris charged, and they toppled to the ground.

Pain filtered through his frenzy, but he refused to stop, channeling all his fury towards the creature that earned it the day it was born.

Magic shot through him, burning like fire. Kris gasped. Another blast, and he fell to the ground. His body roiled with the demon magic, convulsing until the blow faded. He felt himself hauled up by his neck and thrust onto the ground again. His vision blurry, Kris could only see Hannah's beautiful blond hair. Sorrow replaced anger, and he reached out, touching the soft wheat curls.

He'd lost them all. Lilith, Jade, Hannah. Even Andre. He'd not only failed every Immortal that ever lived, he'd failed the only people he'd ever cared for. He lay on the ground, gasping as he tangled his fingers in Hannah's hair.

Rhyn snatched him again and shoved Hannah onto her back. Fury built in Kris again at the disregard for his mate, until he saw her face.

He stared. It was not Hannah lying beside him but a demon with blond hair. Kris pulled his legs beneath him to sit, and Rhyn released him.

"As I was trying to tell you, it's not Hannah," Rhyn said and kicked the dead demon. "Hannah's alive. I've seen her."

"What the fuck is this?" Kris managed at last.

"Shapeshifter demons. Darkyn replaced Hannah and Gabe with them," Rhyn said and squatted. "You're welcome, you fucking idiot."

Kris looked at him, anger building. The muscular half-demon was bleeding from a wound in his chest. His dark eyes glowed like a demon's, though his face was still that of an Immortal.

"I think you helped me," Rhyn said. "I couldn't get to my demon powers until you almost killed me."

"Rhyn ... " Kris said, gaze on the nasty wound.

"I only need to live 'til the end of the day," Rhyn said with an unconcerned glance on the wound. "You came instead of sending someone to stop me?"

It took Kris a moment to regain himself. "We came. Hannah, Kiki and me."

"Where's Kiki?"

"Demons grabbed him." Another thought struck Kris. He couldn't tell Rhyn he'd chosen to save Hannah instead of Kiki, only to discover a shapeshifter demon in Hannah's place.

Rhyn's jaw clenched, and he looked up at the sky. He stood and hauled Kris to his feet, indicating the forest.

"You said Hannah is safe?" Kris asked.

"Relatively safe."

"What does that mean?"

"She's in Hell."

"What?"

"She's with Ully and Toby. They're fine."

"How do you incorporate *Hell* and *fine* in the same sentence?" Kris demanded.

"With all your ruckus, you've probably drawn the attention of the demons. We need to move."

"Rhyn," Kris grabbed his arm. "You got us into this mess. We're leaving, before anyone else gets hurt."

"Do whatever you want, Kris," Rhyn replied, yanking his arm away. "But I'm not leaving without Katie and Kiki."

"We can do more good by engaging Death from some place other than where she has absolute power. She has no reason to negotiate with us."

"Or, we can do things my way for once."

Kris watched him stalk away, unable to shake a sense of guilt. If he'd gone after Kiki, he wouldn't have put his half-brother at even greater risk. His judgment had failed him. As he stood alone in the jungle, Kris couldn't help feeling as though he'd failed some test, one Rhyn wouldn't fail.

"Wait, Rhyn. I'm coming with you," he said and trotted after the half-demon. "Do you have a plan?"

"What is it with you and Kiki and your plans?" Rhyn growled.

"We know you're the brawn, not the brains."

"Apparently, you're neither."

"You are totally justified saying that. I almost killed you."

"No, Kris, you deserved that for letting our brother get taken by demons."

Kris slowed, hearing Andre's message in Rhyn's voice.

"What do you care, demon?" he snapped. "You spent your life in Hell after fucking up mine. And now, you're going to do the stupidest thing any Immortal has ever done, and condemn everyone."

"Maybe. Or maybe this will work."

"Negotiating with Death? Even Andre couldn't manage that."

"Have you met her?"

"Of course," Kris said. "Before we left, she talked to me about some dream I didn't have then started to talk about philosophy."

"Sounds about right. Everyone's got a weakness that can be leveraged, Kris."

"What is hers?"

"I'm still working on that, but I think it's Gabe."

"Dammit, Rhyn, I'm serious. What if you bring down both worlds just by forcing us all to come here?"

"You *chose* to be here, Kris," Rhyn said. "You chose to leave Kiki. You chose to let Jade go and turn a blind eye to him being a traitor. You chose not to see Hannah was a shapeshifter."

"I put my duty first." Even as he said the words, Kris couldn't ignore the part of him that pointed out where he'd failed. "I can't say your choices have been any better."

"We both tried and fucked up. At least I have the backbone to admit it."

Kris said nothing. Rhyn's assurances that Hannah was safe in Hell didn't sit well with him. Kris followed the half-demon without knowing where they might be headed, instead thinking of just how bad of a situation he'd left Kiki in.

Death was right. Kris didn't have what it took to keep the Council together. He may have just lost one of his brothers, because he lost focus of what he should've done. Maybe he should've known Jade was a traitor or Hannah was a demon. He hadn't known of Andre's danger or been able to bring the Council together to fight the demons that threatened them all. He hadn't been able to keep Hannah safe or Toby or Katie.

His eyes went to Rhyn's back as his half-brother hacked through a few branches in their way. The sense that the exiled half-demon could do what he couldn't returned. Kris touched his collarbone, the one Jade had broken. If not for Rhyn, Jade might've killed him a few days ago.

He didn't believe Rhyn would've made the right decisions all along, but he couldn't deny that the half-demon wasn't the creature he remembered Andre sending to Hell.

None of it mattered now, however. Kris had responsibilities, and he had to find a way to fulfill them the best he could.

Rhyn stopped and knelt, placing his hands to the ground. Kris crossed his arms. A blast of energized air swept over him. Rhyn sat back.

"What did you just do?" Kris asked, looking around for any change in their surroundings.

"One person can help us. I just encouraged her to come find us."

Coldness settled over Kris. He gazed around warily. Rhyn rose and flipped the dagger he held in the air, catching it effortlessly.

"Did you tell her off or ask nicely?" Kris asked. The jungle stilled around them, and the snake-like branches froze.

Rhyn responded by pulling a dagger from the small of his back and tossing it. Kris caught it by the hilt and waited, the sound of his heart pounding loud in his ears.

They waited.

Chapter Thirteen

Katie heard Deidre's footsteps stop abruptly and turned around. The woman was facing the opposite direction.

"Deidre, we should hurry," she called.

"I hear something."

Katie listened hard and soon heard it as well. It sounded like a herd of horses plowing through the jungle.

"Demons," Toby said. "We can take the trees, but sometimes they drop you."

"Sounds like hundreds of them," Deidre said, troubled.

"I told you there were—"

"Not now, Toby," Katie said. "We need to get to safety, and I don't have enough food to blow up the amount of trees it'll take to stop a herd of demons."

"Trees!" Toby yelled. "Hold onto them, Mama."

Before Katie could respond, one of the nearby trees snatched her and flung her into the air. She soared above the treetops and let out a cry when she started to fall. A branch caught her and flung her back up. She saw Deidre and Toby sailing through the air in a similar fashion. The second branch almost missed her and snatched her around the leg before throwing her back up.

She gritted her teeth in pain and sucked in a breath as she started to fall again. She glimpsed demons hovering a short distance away over an opening in the jungle. They looked like massive, angry hornets before disappearing from her line of sight. A branch grabbed her arm this time and threw her back over the treetops. This time, she faced a different direction and saw a sprawling palace the size of a mall. They were closer than she thought.

Deidre screamed, and Katie twisted in midair. The woman was tumbling towards the treetops. Branches snatched at her and missed, and Deidre fell through the canopy to the jungle below.

"Toby!" Katie cried. "Toby, Deidre —" A branch grabbed her around the chest, squeezing out the air in her lungs. When she was sailing again, she looked around for Deidre and Toby. The angel was soaring through the air, head over feet, but Deidre was nowhere to be seen.

Helpless until the trees finished flinging them around, Katie struggled to grab the branches, so she didn't end up like Deidre. Finally, a branch wrapped around her and pulled her through the canopy, dumping her at the edge of the jungle. Toby landed with a grunt beside her, and she lay still to catch her breath, still hoping Deidre reappeared.

"Deidre's okay," Toby said.

"The trees got her?"

"More or less."

Katie rolled onto her stomach, almost too tired to get up. The sky and jungle were growing dark. Through the bramble, she saw the marble palace. Death's palace. Katie's heart beat harder as she looked at her destination, not at all certain this was where she should've gone but not knowing where else to go.

The sound of the demons' pursuit reached her again. She stood on wobbly legs and all but dragged Toby to his feet.

"Toby, come on."

The angel found his footing and took her hand. They raced through the last of the jungle and across the expanse of grassless yard between the jungle and the palace. The sounds of demons grew louder.

Katie sought an entrance into the palatial estate, not seeing one along this side. She ran alongside the marble structure. It was well over quarter mile in length. Toby pulled away from her suddenly, and she stopped so fast, she tripped.

"Dammit, Toby, come on!" she yelled.

He faced the jungle. The trees were battling demons, but one then a few then a dozen of the creatures escaped the jungle's grip to pursue.

"You know any more tricks?" she asked him, taking his hand again.

"I'm a failure!" he wailed.

"Jesus, Toby, it's no time for a fucking meltdown. Come on." She pulled, and he ran.

Katie felt the ground shake beneath them as the demons pursued. Several flew overhead and dropped directly in their path. She stopped and shoved Toby behind her, drawing the knife Gabe had given her. Before long, they were surrounded.

"Toby!" a male voice yelled.

"Gabe!" the angel cried.

Katie pressed back against the wall of the palace. The demons gathered around them, and she saw the flash of Gabe's weapons as he tried to cut a path through the creatures towards them. The death-dealer went down as three demons dog-piled him.

"Gabe!" Katie shouted. He reappeared, blood flying with his weapons.

"Oh, no." Toby tugged at her arm.

Katie tore her eyes away from Gabe to follow where Toby was pointing, hoping to see Rhyn. It wasn't Rhyn or anyone else she expected to see, and she gasped.

"She'll be killed!" she exclaimed, watching a disheveled Deidre march from the forest towards them.

The petite woman started to run, ignoring the demons that swiped at her with talons large enough to take off her head with one swipe. She seemed immune to the demons' strikes. They fell away, as if hitting an invisible shield. The bizarre display drew more than Katie and Toby's attention. A ripple went through the demons, and they turned to watch the tiny woman sprinting towards them with flashing blue eyes.

"Is she insane?" Katie breathed. "What is she doing?"

"She's pissed," Toby said and sank behind Katie.

Deidre reached the group of demons. Rather than attack her, they parted, inching away from her. Speechless, Katie watched her approach. The demons fell silent, and even those fighting Gabe stopped.

"Go inside," Deidre said, stopping in front of Katie. "I'll take care of this."

"Nice of you to show up," Gabe snapped.

"You're … Death," Katie said, stunned.

"To you, I'm Deidre," Death said. "I liked being Deidre."

"I …I liked you being Deidre," Katie stammered. Her gaze traveled to Gabe, who was bloodied and beaten. Suddenly, Deidre's vague story of lost love and Gabe's bitterness towards her clicked.

"Go inside and wait for me."

Katie turned away and snatched Toby's hand. They approached the demons tentatively, waiting for the quiet creatures to attack rather than move. As if under a trance, the demons moved away in synchronized steps. Katie ran.

"Gabe, clean up this mess," she heard Death say.

"Working on it," Gabe growled.

Toby took the lead, and the demons, Death and Gabe disappeared as Katie rounded the corner of the palace. The angel released her and raced into the palace and up a set of stairs. They ascended several floors, until Katie was sucking wind bad enough to stop. Toby didn't wait for her, and she stumbled forward. The interior of the palace was unlit, and the darkness of evening crept into the hallways.

She stopped, but Toby yanked her forward.

"We have to *go!*" he shouted.

"She said to wait."

"Mama, if Death –"

"If Death what, Toby?" Deidre demanded, materializing beside them.

Toby mumbled. Katie made out the words *dead-dead* and *underworld*.

"What he's saying is that I'll kill you," Deidre said. "Toby, I could've done that yesterday."

"Worst. Angel. Ever," Toby said, his eyes watering. "I'm so sorry, Mama."

"But I won't," Death added. "You have a lot to learn, Toby, but you've done the best you can. It wouldn't have been enough, if there weren't other issues, but you got lucky. Sometimes, that's half of what Fate is."

"I'm proud of you, Toby," Katie said, seeing the look that crossed Toby's face. "No normal ten-year-old would've come to the underworld to find me."

"I'm twelve," Toby said miserably.

"Seriously?" Katie cleared her throat, not sure what else to say. She looked from Toby to Death. "What happens now?"

"I want you to remember Deidre, not Death," the petite woman said. "It would be nice to be remembered for something other than stealing the souls of loved ones."

"I can do that," Katie said. "We made a good pair in the jungle."

"We survived," Deidre said with a small smile. "I don't have much time. Toby, take her to the portal."

Toby gasped. Realization broke over Katie and with it, joy. She flung her arms around Deidre and hugged the small woman tightly.

"Mama!" Toby cried in shock and pried her away.

Deidre offered one of her amused smiles. "You should go quickly, before I change my mind, my dear."

"One more question," Katie said. "What about Andre? I know I saw him."

"You saw his ghost. I took his form first but found it lacking."

"So he's dead-dead."

"But you are not. Hazel is safe. She'll be a beautiful woman – if you leave now."

Katie couldn't help the bubble of happy laughter that escaped. Death chuckled with her then motioned to the stairwell Toby was desperately trying to pull Katie towards. They ran through the palace. Katie trailed the angel until they reached a small chamber she would've mistaken as a janitor's closet on the top level. Toby wrenched open the door and ducked into the dark room. A portal glowed in the center. Katie entered, overwhelmed by the thought of leaving.

"Toby," she managed. "What about Rhyn?"

"That's between him and Death," Toby said. "She's breaking Immortal Code to let you go. We have to leave, before she changes her mind."

"I don't want to leave without Rhyn."

"He has a better chance of making it if you're not here," Toby said. He tugged her towards the portal. "Everyone has to deal with Death on their own. Please, *pleeeeeeease* come with me, Mama! We have to take you to the Sanctuary. You're still not alive or dead yet. We have to make you alive."

"Can we come back through for Rhyn?"

"Um, yes."

Katie had never been so happy to step into the eerie shadow world.

Chapter Fourteen

Death didn't come. Darkness fell, and Rhyn waited. He paced and stretched, imagining there would be some kind of a struggle. At long last, he forced himself to admit she wasn't coming. No one could've overlooked the blow he dealt her underworld. The trees all around them had died off with a tear forming in the earth that led in the direction of the palace.

"How long are we staying here?" Kris asked at last. "Not that I don't enjoy your company."

Rhyn snorted in amusement. "The feeling is mutual. You're the reason I spent so much time in Hell."

"You earned your place in Hell, Rhyn."

Kris's confident response rankled Rhyn. He leaned his back against a tree and faced his eldest surviving brother.

"I promised Kiki I'd tell you something," he started. "But I don't want to. It won't help you in your duties."

"I do my best, but I'm as flawed as any Immortal. I just hope our brothers see that I'm trying."

"They see it. And they know you're wounded by this business with Jade and Andre. Anyway," Rhyn said. "That's not what I promised to tell you."

"What is it?"

"Lilith."

Kris's sigh of aggravation came out as a hiss.

"She was working for the Dark One," Rhyn said.

"Let her serve out her eternity in peace, Rhyn. I don't appreciate you dishonoring her more than you did."

"I swear it, Kris. She was planted by the demons. I don't know why they chose you, but they did, and you're the one she came after. She reeked of demon, Kris. I'd be surprised if the hatchling she carried was yours."

"Stop there, Rhyn. Whatever reason you have for talking about her this way – just stop."

"Why would I lie about this now?" Rhyn challenged, irritated. "I served fucking *lifetimes* in Hell and kept my mouth closed. I killed her to protect you. Andre always taught me that loyalty was all that mattered."

"You want me to believe you killed my lover to protect me, never told me she was a demon-spy, and you went willingly to Hell. It's ridiculous, Rhyn, even for you!"

Rhyn clamped his mouth shut. He'd done what Kiki asked him to, and Kris didn't believe him. He was ready to go silent on it again for the rest of eternity. He turned to leave then stopped.

"I saved your life twice, and you continue to treat me like shit," he said. "You care more for the honor of a dead-dead woman who betrayed you."

"While I'm grateful you saved me from Jade, you're still half-animal, Rhyn."

"I'm also half-Immortal. I have as much of our father in me as you do," Rhyn said.

"Look, Rhyn, none of this matters. I'm willing to go ahead and forgive you for what you did so long ago. It's still hard for me to think I could've raised a successor and not buried a son," Kris said.

"I don't give a shit about your forgiveness, Kris. Think about it. What do I have to gain by telling you about Lilith now?"

"Maybe you just want to hit me while I'm down."

"Down?" Rhyn echoed and looked at Kris. "If this is what you call down, you need to spend some time in Hell. If you don't believe me, I don't give a shit. But I fulfilled my part of the deal I made with Kiki."

"What does Kiki know about this?" For the first time, Rhyn heard a note of uneasiness replace the self-assuredness in Kris's voice.

"He knows Lilith was evil."

"He's not here to defend himself from whatever you say about him."

"Andre knew," Rhyn said quietly. "Andre always knew. It's why he didn't kill me. You ever wonder why he let me live, even after what I'd done to you? I didn't know it at the time, but he was doing me a favor. He was putting me some place safe. He knew I deserved a second chance, long before Katie, long before I realized it myself."

Kris was silent for a moment before saying slowly, "Kiki said I always had a penchant for traitors."

Rhyn could almost see him thinking. In the end, Kris said nothing else, and Rhyn shook his head. For the first time, he'd tried to reason with Kris. He'd never do it again.

"I'm sick of waiting," he said.

"I have a feeling she's waiting for you to come to her," Kris said at last. "And she'll never let us leave her alive."

"Back to the palace," Rhyn said with a glance towards the dark sky. It was the last day he could press Death for a favor. If they didn't leave tonight, they may never escape with Katie alive. He took off running toward the palace, his demon vision guiding him in the darkness. Kris followed closely, and they burst onto the yards surrounding the palace.

Gabe and a few other assassins in black fought off hordes of demons. Surprised, Rhyn launched into the melee with his dagger. He slashed through several demons before the creatures realized he was there. Wanting to keep them off balance, he morphed into his demon form and shredded the creatures with talons and fangs as deadly as theirs.

Only when he reached Gabe did he return to his Immortal form. The death-dealer's clothing was tattered from demon strikes, his body smelling of blood sure to incense the creatures he fought. Despite this, the assassin's speed and strikes didn't falter. Each was sure and powerful. Rhyn maneuvered until his back was to Gabe's, and he reached back to snatch the knife Gabe kept strapped to one thigh. While Gabe showed no sign of slowing, Rhyn could feel the wound Kris inflicted slowing his movements. At least Kris hadn't stabbed him with the enforcer dagger, or Rhyn would be dead.

"Thanks for … dropping by," Gabe grunted with his dark humor.

"I'm always late, but I always show." Rhyn flung one knife, catching a demon in the eye. The demon that had been ready to run Kris through dropped, and Kris shot him an angry look. "You're welcome, jackass."

"Still fighting?" Gabe asked.

"Where's Death?" Rhyn demanded.

"Inside. Or wherever. She left us to deal with the demons. We've lost five assassins already. I hoped she'd recall more but …"

"She's pissed at you."

"Yeah."

"She want you dead-dead?"

"She wants to make sure I suffer," Gabe answered.

"An eternity of her nagging you wasn't enough?"

Gabe snorted. "Kris! Form up with us. Rhyn's slow on his left. Pick up his slack."

"I'm *slow* because someone stabbed me."

"You had that coming," Kris snapped and joined them, following Gabe's direction.

"Rhyn, Death's got Katie inside."

Fear made Rhyn's chest seize. No sooner had Gabe spoken the words than the demons fell away. Coldness snapped over Rhyn, and his surroundings blurred. He blinked, uncertain what happened until he found himself standing in a dimly lit chamber. Kris and Gabe were still beside him, and instead of demons, there was only Death.

He heard a groan from nearby and lowered his weapons, the first to step away to see whose body lay before Her. It was Kiki's. Rhyn smelled blood before he saw the soaked clothing of his half-brother. Ignoring Death, Rhyn rolled Kiki onto his back. The Immortal was alive, but barely. Satisfied, Rhyn rose, towering over the tiny woman with flaxen hair.

"Darkyn won this round," she said.

"What did you do with Katie?" Rhyn demanded. A quick look around the chamber showed no sign of his mate.

"You led him here, Rhyn, a sin made worse by the fact my own weakness made my domain vulnerable. But, I'm going to remedy this."

"I don't give a shit! Where – "

Death held out two small emeralds, and Rhyn's breath left him. She snapped them back up in her hand and put them in the pocket of her pants.

"You *swore* you'd free her!" he whispered, stricken.

"I can give her back to you," Death said slowly. "But it means this." She held out her hand again. A hologram-like image appeared in her hand.

Rhyn saw the demons pouring from the skies over major cities in the mortal worlds. He turned away, not wanting to care about the cost of getting his mate back.

"Look at it!" Death commanded.

His body obeyed her, and he found himself struggling against himself not to turn around. Death won the fight for his body, and he watched. Demons slaughtered humans and Immortals alike, razing the mortal world.

"This happened once before, long ago," Death said and held out her other hand. "Gabe remembers. This is when I found him."

Rhyn saw the young man he assumed was Gabriel fighting demons.

"It was stopped by the Dark One, who knew what I'd do if he didn't stop it," she said. "Darkyn led this assault without the Dark One's permission. He was banished deep into Hell. This time, I can do nothing, and they know it. If you ask me, I will give Katie and your child back to you. The price will be this." She held up the hand holding the scenes of demons destroying the mortal world.

Protect what's left of good in the world.

Rhyn gripped and released the dagger, struggling between the tiny voice that reminded him of his promise to Katie and the vision before him. If he took back his mate and child, there would be nowhere safe for them to go. But he didn't want to live eternity without her.

"Rhyn … " Kris murmured. "You have a duty to protect all mortals, not just one."

"Will you take my soul in exchange for Katie's?" Rhyn asked.

"If she were alive, that might work. Once I claim a soul, the price climbs. And in this case, the price is beyond my control," Death answered.

Rhyn stared at the scenes playing out in Death's outstretched hands. His heart grew heavy as he watched demons kill humans by the hundreds. The promise he'd made to keep Katie happy made him feel sick, and *duty* would never fill the hollow part of him that would remain during a lifetime without his mate.

"Choose, demon," Death ordered him. "Your mate or the fate of humanity."

Maybe Katie had known this was how it would end when they'd last met in his dream. Maybe this was his penance for being what he was. Rhyn didn't know, but he knew he couldn't choose his own interests over those of humanity.

"Is she safe and happy?" he asked.

"She is," Death answered. "I made certain of that."

"As much as I love her, I can't condemn her kind to the demons."

Death lowered the hand displaying the end of the world scenario. The images of Gabe fighting demons switched to those of Katie on the beach under the moonlight. Rhyn's breath caught at the sight of her. She appeared exhausted, tattered, and drenched from the underworld rain. She'd never looked as beautiful as she did, even if she looked as if she'd just left the underworld. Toby was with her, pulling her from the beach towards the Sanctuary.

"What the fuck is this?" he demanded.

"You let her go?" Gabe asked in surprise.

"You were right, Gabe," Death said. "You'll never hear those words again."

"She's not dead-dead," Rhyn said, afraid to believe the images he saw. He searched Death's impassive features.

"I had to know you could serve a purpose greater than yourself," Death said to Rhyn.

He stared at her, certain he'd throttle her if Gabe didn't eventually.

"But, that leaves us in a difficult position. There are four of you here. A contract was put out for two souls, and two souls were sent to my underworld. Unfortunately, they left before I could claim them. Which means, I need two souls to fulfill the contract."

"I can't believe you freed Katie," Rhyn said. "Is this a trick?"

"I made you a promise, didn't I?"

"You broke rules older than you," Gabe said, moving to stand beside Rhyn. "Even you are not allowed to so without some sort of consequence."

"I never should've interfered, Gabriel. I set things right. So what if I broke a Code or two to right things?" Death said with a shrug.

"You are sworn—"

"No time for a lovers' spat," Rhyn interrupted. "Tell me what it'll take for us to get the fuck out of here."

Death turned her attention to him. "I told you. I need souls."

"Easy. Mine," Rhyn said.

"Not yours."

"Mine is the most obvious choice."

"I get to choose who I take, and I don't want yours. Maybe the Immortal who issued the contract for two souls should step up," Death said. "It would be a noble death for a good cause."

"I don't have time to track down whoever it was that crossed you," Rhyn snapped. "Take mine, send everyone else back."

"Even if I took yours, that's *one*. Or do demons not know how to count?"

"Demons aren't known for thinking," Gabe said. "You've got a mate and child, Rhyn. Take mine."

"It's raining souls now," Death said and pursed her lips. "I own you already, Gabe."

"*You* own me, but I'm not dead-dead," he argued. "If I'm not mistaken, the souls of your assassins are more of a personal collection than an official one."

"Minor details."

"Mine," Gabe said, stepping closer to her.

"Fine. That's one," she said. "Another soul, or I can still claim Katie or her child."

"Am I the only one who hears me?" Rhyn demanded. "Take. Mine. Be done with this nonsense. Leave my mate and my hatchling alone!"

"Not yours!" Death snapped. "You're making me second guess myself, Rhyn. Don't be so stupid."

"There *is* no one else!"

"Mine."

Rhyn turned, surprised. He'd forgotten Kris's presence. The Council leader stepped forward.

"No," Rhyn said. "You'll take mine, Death, if you take anyone's."

"It's my choice, Rhyn," Kris said. "It's the right thing to do."

"The Council needs you."

"The Council needs *you*."

"As you and everyone else like to remind me, I'm the brawn, not the brains," Rhyn said.

"I issued the contract to Gabe."

Rhyn stared.

"It was for Katie and someone else, someone you killed. I didn't know about your child. I didn't know Katie would end up your mate. In truth, it might not have altered my decision, but it's a little late for holding millennia-old grudges," Kris explained. "You chose your duty over your mate. You are more fit to lead the Immortals than I'll ever be."

"Done," Death said, pleased.

"Wait, it's *not* done," Rhyn said and approached Kris. "You can't be serious, Kris. I'm the last person you want in charge of something important."

"Andre always saw something in you that I never saw, until now," Kris said with some difficulty. "You made a selfless choice, one I've failed to make more than once. Besides, I ordered Katie killed. I alone can make this right."

"Kris—"

"I thought about what you said in the forest, about Lilith. Kiki said something before he left that makes me think you're not lying. If what you said is true, you do deserve a second chance, Rhyn," Kris continued. "Swear to me you'll keep the Council together. Father and Andre always said we were stronger together than apart. I was unwilling to do whatever it took to keep them together. But you will."

Rhyn saw the resolution on Kris's face.

"I swear it," Rhyn said.

"And, free Hannah from Hell."

"I'll march into Hell and confront Darkyn myself."

"Don't make me regret this," Kris said and shook his head. "Just get her out."

"I will, Kris."

"Oddly enough, I believe you." Kris said. He strode past Rhyn to stand before Death.

Rhyn watched, torn between defending his brother as he'd done before and letting Kris go. Even in Hell, Rhyn comforted himself with the knowledge that he'd protected his brothers.

"I'm happy to call you my brother, Rhyn," Kris said. His gaze focused on Death. "I'm ready."

His words made Rhyn's throat tighten. He'd never acted in order to gain his brothers' favor, but Kris's words affected him more than he thought they would. There was a flash of light and Kris was gone. Gabe jerked, as if surprised to find himself still standing.

Death held out her closed hand to Rhyn. He crept forward warily and extended his. She dropped a small green gem into it.

"You can keep it," she said.

He looked at it hard, not sure what to think about holding Kris's soul in his palm.

"Why am I still here?" Gabe asked tersely. "You got your two souls."

"I'm sure you noticed that my domain in overrun with demons," Death said casually. "My ... interference put the underworld—and all the little humans' souls—at risk, weakened the barriers between here and Hell. You were right, Gabe. Even my actions have consequences."

Rhyn lowered his hand, the strange note in her voice warning him the game wasn't over.

"Darkyn won this round," she said again. "I can dispel the demons, but they'll return. As long as I am here, the barrier will remain weak. There are Codes older than me, older even than my predecessors. I have no choice. I interfered, and now I must relinquish my title. I'm leaving."

"Leaving?" Gabe echoed, gaping. "What do you mean you're leaving?"

"I'm going through the portal. Wherever it takes me, is where I'll go."

"And the demons and souls?" Rhyn asked as Gabe stood, speechless. "What about them?"

"I always thought Gabe's humanity made him weak. It appears my inhumanity did me in," she mused. "The underworld will still exist. It just won't be my problem anymore."

"Whose problem will it be?" Rhyn asked, his gaze going to Gabe.

"It looks like I'll be promoting my best assassin before I leave," Death responded. "Don't make the mistakes I did, Gabe. And get rid of the demons." And with that, she strode past them both, towards the door. "I'm leaving now. Rhyn, you'll want to be gone before I cross through the portal, or Gabe won't be able to send you back. Gabe can't break that many Codes his first day on the job."

Rhyn grunted as he pulled Kiki over his shoulders. He feared the palace would go down with Death, what with the nonsense she was spouting about leaving. He took in his best friend's features, uncertain whether becoming Death was a good thing or not. Gabe looked the same, and hopefully, he wouldn't turn into the riddle-talking sociopath that preceded him.

Gabe shifted finally and faced him. "What the fuck just happened?"

"Don't change, Gabe," Rhyn said. "I'm getting out of here. If what she says is true, you can come visit whenever you want."

The death-dealer looked around, lost. Rhyn moved away and drew off his demon power to call forth a portal.

"Gabe," he said, pausing before he stepped through. "You'll make a good Death."

"I fucked up this time, if this is what I get," Gabe said, regaining himself at last. "Eternity at the day job I was trying so hard to leave."

"No, I think she fucked you up."

"She'll be the first soul I hunt down."

"If the Council can help, let me know," Rhyn half-joked.

They gazed at each other, and Gabe shook his head, a smile spreading across his features.

"At least we're a good match for Darkyn," he said.

"Maybe that's why things ended up this way," Rhyn said, his humor fading as he thought of Kris. He looked at the emerald in his palm.

"You can't save him, but you can save Kiki. Get going, Rhyn."

"We'll see you around, Gabe."

"Yeah."

Rhyn stepped into the portal. He crossed fast and leapt through the portal leading to the Caribbean Sanctuary. No sooner had he hit the sandy beach than the restraints of the underworld fled, knocking him off his feet. His body bucked under the influence of power. Sudden pain shot through him, followed by the sensation of his magic snapping back into a bond too strong for him to access.

Rhyn gasped and struggled to sit. Kiki's still body lay a few feet from him, the ocean lapping at his brother's feet. The Caribbean night was humid and warm, and the moon large over head.

"I told you that you needed me," Toby grumbled. "You've got a couple hours until midnight."

Disoriented, Rhyn glanced down and pulled the syringe out of his thigh, where the angel had stabbed him.

"Where are you getting these fucking things?" Rhyn gasped.

"Well … maybe you should get Hannah and Ully out before Jared eats them. I can tell you that stuff later."

"Where's Katie?"

"I brought her back!" Toby said, beaming. "She's at the Sanctuary."

"I want to see her."

"No. Go get Hannah. If Death let you go, then Darkyn's pissed. If Darkyn's pissed then—"

"Hannah and Ully are in trouble," Rhyn finished and rose. He looked at the wound in his chest. It might be tough taking on the demons of Hell, but he had a promise to fulfill. "Take Kiki back to the Sanctuary's healer."

"Me?"

"You see anyone else here?"

Toby looked at the unconscious Immortal twice his size and back up at Rhyn. Rhyn pointed. The angel sighed and crossed to Kiki. Rhyn opened a new portal, took a deep breath and crossed through to Hell.

He emerged outside the jailer's door and readied himself for a confrontation. The sounds of activity were thick in the hallways behind him, and he listened, trying to determine if he could hear any sounds that the demons were victorious in the underworld. His instincts warned him to hurry, that he had a reason to grab Hannah and go instead of sticking around to see what was causing the activity.

Rhyn opened the door, surprised to find the jailer's room empty. He'd expected Jared at least. He closed the door quietly behind him. He snatched the talisman hanging near the door, the one that freed inmates from their cells. He ignored the quickening of his pulse as he entered the familiar cell block.

He heard Hannah crying and smelled the unmistakable scent of human blood before he took a step onto the block. He strode down the block and paused in front of Hannah's cell. She was curled up on the bed, sobbing. When he looked at the cell across from her, he saw why. Jared stood in the cell, covered in blood. The cell looked as if a human had exploded, and Rhyn saw a pile of bones Jared had gnawed clean then stacked neatly.

"Ully didn't make it," Jared said.

"I see that."

"I didn't touch the cupcake."

"Good for you," Rhyn said. He placed the talisman on the door frame of Hannah's cell. The door opened.

"Are we still good? You taking me with you?" Jared asked.

"I'll do you a favor," Rhyn said. He grimaced at the pain in his chest as he hefted Hannah into his arms. "I'll leave you right there instead of tearing you limb-from-limb."

"Fuck you, Rhyn."

Rhyn ignored the demon and left the cell block, returning to the hallway before opening a portal. He crossed through the shadow world to the beach of the Caribbean Sanctuary. Toby was dragging Kiki up the beach by one leg.

"What the fuck, Toby? Go get help if you can't lift him!" he shouted at the young angel.

Toby dropped Kiki's leg and took off for the Sanctuary. Rhyn strode through the loose sand of the beach and paused beside Kiki. He set Hannah down.

"Hannah, walk," he ordered. "I can't carry you both." He hefted Kiki once again. Hannah sniffled and crawled to her feet. Rhyn hurried towards the Sanctuary, concerned for Kiki but even more anxious about making sure Katie was alive and well.

The convent members who managed the Sanctuary had replaced the wall Rhyn knocked down with a row of brown tents that matched their dresses. Rhyn eased between two of them, aware of Kiki's fading pulse. He set his brother down on the ground and looked around wildly, hoping they hadn't sent Katie's Ancient Healer, Lankha, home to the underworld.

"You!" he yelled at a member of the Sanctuary entering the courtyard. "Where's Lankha?"

"Sleeping. You're not— "

"Go get him."

The woman pursed her lips and crossed her arms, eyeing him.

"I'll get him," Toby shouted from across the courtyard.

Rhyn paced under the watchful gaze of the convent member, itching to leave Kiki to find Katie. Instead, he forced himself to wait. He'd lost one brother this night. He wanted to make sure Kiki was okay before leaving him.

Toby reappeared after a few minutes, tugging a reluctant Lakhna with him. The otherworldly creature ducked and covered his head from the moon and crowded Toby as they crossed the courtyard. Rhyn pointed to Kiki, and Lakhna cringed. Rhyn was about to demand to know where Katie was when he heard her agitated voice.

"You had to leave Hannah on the beach?"

Rhyn stopped in place. He'd never thought he'd hear her voice again, and he couldn't remember the last time he'd heard anything that stopped his world in place. He turned to see Katie supporting Hannah as they entered the Sanctuary courtyard. Katie wore simple jeans and a t-shirt. Her dark curls cascaded down her shoulders, and her face glowed. Her bright eyes locked on his. She stopped too far away for his comfort, struggling to support her sister.

"Toby. Get Hannah," Rhyn barked.

"Rhyn, I'm too little!" Toby whined.

"You've got to the count of five to have you both out of my sight."

Toby hesitated.

"One."

The angel darted forward and clumsily took Hannah's arms. Katie helped him stabilize Hannah then watched them walk away. Rhyn stared at his mate, heart beating fast. Of all the words in his head, none of them made it to his tongue.

"I see you made it back," Katie said awkwardly.

"You look better than I expected."

"Gee, thanks, Rhyn."

"I mean, you look beautiful for a dead woman."

She crossed her arms.

"I told you I'd get you back," he said and took a step towards her.

"Toby brought me back," she pointed out. "He said if you listened to him, you could've found me faster."

"That little shit."

Katie fought back a smile at the irritated look on Rhyn's face. He was in raw form: bloodied, drenched with underworld rain, disheveled, in need of a good shave. His thick frame was still on edge, as if he expected one of the Sanctuary's nuns to turn into a demon and fly at them. He looked every bit the muscular, powerful, glowering half-demon the nuns wanted to throw out of the Sanctuary.

She stepped closer to him as she had in their dream, gazing up into his molten silver eyes. He'd gone to Hell for Hannah and confronted Death for her. He'd killed demons to protect her and defied his family to find – and keep – her. Katie fought to keep the emotions tumbling within her from leaking out, instead reveling in the sight of her mate. While in the underworld, she'd lost all hope of ever standing next to him again. Part of her was convinced this was another dream, and Rhyn would disappear all too soon.

"It's not a dream," he said. "Not this time."

"Doesn't quite seem real yet, though."

He hesitated and then held out a hand. She took it. His warm hands were rough and large. He squeezed hers. He led her away from the courtyard and lights into the dark night. They walked hand in hand for a few moments, alone under the full moon. She'd walked with him before, but this night, it was different. She felt the shift between them.

"The hatchling really is a girl?" he asked.

"She's not a hatchling, Rhyn."

"I hope she comes out better behaved than Toby."

Katie laughed loudly, unable to help herself. Rhyn pulled her into his arms, swallowing her in his warmth and scent. Katie wrapped her arms around him.

"It's really over, isn't it?" she whispered.

"It's just us tonight. I've gotta go kill some demons in the morning."

"But you'll come right back."

"Every day. I swear it. We won't be apart anymore. We'll stay here until I can get the castle cleaned out and beat the shit out of my brothers. They'll be moving in, even if they don't know it yet. And that's where Hazel will hatch and live."

Katie's eyes watered, and she squeezed him harder. The nightmares of the past few weeks seemed to fade away while she was in his arms. She'd been too afraid to think about what kind of life they might possibly have, but she found herself wondering how it would feel to wake up and go to sleep with Rhyn beside her.

"Our life together starts right now. Unless you want to send me away," he added.

"Depends on how you behave," she said, smiling up at him through happy tears.

Rhyn grimaced. "I'm not promising any miracles. We got a lot to do to prepare the world for Hazel."

"I have faith in us."

"Right now, I owe my mate a rowdy night on the beach under the moonlight," he said. He swung her up into his arms and strode towards the water.

Katie laughed, happiness and hope bubbling within her. She took in Rhyn's strong profile. If anyone could save the world, it was him.

In Hell, Darkyn stood before the hourglass perched on a window sill in his study. The black sand had run out. He'd missed his window. Rather, he missed *this* window. He looked over at the demon standing before him. At least one of his super-demons had survived. This one still wore half a face, that of Death's favorite assassin, Gabriel.

"Chances are, the demons will be defeated this round," Darkyn said. "And Death … you're certain she walked away?"

"Yes, my lord. She quit and appointed Gabriel in her stead."

"Interesting. A Death with a history as a mortal. Not any mortal, but one you say she was in love with. I'd heard rumor but never thought a deity capable of such a thing."

"Rhyn's mortal was convinced of this. She said Gabriel had been the lover of Death for thousands of years."

"And now she's gone," Darkyn said.

"As far as we know. I didn't see her enter the portal, but one of our spies was in her fortress when she entered the chamber you indicated."

"Where would a deity in love with a mortal go?"

"To the mortal world," the super-demon guessed. "She's no threat to you, master."

"True," Darkyn said. "But the new Death is her lover. That makes her someone of interest to me."

"The immunity blood worked. We can have the Immortal scientist make us more. We could slide right into the – "

"Ully is dead-dead, as you will be by the time the day is over," Darkyn said. "I cannot have anyone else find out about the power of the immunity blood."

The demon before him looked down but didn't object, understanding his place. Unlike Immortals, demons obeyed their leaders. But maybe, next time, lack of discipline in his enemies would work for Darkyn. He'd failed to takeover Death's domain or to kill her. It would take Gabriel a very long time to learn how to rule over the dead, and Rhyn was a loose cannon as a leader for the Immortals. In the meantime, all of Rhyn's Immortals and Death's assassins would be a disorganized mess.

All Darkyn had to do was wait and watch for his opportunity. While he did so, he had a new plan: To pursue a certain deity who'd left her position to her lover. In all his dealings with Immortals and mortals, Darkyn long ago learned the weakness Immortals and mortals had for a beautiful woman. Gabriel would be no different.

"Leave me. Report to the executioner."

The super-demon bowed his head and left. Darkyn watched him go then looked again at the hourglass. He hadn't expected Death to quit, but she was about to give him a new window of opportunity, one that might be more powerful. He might soon take over the underworld and its army of souls.

Chapter Fifteen

Two weeks later

"Watsup, Gabe?" Rhyn's familiar voice interrupted Gabe's concentration.

"You're forbidden from entering, Rhyn."

"Sure, Gabe."

Gabriel looked up from his stance peering into the murky Lake of Souls. The half-demon appeared unconcerned about sliding through the barrier Gabe had been working hard to patch up. Rhyn looked happy and healthy, the opposite of how Gabe felt.

"You clean up good," he said. "You know I can claim your— "

"But you won't. I came to see how my only friend is doing," Rhyn said. "You need help killing demons?"

"I recalled all the assassins and put a hold on all soul collections for a week or so," Gabe answered. "The queue to get in here is longer than you'd guess."

"We're almost done exterminating the castle. I can send some help your way."

"I imagine you have your hands full dealing with the Immortals."

"Nothing I can't handle. I have Kiki, Tamer, and Erik on lockdown. A week without food, and they're happy to help. Kiki is running most things, until I figure them out."

"Sounds like it's going well," Gabe said, truly pleased to see his friend, despite the poor timing. "How's Katie?"

A small smile crossed Rhyn's face, answering Gabe's question without words.

"Then everything is going well. Good for you, Rhyn." He couldn't help but feel envious of his friend, who wasn't trapped in a world where he didn't belong, fighting demons.

"Katie sent these back with me," Rhyn said and held out a familiar necklace. "We're still working with Hannah. She's in denial about everything. I almost pity the girl."

Gabe took the necklace, looking at the two emeralds on the black leather-like cord. He'd missed his necklace after eons wearing it. He'd missed his mother and baby brother. He squeezed them in his hand in the only hug he could give his dead family.

"We're twins, now, though I think you liked your family," Rhyn said and pulled free an emerald on a chain around his neck.

"You're all the family I got now. I got a long way to go to figure out how to be a proper Death," Gabe said, looking again at the lake.

"You hear from her?"

"No. I don't expect to. I should've sent someone after her, but … " Gabe met Rhyn's gaze and managed a smile. The half-demon's sharp silver gaze missed nothing, even how unhappy Gabe really was.

"You never stopped loving her," Rhyn said.

"I tried."

"Yeah, you're fucked. Gods know I tried not to fall for Katie."

"Appreciate the pep talk," Gabe said drily. "I did tell you I can legally claim your soul if you come here, didn't I?"

"Why don't you come up for air sometime?" Rhyn asked, ignoring him. "Katie and Toby will be glad to see you, and you can scare the shit out of Tamer. It'll be fun."

"I'd like that. I have to fix this first," Gabe said and motioned to the Lake.

"What's wrong?"

Gabe stepped closer to the Lake. Even through the black water, he could see the green souls at the bottom. They glimmered faintly, like lights shrouded by fog.

"They're moving," he said. "They shouldn't be. I heard a story once about the Army of Souls. I'm wondering if they are what Darkyn was after, not killing Death."

"Never heard of the Army of Souls."

"It led to the last apocalyptic age that predated my predecessor here. It was not a good time, Rhyn. I'm hoping I can calm the waters down."

"If anyone can, you can, Gabe." Rhyn studied him a moment longer.

"I'm fine, Rhyn," Gabe said. "Really."

"Come by when you need someone to kick your ass."

"I will. Rhyn, thank you."

The half-demon shook his head, turned and strode away, disappearing into a portal. Gabriel watched him, envious and proud of his friend. He'd always had faith in Rhyn. Gabe's faith had cost him everything, but it was worth it. If only he could find peace as well.

He moved away from the Lake. He had a long journey ahead of him, one he didn't relish taking. But, if he was to be the honorable Death that mortals and Immortals alike deserved, he had to do it.

Gabe's thoughts went to his predecessor once again. He couldn't help wondering what happened to her. He'd expected her abandonment of the underworld would grant him some sort of peace or reprieve. However, after thousands of years with the vexing deity, he found himself lonely instead.

He replaced the necklace around his neck and strode back to the fortress, his new home for eternity.

RHYN TRILOGY: ORIGINS

RHYN TRILOGY: ORIGINS

The demons came with the night, sweeping across the hills with fiery swords that tore through darkness and the bodies of the villagers they left in their wake. Gabriel gripped and released the hilt of his broad sword as he watched the flames of Hell envelope hill after hill, each one closer than the last. At seventeen, he was bigger than any other man in his village, and still he feared the fanged creatures.

"Is this all there is?" his father, the village elder, hissed as three more men joined their small army overlooking the valley.

"Aye, 'tis everyone."

Gabriel turned to see the restless shadows that were his family and friends. There were only forty men from their village in any shape to fight, and several more who had not lifted a sword in years. The rest of their village fled for the caves in the cliff, where they hoped the demons would not follow.

"We only need to stay alive long enough for our women to make it to the cliffs," his father said. Several men murmured in agreement. Gabriel's gaze returned to the demons. Fear chilled his insides and adrenaline made him fidget.

"We'll ambush 'em in the valley, then run for the cliffs," his father went on. "Son, you'll stay here."

"No, Papa," Gabriel said. "I'm the biggest man in the village. I'll fight."

"You're no warrior, boy. You'll stay here. Hide yourselves, men!"

The villagers—only a few armed with swords and the rest armed with iron tools or wood—hurried past him to take up their positions hidden in the tall grasses of the valley's sloping walls. He started forward, determined to fight the beasts that threatened his mother and younger brother.

"No, boy," his father said and pulled him back. "Listen to me."

"Papa, I—"

"I swore to your mother you'd come home, even if I didn't. Listen to me, boy."

"I am, Papa!" he said, eyes going to the demons again. His father gripped his chin and forced his attention back to him. The dim light from stars made the creases appear deeper in his father's leathery face, and Gabriel gazed into eyes as dark as his.

"If Death comes for you, you tell her she can't have your spirit. You hear me?"

"Papa, I'm not going to die! I'm going to kill all the demons and go home to mama!"

"Boy, you tell her, she can't have your spirit."

"Papa, enough!" Gabriel snapped. "They're coming!"

His father looked towards the demons, resignation crossing his features before he darted down the hill. Gabriel followed as far as he dared before the first of the demons crested the hill on the other side of the valley.

Their flaming swords were longer than he was tall and clutched by hands with talons the length of his forearm. Moonlight glinted off fangs and the scales that lined their bodies beneath tufts of black fur. Even their horses were twice the size of any horse he'd ever seen with eyes that glowed like the harvest moon. His mouth dropped open and for a long moment, he forgot to breathe.

"Now, men!" his father shouted and charged out of the grass towards the low point in the valley.

A demon launched itself off its horse, snapped his father's arm with one bite of its powerful jaws, and broke his body in half. Horrified, Gabriel watched the demon rip the flesh off his father's bones before tossing the carcass aside. The fiery swords of the demons mowed through his uncles and cousins while several more tackled his friends. Blood soaked the earth.

Paralyzed by fear, he saw the demons ride towards him, but it was as if he watched someone else. He screamed at the youth on the hilltop to raise his sword, to fight for his family, to die with honor, but the fool did not move. He stood there with the sword at his feet and his jaw slack as the demons thundered up the hill to claim his head. As the sword descended, he moved his lips in a scream that echoed into the night.

"You cannot have my spirit!"

Fire, darkness, silence.

Sweet smelling grass tickled his cheeks and rustled in the ocean breeze. Gabriel swatted it out of his face and opened his eyes, squinting at the bright midmorning sun. He rolled onto his back. Smoke billowed into the sky from the direction of his village.

Demons!

He scrambled to his feet, his stomach turning at the sight of the carnage in the valley. Memories of his father being cut down were fresh in his mind. He remembered the demon charging him as well, the sword descending then…nothing. He ran his hands over his body to make sure all his parts were there and stopped to stare at his palms. They were covered in blood. So was his clothing and the grass around him. It looked as if he'd died last night, yet he was alive.

His thoughts flew to his mother and the caves. His pulse loud in his ears, Gabriel ran down then up the hill separating the village from the valley of death to the hill overlooking the home he'd meant to defend. Everything was burnt to the ground or still burning, from the dwelling he'd shared with his family to the horses in the smithy's corral. His eyes followed the path the demons took, marked by a swath of scorched ground that snaked through the grass from the village towards the cliffs—the same path his mother would have taken.

He ran until he reached the scorched earth then slowed to take in the bodies lining the demons' path. His panicked gaze flew from body to body as he made his way to the cliff's edge. He caught a blur of white from the corner of his eye but dismissed the fleeting image as nothing more than a lucky sheep, until a sweet, sing song voice penetrated his maddened search.

"Come with me, my darling."

He faced the small woman with white robes and hair that shifted in the wind without disturbing the grass. His hands clenched and released, but he'd left his sword on the hill. She knelt beside the lifeless body of a woman, and he drew a sharp breath.

"Mama," he whispered.

The woman in white turned. One moment her eyes were white then black then every color in between. In her hand she held green gems. His gaze went from her to his mother, and he dropped to his knees, tears blurring his vision.

"Mama."

"I fear she's dead-dead," the small woman in white said. "I've harvested her spirit already." She held out the gems and pointed at one. "This one is hers."

He reached for it numbly and held the transparent emerald in his hand.

"She's so small," he said in a choked voice. Tears streamed down his face, and he wiped snot from his nose. His chest was so tight, he thought he'd suffocate.

"Your brother is over there."

He followed her pointing finger with his gaze. His little brother lay spread-eagled on his belly, his back torn open down the middle. Gabriel wiped his face again and went to his brother. He squatted to run his fingers through his brother's hair just as he had done yesterday morning.

"They're never really gone forever," the woman said. She held out a hand to the boy's ear. A tiny whirlwind of green dust swirled free of his brother, danced around her hand like smoke, and crystallized in her palm. She held it out to him.

"Where do they go?" he asked.

"To the underworld, where I keep all the souls. Your family will be together down there. There's no more pain once I take them from their weak mortal bodies," she answered. "One day, I'll teach you."

"Teach me what?" he asked and took his brother's soul. He closed his fist around what remained of his mother and brother, protecting them as he had not been able to the night before.

"How to gather a human soul once one is dead-dead." Her voice was cheerful, as if she plucked daisies in the field and not the spirits of his family.

"What are you?"

"You spoke to me last night, Gabriel."

"You know my name."

"You knocked on my door and refused to come in. I'm not accustomed to that, Gabriel," she chided him gently.

He stared at her and stood, ready to flee the madwoman and take his mother and brother with him. She drew nearer, and he caught her scent, like sunshine and grass. Her rainbow eyes seemed to see right through him. At half his size, she seemed delicate and small, but he felt the warm power that made the air around her shimmer. He'd spoken to no one last night except…

"Death," he said at last, his voice barely a whisper. "My father warned me about you."

"And see where that got you?"

"Dead?"

"Yes and no. Because you refused to give me your soul, I had to turn you into an Immortal. I don't like leaving mortals in the shadow world. Nothing good ever comes of that. I can always make you dead-dead…" She raised her eyebrow in inquiry, but he shook his head. "Very well. Come on."

"Where are we going?"

"You're mine now, Gabriel, and we have more souls to gather."

He looked down at the gems in his hand. Pain and loss crippled him, and he doubled over to retch. Death placed a cool hand on the back of his neck. His stomach settled.

"Come, young one," she said, not unkindly. "I have great plans for you."

He watched her walk away and forced himself to his feet. He faced the bodies of his mother and brother one last time. Cold desolation lingered within him like a thick fog.

"I want to bury them," he said.

"We have to gather the souls before nightfall, or the demons will return for them."

Such creatures would kill the innocent then harvest their souls? He never knew such evil existed.

"I will kill them if they come!" he vowed.

"Not this day. I saw you on the hill last night. You did not even lift your sword," Death said, bemused. "You must learn to fight, and you must learn to bury your human emotions. They make you weak, Gabriel, and I cannot have that."

"I cannot help what I am!" he said, his face hot with shame and anger at the reminder that he'd done nothing when the demons attacked.

"You can, and you will. You will be known by many names. Death dealer. Assassin." She stooped to coax another stream of green sand free from a fallen villager. "You will join the others who bring me the souls of mortals and immortals."

"I want to kill demons."

"You will. Come with me, Gabriel. We're going home."

What looked like the mouth of a cave materialized in the air before her, and she stepped into it. He gazed around once more while hot tears burned down his cheeks. He wiped them away and squared his shoulders. His family died because he was too afraid to act.

I will become the strongest and fastest and bravest. I will avenge you mama, papa, I swear it.

His heart pounding, he followed Death to the underworld.

1,000 YEARS LATER

Gabriel lopped the head off the last demon and stood ready to take on more. The demons, however, were done playing his game, and those remaining disappeared. He stood knee deep in demon body parts and straightened. He'd happened upon the demons on his way to kill those on his list of souls to claim this cold night.

He cleaned his sword methodically and replaced it at his back. While he never passed up a chance to behead a demon, he no longer burned to kill them or felt any sense of satisfaction afterwards. He'd all but lost his human emotions after a millennium, much to Death's delight.

"I'll take your head, assassin!"

He whipped around and saw the small form dart from behind a tree nearby. The sword was larger than the boy bearing it. The boy's first strike came nowhere near him, and the second almost reached him. He stepped away from three more strikes. The boy paused, puffing with effort.

"Wait there, assassin. I must kill you," he ordered. Gabriel watched him run behind a tree. He normally killed witnesses, human or otherwise, but hesitated, reminded of his youngest brother, who was near the same age when he was killed.

Suddenly, the tree behind him exploded into flames. He spun, sword in his hand. Another one exploded then a third. Soon, all the trees nearby crackled with flames. Magic hummed in the air around him.

"Boy, you should leave before the fire gets you," he called.

"I will not!" the boy shouted, poking his head out from behind his tree.

"If you're foolish enough to attack a full-grown assassin, you're foolish enough to burn yourself to death."

"I'm a demon. I can eat a full-grown assassin!"

"I don't know who told you this, but Death has domain over mortals, Immortals, and all the Hell-beasts," he said and approached the child, whose arms were crossed and whose grubby expression was fierce. The boy's eyes were silver like a wolf's. Gabriel knelt in front of him. The raw, wild magic that made the hair on his arms stand on end emanated from the boy. The child was a half-breed demon, though Gabriel hadn't met many full-blooded demons with such raw power.

"Where is your mother?" he asked.

"I have none."

"And your father?"

"I have none."

"What are you doing here? Setting trees on fire?" Gabriel studied him, his curiosity piqued by the little demon boy.

The half-breed hesitated before saying, "I was aiming for you."

"I've killed men for less."

"I've never killed anyone, but I'll keep trying."

"You shouldn't be out here alone," Gabriel said. He rose to leave. "Go home, boy, before I change my mind and take your head."

"I have no home, assassin." Though the words were brave, the tortured look that crossed the demon boy's face bade Gabriel linger. "Do you go to kill someone?"

"I do. I have three on my list," Gabriel replied.

"What list?"

"The list of souls Death has ordered me to take to the underworld."

"I can help you," the demon boy offered. "I can burn their houses down."

Gabriel wasn't sure what to do with the demon boy who was clearly a menace to the mortal world. The more he thought, the more he wondered how the boy had gotten out of the Immortal world in the first place. Demons were known for killing half-breeds or tossing them into one of the bottomless seas in the underworld. He'd never heard of a half-breed being stranded among the humans.

Something about the brave, unkempt boy glaring up at him disturbed him more than he liked. After years of Death's brutal efforts to banish his human weaknesses, he couldn't explain the instinct that urged him to take care of the boy.

"You can come with me," he said at last.

"To hunt souls?"

"Yes, then to the Immortal world, where you belong."

"I came from there," the boy said with a frown. His eyes welled with tears.

"You cannot stay here in the mortal world. They'll kill you."

The boy looked torn. Gabriel sheathed his sword and walked away, puzzled as to why such a young creature with so much power had been abandoned in the human world. Another tree exploded, and he tensed without turning. He remembered his own brother's willful tantrums and refused to respond to the half-breed.

"Wait!" the half breed said, running to catch up to him. "What are you called, assassin?"

"Gabriel."

"Gabriel, I'm going with you."

"Keep up. I do not have all night to fetch the souls," Gabriel said with a glance down at the boy whose head barely reached above his waist. At close to seven feet tall and wider than most trees, Gabriel was accustomed to seeing most full grown men run when they saw him. Even demons hesitated before attacking. The boy hadn't been intimidated in the least by his size. Occupied by the little demon, he didn't notice his enemies massing in the forest around them.

"What does Death—" The demon boy was interrupted by shouts from the forest and a fiery volley of arrows. Gabriel dropped to the ground, snatched the boy and rolled his small body beneath his. He grunted as arrows pierced his back and legs. He expected the boy to cry out in fear or pain at any moment and heard the half-breed mumbling in agitation.

A sudden shockwave made Gabriel's teeth chatter as a burst of demon power rolled through him. Demons roared, and more arrows fell. Gabriel hunched his shoulders, expecting to feel the demons' swords pierce his body. Quiet fell instead. He waited a long moment then unfolded his body with some difficulty. The number of arrows lodged in his back and legs made it impossible for him to stand. The demon boy rose and surveyed the damage.

"I did it," he breathed, silver eyes glowing like the moon. "Gabriel, I did it!"

Gabriel craned his neck to look around. As far as he could see on either side of the road, the forest had disintegrated. Piles of ashes were all that remained of demons and trees alike. Proud, the half-breed faced him, his smile fading.

"There are so many arrows."

To his surprise, the demon boy carefully gripped the shaft of an arrow in Gabriel's calf and jerked it free. It hurt worse coming out than it had going in, and Gabriel hissed at the pain.

"Be still, assassin," the boy said with a level of self-command beyond his years.

"I thought you wanted me dead-dead," Gabriel grunted. "You prefer to kill me yourself?"

"No, Gabriel," the boy said. "I don't want to kill you now."

Gabriel gritted his teeth as another arrow was pulled free. He didn't understand the demon boy. One minute, he was the enemy. The next, the half breed tried to help him.

"You saved me. No one else cares if I live, Gabriel." The soft words were filled with unshed tears. Gabriel twisted to see the boy, whose face was stormy with emotions. The child met his gaze, and he felt the connection again. For reasons he couldn't explain, he wouldn't leave the demon boy behind.

"Hurry, boy," he said. "We have souls to claim and demons to hunt."

"You won't die-dead?"

"Not this night."

"I'll protect you if they come back."

Gabriel raised an eyebrow as Death did when he said something foolish to her. The half-breed was powerful yet showed no capacity for control. He suspected the boy could kill him accidentally with another of those bursts. The half breed was quiet, concentrating on the arrows. Gabriel bore the pain in silence.

"Done, Gabriel," the half-breed said and sat back, a frown on his face. Gabriel rolled with a grimace. His body worked, but he hurt and was weaker than he preferred.

"What are you called?" he asked as he pushed himself up.

"Rhyn."

"Rhyn," he echoed. "Is that not demon for flower?"

The boy's eyes narrowed in response. Gabriel snorted and limped onto the road.

"C'mon, boy. We have souls to fetch."

"Do you think we'll be friends for all time?" Rhyn asked and fell into step beside him.

"Eternity's a long time, Rhyn," he said.

"Yes, but there are a lot of souls we can hunt."

"You'll have to learn to fight like I do. Rhyn," he said suddenly and stopped to look down at the demon boy. "You can't come with me to the underworld. Death won't allow that."

Rhyn gazed up at him, hurt in his eyes. The boy belonged in the Immortal world. Gabriel's thoughts went to the Immortals he'd met when they bought death warrants from Death that he carried out. Soon after taking him to the underworld, Death had pushed him into a brutal series of assassinations to harden him against human emotion. He'd wiped out entire cities at her command, and killed children as young as Rhyn when paid by Immortals to do so. He didn't care for most of the Immortals, but there was one who'd gone so far as to thank him for his service and buy him a new dagger.

The air around Rhyn shimmered as his hurt turned to anger. The demon boy gathered his power to strike. Gabriel ruffled his hair as he had his brother's, amused by his companion.

"I might know someone who can help," he said and began walking again. "First, we'll hunt."

Rhyn released the breath he'd been holding. "I trust you, Gabriel."

"You ever take a soul from a human?"

"No."

"I'll teach you how."

As they walked in silence down the road, Gabriel had the uncanny sense his fate was now tied to that of the creature he'd saved.

ABOUT THE AUTHOR

Lizzy Ford is the hyper-prolific author of the Rhyn Trilogy, Foretold Trilogy, and War of Gods series as well as multiple other single-title paranormal romance and YA fantasy novels. Lizzy published 10 books in 2011 and plans another 10 for 2012. She loves to hear from readers.

Contact her:

Website: http://www.guerrillawordfare.com/

Amazon author's page: http://www.amazon.com/Lizzy-Ford/e/B004XTTYOC/

Facebook: http://www.facebook.com/LizzyFordBooks/

Twitter: http://www.twitter.com/#!/LizzyFord2010

Google+:
https://plus.google.com/b/106728579413949863215/#

Email: LizzyFord2010@gmail.com

Also by Lizzy Ford

The Rhyn Trilogy
Katie's Hellion, Book I (May 2011)
Katie's Hope, Book II (September 2011)
Rhyn's Redemption, Book III (March 2012)

Rhyn Eternal Series
Gabriel's Hope (September 2012)

The War of Gods series
Damian's Oracle (October 2011)
Damian's Assassin (November 2011)
Damian's Immortal (December 2011)
The Grey God (May 2012)

The Foretold Trilogy
Elle's Journey (December 2011)
Shadow Rising (Winter 2012)

Anshan Saga
Kiera's Moon (June 2011)
Kiera's Sun (July 2012)

Single-titles (2011)
A Demon's Desire
The Warlord's Secret
Maddy's Oasis

Single-titles (2012)
Rebel Heart

New series being launched in 2012

The Original Beings (War of Gods spinoff)
Xander's Chance – summer 2012

The Witchling Trilogy
Dark Summer (late summer 2012)
Autumn Storm (autumn 2012)
Winter Kiss (winter 2012)

Made in the USA
Charleston, SC
04 November 2014